To Cimean

I hope you
enjoy the
journey!

Best regards,

Karen Johnson

TORN THREADS

By Karen Lynn Johnson and Kathryne Willison Sackett

authorHOUSE®

AuthorHouse™
1663 Liberty Drive
Bloomington, IN 47403
www.authorhouse.com
Phone: 1-800-839-8640

First published by AuthorHouse   10/19/2009

ISBN: 978-1-4490-1706-4 (sc)

Library of Congress Control Number: 2009908195

Printed in the United States of America
Bloomington, Indiana

This book is printed on acid-free paper.

ACKNOWLEDGMENTS

There are many people who assisted us in the research and editing of this book. We thank the following for their assistance:

The kind people of London who answered our questions willingly, especially the employees of the Ministry of Defence, the War Records Department, and the historian at the Royal War Museum; the bus drivers and tour bus operators of Oxford; the Police Department of Croydon and the staff of the Fishery Inn in Hemel Hempstead;

Mr.John Laughton of Salisbury for sharing his own invaluable story of childhood evacuation and his son, Darren, for introducing us; Mr. Frazier Wright of HRM Mail of London for his insights and information on telephone and mail communication during the war; Ms. Kristen Swett, archivist for the city of Boston, Massachusetts;

The sisters at Tyburn Convent for their kind tour and information and their follow-up booklet, Tyburn in War-time;

Miss Joan Firth of Cleckheaton, West Yorkshire, for her first hand descriptions of train stations and daily life in England during the war as well as the role of women in the military services;

Lisette Johnson, Hillary Johnson, Jim Johnson and Linda Johnson for their editing efforts, and finally we thank our husbands, Jim and Mark, for their support and encouragement in this endeavor (including our trip to the U.K.!)

ABOUT THE AUTHORS

Karen Lynn Johnson holds a Bachelor of Music Education degree from Valparaiso University and a Masters Degree from Indiana University. She taught many years in public schools and has spent much time volunteering for church and community organizations. She is currently a part time preschool teacher and church musician and is involved with Habitat For Humanity. She loves traveling with her semi-retired husband, Jim, and their Bichon dog. She's the mother of two grown daughters, Lisette and Hillary who, with her husband, continue to inspire her to reach for new heights and explore new adventures. She and her husband live part time in Cincinnati, Ohio and part of the year in Emerald Isle, North Carolina.

Kathryne Willison Sackett holds a Bachelor of Science Degree from the University of Cincinnati's Design, Art, and Architecture department and is currently taking courses at The Art Academy of Cincinnati. Along with pursuing her artistic abilities, she enjoys being a Jazzercise manager and volunteering for the Arts and her church. She and her husband, Mark, reside in downtown Cincinnati, Ohio.

CHAPTER ONE
Amersham, England
November 1931

The rain wasn't coming *down*, it was blowing horizontally across the Green, whipping against rickety gates, pelting the ancient stones of the cottages, rattling window panes. The greengrocer was already locked up tight, having closed early in the day as was the way with most shopkeepers on a Wednesday afternoon. Still, Sister Joan hoped the chemist shop was open. Mother Superior had sent her on a mission to retrieve some lavender powders, a remedy she used for migraines. She knew she had left the convent too late to complete her errand, yet she had made her way to the village anyway. She could wander around and think. At least there were other people here, signs of an active life outside the restrictions of the convent. Something besides quiet and emptiness. Even with the sheets of cold water drenching her thin coat, it was worth the walk.

The village was quiet this day in a different way from the cloisters of Wycombe Convent. The village held evidence of children, their toys strewn about in back gardens. Here was washing pegged out to dry, now drenched in the sudden squall. Old people were sitting by their front bay windows, gazing out with tired faces. Sister Joan accepted the stinging rain as penance for her untoward thoughts. Here was freedom. Here was opportunity. Regret now weighed on her conscience like an unpardonable sin. Her remorse was purely personal, purely selfish. How had she come to this point? Once, it had all seemed so clear, so easy. Now her life choice seemed almost unbearable.

She looked down at her soaked shoes, wishing she had pulled on her boots before leaving the convent. She had left in a hurry, running late as usual. When was the last time someone had hurried her along or given her clear direction? When was the last time she'd even asked? She stopped to stare at the village Green. Its carefully laid out square settled in her vision like a picture frame as the rain smeared the colors into a blurry photo.

Sister Joan drew her wet hands across her face and sighed deeply. The wind had died down a bit but the rain continued falling as she shook her head, trying to refocus. Moments of her silent reverie stopped time in its tracks; there was no way to tell how long she'd been standing in the rain, staring at pictures that only she could see. Finally, she crossed the Green and rounded the corner toward the chemist.

"Go'mornin' to ya, Sister Joanie!" came a voice from across the walk. It was old Mr. Brown.

Joan smiled and waved but her mind wandered to the passages in her daily journal that were written at the time of her walk into Wycombe Convent. Most of them were filled with exciting promise, with hope and reassurance. Yet some entries were full of doubt about the wisdom of her choice. Now living a lie while surrounded by so many wonderful women pressed down on her. They were her family. They were her future. But on this early November day, they were an intrusion into her life. The convent felt like an albatross around her neck, stifling the very air she needed to breathe. Resentment led to guilt and guilt led to anger. She walked faster against the rain, hoping to hide from herself the tears of frustration that streamed down her face.

The chemist shop was indeed closed. Now she would have to return to the convent for there was no logical reason to stroll the village in this inclement weather. She stood still and let the wind and rain pelt her face. Then, turning the opposite direction from the convent in Amersham, she doubled back and headed toward Hempstead, toward the Royal Infirmary.

"Why Sister Joan, you are positively drenched. Do take off that dripping coat and come and set yourself down for a cuppa tea."

The hospital receptionist, Mrs. Markham, had a gruff yet grandmotherly way about her and the young nun followed her to the Infirmary café where tea and coffee were always brewing.

"Whatever can you be doing here at hospital on such a dismal day as this? Have you business here?"

Joan picked up the teacup nervously.

"Not business exactly, Mrs. Markham. I only came to check on a few patients that I've been praying for. I haven't seen them for a few days."

There it was. Another lie.

"Yes, dear. Well anyway, the patients will be glad you are here. Just make sure you warm up a bit and dry off before heading back to the Convent."

Mrs. Markham left quickly. A hand touched the Sister's shoulder and she jumped.

"What are you doing here on a day like this?"

The voice was deep and smooth and Joan knew exactly whose it was.

"Dr. Bennett, hallo! I haven't seen you for a while. Were you on holiday?"

What a stupid thing to say!

"Yes, I was. A friend and I took a skiing trip to Austria. It was wonderful and reasonable I might add. Their currency's more worthless than ours!"

His eyes are such a dark brown – and he's staring at me. Or perhaps I'm staring at him!

Sister Joan awkwardly pushed back strands of hair from her face.

"Sister, are you all right?"

"Oh yes, yes thank you."

"Well then, I must be off for afternoon rounds. Do stop in for a chat the next time you're here. I'd like to talk to you about a new nursing ministry for the sisters at your convent. I'm in the process of putting it together and I think with your experience and your faith, you could be an asset in developing our program. It would help ease our shortage of regular nurses. Do you think you'd be interested at this point in time?"

The doctor's tall frame stood perfectly still, waiting.

"Yes, I think I'd be most interested, at least for the immediate future. After that, I'm not sure where I'd fit in…."

"I see…should I ask why?"

"Not now, please."

She was beginning to perspire under her black habit.

"Well then, we'll let it be at that."

"I'd better be getting back to the convent."

They exchanged good-byes and Sister Joan nervously headed toward reception, then stopped. It dawned on her that Mrs. Markham might find it odd that she had not yet visited any of the patients she had mentioned. *She* knew the real reason for diverting from the chemist shop in Amersham to the hospital in Hempstead, in the pouring rain no less. She slipped out the side door. It was time to go back.

Colin Bennett walked into his office but he did not sit down. He paced back and forth on the hard linoleum between his desk and the small window that overlooked the well-worn public footpath leading to

Wycombe Convent. Though his feet kept moving, his mind lingered on one thing. *God, her eyes are so blue.*

The Mother Superior was asleep when Sister Joan arrived home at the convent, for which she was grateful. Not only was she unable to get the headache powders, she may have had to explain her tardiness. After drying off, she entered the chapel to pray until late evening vespers. The floor beneath her knees was hard and unforgiving.

CHAPTER TWO

Hempstead
March 1932

Sister Joan approached the hospital steps with some apprehension. Mother Mary Catherine had approved the nursing program for the convent sisters in January and it was now in full swing. Still, every time Joan came for classes nervous tension rose in her throat. She secured some wispy hairs under her guimpe, stepped inside the reception area and quickly took a seat. The ache in the pit of her stomach had never diminished since that depressing November day. The day she had accepted the mistake she'd made with her life. Every visit to the hospital made her life more surreal. Someone else was living it.

She stared at Mrs. Markham who was greeting other sisters coming in the door for their nursing duties and more training. Mrs. Markham had such an easy way with Dr. Bennett, keeping him on schedule with the training classes. Occasionally a veteran nurse or another comparable surgeon would give the lecture and Mrs. Markham kept her eye on them also. Sister Joan looked around for the Dr. just as he strode into Reception and Mrs. Markham handed him a cup of coffee.

"Good morning, sisters, I'll be with you in a bit. Sister Joan, I need to speak privately with you for a few moments."

Joan followed the doctor into his office feeling both uncomfortable and exhilarated.

"Please sit down, Sister. I just wanted to thank you for being instrumental in getting this program airborne. I wondered if we might have dinner here at the hospital tomorrow evening, after my duty hours end. I thought we could begin planning our next set of training classes. Are you available after vespers?"

The doctor's gaze fell from her face to her hands fidgeting with her black habit. Her hands began to tremble. She rubbed them together, dropping her notebook. When she looked down to retrieve it, a large strand of hair fell from her guimpe, blocking her view. Before she could push it back, his hand did it for her.

"Allow me."

She had witnessed his gentleness on other occasions, though it had been in his manners and in his voice. This time it was in his touch. He smiled as he reached down for her notebook.

"You haven't answered me, Sister Joan, is that a 'no'?"

"Oh, uh no. I mean yes, Dr. Bennett. I'm available. But I must be back at the convent by half past nine."

"Or you turn into something else?"

He started to laugh but stopped as she stared in silence. The wall clock ticked for several uneasy moments before he spoke again.

"By the way, Sister, please call me Colin. Since you haven't mentioned anything more about other plans for yourself, I hope we are to have a long working relationship here. I believe it's proper for you to call me by my given name."

"Oh, right doctor, I mean Colin. And *my* given name is…"

Sister Joan stopped mid-sentence, her face flushed. She hadn't a clue why she was going to say that.

"Yes well, anyway, I shall be here about sixish tomorrow evening, Colin. I best check the duty roster now and get to work."

She felt there were a million eyes upon her as she left Dr. Bennett's office.

Colin Bennett sat in his office long after Sister Joan had gone. He rearranged papers on his desk that were already in neat stacks and pulled open drawers for no apparent reason. He twirled a pencil between his fingers and thought again of the chestnut strand of hair he'd brushed from the Sister's face. Why did nuns need to cover up so completely? If God had made a woman so beautiful, why did she need to hide that loveliness? He smiled at his unspoken question and laid the pencil down. Blonde. The last woman he'd been with was blonde. Not the bottle variety that many London girls experimented with, but the genuine article. God, he hadn't thought of her in a long time. She'd been anxious for excitement in her life. Maybe too anxious. He leaned back in his chair and spent the next hour going backwards in his own timeline, nodding at the good parts and excusing the rest. His life was so full now. And so empty. *Geez, a nun. Was he crazy?* He stretched his legs under the desk and finally stood up to leave, but his mind was still wondering what the nun turned into if she were late getting back.

Joan looked around the sparsely furnished hospital dining room. She wasn't sure if her dinner with Colin would be a welcome relief from the blandness of the convent fare or another uncomfortable diversion into the secular world, into his world. It was a thought that had plagued her since the doctor's invitation. She smoothed out the small wrinkles on her habit and shifted in the tall-back wooden chair, anxious to get the initial greeting over with. She lifted her eyes to look across the room for him and was startled to find the doctor standing in front of her.

"Sorry, Sister. I didn't mean to surprise you. I guess you were deep in thought and didn't hear me approach. How are you this evening?"

"I'm doing well, Colin."

Her eyes followed him as he sat in the chair closest to her.

"You know, Sister, I always have more work than I have hours to do it in, which is why I've been excited about this new nursing ministry. I think it's already been a wonderful improvement in patient care. How about we celebrate with full plate dinners before we get down to the details of the next training?"

"That would be lovely, though *celebrating* in the hospital's cafeteria may be a bit overstated. Still, you can't imagine what a nice respite this will be from the predictable convent meals." The sister laughed.

As they sat back down with filled plates, there was a long minute of silence as the sister bowed her head. It was the kind of quiet that good friends and long-married couples are comfortable with, but one that usually feels like an eternal void with acquaintances uncertain of boundaries. Joan struggled to focus on her short, softly spoken prayer. Colin struggled to keep from focusing on the mere sound of her voice. When she raised her head, he gazed at her before speaking.

"So what do you feel is the best aspect of this new program?"

"For the hospital, the answer is obvious. More nurses, better care for the patients. For the sisters, a chance to minister in a setting outside of the convent. I know there are more than a few who feel too isolated from God's work in the *real* world."

"And what about you, personally? What do you hope to gain while you're giving your time to all of this?"

She mulled the question before the answer formed on her lips.

"I need more in my life, Colin. I need to feel more connected to life on the outside. Connected to life in the way that my mum was."

"You make Wycombe sound like a prison."

She shrugged her shoulders.

"I sure don't mean to. It's just that...I guess I need a little more in my life." Sister Joan bit her lip, swallowed, and went on.

"You know, my earlier intentions were to get out of this area and find some place with more activity. Somewhere that has more going on, more parks and a theatre and a choice of restaurants...."

Colin smiled and she stopped before saying more.

"Sister, that doesn't sound like a realistic plan for a nun, if you don't mind my saying."

"You're probably right. Anyway, at least working and learning here at the hospital gives me new opportunities. I mean, gives all of us a chance to serve, of course."

"Of course."

Colin's deep eyes danced with amusement and Joan smoothed her habit again.

"On a different subject, Sister, I never really got the chance to tell you that I admired your courage and positive attitude when your mum was ill. The way you just kept going and never complained about the hand you were dealt. You must have a secret way of coping that you should bottle and sell."

"Thanks. I never thought I'd get through all that, which may be odd for a nun to say. You know, we're supposed to have unquestioning faith."

"And do you? Have a strong faith, I mean."

"Colin, the one thing I've learned in the past few weeks is that vows and a habit don't guarantee unquestioning faith. Those of us 'on the inside' struggle just like everyone else."

"You know, Sister Joan, you're not like any nun I've ever known. Doesn't seem that you're hiding behind that habit."

The nun blushed and scooted back into her chair as he continued.

"Though I must admit that I've often wondered what you actually look like without your normal garb."

Joan let out a small giggle.

"Oh, sorry, I hope I didn't offend you."

"You didn't offend at all. Everyone wonders what nuns look like without all this cover-up. Truth is, most of us wonder ourselves!"

This time they both laughed. Colin pushed the food around on his plate before speaking again.

"Joan, if you don't mind my asking, your comment about struggling... what I mean is, are you struggling with something right now?"

The dining room became eerily silent as she pondered her answer. There were so many conflicts raging inside her, yet the one that was laying claim to her soul involved the very person in front of her. How could she give him an honest response?

"Actually, yes. I can tell you that my faith is being tested and I'm not sure how to handle this one. It's confusing and unsettling, not knowing the answer."

"I think I know what you mean. I'm used to knowing all the answers and just now I don't even know the question!"

Joan's gaze went straight to his.

"Sister, is it really your faith that's being tested, or your commitments? Is this nursing ministry laying heavy on your mind?"

This man unnerved her and captivated her at the same time.

"It's not the program at all. It's something heavy on my heart, not my mind. It's about the commitment I've made with my life."

She pushed her plate away, then held her forehead in her hands. *How could I have been so bold?* She began to perspire as silence filled the nearly empty room. Colin broke the quiet.

"I see."

He sat back and placed his hands behind his head, not taking his eyes off her. More quiet moments before he sighed and spoke again.

"Sister, you almost told me once before but just out of curiosity, what is your given name?"

She looked up and hesitated.

"Doreen."

"Doreen....beautiful name. So, is there anything I can do to help you, anything I can say to help clear up your confusion?"

"I don't know. Probably not. This is something I need to work out on my own. But thanks. I just need some time to think and sort through things, and pray, of course."

The Sister tried to smile as she spoke the word 'pray.' The very act of praying had become more and more difficult.

"Well, if you change your mind, you know I'm here."

"Thank you, Colin."

Joan tried desperately to move the conversation on, but her voice wouldn't speak. Her mind was registering a blank except for noting yet again how deep brown his eyes were. That, and his comment about seeing her without the habit.

Dr. Bennett left the hospital with a lively gait and headed toward the Three Blackbirds pub. He sat on a brocaded bench in the back corner and his spirits quickly dampened as he watched the loud, obnoxious antics of the local drunk. Once he'd seen the old guy take a swing at a much younger man who seemed bent on getting him out of the pub. On this night there was no one else paying attention to the drunken slurs and curses and Colin turned his thoughts to his own problems. His mind was reeling with Sister Joan's – Doreen's - words about her confusion. Had she really hinted at having feelings for him, or was it just wishful thinking on his part? *God, you idiot, she's a nun! You thought all this through just yesterday and the answer was the same. You can't get interested in a nun!* Colin gulped his beer, strode up to the bar and ordered another just as the drunk staggered out the door yelling something about a skinny assed runt.

CHAPTER THREE
Amersham,
April 1932

Whispers of spring floated through the cloisters and danced on the breezes that surrounded the convent. Sister Joan picked up her long, black skirt and walked out into the sunshine. Though light now bathed her face, her heart was as heavy as a stone. Walking the convent grounds was the best way she knew to sort through the nagging thoughts and feelings that had twisted her stomach into knots. She hadn't eaten a full meal in days. Anxiety raced through her veins, undefined yet not unwelcome, as though physical ache would pay for her confusion. She headed toward the Sisters of the Holy Cross Cemetery as it had always brought her a strange sense of beauty and order. Not the kind of stifling routine she now felt inside the convent walls, but a larger picture of life, unfolding as it should in a kind of cosmic plan; a picture one could add color to. Staring at the stones and now stepping through the manicured gardens, she heard a quiet and soothing voice. It almost sounded like her mum's and seemed to possess a holy quality that was born of the ancients and carried on the flutter of the leaves that shaded her path. Her heartbeat quickened yet a strange calm flooded her. It was both unnerving and comforting. A kind of immediate catharsis that she hadn't experienced before.

She sat down and laid her head back on the trunk of an old red oak, her eyes staring ahead, unfocused. It was so very still in the cemetery, a peaceful place to reflect and gather strength while surrounded by so many souls. Only the chattering of a bird overhead interrupted the silence. Just behind her shoulder lay her chosen home for the past two years. She knew, without looking, every detail of the ancient stones that made up the small community. She could see the winding, narrow hallways, spotted with the moss and residue of time, leading to cloisters where she had worked and meditated. She could feel the dampness of the chapel walls and smell the pungent odor of candles mixing with the perspiration of heavily covered confessors on humid days. She could hear the trickle of water as it poured over the rocks of the small memorial fountain, set in the gardens just beyond the public's eye. Tears began to come from somewhere deep inside her and made their way slowly and painfully to her eyes, spilling onto her habit, her skin stinging from the sweat. In her mind, visions of her past began forming behind those tears. It was time to go backwards, to sort through her past and try to understand how she had come to this point. What had shaped her choices and were they ever even hers? Had she compromised her life for security, for company, for what? Now she could see her mother's face and hear her voice. It was such a long time ago, so many worlds away, but the scenes racing through her thoughts were clear and complete. Memories forced their way through broken barriers, puncturing her fragile spirit, yet she let them flood over her like cleansing waves.

Chapter Four

Hempstead, England
April 1924

"Doreen Anna Bailey, get your boots and gloves on this moment, or we'll be late for Mass!"

"I'm coming, Mum. Anyway, Father Loughry never starts on time".

"Never mind the commentary, young lady. You'll soon be of age to make your own decisions on time and tarry. Besides, I've asked the Father to speak with you beforehand. He'd like to employ you to call in and see to the needs of his sister, Mauve. She's had a bad fall and won't be up and about for awhile."

"But I promised I'd walk Miss Butler's dog for the next fortnight."

"Please, Doreen, do it for me."

"Mum, his sister always looks at us as though we've done something wrong. I hate it when she does that."

"Lamb, don't speak so of the aged. I'll be there soon enough and I pray on Mary's name that you won't speak ill of me."

"You know what I'm talking about and it has nothing to do with her age. She's a crotchety lady who just doesn't like us. We're not like everyone else."

"I know what you're saying, love, but never mind. We both know that your father deserted *us*, we can't help that. Maeve's from the old school, thinks I didn't do my part. We know better. Just swallow your tongue and hold your head high. Do remember that we're not the only fatherless family about here. Plenty of others who lost men in the Great War. I'm not totally convinced that some of them didn't just settle some place else a bit more exciting than this small town. Now stop squawking, we'll just make the Mass."

Saint Mary and Joseph Catholic Church stood stark white next to the sooty- darkened brick cottages that lined St. John's Road in Hempstead.

13

Its doors were opened wide to let in fresh air, unlike the doors of the Three Blackbirds pub that stood directly across the street. Its doors would not be open for another three hours and no one inside would be too worried about fresh air. Doreen glanced at the pub as her mum's sure arm pulled her inside the small church. She knew William's father would be occupying his usual place at the bar soon after the noon bells rang through the village. She wasn't sure why she'd thought of William, maybe because she felt sorry for his family situation. She liked him- they'd been friends for a long time.

After the service, there were children already playing in the park next to the church, some of them adventurous and making their way up Box Moor. Some were climbing the horse chestnut trees that lined the main street. A few of them, unlucky in their pursuit, would spend the afternoon getting cuts stitched up at the hospital just over the hill at the far end of St. John's Road.

It wasn't often that Doreen and her mum were able to treat themselves to a pub lunch. They took a window table at the Fishery Inn, looking out at the fishermen who lined the canal that ran through the village. Their long poles hung over the murky water like broken umbrella spokes. The trout that ran through those waters were smart; she wondered if their would-be captors were clever enough to hook them. If not, their family would probably forgo any protein for evening tea, save for a white-crusted hunk of cheddar that sat on most kitchen counters in their village.

"Doreen, I want to talk to you about your upcoming birthday. Twelve years old already!"

"You don't have to worry about getting me anything for my birthday, Mum. This is the best present of all, just having lunch out today. There isn't anything I really need."

"Oh love, there are lots of things you need, but I want you to have that special gift, something you can use and enjoy. What is it that you like to do when you have free time?"

"Well..... I like to walk and wander in the fields. I like to watch the seasons change. Lately I've been feeling a bit interested in jotting all that down, you know, some kind of written record of my thoughts and feelings. Sounds a bit silly when I say it out loud."

"Nonsense, I don't think it sounds silly at all. It sounds more like my little girl is growing up. I'm not sure how I feel about that."

"Feel about what, Mrs. Bailey?!"

The tall, lanky lad stood towering over their table.

"Hallo, William, have a seat. We were about to have a bit of lunch. Care to share it with us?"

"Thank you, Mrs. Bailey, but I can't stay. Mum's expecting me back for our own meal soon. She just sent me down this way to check on Da and I saw the two of you through the window. I have to go make sure he gets home all right. Of course by now, he already has a couple of hours of his own private lunch under his belt, if you know what I mean…."

His bluntness brought an uncomfortable silence. Doreen stared down at her menu.

"I'm sorry you have such a job of looking after your Da, William. It must be a strain at times."

"Oh, it's alright, Mrs. Bailey, I'm used to it. Besides, someday I'll get out of here. Travel and see other places."

"That's a fine goal, William. Keep thinking that way. God has His way of working it all out, even if we can't always see that."

Doreen raised her eyes and smiled. Her mother always looked to the positive, even when it came to Wilhelm Strucker. Everyone knew what a mean-spirited drunk he was, not to mention his ugly rhetoric on Jews and other immigrants.

William stood up quickly and tipped his well-worn cap.

"Got to get on with it now. Need to get 'im home before he gets into a right brawl over there. I'll see you later, Doreen."

She felt the blood rush to her cheeks.

"See you later, William. Tell your mum hallo for me."

"Aye, I will. Oh, and thanks for the word, Mrs. Bailey."

Anna Bailey turned and watched William leave.

"You know, Doreen, he shouldn't feel responsible for his da's behavior, nor his horrible prejudices."

"I know, mum. I know."

William disappeared out the front entrance. They both watched as he crossed the street and walked into the Blackbird Pub.

It had been a hot August in 1925. The lush trees in the local park had been decorated with festive streamers for the biggest Catholic event Hempstead had seen in a while. It was the 200th anniversary of Saint Mary and Joseph Church and the side street had been closed off to accommodate the overfill of parishioners and special guests, including a Cardinal from London. The church doors were opened and rows of chairs extended out into the street and even onto the grass in the park. Doreen checked her dress pocket for the diary that went everywhere with her. This would be a day to write about! She smoothed the pleats and tried to forget that some of her friends had new outfits for the occasion. Her mum's eyes focused straight ahead as the sermon and accompanying lessons, hymns, and "special messages" droned on for what seemed hours. Still, it was exciting to know that soon the real festivities would begin with lots of food, dancers, and musicians. She smiled at her vision of Father Loughry and the guest priests making their way about the crowds with elegant tankards filled with something other than consecrated wine. She turned to look at Mauve Loughry, sitting rigidly with a half-smile frozen on her face. She seemed quite pleased to be sitting next to a group of nuns from the nearby Amersham convent, as though being next to so much piety would suffice for a couple of Hail Mary's!

William was sitting with his mum and two sisters in the row of chairs behind them, but Doreen dare not turn around. She could feel his eyes on her occasionally, though perhaps it was just the warmth of the sun on her back. His da would be across the street soon, "worshipping" in his usual haunt. It must be awkward to have a family so divided. At least she and her mum were a solid unit.

Doreen felt a hand tapping her shoulder as the last strain of the final hymn floated through the air.

"I'll meet you by the big tree and we can eat together," William whispered in her ear. "Your mum won't mind, will she?"

"Don't think so, as long as you behave yourself!"

He laughed at her comment and then glanced around. His sisters were already running off with some friends and both their mums had left to help with the serving.

"Come on, let's get some food and go off a ways."

"What do you mean I can't join in this feast?!! You lousy, damn hypocrites! I'll eat here if I want to-just try and stop me!"

Doreen whirled around to see where the loud, angry voice came from. She knew right away whose it was. The man's eyes were red and swollen and his arms waved wildly as he continued with his tirade.

"By God, I helped pay for this party with my hard-earned money that my old woman keeps throwing away on the likes of you! Get out of my way!"

A hush fell over the crowd as Wilhelm Strucker pushed Father Loughry out of his way. His words grew louder and more slurred as he stumbled over to the food line. Doreen turned back around to William, but he was already making his way toward his father.

"Come on Da, I'll take you home and make a right, nice sandwich for ya. Never mind what's going on here."

"Get out of my way, Will, why you're nothing but mummy's little boy! Look at ya, ya skinny little runt!"

The drunk's large arm thrust toward his son. William ducked at his swing, then reached forward to steady his Da who was reeling from the effort.

Doreen's eyes filled with tears as she watched her dearest friend struggle to avoid his father's punches while leading him away from the celebration. What kind of life was that? What kind of future would any girl have with a boy whose role model was a drunken mess? She ran in the opposite direction to the comfort of the chestnut tree, leaned against its trunk and sobbed.

A firm hand touched her shoulder. Doreen slowly turned around; it was Father Loughry.

"Now, now, my child. Dry those tears. Here, take my handkerchief."

"Father, I guess I don't understand how William can live like that all the time. I don't see how he sees any hope in it."

"He keeps going because that's what he must do. I think all of us find that wee bit of hope with the rising of the morn. I shouldn't worry about William, if I were you. Now his Da, there may be another story, but it's not yours to worry about."

"Maybe I'm more concerned about myself. Things seem to be turning every which way these days. It's all so confusing."

"Aye, it is. It may be that you're just more sensitive than most, or perhaps it's because you care for the lad."

"I do like him, Father. I just don't know if I want to get involved with all the things he's got to deal with. You know, his father and all…"

"Ah Doreen, you're young yet. I know you'll figure out that one for yourself someday. You've got a good head on your shoulders – and a heart to match."

The priest patted her head and moved towards the circle of nuns who were lost in their own chatter. The uncomfortable scene replayed in his mind. *Whose responsibility was it to keep an eye on Mr. Strucker?*

Doreen watched him for a few minutes, then walked up Box Moor. She sat down and tried to imagine what it may have been like holding hands with William for a whole afternoon.

Sister Joan arched her back against the oak tree as her thoughts flashed back to her first real job. It had been late winter in 1926 and it certainly hadn't been what she would have chosen. But jobs for young women in small towns were scarce so she'd settled with sewing in Miss Norton's seamstress shop. The click clack of a simple machine was the only sound to break the silence in the cluttered room. Actually, it wasn't really a shop, just a small space in the back of Ethel Norton's home, but she called it her shop. Doreen's fingers worked slowly and carefully as she finished the hand stitching on the hem of a dress. She paused now and then to glance up at Miss Norton as the plain woman pulled material across the sewing plate. Finally, Doreen's curiosity had prompted her to speak.

"Miss Norton, can I ask you a question?"

"Yes, my dear. What is it you want to know?"

"I've just been wondering....how you work all day with these temperamental machines, without talking to people very often. Don't you get bored, I mean, don't you miss being around others?"

"I suppose there are times I do. But all in all, it's not a bad job. It's also one that I can have a bit of control over. I take the orders I want and can vary my hours when I need to."

"I guess I see your point. I know I'm not very good at this, but it may be that I just get bored with a bolt of cloth I push around."

Doreen looked down at her boots, then rushed through an apology.

"I'm sorry, I didn't mean that the way it sounded."

"No harm, my dear. Not everyone is meant to do this. What is it you *really* would like to do?"

"I'd really like to work at the chemist shop. I love watching Mr. Spence fill prescriptions and give advice on all that medical stuff. It looks so fascinating!"

"I can see that you might find that interesting work. I'll tell you what, I'll keep my ears to the ground for any openings there, if you can find someone qualified to take your place *here* – deal?"

"Deal. Thank you, Miss Norton."

"Now get going with that dress that's lying on the floor."

Doreen sheepishly picked it up and smiled as she put it under the footplate of the old machine for its final decorative stitches. Her mind was already racing with a plan to stop by the chemist shop before she looked in on Mauve, who was still poorly with a cold.

Joan had written about that first job in her diary. She'd written just about everything in that small, leather book. It had become a constant companion. Some entries became almost mantras and she could recite them from memory. One in particular had often soothed her and now the nun let those words and images flow through her as more tears streamed down her face.

October 26, 1926
Dear Diary,
The amber leaves of autumn have certainly dressed up this drab town. I know I should appreciate all the history of these ancient stones, but sometimes I only see the years of neglect. It is nice, at least, to have the gardens strewn about that the Town Hall Greening Ladies care for. William and I took a long walk today, as neither one of us had to work until teatime. We took the footpath that begins at the fish-n-chips shop on St. John's Road and winds about the town, then up into the fading meadows on the moor, taking in some lovely views. The darkened buildings of Hempstead are in stark contrast to the beauty of the open fields. We stopped at the crest of Wickens' Hill, just beyond the Batley's farm and, oh, what an incredible sight! The golds and yellows of grasses preparing themselves for the winter waved against the few white sheep still left grazing on small mounds above the slowing creek. Unlike the flowing canal, Stillwater Creek looks so pathetic, as it has long been dammed in places to provide shallow watering holes for any grazing beast. Still, in autumn's light, the stream looked somehow alive with secrets it wanted to tell. I hope that someday I have as many secrets to tell you. William and I sat down under a tree on the side of the hill and stared for a long time at the vista spread before us. The stone farm buildings are starting to crumble in places, yet they seem close to reverent by the passage of time. Most of the cottages dotting the distance have long been covered in some kind of climbing ivy. The ivy's green fingers envelop the doors and windows; I wonder how some folks see outside! Way off in the distance we could just make out the shapes of buildings in Amersham. William says he thinks there's a hermitage of some sort just outside of town. I started laughing at his idea of hermits and told him that's where all the nuns live. He cuffed me gently on the top of my head and I felt very warm and uncomfortable, yet in an exciting sort of way. I knew mum would be angry with me, but I let him put his arms around me. I thought he might kiss me and I got so nervous, but he didn't. It was so nice looking out over all that beauty with someone special holding me. The only thing that almost spoiled our time together was a disagreement we had about immigrants. William said that most of them should go back to their own countries. I told him that wasn't very charitable, but he insisted that they are all troublemakers. He thinks England shouldn't let so many immigrants settle here, and I told him he was being narrow-minded and prejudiced, especially since his father immigrated! Would he want to be sent

to Germany? And if we enforced that idea, half of our town would have to return to Ireland! Anyway, we agreed to disagree on that point. But the rest of the day... I will remember for a long time. Unfortunately, days like this don't last forever. This season moves on, as do they all. Then I always feel a bit saddened by the fields' and gardens' demise. Yet every spring they come back, splashing their bright colors across the countryside and the walkways and pavements of town. Still, there is something quieting about October, a peacefulness that I don't feel the rest of the year. Perhaps it's just knowing that soon the drapes and doors will be closed all day, keeping out the chill and secluding me in our cottage. A perfect time to think and write. A perfect excuse to shut out the rest of the world for a while. Lamb

CHAPTER FIVE

On a breezy, temperate day in March of 1927, the sounds of boisterous laughter had filtered out from the Hempstead Town Hall and passersby smiled with amusement. There'd been a Pantomime in progress and the Hall was filled with giggling youth of all ages. Even the old men who sat dazed on bar stools in the nearby pub could hear the raucous, prompting them to order more drinks than usual. The thought of children having so much fun brought either fond reminiscing or disdain from those who had struggled through life in the small village. Posters announcing the upcoming Ides of March observance sat propped up in shop windows, their message perhaps accounting for the growing tensions that seemed to float through the village like unseen ghosts. This was a place filled with mystical, Celtic stories passed down through generations like a set of fine jewels. Even those whose heritage did not include such tales treaded more softly when the Fifteenth of March approached. The local tailor, Mr. Booth, often told his patrons that it was best not to tempt the demons that the Irish had brought with them. Too many centuries of unexplained mysteries and unresolved anger to tempt fate. Still, this day any gloom or doom had been lost to the unrestrained merriment that shook the old single-glazed windows of Town Hall.

Sister Joan adjusted her back against the oak tree once more and smiled slightly, recalling her favorite knit hat she'd worn to the Pantomime. That day had been one turning point, hinting at a future she and her friends couldn't have seen. The vision and their conversation played again in her mind. Louise. Louise always spoke first – and fast. Her friend with so much to say and so little sense.

"It really was a good show this time, much better than the last one."

Doreen had nodded in agreement as she looked up at her friend. Louise always had her face made up and on that day she looked rather like a clown.

"Let's go to Miss Logan's Cafe for some salad sandwiches and cakes."

Miss Logan's Cafe was small but cheerful, its tables set with printed cloths and small glass jars filled with the early wildflowers. The smell of baked goods and cheese mingled together with the scented powders of the patrons. The girls took a seat by the window, giggling and pointing to Miss Logan's cat that occupied its normal place on the windowsill. When the tea and sandwiches were brought, they took turns covering the cream pitcher with their hands to keep the cat from leaping on their table, a ritual that many patrons performed out of past experience.

"So Doreen, how are you getting on with both of your jobs?"

"I love my job at the chemist. Mr. Spence's work is so interesting and his shop always smells fresh and clean. But I should've stayed on at Miss Norton's instead of moving on to tailor Booth. It's not that I dislike Mr. Booth, but I think he needs to bathe more often and open up the doors and windows!"

All three girls laughed a little more loudly than was proper, covering their mouths with the printed cloth serviettes.

Betty's face grew serious before she spoke.

"Doreen, thanks for giving me your job at Miss Norton's, it's been great. Have you thought about what you're going to do with your schooling in the next two years? I mean, are you going to stay in school or go to work fulltime?"

"I'd really like to continue in school, but I'm not sure if that will be possible. My mum is working more hours and doing a lot more volunteering at the church. I feel like I should consider going to work fulltime to help out, but I'm not sure yet. What about you, Louise? What do you plan to do?"

"I plan to find a handsome boy who has a good job and get married as soon as I can! I'll even settle for a not-so-handsome lad, as long as he works and stays out of the pub!"

Betty leaned toward the center of the table and whispered.

"Speaking of reasons for getting married, Louise, you'd better start watching how you spend time when we're not around you."

"Betty! What are you talking about?!"

"Oh come on, Louise, you don't exactly make a secret of your late night activities."

Doreen's eyes widened and she shifted in her chair as she spoke.

"Betty! I can't believe you said that! That's a gossip tale if ever I heard one."

"Oh Doreen, you can't be that naive. Besides, we love you anyway, Louise."

Doreen sat back and sighed.

"That we do, but you probably should be more careful. Maybe you just want extra attention."

"I don't think that's all she wants!"

Despite their best intentions, all three giggled.

Over cakes, Doreen let her mind wander back to Louise's comment on marriage. She'd never considered having a husband as a goal. Perhaps it was because it had always been just she and her mum, and their home was filled with love. It didn't seem as though they were missing anything. Still, again she *had* wondered what it would be like to be married to William...

Doreen had stopped by the church on the way home that day to see if her mum was there, but everything was quiet and closed up for the evening. The sun had slipped down and the clouds had cast a dark pink glow on the stained glass window above the front doors. She'd stood wondering what Father Laughry was doing as he puttered around in the small parish flat that was attached to the church, musing that it must be lonely for priests and nuns. She'd shaken her head, readjusted her hat, and briskly walked home as the colors in the sky faded to gray.

CHAPTER SIX

Sister Joan stood briefly and looked out over the convent cemetery, wondering for a moment how long she'd been there. *It didn't matter. Time didn't matter right now.* She placed her hands behind her head and looked up at darkening clouds. There had been other clouds hovering over her many times before! She lowered herself against the red oak once again as her mind wandered onto one such time.

The winter of 1928 had been a cold and confusing one. The topic of rising unrest in parts of Europe had been table conversation more than once. Doreen faced decisions on her schooling and there was always the question of William and where their relationship would lead. One afternoon in early January had ended badly when the conversation touched on her mum's visit to William's house to help with the children. His mum had been ailing and Wilhelm had left for Germany several weeks ago. William had insisted that his father had gone to get more involved with the rising political movement that was divisive and intolerant. Doreen was uncomfortable with his harsh criticism of his father and her response still echoed in her mind.

"But William, when you talk about your da without knowing the whole story, aren't you being just as intolerant? Not all Germans are like that! You can't question his motives without looking at your own!"

William had defended himself with more angst than necessary, telling her that he lived with the man and knew him better than she. They had ended the subject abruptly, but their disagreement had spoiled the outing.

Although it was a public footpath up to Wickens Hill, there'd been no one else around on their next trek up the path, most likely due to the blustery weather that had blown in from the north. The young couple's gloved hands were clasped together and their shoulders nearly touched as they slowly ambled up the path. The wind made mournful sounds as it whipped across the moor. A little time and youthful optimism had nearly erased the hurt from their last ugly scene but Doreen waited for William to speak first.

"So, you and your mum had a fun New Year's Day?"

"Oh, William, we really had a good time. We started at the parish house to greet Father Laughry, then made the rounds from there. My mum was in a rare mood, laughing a lot and even taking a few sips of holiday punch at Miss Norton's place."

"How about you? Did you get any of her nearly famous punch?"

"I'll never tell! Besides, the visiting was all about having a good natter."

William had gently knocked her new wool cap off and they'd both laughed, a comfortable kind of playfulness that growing up friends share.

"Aye, I know what you're saying. I've just never got anything to say back. I'm not very good at this talking and sharing business. Just look at my da, the only thing he shares has a bottomless tap and a foam head on top!"

Doreen glanced at William to see if his mood had changed to the serious, but he was smiling broadly.

"So, what exactly did you do while Mum and I were making the rounds that day?"

"I didn't really do much of anything except keep an eye on the wee lass. My mum was in a bit of a state, but I calmed her down in time for tea, which I may say, was entirely my project."

"Really? I'm impressed, William. You're not anything like your da, are you?"

"I certainly hope not!"

They shared the comment in silent understanding. William motioned for Doreen to sit on the hard ground under the branches of a plane tree that tenaciously held onto its leaves.

"William, don't you ever wonder if marriage is really worth it? I mean, with all the struggles many folks have, I just don't know..."

"Aye, I do sometimes. I mean, look at my mum. She's tired all the time and doesn't have much to show for her life."

"She's got you and your sisters. That's quite a bit I'd say. Yet I have to admit that for me, I'm not sure that would be enough. Not to sound selfish or anything. It's just that men seem to have the upper hand in this world. I'm not sure where I want to fit in to all of that."

Doreen expected a quick reply, but none came.

The wind was now howling across the moor and Doreen pulled her hat back on. They sat huddled in silence like a couple of Jerseys, listening to the trees bending and moaning. Doreen could hear the sound of her own heartbeat quicken as William reached over and turned her face to his. She knew what he was about to do and she wasn't sure it was a good idea, but she couldn't turn away. It wasn't a long kiss, but it was warm and sweet like innocence should be, and Doreen was powerless to move. It wasn't too long before the cold forced them to break their awkward silence and stand up.

"I'll treat you to a hot cocoa at Miss Logan's, if you want one."

Doreen knew that William was trying to make idle conversation after the unexpected kiss. Drinking hot cocoa at Miss Logan's was a treat they had routinely enjoyed and seemed to put aside the meaning of the moment on Wickens Hill.

"I'd love some, thanks."

"You started to tell me about your uncle that wants to help you with schooling costs. Are you planning to continue your studies?"

"I sure am. I've got to get out of here someday, Doreen. I don't want to end up stuck here. Not that there's anything wrong with this town, I just need to get away. I'm hoping to study engineering at a university."

"That sounds wonderful. I know you'll succeed. The only thing is, I guess that means that it won't be long before you're gone."

As soon as the words were out, Doreen regretted having said them. She swallowed and went on.

"But actually, *I* probably won't live my whole life in Hempstead, though I'm sure I'll be here for a while. I don't know if I'll have any money for living at university. Lately I've been delivering the parish news to the hospital, helping mum out with some of her church duties. It's fun watching everything that goes on at hospital, but it seems they are a bit outdated in some equipment and procedures."

"Likely right on that score."

William took a long sip of cocoa, then awkwardly placed his hand on top of hers. Doreen didn't move. She thought it best to just keep talking.

"What I'd really like is to have the means to move mum and myself into a nicer cottage outside of town or even in another village. I'd love for her to have the time and space to tend a large garden as it's always been a dream of hers. You know how well she tends that flower bed at the church."

"Aye, she's good at that."

The evening shadows were already darkening the streets when Doreen and William walked home. Only their shoulders were touching. They both sighed at the same time, then smiled and turned away to step inside the reality of their own homes.

The earlier sunshine had disappeared and the spring breeze had shifted to a damp wind that caused Sister Joan to shiver. She stood up and brushed off her habit and walked toward a row of newly sprung flowers. Their colors were so young and bright, untainted as yet by the harshness of rains that often pelted the English Isles in any season. Their perfection caused a catch in her throat. Their petals were all intact and the stems were straight and sturdy. They looked as though they could weather any rainstorm. Joan suddenly felt very small and weak. It was the same feeling she'd had on her sixteenth birthday in April of 1928.

The day had started out well with a lovely ring from her mum. It was after realizing that William wasn't even going to remember her with a card, let alone a visit, that the day had taken on a sadder note. She'd known he'd be starting university classes soon and her mum's question about their relationship had thrown her off guard. She'd told her mum that he'd been selfish with his time and attention of late, but that she wasn't bothered by that. Her mum had only smiled, knowing full well that wasn't the case. She'd changed the conversation, telling her mum about her visits to the convent at the request of Father Loughry. Her mum had seemed pleased.

Joan stepped around the flowers and folded her arms against the growing wind. She walked aimlessly for a few minutes and settled down beneath a different tree, next to a row of headstones. The date of death on the grave marker closest to her read December 15, 1928. That was a month she'd never forgotten. Its events laid out in her mind as though they'd never been replaced. That year's festive Christmas holidays had lost their luster for her after the ill-fated winter ball. It was strange to think that one evening so many years before could still be so fresh and hurtful. She'd come out to the cemetery to find solace, but the conversations of that December evening wailed through her consciousness, replaying like an old cylinder.

That dark winter evening had set in with usual dankness as Doreen slipped on her holiday dress for the big dance. She could hear her mother humming in the kitchen as she set out a small supper for herself. Her mum had moved so much slower of late and Doreen had worried. She'd felt badly about confiding her concern to the convent's Mother Superior. Still, Mother Mary Catherine had spoken words of comfort and reassurance: *it was probably just fatigue or the damp weather.*

"Doreen, you'd better get moving, you'll be late!"

"I'm ready. By the way, did I tell you I saw William at the greengrocer the other day?"

"No, how is he?"

"He looked good – he's taller. We only talked for a minute, but he asked what I was planning to do next. I told him nothing has really taken me in just now. It was the strangest thing though, Mum. I'm not sure how I feel about him anymore. I don't know how we fell apart. I've heard he was in town a few times, but he never came by."

"That happens, Lamb. Sometimes we part with people naturally, the way it should be. Anyway, have a good time, love. Mind your manners and don't come home too late!"

Doreen shook her head and smiled at her mum's admonition. It was an all too familiar phrase, spoken each time she went out with friends. Still, it was comforting that her mum cared enough to say those words, as not all of her friends had mums who knew of their daughter's exploits.

"I'll be home by 11:00, I promise."

Doreen braced herself against the blowing drizzle and quickened her steps. The annual Christmas Dance at the Town Hall was the biggest event of the year for Hempstead youth. The young people donned their very best and spent the evening eating, eyeing one another, and even dancing occasionally. No one ever worried about having a date and that made it well attended. She stopped at Betty's house and the two of them walked into the Hall together. How beautifully decorated! The dance committee had certainly gone to great lengths to transform the large, sterile room into a winter wonderland. There were gold and silver garlands hanging from the lights and evergreens draped across the front stage area where the orchestra sat. The food and punch tables were filled with festive platters and splashes of red ribbons donned the cracked walls. The musicians had come from Oxford University, looking very sophisticated in their suits. She'd strike up a conversation with at least one of them at their first break!

Her thoughts were interrupted by a familiar voice.

"There you are, Doreen. I thought you and Betty would never get here!"

"Hi Louise! I haven't seen you in a bag of fortnights! Where've you been keeping yourself?"

"Oh, Louise has been out and about alright. She's been avoiding us."

"Betty, that's not fair! I haven't been avoiding anyone, I've just been…. caught up in some things. Doreen, perhaps we can have a serious chat soon. Like tonight."

"I don't know, Louise. Tonight I'm in the mood for dancing and fun!"

"Well then, I'm going for some punch so I'll see you later."

Doreen and Betty watched their childhood friend make her way through the crowd to the refreshment table.

Doreen looked at her closest confidante, expecting to hear Betty's explanation for Louise's absence from their escapades.

"Are you going to tell me *why* you said Louise has been 'out and about'? What does that mean?"

"God, Doreen, you don't really know, do you? All this time I thought you were just avoiding the topic, waiting until I brought it up. Did you get a good look at the dress Louise is wearing?"

Doreen strained to see her friend through the dimness and the crowd.

"It's beautiful, Betty. Certainly a store bought one, unlike yours and mine. Besides, what does her dress have to do with anything?"

"I'm talking about extra roominess, especially around the middle. Doesn't that give you a clue?"

Louise had moved away from the table and was heading towards the dance floor. Doreen stared at her and nodded her head in silence. It was frightening to think of Louise facing such a difficult situation.

"Does she even have a boyfriend?"

"Yes, well, how can I answer that? Do you want to know the rest of the details?"

Doreen's stomach felt a bit queasy as her words tumbled out and the music blared too loudly.

"No, not really, I guess. I feel sorry for her. I suppose she'll be visiting a 'sick aunt' soon, disappearing from Hempstead for several months and returning at least a stone lighter."

"Doreen, don't you really want to know the rest of the story? I mean, I think it's important for you to hear the news from me."

"What are you talking about?"

"I'm talking about who they say the father is."

"Betty! I don't want to hear this. I don't care, and I don't want to know! Now, come on, let's dance before they take a break."

She grabbed Betty's arm and whirled her onto the floor, lost in the mix of colors and scents and sounds.

Later, Doreen and Betty sat side by side uneasily as they all donned bright, paper crowns and toasted to Father Christmas. Doreen left the table suddenly, trying to get to the bench on the back wall when she felt an arm take hers gently.

"Doreen, I wondered if you were here. We must have been on opposite sides of the room."

Doreen knew it was William even before she glanced up. He was wearing his hair differently, making him more handsome. He looked so much more mature and his clothes were well tailored.

"Hallo, William. How are you?"

Her question sounded stupid, but she couldn't think of anything else to say.

"You look beautiful, Doreen."

"Thank you."

"And to answer your question, I'm fine. I'm sorry I didn't have time to really chat at the greengrocer the other day. I wanted to tell you that I've really enjoyed university and I appreciate all your encouragement you always gave me."

I'm glad your schooling is working out for you, but I must admit that a lot of us miss having you around."

She didn't know why she'd said that. The truth was, William had never had a lot of friends. His father's boisterous behavior had scared off most of them.

"Doreen, how's your mum?"

"Fine, just a bit worn out sometimes. And your family?"

"Alright, I guess, though I can't say about my da. He's still in Germany. Doreen, there's something I need to tell you. I'm not in school anymore, at least not right now."

"What do you mean, you're not in school? It was always what you wanted and you've barely started. You just said...."

"I know. I was doing great and I loved it. I've come home to visit and help my mum several times in the past few months. I'm sure you knew when I was here."

"I did. I figured you were busy and our friendship had.....well, faded I guess."

"Our friendship was always important to me, Doreen. It's just that I sort of got involved with another girl and I didn't want to hurt you."

Doreen glanced around before turning her eyes to the floor.

"I see. So, are you and this girl getting married?"

"I don't know. Honestly, I don't think so. Her parents aren't thrilled with her marrying into a German family, especially one with a drunk. They do seem keen to have her marry *someone* as soon as possible, though. Anyway, *she's* not bothered by my tainted family, so everything's up in the air, as they say."

Doreen raised her eyes and looked into his face. It bore a sadness she'd rarely seen in him and for a moment, a small pain shot through her chest.

She realized how much she had truly missed him. Before another word was spoken, Louise came up behind them, her voice nervous and agitated.

"Here you both are. William, have you told Doreen....about us, I mean?"

Doreen swallowed, her mouth half-open.

William fidgeted with his cravat.

"I was getting to that."

Without thinking, Doreen's eyes went straight to Louise's stomach. William stepped backwards and looked over his shoulder awkwardly.

"If you want to dance, Louise, now's the time. I'm not staying long. I'll meet you by the stage."

Louise paused and turned to Doreen.

"Doreen, I'm sorry. I really am. It's just that you were so busy and William stopped in town ever so often. I never meant to hurt you."

Louise turned and headed toward the source of the music, her dress ballooning like a parachute from a sudden draft.

"Doreen, I don't know what to say."

"Damn it, William. With Louise? How could you just fade from my life and reappear as Louise's....whatever you call her?"

William stood silent for a moment, his feet shifting back and forth.

"I don't know if we'll marry. I'm really sorry, Doreen. But what you and I had was...a while ago. I should have done things differently. I should have told you sooner."

"Bloody hell, I'll say!"

Doreen's voice caught and her mind whirled as she heard more swear words escape from her own mouth. She took a deep breath.

"William, I really hope you can get back into school, it's where you belong. You know that I've always....well, at any rate, I guess I wish both of you the best."

Doreen's voice began to waiver and the lie she'd just spoken stuck in her throat. William took her hands and kissed the top of her head, then walked away, turning around once to stare at her. Taking a seat on the bench by the wall, Doreen sat out several dances before returning to the floor with Betty to finish out the evening getting lost in the movement of young bodies. Getting lost in the blur of her own tears.

CHAPTER SEVEN

Sister Joan clicked off the months following that holiday dance until she reached June of 1929. Another concern had taken over her by then and at times it consumed her thoughts. She'd even taken up the subject with Father Loughry at an awkward time and place and hadn't been pleased with his response.

There had been a slight breeze that summer day which blew across the garden near the cloisters of Wycombe Convent. It rustled the papers in front of Father Loughry and he'd secured them with his teacup. She would have preferred a cold drink that afternoon, but tradition demanded otherwise. It'd felt a bit strange to be visiting the convent on the day that her priest came to discuss his late sister's personal effects, but both he and Mother Mary Catherine had asked her to stay. She had visited the Hempstead Royal Infirmary earlier in the day and arrived at the convent to give the sisters and the Father an update on Sister Agnes' condition. But there had been more on her mind than Sister Agnes' health and in a conversation lull, she changed the subject.

"Sister Agnes talked today of some serious things going on in Germany. She called them 'unpleasant events' and genuinely seemed upset. I remember when my mum looked in on William Strucker's family last winter. His father, Wilhelm, had gone back to Germany and has never returned. It seems like there are some dark secrets over there, but I hate to judge what I don't know much about. Have you got any thoughts?"

Neither the Mother Superior nor the priest spoke right away. They continued sipping their tea, looking at each other for an answer to her question. Father Loughry leaned back and stretched.

"Doreen, there are some peculiar and yes, quite unpleasant things going on there. But it's very far from us and we don't really know the whole story."

"But does that excuse us from paying attention, or at least *trying* to know more?"

"Father Loughry's right, my dear. There are so many things here in the U.K. we should be focusing on. You're too young to be worrying about political activities over on the continent. You should be thinking of your own future. Do you have any plans?"

Doreen had sighed audibly before answering.

"No, not exactly. I suppose I'd like to work at the chemist full time."

"That's fine, my dear. But take your time and make sure it's right for you."

With evening setting in, she'd excused herself and headed home feeling that her future and her concerns were more unresolved than ever.

A figure clad in long, black clothes stood at a distance and stared at Joan as the young nun wandered away to a different section of the cemetery. The unseen visitor turned back to the convent, her shoulders slumping and her eyes watching shadowy patterns on the stone path.

Joan had been struggling through memories for hours and the threat of rain now loomed above her. *It wouldn't matter.* The rain might even wash the salt of tears from her face. She ambled the walkway, searching for a stone with a date of November, 1929. Why was she doing this? Would it really make a difference to relive the moments when her very own words sealed her fate – determined her future?

November 1929

Anna Bailey had turned over the flowered plates, examining them as she set places on her kitchen table. There were chips and scratches that indicated years of use and the plates were brittle in her hands. There was rarely extra money for luxuries like new dishes. She'd watched her daughter's young, strong arm move in a circular pattern as she stirred the mutton stew. She knew it wasn't Doreen's favorite meal, but recently it was the only thing they could afford.

"Do you want me to wrap up the bread yet, Mum?"

"Sure, love. I think we're just about ready to eat. Let me just pour the milk."

There was no further comment for a while, a sure sign that both were absorbed in their own thoughts.

"So Mum, do you really think our banks are in danger, like the ones in the States? I've heard some people say that folks in America are already trying to take out their savings, even though that probably just makes the situation worse."

"I don't know, love. It's a hard thing to predict. I really don't understand most of it. All I know is that what's going on in America will very soon affect us here, as well as the rest of Europe. It's only a matter of time. I fear that we're headed toward a rough swell."

Doreen knew what her mum meant by the term "rough swell." Mum had often used seafaring terms as her father had been a fisherman on the North Sea. You could hang on and ride out a rough swell if you were lucky. If you weren't, the sea claimed you for its own. The thought had given her a sudden chill and she lowered her face to feel the steam rising from the plate of stew.

"Do you think we should take our savings out of the bank, Mum?"

"No, not yet. We need to hang on for a bit and see what happens. We'll have to batten down the sails though, and not spend foolishly. But don't you worry your mind about any of this right now. You just concentrate on making a decision about schooling or keeping your two jobs. I know you'd rather work at the chemist's, but Mr. Spence just can't hire you for all day. Please don't let any dismal news affect your decision. You can still go to university for just the cost of meals and extras. We can make it work."

Doreen had known it pained her mum to always have little means for "extras." She'd always tried hard not to let her mum see any disappointment over their inability to afford new clothes or train trips into London. They were a team and had ridden out many "turbulent waves." That wasn't the time to get selfish and worry about extra schooling, especially when she'd had options that some girls didn't have.

"Well, here's to jobs, whatever they may turn out to be."

They'd both laughed, each raising their glass of milk in a silent toast. The rest of dinner was spent in light conversation. They took a seat in the front room, each one setting a cup of tea beside them and picking up a book to read. It was a ritual they enjoyed at least twice a week, letting the sounds of the ticking grandfather clock and the hum of the gas fire sink into their souls, a quiet retreat that Anna Bailey proclaimed as "absolutely necessary." Doreen had always liked these evenings, often using them as an excuse to avoid the usual idle traipsing about with friends.

It was nearing bedtime before Doreen found what she hoped were just the right words to convey what she'd been considering for the past few days.

"Mum, I have been thinking about another option for my life. I wanted you to hear my thoughts before I made a final decision. I know it's probably not exactly what either of us had planned for my life, but..."

"Doreen, I'm not the one that's going to live your life, *you* are. I've never yet planned your future and I would never be disappointed in any path you chose. You are bright and ambitious and have quite enough sense to plan your own."

"Thanks, Mum. What I mean is, I've actually been considering going into the convent, you know, becoming a nun. I know it sounds a bit sudden and all, but I truly enjoy their company and I've really felt a calling to that place. Wycombe Convent is where I've felt most comfortable lately, except for here of course."

Doreen expected to see a look of surprise and concern, but there was only an expression of pride.

"Doreen, that's wonderful! I'm so very proud of you! Nothing could make me happier than seeing you as a bride of Christ. I have always thought that you were destined for great adventures in your life. Serving as a sister in the Church must surely be the most special of all pursuits. I'm so happy for your decision, that is, if it's what you *really* want for yourself and not just something you've decided to settle on."

The clock chimed loudly in the stillness of the room. Doreen felt a strange ache in her stomach. Her mum's words were almost too accepting. Too encouraging. The real truth was that Doreen *did* feel a calling to become a nun, but it wasn't really her first calling. She didn't know yet what her heart most longed to pursue. Perhaps medicine? There was something else waiting for her, she just didn't have time to wait until that something became crystal clear. Joining the convent would give her life purpose and direction. It would also give her a long term home and three meals a day. It would most certainly ease their financial burden and lessen her mum's worries. And too, Wycombe Convent exuded an air of refuge and peace, of camaraderie without judgment and contentment without pressure. She already knew several of the sisters quite well from earlier visits and they had been uncharacteristically lavish in their kind comments about her. It was the perfect solution. The perfect path to take. It just felt right, as though God were truly taking her hand to walk down this new path. The clock ticked loudly in the quiet room and Doreen's attention was once more drawn to the one person she would have to leave behind when she walked through the doors of the convent.

"My dear, are you all right? You seem quite lost in your own thoughts. Did I say something that upset you?"

"No, of course you didn't. Mum, You've always believed in me. I know I wasn't the easiest child to raise alone, but..."

"Hush Lamb. Now what's *really* bothering you?"

Doreen smiled and studied the creases in her mum's face. Perhaps those lines were a beautiful right of passage for a parent, a privilege that she herself would never know.

"I guess it's just that I'll never be a mother. I'll never experience what we have together or share the kind of bond that you and I have known."

"Never mind, love. God has called you to be one of His own and that, in itself, is enough."

"So you truly think I've made the right decision, don't you?"

"I think only you can answer that, but I *will* tell you that I believe you'll be a remarkable nun and a blessing to everyone whose lives you touch."

Her mum's words were overly sentimental for a woman whose own life had been filled with the practical and harsh realities of living. Doreen glanced down at the cold cup of tea still cradled in her lap. It was time to pour a fresh, hot cup before turning down the gas stove for the night. The bedtime rituals she and her mum had followed for years came into sharp focus, painting an invisible mural before her eyes as Doreen walked slowly into the warm kitchen, her hands still clutched around the cold cup.

February 23, 1930

The clean, crisp air of the late winter day made everyone move quickly into the chapel at Wycombe Convent. The previous night's weather had made ice crystals form on the bare trees and the fields surrounding the ancient, stone buildings. The few ornate, sculpted figures on the roofs were adorned with the sparkling ice, giving the gargoyles a strange, festive appearance. Doreen stood outside and stared at them before going inside to take her vows as a novice. The stone faces were looking off into the distance, as though they were guarding some other home and not the one they had been assigned to. She always thought they had looked quite out of place on sacred ground with their scowling expressions just on the verge of appearing evil. She knew, of course, that their appearance was precisely for that purpose, to ward off any evil spirits that might approach the house of God. Still, as Doreen watched the ice crystals slowly melting and dripping from their stone faces, she couldn't help but wonder if anyone really knew what evil looked like and if it had already made its way inside the door. She felt a cold shiver as the wind picked up, swirling her long skirt around her legs. It was time to make this promise. Time to start a new life. Time to embrace a love that would forever be her intimate soul mate. A mate that would never abandon, but might often confuse. A mate that would carry her when she could not walk under her own power, but would require her to hold others when necessary. It was a paradoxical lover. A demanding, forgiving, intense, gentle, smothering, yet freeing lover. Not at all the kind she had imagined she would embrace when sitting under the tree on the top of Wickens Hill. It was a love that would give her purpose, constancy, and immense personal satisfaction. Yet, not a lover who would grace her with *human intimacy* and the opportunity to bond with a life that she had brought into this world. It was not a loss, really. Just an empty spot she hoped would be filled.

Doreen shook her head to clear away the vision of the stony faces standing guard. She walked into the Chapel, her eyes unfocused and bleary. She made her way to the front altar and stood next to the Mother Superior Mary Catherine and the visiting Cardinal. She glanced at the Baptismal Font. The colors of the clerics' robes blurred like a painting smeared with water. Her head turned to see Father Loughry, sitting straight in his chair, a smile on his face and eyes welled with tears of pride. It was a shining moment for him. One of his own flock joining the sisterhood; every priest's dream. She was drawn back to reality at his gaze, but a veil quickly covered her presence of mind.

She took her vows as though they were someone else's. Someone whose voice she recognized, but whose words were that of a stranger. She felt the ring slip on her finger and stared at the cold circle of gold. It was so plain. So unadorned. It fit perfectly but her hand felt oddly heavy. It would forever be difficult to hold anything without feeling the weight of that circle. The stones on the chapel floor were uncomfortable, even through her layers of clothing, yet she hesitated before rising when the kneeling part was over. It seemed appropriate to let the pain of the jagged blocks dig into her skin, as penance for sins yet unknown. She finally stood as *Sister Joan*, still lost in the maze of sights and sounds and the smell of the incense, her mind not yet able to process the magnitude and meaning of the chants punctuated with phrases of sacred promises. This was right. Whatever evil was lurking inside this place, inside of her, was surely banished on this frozen, sunny morning. While everyone moved from the chapel to finish with a celebratory luncheon, her consciousness had slowly returned.

"Thank you, Mum, for getting me to this point, and allowing me to pursue this path. I love you."

"My sweet lamb, you keep forgetting that it was not anyone of us that brought you to this point. It's always been just between you and God. Oh, and dear, I love you, too. I love you so very much."

The rest of that afternoon had gone swiftly with lots of chatter and tours of the Convent and enough food to feed a small country. When at last she'd fallen on her knees in her small, private room, the sun had long disappeared from the sky and the cold air outside had crept through the stones. She'd shivered as she said her prayers and as she jumped into the narrow bed, a picture of the gargoyles flashed across her mind. They were still outside on guard duty, their faces once again frozen over from the damp chill that February brought. She couldn't help but wonder if they had fallen asleep on the job. Had anyone searched their expressions for any sign of turmoil? Had she glanced at her own reflection before walking into the tiny, mirrorless room she'd tried to claim as her own sanctuary?

The air in that small room was heavy from the weight of an ominous warning. Perhaps it was only the weight of the responsibility she'd promised to bear. A responsibility symbolized by the ring that had immediately become too tight. She'd drawn the extra covers up about her neck and fallen asleep struggling to twirl the ring around and around.

CHAPTER EIGHT

Joan moved from the tree to the damp grass and laid her head against a headstone knowing that it surely was some sort of sin to invade a space that held a nun's remains. Still, the stone was smooth and strangely comforting. The months following her vows had brought more confusion and fear as her mum's health declined. She recalled with clarity her entrance into the Hempstead Royal Infirmary in February of 1931. Her mum had been adamant about avoiding the hospital, as if not knowing the cause or the outcome would make her illness disappear. It had been a frustrating year. The sisters had been more than supportive, especially when she'd been absent from her convent duties. She'd worn a path between Hempstead and Amersham as she tried to keep watch over her mum's failing health and Mother Superior Mary Catherine had been very generous in giving her leaves of absence. It had gotten much easier when she was no longer a novice and could enjoy the full privileges of the sisterhood. Still, she'd felt a pang of guilt making her way to the hospital reception desk that cold day in February. She'd counted on getting some answers that time!

"Good morning. May I help you, Sister Joan?"

She'd known the middle-aged receptionist from her earlier visits to ailing nuns, but she'd never really had a real conversation with her. Mrs. Markham brushed a lock of graying hair aside and smiled.

"I hope so. I've an appointment to speak with a doctor about my mum, Anna Bailey."

"Oh yes, Sister, Dr. Bennett is expecting you. I'm afraid he's still in conference at the moment, but he should be out soon. Would you like some coffee while you wait?"

The woman's eyes still danced with a spark of youth and her voice was light and soothing, not hoarse or tired like most women her age.

"Oh goodness, please excuse my manners, won't you sit down in that comfy chair and I'll be right back with a pot of coffee."

Joan couldn't help but smile as she fell into the only soft chair in the otherwise clinical room. She realized that she hadn't even answered the woman's offer before the click of her matronly shoes briskly echoed down the hall. Mrs. Markham emerged as quickly as she had disappeared with a tray of coffee, two porcelain cups and a small pitcher of milk.

"Sorry love, I forgot the sugar. Don't use it myself so I never remember to put it on the tray."

"That's fine. I only take a spot of milk in mine. Thank you very much."

Mrs. Markham poured two cups of the aromatic, steaming liquid and sat down beside Joan on a straight-backed chair.

"So Sister Joan, you're here to talk to Dr. Bennett about your mum's condition, is it?"

"Yes, my mum has been quite ill for some time now. We're hoping to get some answers soon so she can begin a recovery before summer sets in. My mum loves to garden and it's going to be such a disappointment for her if she's unable to get into the flowers by June."

"Flowers. I know exactly how she feels. I just love to garden; have quite a nice one myself just over the way a bit. My cottage isn't much to speak of, but my flowers are quite lovely, I must say. I know exactly how your mum feels, I do."

Joan had stiffened a bit. Had she really known exactly how Mum felt? It had been so long since her mum had been able to do much of anything. Yet it certainly wouldn't do to hurt this woman with an unkind word.

"Mrs. Markham, please tell me about Dr. Bennett."

"He's quite knowledgeable, Sister Joan. You and your mum have nothing to worry about. He's the best around Hempstead. He practically lives here at the hospital. Can't figure it out. He's a fine looking man, should be quite married by now."

The sound of heavy footsteps had interrupted their conversation as a man in a knee-length white coat strode across the room and stood before them.

"I see that Mrs. Markham has you drinking that stiff juice she calls coffee, right on target for her."

He'd winked at his receptionist, then offered his hand to Joan.

"I'm Dr. Colin Bennett, Sister. I've been assigned to your mother's case. Let's talk in my office."

He'd motioned her into his office and she'd followed him, turning once to give a small wave and "thank you" to the woman who had already resumed her position at the front desk.

His office was stark, undecorated and immaculately clean. His desk was piled with neat stacks of papers and the books on his shelf were lined up in exacting, symmetrical rows. He was obviously a man of some perfectionist qualities.

"I've reviewed your mother's medical file and talked extensively to the doctor who treated her several months ago. I'm afraid it doesn't look good. Your mother needs an operation immediately. Only after we open her up can we determine the extent of the damage. We may be able to rid her of the bad tissue cells, but there's no guarantee. Your mother must be a very brave woman, to be able to hide such an illness for so long."

She had stared wordlessly at the doctor unable to speak, lost in her own thoughts. The finality of his words seemed harsh, yet he managed to deliver them with softness, his eyes heavy with compassion. He was certainly professional, yet his shoulders dropped with his final words.

"I believe your mother will only get worse with time, eventually needing round the clock care. I will do my best with the surgery to make her more comfortable, but I'm afraid that her immediate future is really in God's hands."

She'd swallowed hard, shifted in her seat and stared at the floor for a minute.

"Are you all right, Sister? I know this is hard news to take. Can I get you a glass of water or some more coffee?"

"No thank you. How soon can we schedule the surgery?"

"I'll get back to you tomorrow about that."

The rest of the time in his office was spent discussing the logistics of her mum's surgery and recovery. The doctor seemed pleased that she was so knowledgeable about medicines and procedures and it made her feel oddly proud to be able to speak intelligently with him.

She'd waved and spoken to Mrs. Markham on the way out and noticed that the wedding band was on the older woman's right hand, an old-fashioned sign that her husband was deceased. She had pondered that as well as the sound of Dr. Bennett's voice all the way back to the Convent and well after she should have been repenting for her daily sins.

Joan turned around to face the headstone and moved her hand in circular patterns across the cold engravings, trying to erase years of weathering. Once again, the mantra of her diary entries flowed, their words repeating like a sad dirge.

April 22, 1931

My heart is so heavy it is hard to breathe. Here I sit in mum's hospital room, glad that I brought you along to unburden my thoughts. Her recovery is not going well at all. Dr. Bennett checks in on her regularly and gives me his sense of her situation, even though he is not assigned to her anymore. As a surgeon, he did what he could. I don't believe mum is going home this time, at least, not home to our cottage in Hempstead. S.J.

June 11, 1931

Mum died today. Lamb

June 13, 1931

We buried mum today in the old churchyard. It was the hardest thing I've ever done. Everyone was there, including Dr. Bennett, a true kindness indeed. We laid her to rest by the cemetery garden that she and Mauve had planted years ago. The flowers are blooming and their fragrance softened the black stones of the ancient church. I've arranged for a simple stone to read "Anna Bailey- 1891 to 1931- Loving mother." I'm trying hard and praying harder to seek a reason for mum's passing so soon. God knows that we were all each other had. I feel so alone and even betrayed. I just can't help feeling angry.

After everyone left, I walked up the footpath to the fields overlooking Batley's farm. The summer blossoms are nearly in full bloom on the berry bushes, and the sun sparkled on the tiny creek that meanders its way across the farmland. It was as if the creek were talking to me, babbling and then whispering as the breeze changed directions. I could almost feel Mum's arms around me, almost hear her voice. The bleating of the sheep in the grasses below was a strange intrusion upon my refuge. How could every detail of this vista look so unaffected? How could the sun feel so light and warm and my heart feel so heavy and cold all in the same place? I tried to capture a picture in my mind of Mum's face. I stood there a long time and finally called out loud, "God, where is your mercy, your comfort, where are your answers?!" But I heard only the incessant sounds of bleating and tree branches swishing in the wind. I came back to the convent at dark, skipped devotions, and now I sit alone. So utterly alone. Oh, Mum, I miss you terribly. And I love you. Your lamb forever, Doreen

CHAPTER NINE

Sister Joan had no idea how long she'd been sitting on a gravesite, leaning against the headstone, but her skirt was wet from the damp grass. She'd been lost in her own private reverie while the April evening turned to darkness and the wind now whirled around her with growing intensity. Perhaps she'd come out to this holy place to see if she could fill her emptiness with the ghosts of others' lives. Those early years held so much of who she really was, but at this moment her life seemed devoid of her past and without vision for her future. The stinging tears had long since dried, but the stabbing pain was still there.

She placed her hand on the headstone and slowly stood up, her heartbeats drowning out even the cries of roosting birds. New tears escaped as the wind blew her habit back and forth in rhythmic pulses.

"Sister Joan."

She whirled around at the sound of the deep voice behind her.

"Sister Mary Catherine told me I might find you here."

"Colin!"

"I'm so sorry to intrude on you, but I ....I just wanted to make sure you were alright. You've not been back to the hospital since our dinner there weeks ago. I was worried about you."

Doreen placed her hands over her skirt that was dancing with abandon. How long had he been there? Had she spoken any words out loud, or were they only inside her head? What did he know that she herself had only come to realize moments before? She found her voice and raised her eyes to his as she spoke.

"I must look awful."

She wiped her face with her sleeve and continued.

"Have you been here long?"

"No, not too long. And you don't look awful at all. Just upset. This is really a beautiful spot, Sister. I can see why you came out here. It's not dismal or depressing. Seems somehow, I don't know, comforting I guess."

"Yes it is. And please, Colin, just call me Doreen."

"Doreen? Are you sure?"

"I'm sure."

"You know, I feel a bit awkward asking you this, but is it okay that we're out here alone?"

Doreen paused, gathering her composure.

"Yes. I believe it's very much okay. It seems very right to me. I mean, you being here- with me."

Colin moved closer to her and nodded before speaking.

"That's perfect, because it sure seems right to me, too. I've missed you, Doreen. I mean, I've *really* missed you. God help me, but I have. I just don't know how to handle this. You know, this thing between us. If you've insight from the Man upstairs, I'd sure like to hear it."

Doreen smiled.

"I've missed you too, Colin. I'm not quite sure what to do with all these feelings, but I do know something. I believe my life isn't here at Wycombe Convent."

"Do I have a right to ask what you're going to do now?"

"You do. But I can't really say the answer out loud just yet. I have to keep it inside for awhile, until my mind wraps around it all."

He took another step toward her, reached over and wiped an escaping tear. He let his hand rest on her cheek, nearly touching her lips, then drew it away and stepped back.

"I understand. I should go now. I'm not much of a praying man, Doreen, but I'll sure try to send one up His way for you. And one for me."

They both managed a smile, then he turned around and stepped onto the stone path that meandered between the gravesites. She watched him walk away while her skirt rose and fell in the wind. The mournful sound of one lone night bird pierced the silence and she could hear the murmur of those ancient voices dancing on the shifting winds, filling her head until she could no longer hear the pounding of her own heart.

Sister Mary Catherine was at her desk writing when Doreen knocked on the open door two days later.

"Sister Joan, do come in. You look as though you've spent a bit too much time in the gardens. The sun is quite hot today, you should be careful not to get too warm."

Joan paused before entering, waiting to respond.

"Mother Mary Catherine, I've come here to tell you that I cannot remain at the convent. I'm asking for a dispensation from my vows."

The silence was deafening. Mother Superior stood up and walked toward her.

"I see. When is it you came to this decision? It seems rather sudden, my dear."

"I can assure you that it is not. I know I should have come to you sooner, but I felt as though I needed to work this out by myself – with God's help of course."

"Sister Joan, how can you be so certain? It's been less than a year since your mother's death, and you've been so busy with the Sisters' Nursing Program, you need to give yourself more time to adjust to life here in the convent."

"Mother Mary Catherine, I've been so unhappy for several months. I know that taking more time will not change how I feel. The only reason I've not spoken sooner is because of my love for you. You have been such a comfort and inspiration to me, I can never repay all your kindness. But God and I both know that this is no longer the place for me to be. I can no longer in good faith and conscience call this my home."

Mary Catherine nodded

"Oh, child, how you must have struggled with this very difficult decision. You should have come to me sooner. Although I'm saddened by your choice to leave us, I'm more concerned with your mental health and happiness. Is there anything in particular you really want to do on the outside?"

"I've always been fascinated with medicine, even as a young girl. That's why I was so keen on the convent's hospital nursing ministry. Beyond that, I'd like to get even more involved in the medical profession. It's been a dream that I set aside, thinking it would fade."

"Dreams rarely fade, my dear. They find us in our sleep and awaken us with their persistence."

Doreen was helpless to stop the tears from once again streaming down her face soiling her habit with brackish spots.

"There now, dear, you mustn't shed any more tears on this. I'm sure our Blessed Mother Mary, as well as the Holy Ghost has guided you, and you must always honor that. Remember, God can and will use you in many different walks of life. Please know that we all will miss you, but I will attend to your request as soon as possible."

"Thank you. I'm so sorry, please forgive me."

"No need for apologies or forgiveness. One more thing: you will always have the love of this Order. May God go with you."

Doreen's footsteps echoed down the hall as she headed outside. The rest of the day could only be spent in solitude as there was so much to think about. So much to plan for. So much to cry about.

CHAPTER TEN
Hempstead
June 1932

June 24, 1932

It is turning out to be a lovely week here. The roses are blooming and the trees have shaded the walks and streets of otherwise drab Hempstead. The trees along the canals are in full greenery, spreading their shadows over the fishermen who cast their lines for trout by the old Fishery Inn. There are times, though, when I miss the beauty of the Convent grounds. Though I must admit, I have never been happier, except for my growing up years with mum. It's hard to believe it has been a whole year since her passing. Colin has been ever so kind of late, recognizing the time of her death, I suppose. We've not spoken again of our feelings though I'm not sure why. Perhaps he's waiting for me to broach the subject. I just don't have the courage. At any rate, we're enjoying our work together at the hospital. I'm so grateful I was able to keep on with the nurse's training, though I miss having classes with the sisters. We have quite a few new younger girls from surrounding villages who have come to train. I think they are finding it increasingly difficult to get work and want to have other options in their lives. I often wonder what's become of William. I'm excited about the next term though, as I can teach some of the basic classes. Colin says I have a real knack for this! I know mum would be proud of me. Doreen

January, 1933

The steps of the Hempstead Infirmary seemed steeper than usual and Doreen stood hesitantly before going inside. She knew that Mrs. Markham would be seated at her usual place, cheerfully greeting all who entered. She also knew that this conversation would be difficult at best, a conversation she hadn't expected to have so soon. Hempstead had been her home for twenty-one years. Her mum was laid to rest in this town. She had remained friends with a few of the sisters from the convent, especially Mary Catherine. Yet she also knew that those ties were not enough to keep her in a dying town. Saying "goodbye" to Mrs. Markham would be a painful realization that every new experience comes with a price. She had already paid for new choices before in her young life, but it seemed harder this time. She was luckier than those living in the northern regions of Yorkshire and Lancashire. Their towns had been economically devastated by the closing of coal and textile factories and didn't have the same advantages as London and its immediate locales. Still, she knew the hasty ban on trade with Germany after The Great War had brought the south to dire straits as well. Leaving Hempstead to move closer to the City of London was a chance to personally fare at least a bit better. This move would give her the chance to work in a larger, better-equipped hospital. She would have more opportunities for private nursing duties and more schooling as well.

Mrs. Markham smiled and took an envelope from her desk as Doreen approached.

"My dear, I was hoping you wouldn't board the train without saying 'goodbye.' Dr. Bennett said to tell you that he would meet you on the train. He had some last minute items to attend to. I must say, you look lovely. Quite posh for train travel."

Doreen blushed as she took a seat across from Mrs. Markham and placed a colorful package on the desk.

"This is for you, dear Mrs. Markham. It's not much really, but I wanted you to have some small remembrance of me. I'm going to miss you dreadfully."

"Now please don't start talking like that or I'll never get through the rest of the day. Whatever have you done?"

Mrs. Markham carefully opened the gift and covered her face in her hands.

"It's just a small door hanging that I made from dried flowers. My mum had kept a whole drawer full of pressed and dried bits from the garden she tended at the church. When she died, I took them with me to the convent and spent evenings making small arrangements. It seemed like a way to preserve a memory of the hours and devotion she'd spent lovingly digging in the dirt. I wanted you to have my favorite, as you've been so dear to me."

Mrs. Markham picked up the delicate arrangement, then pulled a linen hankie from the pocket of her skirt.

"It's truly lovely, Doreen. Something I shall cherish always."

The two women absorbed the moment in silence.

"You do think I'm doing the right thing, don't you?"

"Oh yes, my dear. Certainly the right thing for a young person. You have so many talents and your whole life is before you. Don't look back."

"What about you? Will you continue on here or could you possibly join us in London? I'm sure there'd be a place for you."

Mrs. Markham smiled and placed her hand on Doreen's.

"I've been here a long time. It's difficult to teach an old dog new tricks, you know."

Doreen studied her face for moment, trying to discern just how old Mrs. Markham really was.

"Please don't worry about us here, Doreen. We'll be fine! Oh, I almost forgot this."

She handed Doreen the envelope from the desk.

"All the nurses and other staff chipped in a bit and want you and Dr. Bennett to split this gift. We figured you both could use a bit of spare change, what with going to the big City and all. I'm afraid it's not much, with times being what they are right now. But it should help you with lodging and meals for a wee time, anyway. Take it with our best wishes and blessings."

Doreen took the envelope and opened it. Her eyes grew wide as she stared at the contents. It would indeed help to cover costs of the move. She suddenly wished Colin were beside her to share in this moment.

"Thank you so very much. Please express my gratitude to everyone else. It's a wonderful gift. I wish I didn't have to say this, but I really have to leave now before I miss the train. Colin and I are meeting with the new hospital personnel about the rooms they rent out. We don't want to miss that appointment!"

"Certainly not, my dear. You will let me know both of your new addresses soon?"

"Of course."

"And if there should be only one address in the future…"

Doreen blushed.

"Mrs. Markham!"

"Well, he's a right slow mover, that one!"

The two women laughed and exchanged a brief but heartfelt hug. Doreen turned around just once to wave as she closed the doors behind her and headed to the station. With three small cases in tow, she presented her ticket and boarded a train at the Hempstead Station. She moved to the coach car and sat down next to Colin. He took her hand briefly and they settled in for the short ride to the outskirts of London. Colin unfolded a newspaper and Doreen took out her diary.

January 31, 1933

    It is with mixed emotions that I sit here in this train as it pulls away from my roots, from the places that have defined who I am. Yet, at the same time, I am so anxious to be heading toward London with Colin! We have spent a great deal of time together, and I have learned so much from him. I'm almost afraid to admit that my feelings for him grow stronger each day. I hope he feels the same. Still, even if nothing more comes of our relationship, I believe that moving on to a new place is the right decision. I will be working as a nurse in a hospital in Croydon, which is just outside of London. Colin has signed on as a surgeon there. It is so much better equipped than Hempstead and I'm looking forward to learning new things, especially learning from Colin. We really work well side by side and have developed a deep respect and genuine affection for each other. I'm not sure Mum would fully approve of my latest decision, but she would likely have still given me her blessing. I still miss her so much. The hospital has small flats next door that they rent to medical employees for a small sum. I will finally be truly on my own and it is more than a little unsettling! I can afford the flat, though, and a few simple meals a week, so I should be fine. I'm as happy as if I were going to settle in at the Savoy! The only thing that has made me feel peculiarly troubled today is an article in the newspaper, a Times article about a radical man that has taken over as Germany's chancellor. I remember what Sister Agnes said about the rise of angry, nationalistic groups in Germany, and how intolerant they are. Also, I remember Mum's bad feelings about Mr. Strucker and his involvement in one of these groups. The news of this man's accession to power has been nagging at me for quite some time and I don't understand fully why. Yet, all in all, I am so excited to be starting a new chapter in my life, maybe one that Colin and I will share together!

Doreen

CHAPTER ELEVEN

Spring 1933
Croydon, England

The economic depression had made most Britons cautious spenders. London was far too expensive for the average person to live in. Just the ability to use public transport and go into London, even if it was only to walk about the streets and peer into the shop windows, was incentive enough to settle in towns like Croydon. Most of these outskirt towns grew in stages without much planning. They were a mixture of ancient and new, quickly fabricated, somewhat preserved. Croydon wasn't particularly charming or even pretty by country village standards, but it lay just to the southern edge of London, was bustling, productive, and *affordable*. Hills in the distance stood in start contrast to the dark and sooty buildings and attached houses on small mews.

Colin and Doreen settled into their separate flats by the hospital and worked together by day. Evenings were spent together in one of their flats, enjoying sandwiches by the fire. Sometimes they met at the local pub for a hot meal and some lively conversation with the folks gathered there. On evenings when the work load was heavy, or one or both of them were teaching classes at the hospital, they met at the fish-n-chips shop two streets over, or the nearby cafe for a quick bowl of soup.

The town had a few lovely gardens, sometimes trampled by unleashed dogs, but blooming in defiance of rubbish that swirled about them in the seasonal winds. Old men sat on benches outside of news agents' shops, reading newspapers, plagued with concern, apprehensive because of their own ignorance of rising unknown leaders. Talk in the local pubs grew defiant. Angry young men bantered back and forth expressing their opinions on the growing turmoil on the continent. Even the women spoke out. The teashops were filled with old ladies complaining about the price of produce and quality of meat in the market stalls. Yet amongst their fears and concerns, the gardens bloomed – a safe haven for those who wanted an escape.

Doreen took a last glance at the flowers around her and rose from the park bench.

"I think I fancy stopping by the art shop on the way home. I'd like to find a frame for that photo of the two of us, the one taken at the employee dinner last month. I have a perfect spot to hang it, just over my gas fire. Do you mind if we stop there on our walk back?"

"No, I guess not. I just want to be back at my place early enough to write up a report that's due tomorrow. We could take in an ice cream at the sweet shop, if you'd like."

"Sounds good to me. Oh, by the way, we've been invited to an intern's flat for a small party on Saturday night. Would you accompany me?"

"Doreen Anna Bailey, I've never known anyone to be as bold as you. Just what *did* they teach you at that Convent? Men do the asking. I'd have thought at least your mum would have put the fear of God into you for your lack of tradition."

Doreen pulled back a bit, shook her hair loose from the nurses' knot, and laughed heartily.

"I can tell you didn't know Anna Bailey all that well! She may have been somewhat traditional, but she always taught me to speak up for myself! Honestly, Colin, you're hopelessly behind the times!"

"No, I'm not behind the times, you have always been ahead of them. For growing up in a small town, you sure know city ways. But I'm not complaining, mind you. I like your forthright, bold approach. It's flattering, actually. It's also one of the things I like best about you. There's no pretense with you. I am forced to be my own bungling, socially inept person. If I were anything but myself, you'd topple me in an instant. Why is it you still keep company with the likes of me?"

"Now wait a minute – First, I confess I don't know city ways at all, at least the ones my mum always talked about. And secondly, although you may not be the most gregarious person I know, I'm not looking to spend time with a socialite. I just like hanging onto your arm. And I like your eyes."

"What else would liven up your existence? And please don't make it too complicated."

"Colin Bennett, if you can't figure that one out, then I'm not recommending you for any more surgical procedures! Where is your head?!"

"Here," he said, pointing to her chest.

They stopped walking. Suddenly the air seemed very still as the blossoms' fragrance penetrated their space. Doreen stood on tiptoes and took Colin's face in her hands.

"Colin…if you don't kiss me this instant, I will be forced to kiss you, and I know you won't find that in any book of etiquette."

There were no more words. The sun warmed Doreen's eyes, a breeze picked up, tangling her hair in soft waves across her face. Colin's hands trembled as he brushed her hair away. Taking her hands from his face, he pressed them against his chest. He bent over to kiss her, tentatively, but *she* was certain of this moment as she urged him on.

The ice cream shop was forgotten. The frame would have to wait for another day. The report sat half-written in the typewriter. The chill of the evening and the flames of the hearth were enough to fill two lovers' time. Those, and awakened passions that had been too long sleeping.

December 1933

The gas fire in Colin's flat made its usual hissing noise as he worked silently on the Sunday Times crossword.

"Can you give me a hint on 27 down?"

Doreen leaned over and looked at the clue.

"Mae West, all one word."

"Thanks."

Doreen stared at her own newspaper, then glanced up again to see how focused he was on his puzzle. It was a good afternoon to discuss the problems they were having at the hospital, yet it was the only day they could put them aside.

"Doreen, what's the Latin derivative for a music staff?"

"Scala."

"Thanks. What are you reading so intently? You've been absorbed in that article for the past thirty minutes. You must have read it three times."

"No, I've only read it twice. I'm just sitting here thinking about it. It frightens me, this situation in Germany. It's all wrong, I tell you."

"What do you mean, 'wrong'?"

"I'm not sure exactly. But I felt this feeling two years ago when we left Hempstead. I'd read a newspaper article about Hitler becoming Chancellor and President of Germany. I don't know, Colin, but something about him scares me. It has for a long time. I even spoke of it to the sisters and Father Loughry once, but they just dismissed it."

"Doreen, the Germans have had a rougher time than we have, struggling with unemployment and a horrid economy that's worse than ours. I think you're taking women's intuition to an extreme."

"Maybe. Anyway, I guess it's a dismal subject."

"Speaking of dismal subjects, how are you coping with the latest nursing crisis?"

"We're managing, I guess. It's getting harder, though. Our patient load is increasing and our budget is shrinking. We see a lot of malnutrition cases, especially in the aged. We've also got a few patients who haven't been able to mentally cope with going on the dole. What about you?"

"I'm fairing okay. I've got the critical surgeries, but some docs get much less on their schedule because of lack of experience. Their pay's been cut by half."

Doreen stood up suddenly, wanting a change in the conversation.

"I'll tell you what, let's go over to my flat and I'll make us some dinner. I'll even get out a jar of preserves that Mrs. Markham sent to me a few months back. She always made the best preserves in Hempstead. I miss her sometimes."

"Me, too. I especially miss her at the hospital. She may have moved a bit slower than most, but she was efficient nonetheless. Besides, she's a dear friend. I think December has a way of reminding you of folks you miss. Do you still miss the sisters at the Convent?"

"Yes. I mostly miss Mother Mary Catherine. She said in her last letter that she may be coming to London on business for the Diocese, and that she would stop at the hospital to see us."

A fine mist was coming down as they made their way to Doreen's flat. Once the fire was lit and a pot of corned beef and cabbage was warming on the stove, Doreen flopped onto the sofa next to Colin. For a while they sat quietly, arms wrapped around each other. There was a peaceful silence in the room; the walls were waiting for something important to be said.

"Doreen…I know this may not be the best time or even the best day to ask you this, but…."

Colin stopped mid-sentence and looked at his feet before continuing.

"I want to marry you. You are the love of my life, and you always will be. Please, say you'll spend the rest of your life with me. I want us to grow old together."

Doreen stared into his eyes before answering, trying to glimpse into his soul.

"Yes, Colin, I will marry you. I can't imagine my life without you."

He reached over to kiss her and then slowly leaned her back on the couch. Outside, the fine mist turned into a steady drizzle, and in front of the crackling fire, dreams were woven through tangled limbs.

London and its surrounding areas were lovely in the spring and April was an especially nice month for a wedding. Even though the rain was unpredictable, the trees were blooming and the breeze was warm. They had arranged to marry in Covent Garden, London. Doreen's heels echoed down the hardwood floors and their vows reverberated from the vaulted, mahogany ceilings of Corpus Christi Catholic Church. The whitewashed plaster and brick walls stood in contrast to the ornate altar flanked by stained glass. The sanctuary was simply decorated with flowers and ribbons, and on this day of April 30th, Colin Bennett and Doreen Bailey became Dr. and Mrs. Colin Bennett. The weather actually held for the wedding Mass and the picnic reception in the churchyard. It was a small gathering, mostly friends and acquaintances from work and some parish members. There were, however, two unexpected guests that took a train ride to witness the marriage.

"Father Loughry! Mrs. Markham! We're so happy you've come!"

"My dears, you both look positively wonderful. What a beautiful Mass. We wouldn't have missed it."

Hugs were given and received as they joined the line of well-wishers. The priest at Corpus Christi had contacted Father Loughry, knowing how fond Doreen was of him and Father Loughry had called in at Hempstead's Infirmary, asking Mrs. Markham to accompany him. It was the perfect blending of old and new, familiar pieces carefully stitched like a patchwork quilt. For Dr. and Mrs. Bennett, life was very, very good. They turned their attentions to finding an affordable, roomier flat.

September 28, 1935

I don't usually mention things as provincial as a doctor's appointment, but I will mention this one! It's rather strange being married to a doctor and going to another doctor for a checkup, but I felt it quite necessary this time. I didn't want to tell Colin about my recent bouts of sickness, as I wanted to be certain myself before mentioning it to him. We are to have a baby, due next spring! I think he will be quite pleased. He's such a gentle, caring man and he will make an excellent father! I'm so grateful we were able to purchase the Pierce's flat, we have so much more room. I should have the decorating finished by Christmas. I hope I'm able to continue working 'til the baby comes- we need the money. Praise God for new blessings! Doreen

May 1936

The dawn of the fifteenth of May came with storm clouds and blustery winds, an omen according to Irish legend. Nevertheless, the mood in the maternity floor of Croydon Hospital was cheerful. It wasn't every day that a surgeon and his favorite nurse brought their own child into the world!

Meghan Bennett was born just as the sky was trying to brighten between rainsqualls. The baby's squalls echoed down the sterile halls, waking even the soundest sleepers. She had a head full of sandy colored wisps, sprinkled with a hint of strawberry.

It was far too early to tell what color her eyes would be. They should be blue like her mum's, but as Doreen carefully studied her baby's face, she knew instinctively that Meghan would defy convention whenever possible. The new mother smiled at the possibilities but her smile faded as a strange, unsettling fear crept into her being. That same uncomfortable, cold feeling that she could never wrap her thoughts around. She pulled the worn hospital blanket around her and cradled the new life in her arms.

"Colin, I'm glad you're home early. I've some news for you! I got a phone call from the priest at Corpus Christi about a Baptismal date for Meghan. It looks like we can have the service in two weeks. What do you think?"

"That's fine, Doreen. I've some news for you, as well. I found out today about a nurses' childminding rota that's been set up for some time now. It was started by a small group of nurses who wanted to continue working at least a few hours a week. I guess their main concern was finding a loving, qualified sitter. Most of our nurses don't have family close by, so it was difficult. Anyway, they decided to share the task by taking turns watching another's child in return for that person watching theirs. It allows them the opportunity to stay current with their skills and still be assured of their child's well being. I talked to a couple of the nurses today, and they said that if you're interested, you should ring them. What do you think?"

"I think it's a wonderful idea, as long as you're fine with that decision. It would be nice to get out and back to the hospital."

"Good. I'll get the phone numbers for you and you can ring them up tonight."

Doreen closed her eyes and said a prayer of thanks as Colin rose to retrieve the numbers she needed. Her world was now filled with so much wonder and new adventures. Yet even with Colin's good news, her mind kept drifting to the disturbing news she'd heard earlier in the day. The accounts of Hitler's advance into the Rhineland dampened her spirits as surely as a sudden storm. Outside, a wind picked up and blew the heavy drapes aside, revealing the darkening skies of evening. Doreen felt a chill and got up to close the windows, noticing how very black the stones were on the cottage across the way. She had never realized how much the soot had sullied the places around her.

CHAPTER TWELVE

London,
May, 1938

Ethan Hollingsworth rose from his chair and walked over to peer out the dirty windows of his office. The Royal Navy was usually much more particular about the cleanliness of its offices and halls, but not recently. There were a lot more important-and urgent- things to consider. He jumped at the loud knock on his door.

"Captain Hollingsworth, Sir. I have a message from the Admiral. He says you need to respond as soon as possible, Sir."

"Thank you Lieutenant. That'll be all."

"Thank you, Sir."

Ethan Hollingsworth laid a folder on top of the newspapers that spilled over his desk. He knew before looking what most of the folder would contain. The situation in Germany was worsening by the month. Since Hitler seized control of the German army and subsequently rose to the presidency four years before, he had taken over the media and established a cruel and unscrupulous security force, answerable only to him. Most of Hitler's fellow countrymen had not only allowed his domination, they had fueled his rhetoric. The newspapers that now lay stacked with paragraphs circled had boldly detailed Hitler's masterful vacillation of friend-foe ties with Stalin in Russia and Mussolini in Italy. That, and his backing of the Fascists in the Spanish Civil War, had secured his reputation as a formidable leader.

Captain Hollingsworth walked backed to the smeared windows and looked out at the streets below. Everyone seemed to be going somewhere, and in a great hurry at that. He sighed and lowered his head. They were so unaware. Most of them so uninformed about so much, like Hitler's annexation of the Saarlanders that returned the Saar basin to Germany. Most Brits knew little of this land that had been separated from Germany at the Treaty of Versailles in 1919 and given to France, and now was back in German hands. In Hitler's hands. The people below him were too concerned about paying the rent on their small flats and having enough left over to put a meal on the table. Too preoccupied to read about the political chaos caused by the British and French plan to rescue the part of Ethiopia overrun by the Italian army. Most of them were oblivious to Hitler having taking advantage of that turmoil, sending his troops into the demilitarized, pre-World War I German territory on the Belgium-Holland border in March of 1936. Poor slobs. Actually, they were the lucky ones. They didn't have a clue what information was contained in the folder that still lay unopened on the desk.

Hollingsworth shook his head and sighed in disgust. Damn France. They had bailed out of any responsibility, preferring to let England take the lead. Damn Chamberlain. His nebulous stand against Hitler's aggression had stirred up speeches in Parliament, but little else. The powers-that-be seemed more afraid of the Russian Communists than of the radical right factions. The Captain walked over to his desk once again, this time taking a bottle out of the bottom drawer. Since Hitler's troops had annexed Austria two months earlier, further escalation was only a matter of time. Only a matter of time before *he* would be responsible for sending his recruits to fight a war that would surely be more costly than any of the unaware people on the streets or the ignorant politicians could even imagine. He would sign the orders, then wait to receive with stoic resolve the coded memos. Memos detailing the numbers of men coming home in zippered bags or not coming home at all, their bodies rotting in a field somewhere or riding the swells, then bloating and sinking to the ocean's floor.

Ethan Hollingsworth poured a glass of whiskey and chugged it. He picked up the bottle and finished its contents while the glass and the folder lay across his cluttered desk.

May 4, 1938

I can't believe that Meghan is almost two years old! I wish so much that Mum were still here to share these times with us. I sure could use her advice. I got a letter from Mrs. Markham today. It was filled with disturbing news about Father Loughry. He's coming to London to meet with a Cardinal about his declining parish numbers. It's so sad, as he is a proud man who has given his life to the Church. Now he must answer questions concerning the lack of people on the rolls, but numbers don't always tell the story. I hope to have tea with him while he's in the City. Mrs. Markham wrote that the Infirmary is still open for all emergencies and some surgeries. It's important that she stay on there, as she has not known any other job since her husband died many years ago. Her letter makes me long to visit Mum's grave and walk the familiar footpaths up to Wicken's Farm. The years have a way of slipping by too fast. The news from Europe isn't good. I know from news accounts that some Austrians are devastated at Hitler's annexation of their homeland, still others seemed nearly pleased. I don't think I will ever understand world politics. Colin thinks I worry too much. Perhaps he's right. I miss you, Mum.

Lamb

When the sun was shining in London, it was indeed a beautiful place. This day in June of 1938, the gritty air seemed less polluted and the sky was as clear as it ever gets. The few clouds overhead were wispy and scattered like dandelions in the breeze. Doreen fidgeted with the scarf around her shoulders and peered down the track for the 9:35 a.m. train to arrive at Victoria Station from Hempstead. She knew that Father Loughry would have been awake for hours, as his early morning prayers and devotions were a strict priority with him. She was unprepared for what greeted her as he stepped off the coach car and descended the steps. He had aged considerably since their wedding and his coat hung loosely around his bent shoulders, though his genuine smile was the same.

"Good mornin' to ya, my little Doreen. I'm so happy that you've come here to greet me. I'm lookin' forward to spending the morning with you!"

"Good morning, Father. How was your trip?"

"Not so bad. It's a short one, mind you. Hardly seems worth the fare, if you ask me."

"Give me your bag, Father. I took the day off from my nursing job so we could start catching up on all our news. Wait until you see our lovely Meghan. I decided to leave her with my childminder until we get to our flat. She's quite the little monkey these days!"

"That sounds wonderful, Doreen. I apologize for not writing to you more often. My parish duties seem to take so much more of my energy these days, even though I've fewer folks to minister to. You do know my situation with the Diocese, don't you?"

"Yes, Father, I do. I hope you won't feel betrayed, but Mrs. Markham has been worried about you lately. She wrote to me about your appointment with the Cardinal. I'm not sure why His Excellency feels compelled to take this seemingly small matter on, but I suppose he must have his reasons."

"Indeed, I'm sure he does, my dear. If I am in need of other information for His Excellency, I know I can ask you. Even if you have nothing pertinent for me, I could at least confide in you."

"Now that is something I have never considered! Whom do priests go to when they've a need to share?!"

"Other priests, or very close friends."

Doreen stopped walking and stood facing her spiritual counselor. She smiled and wondered if she dare readdress the eerie, gnawing fear she had had for several years. Her fear that there was something to dread. She paused to set down the Father's traveling bag.

"Father Loughry, you are one of my dearest friends. You have always been there for me. You know that I would always be there for you."

Doreen and Father Loughry walked in silence to the bus stand and boarded the 10:15 for the Bennett's flat in Croydon.

Just outside a small hotel next to the bus stand stood a tall, wiry, gray-haired man, holding a battered leather bag. He stared intently at the priest and his friend as they found a seat on the bus. It had been a long time since the stranger had been in England, but he never forgot a face. Especially one that stirred up fierce anger in him. A voice startled him from behind.

"Mr. Strucker, I have a message for you from the reception desk."

The uniformed, young bellboy extended his hand and the older man grabbed the envelope. There was no gratuity offered as the man tore open the envelope and hungrily read its contents.

The Bennett house was strewn with toys and filled with a medley of kitchen sounds and chattering voices.

"Father Loughry, it's been so good to see you. Your visit sure has sparked Doreen."

Colin picked up Meghan and began tossing her into the air. Meghan's strawberry blonde curls bounced up and down as her daddy continued his antics. Her blue eyes, so like her mum's, sparkled when she giggled. She was smaller than her playmates and looked as though she would have her grandma Anna's short stature. Her smile was broad and her laughter infectious.

"Doreen hates it when I do this. I can't remember if my father ever tossed me about, but if he did, I'm sure I loved it!"

"Mothers are usually a bit overly protective. You've got a lovely family, Colin. Protect them – and most of all, love them."

"I will, Father. Best of luck to you on your meetings with the Cardinal. Please let us know if there's anything we can do to help you."

Throwing his cardigan across his shoulders, Father Loughry headed to the kitchen to say 'goodbye' to Doreen. She handed him a packed lunch and told him to write more often.

The Cardinal was sitting down, staring at the picture of the Pope that hung above his desk across the room. He raised his eyes and motioned to a nearby chair as Father Loughry entered his office.

"I know you must think it odd to meet with me concerning your shrinking parish, Father Loughry. I assure you that you have done a magnificent job serving the Church all these years and you are not here for a reprimand. Your meeting with me does *not* concern the size of your congregation. It concerns a former member of your flock."

Father Loughry's eyes lit up for the first time in a week. He studied his superior's face as he waited for further explanation.

"I received a visit from British Intelligence concerning a certain member of your parish who has been away from England for quite some time. They have a keen interest in this man. Wilhelm Strucker is under command of the Third Reich and has been involved with some vicious attacks on individuals and small groups that advocate tolerance of Jews and other minorities. One of our priests from a parish in Munich contacted British authorities regarding some of Strucker's murderous activities. Wilhelm and his "underlings" are targeting some of the more tolerant members of large congregations in Munich. Evidently they see our religion, and indeed others' as a weakness and a detriment to their political cause of ethnic purity. Strucker and his group have been vandalizing homes and church buildings, and in some cases attacking parishioners as they go about daily living. In one case, they kidnapped a child, only releasing him after threatening to kill his family.

"I sadly say that the Catholic churches in Germany have been rather silent for the most part, concerning Hitler and his hate-filled messages. For that, may God forgive us. At any rate, this former parishioner of yours is quite vocal about religion and tolerance diluting the strength of their cause. They seem determined to see the rise of a pure German nation, at the expense of many others from other countries and backgrounds. We believe Wilhelm will soon return home to Hempstead to visit his dying wife. His children live in the same area but are not at all a part of his cause. He is dangerous to you and your parish, precisely because of his past association with you and because of his hatred for the traditional Catholic Church. We want you to watch his actions carefully and report any suspicious activities to authorities immediately, or phone me and I'll contact British Intelligence directly. Some folks from the church in Munich have actually seen him carrying out cruel and unprovoked attacks upon Catholics, Protestants, and Jews alike. I know what I'm asking you to do may seem contrary to confidentiality vows, but I assure you that it is not. He has made his position on humanity quite clear; we are trying to protect you and the ones you love."

The Cardinal got up slowly from the overstuffed chair that for years had occupied the same corner in his office. He walked over to the ancient paned window and stared out. Father Loughry sat, immobilized, and began to rub his forehead in a pattern born of habit. Finally he stood, composed enough to speak.

"I know the man you speak of, Your Excellency. He's had a grudge against me for years. It concerns a confession he made to me that I could not absolve, as he gave no sign of any remorse or repentance. After that, he never came to Confession or Mass again. For years his family took the brunt of his drinking and ugly temper. I wish I could spare them his visit. I'll most certainly honor your request and watch for him. I'm traveling home to Hempstead this morning. One of my main concerns is what I tell my congregation. Should I alert them to the danger Strucker poses, or merely ask about town of his dealings? Should I go to his home and warn his family, or stay away to allow him anonymity, giving me more rein to quietly keep an eye on him?"

Now that the new reality had set in, Father Loughry couldn't keep the questions from coming. The Cardinal listened patiently to every concern and question, answering with a calm, assuring manner. Finally the two men stood silently, both gazing out the window, both hoping the scene outside would erase this horrible reality and the evil that had brought them to this conversation.

The early morning fog was lifting and it was another sunny but unseasonably cold day when Father Loughry left the Cardinal's office. He took a shortcut through back closes to catch the train bound for Hempstead. As the priest walked, he buttoned up his cardigan and wrapped his scarf around his neck to keep out the dampness. He felt burdened with a dreadful secret, and his thoughts kept bouncing from his visit with his young friends to the words of warning from the Cardinal. He knew he couldn't live his life in fear, nor could he expect the rest of his parish to constantly question their own safety. He just didn't know if he had the strength to handle such an immense task. He didn't feel spiritually prepared to face this new enemy. Absorbed in all these thoughts, he walked more slowly than usual, completely unaware of the figure behind him until his nostrils filled with the pungent smell of soured whiskey. He could feel his scarf tightening around his throat.

Trying to turn around to see his attacker, Father Loughry stumbled as blackness spread before him. The hands that gripped his throat were choking off the air he gasped to take in. There was no time to question the meaning or sense of this. The blackness was growing larger. Events and places swirled before him like a carousel out of control. He struggled to get away, but he was no match for the strong grasp on his neck. The blackness soon melted into a strange peace as the priest slumped to the ground, his head twisted and contorted, dropping onto the hard pavement with an unholy thud.

Doreen was still at home with Meghan when the phone call came. This was all wrong - this was not God's plan! Not this time. Not this way. Her head was pounding in pain when Colin arrived home. Struggling to feel protected, she finally fell asleep cradled in his arms with Meghan curled up in her lap.

The funeral Mass at St. Mary and Joseph's Catholic Church was long and solemn. Colin took Meghan out of the church several times, to avoid any disturbances that would detract from the reverence of the service. Most of the sisters from Wycombe Convent were there, as well as many former hospital co-workers and nearly all the Hempstead parishioners. Doreen spoke with Mother Mary Catherine outside the church, as others prepared to follow the procession to the gravesite.

"Mother, I'm struggling to find an answer to this evil. I can't see God anymore. I'm looking, but I can't see Him. I can't feel Him. May Mother Mary forgive me, but I don't think He cares that I'm lost."

"Doreen, this isn't about your being lost. This is about *loss*, not *being lost*. No one can ever be lost to God. And child, remember that God didn't create this evil. Perhaps you're looking for God on the outside. He's inside of you. Look into the faces of your loving husband and precious daughter. Can't you see Him there? Perhaps you can't feel Him because you're afraid to feel anything right now. He's watching over you - and holding you. Let some healing begin."

Doreen let the Mother's words of comfort and wisdom play back in her head as they walked arm in arm to the place where the dust of the earth would be Father Loughry's final blanket.

CHAPTER THIRTEEN

June 1938
London

The chiming of the tower bells annoyed Ethan Hollingsworth as he paced across his office floor. He didn't know exactly when Big Ben's serenade had begun to grate on him, but he was sure it had been a while ago. Their clanging signaled the normality of London life, but now the sound seemed intrusive and out of place. If only he weren't always privy to classified governmental information! That so-called privilege had destroyed any semblance of "life as usual" for him. It was just as well that he lived alone. Just as well that his wife had given up on their "boring and tedious" relationship and moved back to Scotland to live with her sister. It was good not to have any ties just now. He stopped pacing to pick up the latest folder that had arrived on his desk earlier in the day. He'd read its contents twice already, but he still couldn't come to terms with the words that appeared to crumble with weakness under his glaring scrutiny. He spoke his frustration aloud, as though the power of his angry words could cause the very walls to shrink in fear and submission.

"Chamberlain, you idiot! What the hell are you thinking? You let Hitler steal Austria from her own people and now you give up the Czech border to the maniac! God! You won't even ask the bloody French to do their part!"

The Captain continued ranting until he fell into the cracked, leather desk chair, exhausted from his tirade. He was aware of the consequences of involving the French in this latest German assault, but still, he loathed Chamberlain's pandering. No one wanted to declare war on Germany but too many lines had been crossed, too many lives smothered already. The Royal Navy had never shirked Her duty before, even knowing the great cost of her involvement. It was too late to keep backing away. It was time to act. He slept fitfully in the chair while Big Ben continued to remind

Londoners that time would never wait. It would only move on, despite the deepest cries of the human voice to stop and take notice of what the hands on the clock were pointing to.

March, 1939

Croydon

Dr. Colin Bennett carried his packed sandwich to a table in the corner of the hospital lunchroom and grabbed the morning newspaper from a disheveled display. He unwrapped the meat pastie that Doreen had hurriedly fixed amidst Meghan's cries for immediate attention. He placed the sandwich on the table and started in on the raw carrots that now were warm and lacked their usual crunch, his appetite vanishing as he scanned the printed words. He had never considered that Hitler would actually occupy the *rest* of Czechoslovakia! This was insanity, even for a madman like Hitler. What would that mean for Poland and the rest of the Czech neighbors?! He shoved the carrot back into the small, canvas bag and stared out the window in confused frustration.

Doreen kept watch out of their flat window, hoping to see Colin coming down the walk soon. He had been arriving home later than usual in the past few weeks, ever since the invasion of Czechoslovakia. *Did he think that putting in extra hours at the hospital would avoid any discussion of England's response and somehow ward off the impending conflict?* She knew how worried he was, but his inability to talk about the future, *their* future, was causing even more tension.

They ate dinner in near silence, except for Meghan's quiet chattering about something in her imaginary world. Doreen cleared the dishes and set her mum's chipped teapot on the table.

"Colin, we have to talk about this. You know the situation is growing worse each week. I don't believe we'll be able to stay out of this much longer. Chamberlain's offered Poland our protection and you already know men who've been conscripted for military service. We've got to talk about what that means for *us*, as a family. Love, you know I'm strong enough to handle about anything, but we've got Meghan to think about now."

"I know, I know. I'm sorry, Doreen. Everything's just so unsettled. We're already gearing up at the hospital for extra employees and it's been a burden to set up training and new schedules. I don't know exactly where this is all going, but it doesn't look good. If I have to go into service, I want you home more often with Meghan. She'll need that reassurance."

"Well, I agree with that. But in the meantime, Meghan and I need you here for longer than one short dinner hour. I feel that I'm shouldering all the home responsibilities on my own."

"Damn it, Doreen! I'm doing the best I can."

Doreen's look of concern turned into a scolding frown at Colin's profanity as he continued without apology.

"Look, I just can't be in two places at once. I know you need me here – it's what I'd prefer. But we'll be at war soon and I need to get the hospital staff ready for that. I'd think you'd be the first to understand."

They moved to the front room in silence and sat on the sofa to watch Meghan play until her bedtime. Long after she was asleep in her own bed, they drifted off without any words, their limbs lacking any comfort from the human touch, and their minds filling the darkness with frightening visions. The dawn broke with confusing dreams just bordering on nightmares.

June, 1939

The summer sun was uncomfortably hot on Doreen's shoulders and she had already snagged her skirt on the hard, wooden park bench. She shifted her position to watch Meghan playing happily on the slide, her daughter preferring to climb *up* the ramp.

"I'm so sorry I'm late, my dear!"

Doreen knew Mrs. Markham's voice.

"That's alright! We've been having a nice time soaking up this day, though it is getting a bit warm. How was the train – packed with folks as usual?"

"No, not too bad today. I think there's an uncomfortable feeling floating about these days. Folks seem to be staying at home by the wireless. Has Colin heard anything about service duty yet?"

Mrs. Markham smoothed her dress before sitting and took a hankie from her handbag to wipe the perspiration from her face.

"No, not yet, for which we're very grateful. I've no idea how he'd react to being called up. He's such a private man, keeps his concerns and fears to himself. In fact, he keeps a lot of other things to himself."

"Just like an Englishman, that's for sure. My Daryl was the same way."

"You've never talked much about your husband. What was he like?"

"Simple in his wishes and plain in his living. He was a good man. He would have been in a muddle about this whole mess in Europe, though."

The two women were silent for a while as the squeak of the swings and the squeal of children drifted across the park.

Doreen broke the quiet.

"Hitler's demanded that Gdansk, Poland be returned to German hands. Do you think the Polish people will appease him?"

"I'm not sure what the Polish government will do. You know their *border's* under attack from Hitler, but the Poles won't ask the Soviet troops for help. They're too afraid of permanent occupation."

Doreen shot a surprised look and Mrs. Markham smiled.

"I know, I sound like I'm writing the latest news for the wire. I've been listening and reading about all of this as much as I can. I need to have a heads-up at our little hospital for any changes this mess may bring about. I suppose Hitler will talk Stalin into signing a treaty with him, just to keep the man on his side."

"Could be. I think this whole thing is going to be much larger and longer than any of us ever expected it would be. Look at my wee one. What kind of world do you think we're leading her into? I'm frightened, Mrs. Markham."

"Me, too, dearie. Me, too. I guess the only thing any of us can cling to is faith and hope. Hope that all this will resolve quickly."

The older woman stood up and brushed a leaf from her stocking, then clapped her hands together.

"Come now, Doreen. Let's get out o' this sun and go for a sweetie with Meghan and talk of more pleasant things. It's too nice a day for such dreadful thoughts."

Meghan skipped a few steps in front of them, singing to herself and turning around often to make certain they were watching her antics.

September 1, 1939

Colin opened the front door slowly and walked inside their flat.

"I'm home, Doreen!"

"Colin, what are you doing home so early?"

"Haven't you had the radio on this morning? You don't know, do you?"

"No, Colin. What's happened?"

She watched him gently scoop up Meghan from her play spot, lifting her high into the air, then bringing her close to his chest.

"Germany invaded Poland this morning. It looks as if earlier precautions of the past few days were an ominous sign of things to come."

Doreen followed her husband to the kitchen table. His eyes were focused intently on Meghan, as though he were seeing his daughter for the first time. Doreen sighed and took a deep breath before responding to his news.

"This is horrible. This is awful. God, Colin, have we all gone mad? I mean, those ridiculous gas masks and blackout curtains and blinds, they're actually a realistic precaution. I never thought...."

Colin lowered Meghan, silently shooing her back to play in the front room.

"I know. Fighter squadrons, anti-aircraft guns and searchlights, shelters and trenches for air raids. Doreen, what are we getting into?"

She looked up at him and shook her head.

"There's more. Orders were given this morning to strongly encourage evacuation of school-aged children and young mothers, as well as teachers. How do you feel about leaving the city to go stay with Mrs. Markham for awhile?"

"Not on your life. I'm not leaving you or our home. We're in this together, Colin, at least for now. If things get significantly worse, then we'll talk about that."

There was an eerie quiet in the room, not at all the easy kind that often fills a family's place of refuge. They ate without talking, watching their daughter play with her food unaware of the unspoken fear that had gripped the room and choked off any usual conversation.

The next evening was spent in front of the wireless set, absorbing as much as possible from the news reports that changed every hour. They listened with grave concern but without panic. Many hospital wards in the City of London had been evacuated and emergency mortuaries had been opened. Private vehicles were requisitioned for ambulance use. The City seemed prepared for the worst.

The morning of September 3, 1939, started badly for the Bennett household. Colin had overslept and left for the hospital edgy and ill tempered. Meghan was unusually fussy and had finally gone down for a nap. Doreen pulled her chair close to the wireless and took a long swallow of her second cup of tea. She turned the volume up slightly and listened. It was official. At 11:00 a.m., Prime Minister Neville Chamberlain declared war on Germany. There was no more time for last minute treaties and political pleading. Hitler's dark intentions could no longer be ignored in the light of day. There was no going back. Doreen gulped the rest of her tea, wondering aloud if there was any going *forward* in her life. *What was ahead for them?* The realistic answers came flooding into her consciousness like the unwelcome lyrics of a sinister song.

The blackout curtains made night come way too early that evening. Colin stepped inside and walked straight to the kitchen, wrapping his arms around his wife and crying softly into her shoulder. This was not how their lives were supposed to be unfolding. They should be spending autumn evenings in the park with Meghan, planning weekend excursions and household projects. Not planning for war. Not practicing "goodbyes." Certainly not figuring destruction and separation into the scene.

"Daddy!"

Meghan's lighthearted voice broke the painful moment and she ran up to Colin, throwing her arms around his legs.

"Daddy, play with me now."

Colin pulled away from Doreen, wiped his face with his sleeve, and knelt down to answer her.

"And what shall we play tonight, little one?"

"House, Daddy. Let's play house."

"Dinner will be ready in a while. You two play for now. I'll call you."

The simplicity and normalcy of the past few moments were of small comfort to Doreen as she busied herself with the mundane task of setting supper on the table. There wasn't much variety or substance to their meals of late. They'd been cutting back on groceries, as much a factor of their financial situation as it was the growing fear of war rations. She could hear Meghan chattering in the lounge, making-believe with lovely childlike abandon. Her daughter's world would most likely be turned upside down very soon and the ordinary things in all their lives would not be the same. It was more than sobering as the night deepened; it was a sadness born of experience and truth.

Books, crayons, baby dolls, and dressing-up clothes were spread across the floor when Doreen came into the front room to announce that tea was on the table. She looked closely at her husband. He looked drawn and older than his years. His deep brown eyes were glazed like a deer in headlamps. He picked up Meghan for a toss in the air, then stopped almost midair and once again brought her to his chest for a long hug.

"I love you, Daddy."

"I love you, too, beautiful. I will play with you again after supper until Mummy scolds us and makes us go to bed."

Colin tried to grin at his own words, but a smile was hard to force.

"Can we have our tea here by the fire, Mummy?"

Doreen paused at the kitchen door and studied the scene before her. The room was warm and a bit stuffy, yet she wrapped her arms around herself and shivered. She knew now, in this moment, that an overwhelming evil had finally pervaded their lives. The same dreaded fear that had engulfed her so many times before was once again before her. The snug safety of their flat this night would not keep the wolf at bay. It was too late now. All those years of silent foreboding were now crashing down upon her with a painful weight. She silently moved back into the kitchen to prepare a tray to set before the fire.

Meghan went to bed easily that night, too young to know the consequences of the day's events. She curled up with her favorite stuffed toy, a bunny named Max, and drifted off to sleep with a tiny snore. Colin and Doreen stood at her bedroom door for several minutes, afraid to disturb the sanctity of the moment. Afraid to face the discussion that awaited them over a nighttime coffee. When Doreen finally turned around toward the lounge, Colin shook his head and guided her to their bedroom instead.

"Tonight, my love, we will not talk of war. We'll leave that 'til tomorrow. Tonight is ours. No fears, no decisions."

Strange tiny lights from an unknown source danced on the wallpaper above their wardrobe. They accompanied the soft sighs of a passion born from hunger too deep for a mere romantic interlude. The rising and falling of bodies too tightly entwined held a desperation that even light dances could not affect. There was only the sound of breathing and movements. Only the dancing of tears and sweat. A loving ballet that might never be repeated.

It was nearing dawn when Colin awoke to find Doreen sitting up in bed watching him. Neither spoke right away. They stared across the room as if some magic would wash away the reality of the day before. The reality of war. The reality of their small family being torn apart. They heard the milk truck as it went down the street, its milk bottles clanging and the deliveryman whistling to himself. A few birds were singing noisily in the tree outside the window and the neighbor's dog was barking. The whole picture seemed so normal, so ordinary. So lovely.

They rose and ate breakfast together without conversation, sipping their coffee until the pot was empty and their stomachs were full. Meghan was still asleep, giving them the gift of facing their fears and decisions without interruption. Finally, Colin spoke.

"You know, Dorr, that I have to sign up very soon. It's not a choice anymore. Who knows where this conflict is headed? Perhaps we'll be fortunate, and it will end very soon. You know how much I love you and Meghan. You are my life. But you know that we can't avoid this any longer. You know I'm right."

"I don't know what is right anymore. I do know that I love you so much and I can't bear the thought of not waking up next to you each morning. I can't even imagine the effect of your absence on Meghan. But I do agree that at this point, you really don't have a lot of other alternatives. At least if you enlist at the beginning of this mess, perhaps you will be able to come home to us sooner. If you wait, we will all be consumed with the eventuality of your leaving, and our lives would still be torn."

"I know, I know. We'd be living with a heavy cloud over us, waiting for the inevitable. I should be able to enlist as a civilian doctor with the Navy. At least I'll have served. I'll do my tour of duty and then return home to you and Meghan as soon as I can. You'll have your own duties, I'm sure. Just keeping yourself and our Meg safe, and helping in this war effort as best you can."

"We can do this, Colin. You know how hard it's going to be when you board that train but we can do this. We're not alone. So many others will be in the same situation. We can draw strength from each other."

The next few minutes were quiet, save for the ticking of the kitchen clock and the growing sounds of the day outside. Then Meghan began singing from her room, a happy melody, her voice breaking their silence. She was unaware that her daddy would not be working at the hospital all day today. He would spend part of the day registering for service in the Royal Navy.

Doreen felt no need to think about leaving their flat, as only the City of London proper was evacuating children. She would consider that later. Right now, she prepared herself and Meghan for Colin's departure. They would have a few days before he left for the naval base. His exact location after training would not be known, though she and Colin could certainly exchange letters. Letters that would become their lifeline.

It was cloudy and cool when the Bennett family walked to the Croydon train station a few days later. Colin set his bag on the platform and picked up his daughter once more.

"You be a good girl for your mummy, my sweet one. I expect you to eat your vegetables and grow several inches while I'm away. You help pick up your toys before teatime, will you do that for Daddy?"

"Yes, Daddy. Why do you have to leave? I don't want you to go."

Meghan's blue eyes filled with tears and she yanked off her hat in frustration.

"Please, Daddy, don't go. Mummy, make him stay."

"You know why your Daddy is leaving. You mustn't be angry, Meghan. He wants to stay with us, but he can't right now. Daddy is doing something very important for all of us. He will come back to us as soon as he can."

Doreen pulled Meghan from her daddy's arms and the three of them embraced. The engineer's whistle blew and Colin kissed them both. There were no more words.

Slight drizzle was just beginning as the train pulled away from the station and the wind blew the damp mist across the platform. Doreen and Meghan stayed long after the train had departed, as if standing there would somehow bring it back. Meghan was softly sobbing with her bunny, Max, clutched tightly against her chest. Finally, the chill and the emotion of the morning were too much to bear and they walked hand in hand back home. The shrill sound of the earlier whistle was still ringing in Doreen's ears and her head was pounding from unspent tears. She closed all the windows in their flat and removed the teakettle from the stove long before the water was hot.

CHAPTER FOURTEEN

October 8, 1939

My dearest Colin,

It seems as if it has been months, not weeks, since I've seen you. I miss you so terribly. I know that Meghan misses you as much as I do as she asks about you several times each day. I've tried to explain further the reason for your absence, but she seems unable to grasp the concept of separation. We look at photographs each night so your smile is always fresh in her mind. Your touch is always fresh in my heart, no photos needed.

We have been doing mostly our daily routine as much as possible. The blackouts are a nuisance though Meghan and I are always inside by dusk anyway. Still, it is annoying to shutter everything up so early on an autumn evening. I know that they are even stricter in London though I've no idea what they are doing in the port cities where you must be. We have been asked to save some items but so far Meghan hasn't noticed the cutbacks. I'm glad we had a nice store of honey and preserves in the pantry from Mrs. Markham. I shall miss our tea and coffee if the rationing is ever enforced!

I am so very grateful now especially for the wireless set from the staff at Hempstead Hospital. Little did we know when we received that lovely wedding gift how important it would become in our home! Meghan and I sit on the divan and listen at night, sipping hot milk and cuddling.

As I'm sure you know there have been no air raids, no need to be hoarding food as some thought, no real war pressure here in Croydon. It seems ludicrous to me that we are in such a state of panic that I'm not even able to know your location, yet there has been no hint of any German activity, save for the horrible infrequent attacks upon individuals. It is a bit unsettling, as the attacks are unprovoked and unpredictable, just as it was with Father Loughry. I don't understand why a few folks feel they must show their allegiance to Hitler by these attacks. What kind of human nature have we fallen prey to? I worry for our darling daughter and the future life she will have.

Oh, my love, what a dreadfully depressing letter this has been thus far. I'm so sorry! Yet I must tell you my true feelings as you have always been not just my only love and lover, but my surest confidante and best friend as well. How sad for us that our brief years together are now so interrupted, when we should be sharing everything together. Just know, my darling, that I share in your thoughts as you must share in mine. That way we can communicate without words, and without touch, until this whole mess is resolved.

I am forever yours,
Doreen

October 15, 1939

My lovely Doreen,
How desperately I ache for you tonight. I know that you and I are under the same stars, yet I feel as if we're on separate planets. I'm struggling to stay focused on my work, a job that changes daily like the wind. I am struggling to eat as my hunger is only for you. There are times when I cannot get my breath for need of feeling your presence. But oh, to feel your touch. God, I wish I knew when we could be together again. You know I've never been much for praying, but I pray each night that He is protecting you and Meghan and that you are healthy.

I wish I could tell you about my life inside the war, but of course, I can't. I can only tell you that port cities are under the same restrictions as London and surrounding areas. The early darkness outside and the shuttering inside makes my work more challenging, and my spirit as foreboding as Heathcliff's!

I am so excited to get your letters and I hope you are receiving mine. I hope they reach you nearly intact from the censors!

I am also sure you heard on the wireless of Hitler's offer of peace on October 6th. As if he thought France and Great Britain would accept it while he and the Soviet Union continue to desecrate Poland! What a disaster this is turning out to be!

Please give our beautiful Meghan a big hug from Daddy and tell her I love both of you more than life itself.

Your loving husband,
Colin

October 18, 1939

My dearest Colin,

I have been sitting near the wireless all evening, trying to get word of the German air raid over the Firth of Forth two days ago. I know that there were some naval casualties. I am praying that is not where you are. If I don't get any news, I will take that as a blessing. I will anxiously look forward to your next letter, until then I won't be able to sleep!

My love, I must set your mind at ease about one thing. No doubt you've heard about the children being evacuated from London and surrounding areas. Be assured that Meghan is here with me and we will stay together as long as God wills. I do not feel we are in any imminent danger.

The only danger we face is an accident outside in the darkness. The makeshift casualty wards and hospitals are filled to capacity with those injured from automobile accidents and pedestrian injuries from the blackout! What was meant to protect us has turned out to be our worst enemy. At least now they are allowing some hand lit torches when no alerts are sounding. We continue to have our

gas masks with us when outside, yet I feel there
is little threat to ever use them.

I received a letter from Sister Mary Catherine
last week. She inquired of all of us and offered
her assistance if ever we needed her. She said
the other sisters are well, for the most part.
She also said the nursing program at Hempstead is
still intact with more nuns than ever involved,
most likely because more civilians are looking
for wartime jobs. I am glad your legacy there is
still alive!

Your legacy here in our home is still active
and healthy. She is such a joy! She continues to
ask about you each day and we are still in our
nightly routine of pictures and talking about
you.

I have cut back on nursing hours at Croydon,
as my childminding rota is dwindling. Some nurses
have signed up with the Civil Nursing Reserve
of the Voluntary Aid Detachment, so there are
fewer of us in the circle. We are managing with
the government allowance to buy staples and pay
bills. Please don't worry about us, as we are well
and content, though missing you dreadfully. Good
night, my love.

                              Yours forever,
                              Doreen

December 24, 1939
Croydon, England

Doreen lit the fire as the chill of the damp night filtered through the
stone bricks of their flat. Meghan was already asleep, her bunny Max
serving as a pillow. A hand stitched quilt lay crumpled across her legs, a
remnant from the Grandma Anna she never knew. It had been a particularly
long day for both of them, as the weather and darkness of the season and
the blackouts had soured both of their dispositions. It was Christmas
Eve, normally a time of great excitement in the Bennett household. Yet
Doreen and Meghan had attended Mass without much enthusiasm. Father
Christmas had delivered a new doll and a set of paints two weeks earlier
with a note that on Christmas Eve he would leave another small package.
Meghan had whined and cried much of the day and the package was still
hidden in a wardrobe, stuffed in a shirt pocket. At one point in the early

evening, Doreen had announced that Father Christmas didn't visit naughty children, yet even this warning hadn't calmed Meghan's tantrums.

Now as the soup simmered on the range and the teakettle began whistling, Doreen felt utterly defeated. She had failed to comfort her own daughter on the day when God sent the Great Comforter. She had failed to get cards and a few small packages posted back home to Hempstead. She didn't know if her latest letter had reached Colin. The blackout curtains seemed heavy and stifling, drawing the very air from the room. She heard her mum's voice floating about and admonishing her to pick up her chin and deal with the hand she'd been given. It was all too much. It was time to cry. She turned off the range and the soup and the water went cold as she curled up in Colin's overstuffed chair and wept. Father Christmas didn't come that night. It was the first of many Christmas Eves when gifts seemed taken more than given.

December 24, 1939
Dover, England

Colin Bennett sat outside the naval headquarters in Dover and watched the sky darken. It had been a dank and gloomy day and the sky had never really lightened, typical for late December. He had an uneasiness in the pit of his stomach and his mind focused upon the war events of the last month rather than on the holiness of the day. German bombs had actually landed in the Shetlands in mid-November and British soldiers had been killed and wounded at the Battle of River Plate only two weeks earlier. German troops were advancing on the continent, despite former assurances that they had retrieved the territories they wanted. The inevitability of more serious involvement lay heavy on Colin's heart as he saw more clearly his future role as a doctor to the seriously wounded. His visions were of young men, their body parts severed and bleeding, their eyes pleading for help to end their pain while their mums back home keep silent vigil for their safe return.

What an unholy vision on such a holy day! Only after he had shaken those thoughts from his mind could he remember the sights and smells of his own home on Christmas Eve. Doreen and Meghan would be home from Mass, singing carols next to a small tree by the shuttered window. They would be sipping hot soup and enjoying an early taste of Christmas pudding. Doreen would be laughing and telling their daughter stories of past Christmases. Everything would be perfect. He smiled at the picture in his mind. Next year he would be in that picture. That was what kept loneliness from breaking his spirit.

March 22, 1940

My dearest Colin,
It was so good to get your letter, as it always is the happiest moment of my week! I'm glad you are well and taking care of yourself.
The news is distressing this week, with the killing of that Orkney civilian by a German bomb. I do worry at times about the further escalation of this war here on our soil, but we are assured that all preparations are in order. I know from rumors in and around the hospital that we aren't nearly as prepared as we think we are! Our factories seem to not keep up with the demand for plane production and the shipyards are behind in orders as well. Even though many women in the area are

taking wartime jobs, there doesn't seem to be a clear plan to make us truly prepared. I suppose the censors will delete my last few comments!

The rationing that started in January is not as bad as I had expected. We were already consuming less sugar and coffee anyway. The biggest problem will be the cuts in petrol. I'm glad we don't own an automobile, yet I'm afraid the cutbacks in public transport will prove more than just inconvenient. We'll all be walking even more!

Your beautiful Meghan is healthy and getting more clever each day. She is really quite a charmer and has most of our neighbors laughing in spite of themselves. I wish you could see how she's grown! When I save up a few more pounds, I'll get her photo taken. I have looked at buying a secondhand camera so I could send you many photos. Still, the cost is too much for us just now.

I heard from Mrs. Markham again. We've been writing often and I mentioned how Meghan's grown. She said she would bring her old camera with her on her next visit and take some photos that we can send to you!

Meghan has been very happy lately, as several of her friends have returned from evacuation. Their mums said the whole experience was quite upsetting, that they would not evacuate again. I suppose that attests to maternal resolve! School attendance is not enforced just yet, so the gardens are again lively with the sound of children, a lovely sound indeed.

Have you heard anymore about where you are going in the next few weeks? I thought by now they'd send you home for furlough, but I guess they have other plans.

Mrs. Markham wrote the strangest thing in her last letter. It had to do with a man who came into Reception at Hempstead Hospital asking some probing questions. Of course, she had no information for him, but she said the inquiry disturbed her, as he looked like Mr. Strucker. Anyway my love, please don't concern yourself about this on our account. I only tell you this to remind you to be careful. Meghan and I love you so much. You must always remember that.

```
    What should I get Meghan for her birthday? If
you have suggestions, please include them in your
next letter! Take good care of yourself and know
that I ache for you.
```

```
                                    Yours forever,
                                    Doreen
```

March 30, 1940
Dover, England

Vice-Admiral Bertram Ramsay's ships lay waiting in the Dover harbor, ready for another sailing to the northern beaches of France. British Expeditionary Forces, or BEF, had been in Europe for some time and were especially present along the English Channel separating France and Great Britain. The Royal Navy was attempting to bolster the Allied forces. They were there to protect the French sovereignty as well as ensure the safety of Britain's southern coast.

Lieutenant Colin Bennett of the Royal Navy folded his most recent orders and secured them in his official dossier. It was dusk and he was packed and ready to sail. He hesitated to post his letter to Doreen, knowing the censors would delete most of it anyway. Still, he wanted to tell her once more before he left British soil, what she and Meghan meant to him and what he would sacrifice to secure their safety and well being. Censors be damned! He would write 'I love you' seven times at the end, once for each month of their separation. She would understand his message.

He posted the letter and boarded his ship. The channel was rough as spring storms had churned up the waters and the ships set sail rocking and lunging in the twilight hours. The French coast lay waiting eagerly, like a new lover. The beaches at Dunkirk lay waiting, too, like a lover wasted in remorse and pain.

April 12, 1940
Croydon, England

Doreen fumbled with the door latch, hurriedly trying to step into their flat, her arms laden with market items. Meghan trailed behind her, carefully stepping over bugs to avoid their demise, her latest whim. The evening was warm and the fragrance of primrose wafted from the bushes that separated the front gardens. At least it would stay light outside long enough for her to bake her own birthday cake and prepare a special tea.

Meghan would expect some kind of celebration, as she had been singing "happy birthday" for the past two days.

Doreen didn't feel much like celebrating. It had been nearly two weeks since her last letter from Colin, the one in which he had said he was leaving England for an unknown destination. She knew, of course, that he could never divulge his ship's whereabouts, yet she still resented the lack of real involvement in his life, or his involvement in their's. It was all so frustrating!

She prepared the tea and baked her cake and the two of them sang "happy birthday" together. She and Meghan blew out the candles on the cake and laughed when it took them two tries. As Meghan poked her fingers into the cake to retrieve the candles, a shadowy thought crossed Doreen's mind. *My wish won't come true with two attempts to extinguish the light!* She shook her head in disbelief at her own silly superstition. Yet as they finished their small, private party, she couldn't seem to quell the growing fears that engulfed her as the lovely spring day melted into the blackness of night.

The phone rang loudly and Meghan was the first to answer it.

"Hallo, this is 927468."

"Why Meghan, love, is that you? This is Mrs. Markham, how grown up you sound!"

"Hallo Mrs. Markham, I will go get Mummy!"

Meghan ran off to the kitchen, leaving the phone dangling by the rickety wooden stand.

"Mrs. Markham, how lovely of you to ring up! It must have been difficult to get an open line. How are you?"

"I'm quite well, my dear. Just wanted to tell you I'm free from work for a fortnight and I'd thought I'd pay you a visit. I figured you might want a bit of company, as I'm sure your days have been long. How was your birthday yesterday? Did my card arrive on time?"

"Yes, your card arrived two days before and I so enjoyed it. Thank you, by the way, for your local news of Hempstead. I do enjoy hearing about folks. We would love to have you visit- and yes, I could use the company. It's not my days that are so long - it's my nights. I'm still nursing two to three days a week at Croydon Hospital and I tend my small garden out back. That, along with playschool for Meghan, keeps my days busy."

"Oh my dear, how brave you are. Have you heard from Colin since his last letter with his assignment?"

"No, I haven't. I'm sure it's just that no letters are getting through, as it's hard to determine what conditions are like for any kind of regular communication. I don't suppose I'll hear anything for quite some time. I'm frightened by the latest war news. With our forces now in Scandinavia, I fear this war is spreading like a wildfire."

"Never mind, love. Your duty right now is to take care of yourself and your precious daughter. Leave the war details to the generals and just do what you can here to make a difference. I'll be at the train station the day after tomorrow and I can make my own way to your flat. Should be about lunchtime, if all goes well. It's hard to tell now, with interrupted train schedules."

"I'm off work that day! Meghan and I will greet you at the station, as she finishes playschool at half eleven. It'll be perfect! I'll pack us a sandwich and we'll picnic in the town gardens. Do please give the sisters at the convent my greetings if you see them before leaving."

"I shall see them later today when they come for their hospital duties; I'll give them your best. A picnic in the gardens sounds lovely! I'm so excited to spend evenings chatting and sipping tea. And I shall bring a small bottle of sherry that's been waiting to be opened. I just hope we can avoid the too frequent air raid drills and enjoy our visit in quiet. I shall see you the day after tomorrow. Goodbye for now, my dear."

"Goodbye, Mrs. Markham, and take care."

Doreen hung up the receiver as though it held a precious valuable.

The train from Hempstead to Croydon was nearly on time and Mrs. Markham stepped off with only one small suitcase in tow and her worn leather handbag slung over her shoulder. She looked tired yet joyful as the friends reunited, an unspoken fear and anxiety bonding them in a new way.

The next two weeks were spent in a blur of walks in the parks and town gardens and long conversations while watching Meghan play alone or with friends. Doreen felt reunited with her past, having Mrs. Markham about, and a bit more courageous to face the future in an uncertain world. She hadn't yet received a letter from Colin, though she had written to him several times, knowing all the while that he most likely didn't receive them. Still, it quieted her heart to keep writing, giving her the chance to silently verbalize what her voice could not.

Mrs. Markham received a wire at the Bennett's the second week of her visit. It was from a doctor at the Hempstead Infirmary, saying that a 'Mr. S.' from Hempstead had been detained and later imprisoned by the British government for spying for the Germans. The wire was brief, but Mrs. Markham in her wisdom knew how to read between the lines. She understood the message that Wilhelm Strucker had finally been caught. It was the kind of secret knowledge that lay dormant in a small, English town, only to be discussed when the truth could be verified. Mrs. Markham shook her head in sad recognition as she handed the wired message to Doreen.

"Your Mum was right. When I first talked to her during her illness and stay at hospital, she expressed concern to me about Mr. Strucker. She knew there was something terribly wrong in that family, especially with the father. And that poor older boy, what was his name?"

"William."

"Oh yes, well I heard he had a difficult time of it. You must have known the lad."

"Yes I did. We were...close at one time. Actually, he was my best friend for quite some time. But Wilhelm was mean. It was better for them that he left for Germany."

"Anna Bailey was a good judge of character. If only we'd have acted upon our suspicions years ago, who knows..."

"Who knows what, Mrs. Markham? What do you mean?"

"I'm sorry, dear. I shouldn't have brought up the subject."

The elderly woman adjusted the cushion behind her back and smoothed her already secured hair into place.

"Please, you must finish your thought."

"There were many of us in Hempstead, especially the shopkeepers, who have felt that Wilhelm Strucker had something to do with Father Loughry's murder. Possibly he even delivered the blows that sent that poor saint to an early reward. God rest his soul. We've no proof, mind you. It's just that Mr. Strucker appeared in Hempstead after years away in Germany, I think under the pretence of visiting the dying Mrs. He was asking about town as to Father Loughry's whereabouts and I'm sure someone told him the Father was in London. We knew about strange attacks by radical fascists upon certain individuals, especially those of the Cloth so I have a strong feeling that he somehow followed the Father to your place. Why he would actually kill the priest is beyond me. How does anyone explain the actions of a madman?"

Doreen fell onto the divan, her breath coming in short gasps.

"My God, Mrs. Markham, how dreadful! We never knew..." her voice trailed off in a whisper.

Mrs. Markham moved closer to Doreen and wrapped her arms about her. The two of them spent the evening without conversation, watching Meghan play and putting her to bed. They opened the sherry and drank it with only their thoughts and memories to disturb the stillness of the spring night.

May 10, 1940

Doreen sat motionless next to the wireless, her hands folded in her lap and her eyes focused on the window. She and Meghan had spent the day quietly playing and trying to stay busy. Yet the announcement of a national day of prayer had halted Doreen's activities and she now waited for any news that came over the set. She had tried to gently explain the situation to Meghan, how they should say prayers for all the daddies who were far away trying to help other people and bring peace to the world. It was a difficult thing to explain to a four year old, all the while shaking from her mind images of bombs and shells, and mortar attacks chasing men across open fields, cornering them in village buildings, bursting upon them as they lay exhausted in the underbrush. Doreen tried to pray for all the fathers and sons, yet she found herself constantly repeating the same refrain. 'Dear God, please keep Colin safe and bring him back to us.' Selfish as it seemed, she could not help herself. She knew the sisters at Wycombe Convent would be praying regularly for all men and women – while she prayed for the one man who consumed her every waking moment.

She finally moved away from the wireless and poured some tea and milk for the two of them. Meghan seemed to sense her mum's sadness and sat without complaint, leaving the table dutifully to get ready for bed. Doreen sat on the divan trying to remember every detail of Colin, every physical trait, every personality characteristic, every nuance that was a part of him. She smiled at the thought of his habits that had once annoyed her. Oh to be so annoyed again! Just before she turned off the last dim light, she prayed the Rosary. It wasn't a good luck charm. Still, it couldn't hurt.

Doreen and Meghan were looking at picture books, the wireless set humming in the background with lively music interrupted by war news. It was quiet in the area that day as most of the children were at the park, celebrating in a small way the Bank Holiday. She had kept Meghan home because of a roseola rash on her stomach. Meghan didn't seem unwell, yet Doreen feared a fever later in the day. She was only half listening as the deep voice on the wireless interrupted the music for a "special bulletin."

"Today, May 31, Prime Minister Churchill, the War Department, and Admiral Ramsay of the Royal Navy have informed the BBC and the British people of a courageous evacuation of the British Expeditionary Forces from the beaches at Dunkirk, France. We have no details at this time on the number or nature of casualties. We will bring you further details as we receive them. Once again, we interrupt with this report: Today, May 31, Prime ..."

Doreen heard the voice repeating the words, but her mind couldn't seem to grasp what he was saying. Something about an evacuation from Dunkirk of BEF forces. Her mind began to reel. She didn't even know where Colin was. Could he possibly be a part of that operation?! She knew he must be someplace where it was nearly impossible to get mail through, or she would have heard from him by now. If he were in a dangerous spot, surrounded by Germans, there would be no chance to communicate. Of course! All the while, she had been imagining him taking care of the wounded in makeshift hospital tents, away from the front, just beyond danger. Yet, he could have been running just ahead of the Germans and now trapped on a beach, dependent upon a boat in the choppy English Channel to bring him home safely. How could she have been so narrow and naïve in her thinking! Her head was spinning and her heart was pounding in her throat. Meghan looked up from her book and spoke, but Doreen couldn't hear her. Her ears were aching with the sound of crashing waves and wind, beating against the sides of her head like a boat thrashing between high surf and jagged rocks.

June 1940

Captain Ethan Hollingsworth stared at the calendar page on the back wall of the war strategy room. The picture of spring flowers in London gardens looked ridiculous in a room where battles were planned and analyzed. He wondered if the new Prime Minister had brought the calendar from his own kitchen before assuming his duties at 10 Downing Street, or whether Chamberlain had left it behind. Ethan turned around to look at the jowled face of newly appointed Winston Churchill, who sat droning on from a large chair in the front of the room. The war news briefing had been anything but brief. He had been to many briefings over the years, but never one that took so long – and sounded so desperately urgent. He knew the reason for the long and tedious session. All hell had broken loose in the past few weeks. Chamberlain had resigned in duress and Churchill was taking the toughest stand yet against the encroaching Germans. Among other wartime regulations, he had ordered the removal of street names and road signs in and around the London area as well as the internment of British fascists and enemy aliens. Londoners were now keeping vigil for suspected spies and participated fully in the air raid and invasion practices. Ethan nodded with certainty at his own thoughts. The "phony war" was over. The real war had begun.

The captain stretched his legs and cleared his throat, an obvious annoyance to the commanders on either side of him, as was his very presence in this high security briefing. Ethan hadn't felt like explaining the order he'd received from a Rear Admiral, "requesting" him to go in his stead while he attended a family funeral. The sound of shuffling feet and scooting chairs accompanied the Admiral who spoke after Churchill, as he seemed bent on covering every bleak event of the past few weeks in great detail. Ethan only half-listened to the man whose lisp made it difficult to concentrate on the content.

"As you know, sirs, the German advances from the Ardennes to the Somme River have severed all communication between the Allied northern and southern forces. Yet, I'm pleased to report, even with this dire news, we have stirred up the courage and determination of our citizens."

Right, Ethan mused. What else is left for them except their dogged English spirit? What a sham! He cleared his throat and shifted in the chair once again as the Admiral continued.

"You know that the withdrawal of the British Expeditionary Force by sea was ordered by Commander Viscount Gort on May 19th, 1940, as our Allied forces were being encircled by the Krauts. Gort received orders to launch an attack from Arras, France, just north of the Somme River, southward against the right flank of the German line. This attack surprised the high German command, but it was not offensive enough to ensure complete success."

Ethan looked up to see heads nodding in silent agreement.

"The German commandant, Guderian, moved his troops up past Boulogne and Calais, crossing the canal defense line close to Dunkirk. His decision was a real tactical blunder, but one which gave our forces hope for evacuation. At this point, Dunkirk was now the only port left available for the task of shipping thousands of Allied troops from German overrun territory. Our race to evacuate began at that point."

The Prime Minister pushed his chair away from the looming desk and stood next to the Admiral, his strong persona clear evidence of the power he now possessed. At the back of the room, Hollingsworth shifted yet again in his chair, avoiding eye contact with anyone around him.

The information continued as a run-down of events, past and already in progress, already known by those *really* on the inside. The Prime Minister told everyone to stand up and stretch, aware that the long session and the heat of the day was taking its toll on officers that were already sleep-deprived. When they sat back down, the Admiral continued as he mopped his forehead with a handkerchief.

There was a groan from the officers assembled to hear the next devastating news. Ethan sighed in disgust. How in the hell were they going to get anyone out of there?! What was this raging warrior saying – exactly? What would happen to those left behind?! His role as an officer, going home to a flat in London safe and snug, stood in stark contrast to the horrible reality that awaited the men left to a fate surely worse than burial at sea. He tried to shake the news from his mind, but now the sound of the Admiral's voice and the presence of so many bobbing war department heads made it impossible to focus on anything else. Anything that is, except the beautiful calendar page portraying a tranquil London garden that appeared like a taunting harlot in the midst of a city besieged.

Captain Hollingsworth barked out an order to the Lieutenant in the hallway, then stormed into his office, slamming the door behind him. He knew instinctively that he'd been rude to the officer, but his growing frustration had no other expression, except at the bottom of a bottle. He walked over to the window and rammed his fist into the cracked, wooden sill. The latest memo folder lay on his desk, as yet unopened. The Vice-Admiral had already divulged its contents two hours earlier. The information in written form was just a formality, another set of papers to clutter his desk and get filed away with all the other dismal war reports. He walked over to his desk and sat down, covering his face with his large hands, then finally brought out his bottle and set it down in front of him. He opened the folder and stared at the memo. The Vice-Admiral's words played over and over in his mind like a dark poem resounding from an old victrola.

"On the 26 of May, the British troops that had gone southward were diverted to prevent a German breakthrough from Belgium. After closing the gap, Commander Gort withdrew his troops to Dunkirk coast to begin complete evacuation of the BEF. At 17:57 that evening, Admiral Ramsay commenced 'Operation Dynamo' with 35 passenger ships, 62 barges and flat-bottomed Dutch boats, and handful of small private vessels. The sixteen miles of beaches were suitable for assembling men for transport, though indications were that many would not make it to Dunkirk to be transferred to ships before the Germans overran the beach head. Shallow waters just off the coast made docking of larger vessels impossible. Men were ferried out to the waiting ships on smaller, private crafts. Boats returning to our ports from Dunkirk were attacked from the air and shelled by German coastal guns."

Ethan grabbed the bottle, took a swallow of the amber liquid and wiped his mouth on his sleeve. The report was mesmerizing in a sick, twisted kind of way. His eyes glanced down the page and found the place he'd left off.

"Harbor itself was reduced to rubble, breakwater also heavily damaged. After first day of evacuation, virtually no fighting men on board rescue ships, mostly pay-staff and officers.

"Admiral Ramsay assigned Royal navy Captain William Tennat to run Dunkirk beach operation on May 27, then directed the Ministry of Shipping to find more small vessels and send them out immediately. Royal Air Force assigned to give air cover for Dunkirk evacuation and destroyers, minesweepers, and transports were brought in from other locations to help in this operation."

The captain took another long swallow of whiskey, then picked up a pen and drew it across the page. Only 7,669 men had been evacuated by the end of that second day! Since Hitler had secured the surrender of Belgium on May 28, time had been of the essence. Poor bastards - they never had a chance! German Luftwaffe and their cover boats had attacked ships in the channel. Allied troops whose ships were torpedoed and shelled had been transferred to other ships. The waters were on fire and the air had filled with burning fuels.

Ethan stood up and walked to the blackened window and stared. It had to have been a scene of horrible chaos and confusion as unnoticed heroes brought up the burning and wounded men from the water, piling on more men than the ships could safely take on. He walked back to the desk and picked up the last page of the memo, greedily consuming its last paragraphs.

"The wind had dramatically picked up force in the channel, capsizing and swamping smaller vessels. Beaches weren't usable due to high surf and arriving boats diverted to the damaged harbor. Shelling from the Luftwaffe continued and holes in the pier were repaired with loose planks. Two destroyers were ordered back to Dover for repairs; some vessels were towed, many others sunk enroute. More troops moved to the eastern end of the shore in attempt to regroup and board any craft."

He tossed the folder across his desk, then grabbed his coat and walked out into the misting rain. He needed more drink than he left in his bottle.

He walked past his usual haunts and headed to Covent Garden. He didn't know many folks on that side of town, and he could find a table in the back and pretend he was someone else. It would work for a while. He could forget who he was and what responsibilities he had. He could forget how he proudly signed up all those young men for active duty, then sent them to the fires of hell and the icy waters of death. He ordered two pints, took a seat in the back, and drained the glasses without pause. He got up and ordered two more, then took a seat at the bar. It was easier not having to carry the glasses. Easier staying put to drown out the hum of voices around him, though not the voices of crying men that screamed inside his head.

CHAPTER FIFTEEN

On the morning of June 1, Hitler's attacks continued bringing death and destruction on the beaches of the northern French coast and in the waters that transported the Allied fighting troops still alive. The horrible reality was that the Allied men were approaching their breaking point, some having not slept nor eaten in days, living with the constant fear of German attacks on land or dying in the cold, English Channel waters. There were an increasing number of reports that men were losing control of their minds and emotions. The situation was getting desperate. Germans planted mines in the shipping routes and the Luftwaffe continually pounded the beaches and waters. More boats came from England. More boats were shelled and sunk, their hulls breaking like a huge whale in pain, their men screaming from the water as the enemy bore down. Both the Royal Navy and the Royal Air Force requested Operation Dynamo to be halted, as their losses were too heavy, their ammunition running very low, their men not able to withstand much more punishment. At the end of this day, 31 rescue ships, including six destroyers had been sunk or were unable to carry on.

Lieutenant Colin Bennett knelt beside the latest victim who had been picked up from the water only an hour before and taken to the makeshift hospital at Rosendael, France, just a few kilometers from the beaches. He examined the wound that had ripped a hole in the soldier's arm, exposing the sinewy muscles. It had bled profusely at first, but the salt and the time in the water had slowed the bleeding. The young man lay motionless, staring ahead, conscious but not altogether aware of his surroundings. Colin began cleaning the wound as quickly as possible, calling out for help to suture before wrapping bandages. Supplies were already running low, many having been used the day before when the assault in the waters had been particularly bad. He worked without much light as the morning sun hadn't fully risen. He thought of the vision he'd had last Christmas

Eve and shook his head. He could never have imagined the horror of what he had seen in the last few days. He could not imagine ever being able to put it all out of his mind. The idea of celebrating anything after this was unthinkable.

While he stitched the young man's arm, he thought of Meghan. She had just had her fourth birthday a fortnight before while he had worked feverishly into the night on a French boy moving with his division and the British soldiers from the border regions of Belgium back into France. Colin saw the young man's face now, as surely as if he were still there. The fright. The incomprehensibility of a wound so fierce that it could take down such a strong and agile fighter. He had tried to give the boy some comfort that night as the shells burst into fire behind them and flames licked their heels. But he knew the boy could not hear the words, his injuries too extensive, his youthful body too tired. He had finally closed his eyes, the fight gone. The fear gone. Colin had covered the boy with a soiled blanket, pulled off his tags, and turned towards the dark woods vomiting as he ran, his stomach retching.

The morning of June 2 saw two British hospital ships floating in the waters off the French coast. The commanders had done their duty and sent uncoded radio messages, informing everyone in the area, including the enemy, of their purpose. They were only in the waters to pick up and administer to the wounded, Allied or German. The boats' engines sputtered from overwork and the men on board stood by the open decks, weary and sick from too much sea and seeing too much.

Lieutenant Colin Bennett had boarded one of these hospital ships the day before, following orders to abandon the land hospital. Now he paced the ship's deck, unable to rest his body or his soul. The young man he'd worked on during the night had gone into seizures just as dawn broke. It hadn't mattered how carefully and completely Colin had attended him, the soldier's body had not the strength to respond fully. He was pronounced dead just as the Luftwaffe resumed their attacks, the sun just beginning to peek through the clouds, warming the men who lined the beaches looking for their rescue. Colin searched the sky waiting for the shells to fall and expecting constant carnage. Perhaps it would all be over soon. Perhaps some miracle would grace them, and his ship would head towards Dover, granting him a long visit with Doreen and his beautiful Meghan.

He stopped pacing and looked across the Channel, allowing himself one mental picture of home before returning to the injured. It was a strange thought to have, really. It wasn't anything special, or a moment that should have stood out. It was simply the picture of the three of them eating stew at the kitchen table, the teapot steaming and Meghan chattering. The smell of flowers, the sound of the neighbor's dog, the loud ticking of Anna Bailey's old clock, the feel of Doreen's hand as she brushed up against him, pouring the tea. And the dancing, his daughter's feet planted on his as he waltzed across the kitchen floor. God, would the world, his world, ever be right again? In the distance he heard shellfire and his peaceful vision was gone. It would all be gone now.

"Lieutenant!"

Colin's reverie was halted at his commander's voice.

"Yes sir."

"What's the condition of Thompson? Isn't that who you worked on so long?"

"Yes sir. Grant Thompson. He didn't make it, sir. Just too much damage."

"I'm sorry, Colin. How are you holding up?"

"I think I'm alright, Sir. Can I ask you a question?"

"Sure, Lieutenant. What's on your mind?"

"I expected to see troops lined up at the harbor from daybreak on, waiting to board rescue boats. From what I can see from here, there's not been much going on until the last hour or so. Where are our men?"

"Lack of communication. I received a message to be on guard for injured troops trying to reach the boats. Seems that we have boats waiting in the harbor with the men to be rescued waiting somewhere further down the beaches. Damn awful mistake. I think word has finally spread that the boats are waiting in the harbor. From what I can tell, the breakwater is filling up with men who've made their way to a makeshift dock. One message I just received said many men waiting earlier made jetties from the wreckage of abandoned vehicles and these were used to get the men from the beach to boats."

"God, what a mess."

Evening finally crept across the waters, chilling Colin as he stood on the ship's deck and scanned the shore for any further action. Since there were no large ships in the harbor to bomb at this point, the Luftwaffe now turned its attention to the rest of the troops still waiting on the perimeter of the beaches. As nighttime came on, larger ships began to move into the harbor again under the cover of the black sky.

Colin finally settled down to close his eyes for a while, his heart heavier than his eyelids. The sun rose across the harbor, its rays casting colorful hues that looked out of place amongst the debris of war. Colin could feel the warmth beginning to wrap him in a moment of security, when the familiar drone of enemy aircraft assaulted the quiet of early morning. The planes sounded as though they were just overhead and Colin's eyes shot toward the sky. He felt a sudden panic and leaped to his feet, struggling to regain his full capacities. They couldn't be poised to bomb this boat! His ship and one other were clearly marked as hospital ships, whose sole purpose was to lift the wounded from the shores and other sinking ships! What about their non-combat status that was clearly marked and known by uncoded messages?! Surely even Hitler's forces wouldn't attack an unarmed boat whose medical personnel would save German as well as Allied boys!

Colin stared out into the distance at the red cross that marked the sister hospital ship. In that moment it was rocking in the waters, then it burst open in every seam. The sound was deafening! The screams and cries of men, their flesh burning, their bodies being ripped apart, could be heard above the awful groaning and breaking of the wood and steel that had only moments later been a safe haven. Colin was unable to move, but he heard his own voice whispering, " God no, please no…" He repeated the words again and again as if they could make it all go away. He was only vaguely aware of the shouts and orders being given around him and the men scrambling about, trying to secure patients in the holds, trying to hear and follow orders in the mass confusion around them.

"Lieutenant Bennett!! Move your ass and get going!"

Snapping back, Colin raced across the deck and bounded to the lower berth, grabbing life preservers and blankets from stacks as he ran from cot to cot. He felt the ship lurch to one side, then balanced himself and continued moving from bed to bed, lashing the beds to anything solid. The patients moaned with pain as the ship moved erratically. The ship's Captain was trying desperately to move the vessel away from the planes, but a laden ship is no match for an assault from the air.

Colin was now barking out orders as well as listening for them and the scene below was utter chaos. It was no better up on the decks, where officers hoisted lifeboats over the side, grabbing as much in the way of supplies as they could. Then it hit.

The sound of the shelling was so earsplitting that it stunned the men for a moment. Reality set in. The ship was growling and scraping, its hull breaking open and the water coming in. Down below, the force of the hit sent the men, cots and all, careening in all directions.

As though in slow motion, Colin felt himself being hurled against the steel wall, his head stopping the motion. He felt his neck crack to one side and something warm was crawling down his back. He knew he was still alive and he reached for a rag as the ship stopped lunging. Applying the rag to the back of his head, he looked around him to survey the damage.

The ship was certainly in a bad way, but it was still afloat, though for how long it was hard to tell. The orders were coming fast and furious, but most of the men were too injured or too stunned to move. Colin made his way to the steps, checking each man on a cot as he went. Aside from being battered about, most of them were in no worse shape than before. He got to the steps, shouting for any information.

"We have to go back to the shore, Lieutenant Bennett. She's too hard hit to stay out here; we'll sink like the other one. Prepare your patients as best as you can."

"Yes, sir. Does that mean we return to the shore hospital at Rosendael?"

"Hell yes, if we can get them there. We'll be in German territory, but Jesus, we have no other choice. Some of the more able men can head to the rescue points, but the injured...well they just can't make that trip."

"Yes, sir."

"Lieutenant, you've got quite a gash on your neck, you'd better see to that soon, or you won't be any good to anyone."

"Yes, sir."

The ship creaked as it turned toward shore, still taking on water and limping across the waves. It hadn't far to go, which was one small blessing on an otherwise cursed day.

Colin scanned the shore as they prepared to land. The Germans had already advanced through this area and would surely see the renewed activity. One thing was certain, staying behind on shore meant eventual capture by the enemy. It meant either certain, immediate death, or imprisonment, torture, and a slower death in time. Colin knew the only way to survive mentally and physically was to deal with the moment at hand.

As many as possible were carried from the floundering ship through the water to the remnants of the Rosendael hospital. Those who were not seriously injured waded into shore, then left hastily and without order for beaches and other rescue ships further away.

There was more confusion as others who'd been waiting anxiously at Rosendael ran from the hospital to join the exodus. Colin knew he had to stay behind for those injured and dying who had no other choice. He stood at attention and watched until he could no longer see their forms in the gathering darkness, until he could no longer see his own form in the blackness of night. As the piercing sounds of screams and the drone of engines faded, Colin Bennett fell to his knees, his shoulders heaving and his eyes burning as he buried his face in the damp sandy soil.

Captain Hollingsworth walked slowly from his London flat to the offices of the Royal Navy. He passed by a café that boasted hard rolls and French cheese on their breakfast menu. He stopped to stare. It was a peculiar sight for a city that prided itself on British "pub" food, however bland and restrictive that might be. It was obvious the sign in the window was old. There hadn't been any French cheese in London for quite some time. Despite his attempt to avoid the vision, his thoughts turned to his one and only visit to France. It was such a long time ago. Her name was Marie and her eyes danced like the evening stars. She had shown him her Paris and he'd never been the same. He was so young then. So full of adventurous schemes. So full of ridiculous youth and enthusiasm. He knew it wouldn't last, but the memory of that summer crept into his consciousness whenever he needed to escape. Now was that time. The news from the past three days was an account of bravery and some success for the British troops, but it was a dismal prediction for the French people. He didn't let himself wonder where Marie was right now. It didn't matter anyway. There was nothing he could do for her – or for anyone. The reports he'd received had come through sporadically, but their accuracy seemed genuine.

The evacuation of the British Expeditionary Forces had been completed by midnight of June 2 and on June 3 only the French Perimeter troops were left. For some unknown reason, the Germans had ceased their forward movement and the French troops were able to get back to the harbor, to the waiting ships. At 14:00 on June 4, the last of the French rearguard made its way to Dunkirk. At 14:23, Operation Dynamo was completed. The best of the British fighting men were on home soil, but the Dunkirk evacuation had left France virtually undefended. It was only a matter of time before she would fall to the Nazis. Only a matter of time before the Paris still etched in the captain's memory would be raped by a brutal intruder.

The town of Croydon was bursting with the newly arrived soldiers, some occupying the hospital wards and others visiting families on leave. Some came home permanently in bags. The air raid sirens and emergency drills seemed to affect the men more than the townspeople, their minds and bodies having just left the real terrors and carnage of war. Doreen looked into their faces as she made her way home from her hospital duties. She had already put in a twelve-hour shift, her upswept hair now falling, disheveled. She was bone tired and delusional. Perhaps that's why the face of every soldier she attended to took the form of Colin's. She had to get some rest.

It had been two weeks since the end of the Dunkirk evacuation, and still she had not heard a word. She didn't even know if that's where Colin had been. The situation in France had become desperate and very little communication was getting through from Europe.

Doreen stopped at the childminder's, gathered Meghan and her belongings, and walked briskly to their flat. Perhaps today would be the day she received a letter from him! The mail slot was nearly empty when she arrived home, except for one brief note from the Convent, asking if everything was well. Doreen brought in the wash that she had pegged out very early in the day and set out a soup pot on the range. It seemed a good evening for a light supper and Meghan would eat soup and bread without any fuss.

"Meghan, come out back and tidy up the toys in this garden! You've left quite a mess out here, and it may rain before morning."

Meghan didn't respond right away and Doreen sighed with frustration.

"Meghan, I said to come out back and put your things away!"

Meghan appeared at the back door, a puzzled look on her face and her fingers twirling her hair.

"Mummy, there's a man at the front door. He has on a funny uniform, not like Daddy wore. He wants to see you."

Her heart missed a beat.

"Right dear, now put your toys away like a good little girl, while I go talk to the man."

"Yes, Mummy."

Doreen pushed her hair back in place and smoothed her uniform apron as she walked through the house to the front stoop.

"Mrs. Bennett, sorry, but I'm here on behalf of Captain Hollingsworth to deliver a telegram to you from the Royal Navy."

Only after the words were spoken did the true meaning of his visit register in her mind. The Navy did not send out messengers to inform you where your loved one was. They sent the messengers with a telegram, an impersonal typed memo on yellow paper, *explaining their regret of loss.*

The young man in the slightly crumpled uniform left as quickly as he came and Doreen stood on the doorstep, holding the envelope as if it were a lighted match. When her eyes could focus again, she opened it up. Its words seemed to float up in the air like tiny particles of dust or sparkles left over from a fireworks display.

I regret to inform you that your husband, Lieutenant Colin Bennett, has been reported as missing in action following the Battle of Dunkirk. Stop. His last location was at a hospital just down the coast from the evacuation point. Stop. The German army has completely secured that area and our aerial photos show no Allied activity in that location. Stop. The Royal Navy, the War Department, and the Prime Minister send their deepest regrets. Stop.

Doreen stood frozen. Moving about would make it too real. Perhaps if she kept still, this would all pass like a nightmare and she would walk back into their home with the certainty that Colin was fine. Yes, all was fine. That was it. She must be struggling to wake from an after work nap. This whole scene was an illusion.

Meghan wormed her way through the door, coming from behind Doreen's skirt and peering up at her mum.

"His uniform wasn't as nice as Daddy's. That's probably because Daddy's a doctor. He's coming home, isn't he? You said we just have to wait a little longer."

Meghan's chatter broke the spell that Doreen was under. She turned her head to look at her daughter who had become suddenly quiet. Doreen knelt beside her child, gathered her in her arms, and turned back to face the inside of their home.

"Let's go inside, Meghan. Let's go inside and shut the door."

The words that came from her mouth sounded unfamiliar. They came from a person who now felt excruciating pain, though no physical wound appeared. A person whose legs and arms were separated from the body. A woman whose husband was missing. Being interrogated, being tortured. A woman whose husband may already be dead.

Meghan squirmed and tugged at her sleeve.

"Mummy, what did that man say? Why do you look so sad?"

Doreen stared ahead, her mouth drawn down and her eyes glazed. She blinked and looked at her innocent daughter, still holding her close, not wanting to let her go. It took a while longer before she was able to verbalize an explanation that was appropriate for a four year old. It would take a lot longer before she could say it to herself.

Meghan sipped very little soup that night and Doreen's bowl was untouched, as well as the loaf of bread. Instead, Doreen drank a small glass of whiskey while Meghan continued stirring her soup. The drink was a stash of Colin's, usually brought out for joyous occasions. The warmth of the drink helped block the reality and deaden her senses. She finally got up and put Meghan to bed without a storybook.. She knew she should phone their priest at St.Thomas, or Mrs. Markham, or the hospital staff, but she couldn't bring herself to pick up the receiver. The message would have to wait another day. She walked into their room, pulled the curtains shut and lay across their bed.

As the evening shadows turned to darkness Doreen still lay sprawled on the duvet. She tried to see Colin's face, his soft, expressive brown eyes, his strong chin. She could see his smile but the rest of his features blurred together. She tried to remember the touch of his hand on her back, her face, her breasts. She sat upright and slipped out of her soiled clothes and into her nightgown. She could just make out the outline of her own body. The image was reflected in the mirror from the crack of light that made its way from the neighbor's kitchen through the shutters and into their room. Despite the obvious signs of motherhood, she still looked slim and taught. She ran her hands down her gown just as Colin would have done. Her heart always beat faster when Colin's hands caressed her body. But this time the racing pulse was prompted by horrible pictures that now flashed across her mind. Captured. A prisoner of war. Tortured. A body lying alone in a place too terrible for words.

She glanced once more in the mirror as her hands clutched at her chest. She could feel nothing but a searing weight squeezing the air from her lungs. Perhaps she never again would breathe without that pain.

CHAPTER SIXTEEN

In the next two weeks, Doreen stopped in three times at the Royal Navy office in London. Each time meant precious money spent on buses, but she knew no other way to stay in communication with them. The young man who greeted her the third time smiled and waved her to a chair.

"Mrs.Bennett, do have a seat. I'll let the Captain know that you are here."

Doreen smiled at the young petty officer as he disappeared around the corner. It was only a few minutes before the Captain came out and she stood up.

"Why Mrs. Bennett, you're back again so soon. I am so sorry, but I still have absolutely no information for you. As I said before on your last visit, it is nearly impossible to determine what happened to the men in Rosendael Hospital. I do hope you understand that there are hundreds of men missing from various affected war areas and we're trying our best to determine their locations. We just have very little communication coming through from that part of France. Since the French surrender of June 22, there is no information on any troops that were left behind. Again, I'm sorry."

The Captain stopped speaking, waiting for some kind of reply, yet Doreen just continued to stare at him. He motioned for her to sit down and took a chair beside her.

"Mrs. Bennett, isn't there a relative or close friend you can call upon to help you just now? You seem to be all alone in this."

Doreen stiffened and stood up.

"Captain, I appreciate your concern, and yes, I am worried. I'm anxious to find out what's happened to my husband, but I'm not some crazed woman without the means to cope!"

"I'm sorry, Mrs. Bennett. I didn't mean to insinuate..."

"Please Captain, let me finish. I only came here today in hopes of finding out any new information that you might have on his status. I'm sorry if I have wasted your time."

"Mrs. Bennett, I promise you that you will be the first to know when we receive any news of your husband. Believe me when I say that I am truly sorry I can't provide more at this time. I can imagine the pain you must be going through."

She looked directly into his eyes, tears gathering in her own.

"No you can't! You can't possibly imagine the pain!"

Doreen whirled around and left without further comment. She made her way home, exhausted from mental anguish and lack of sleep. As darkness fell she donned her nightgown in the dark and turned away from the mirror that had begun to reflect her pain. She folded her hands upon her pillow and prayed though she was certain that her words sounded stupid and hollow. Tomorrow she would take matters into her own hands and make her own plan of action. She wouldn't wait for answers from this absent God!

Ethan Hollingsworth sat in his office chair in total darkness. He often stayed late to catch up on reports and rarely took the effort to turn on any lights. Now with the blackout enforced, there weren't even the city neons filtering in through his heavily draped windows. He got up slowly and opened the door, letting in a small stream of blue light from one dim bulb hanging precariously on a frayed cord below the transom. Strange, how much brightness the single bulb cast into a room engulfed by the night. He watched the light stream dance as the cord gently swayed in air currents that came from nowhere. He turned back toward his office. The large desk chair resembled the monster that lived under his bed as a child. It had hulking shoulders and a wide stance, as though it could easily swallow you with one attempt. The captain shuddered. It had been a long time since he'd seen that creature. Yet here it was. It was waiting for him. He knew he couldn't escape. There was no place to go except out into the empty hallway where his footsteps would echo loudly and the monster would be able to follow him. There was no one else around to rescue him, no one to hear him grovel for his life. There wouldn't even be anything left to find. The creature would leave no trace. There would never be any evidence that he existed.

He shuffled over to his desk and began methodically putting papers into folders. He gathered up the pens that were scattered about and placed them neatly in the top drawer. Taking the folders over to the cabinet on the far wall, he filed each one carefully, then closed the drawers and returned to the desk. The stream of light had ceased to dance and cast only a single path from the desk to the door. He opened the bottom drawer and removed the whiskey bottle, slowly taking off the cap. Lowering himself into the chair, he waited for the predator to wrap its jaws around him. Instead, there was only the sound of his breathing, a sound that suddenly was out of place. He finished off the whiskey. He couldn't help that woman. He couldn't tell her a damn thing. He didn't know anything. He didn't know where those missing men were. He didn't even know their names or where they had spent their Saturday nights before he shipped them to their fate. Maybe he did know one thing. He knew the sounds of their screams as they faced the evil creatures that tortured them, keeping them from the peace of death.

You can't possibly imagine the pain. He opened the top drawer once again and removed a key. His hand shook slightly as he put the key into the only locked drawer and took out the one valuable thing his father had given him. He ran his hand across the small, smooth barrel, letting his fingers come to rest upon the trigger. He removed the clip and leaned back in his chair, tipping his head back in surrender. He opened his mouth to scream, but the shot was the only sound that rang through the empty building. The only thing he felt was the warm ooze of blood before the monster laid claim to his soul. In the hallway, the light cord twirled feverishly, possessed by a presence darker than night.

July 1940

The sunrise was seen early as the clouds had lifted overnight and the long summer day had begun. Doreen was already at the kitchen table writing when she heard Meghan stirring in her bed. She knew she had at least thirty minutes before her daughter arrived at her side, asking for breakfast of porridge and toast. She wasn't sure why, but earlier in the week she'd felt the need to write to Mother Mary Catherine. It had only been a few days since she had received a letter from the convent, yet responding right away seemed the right thing to do. With Italy having signed a Pact of Steel with Germany, making them Britain's enemy, the war news was getting bleaker by the day. There was renewed talk of evacuating children from London and the surrounding towns and she needed the Mother's advice. Mrs. Markham had rung up Doreen offering to help. Doreen took the pen from her mouth once again, after having contemplated how blessed she was to have good friends to share in this difficult time. She thought momentarily of her mum, and how good it would have been to have her living in their flat just now. A breeze suddenly blew the kitchen curtains aside and a small vase of flowers nearly toppled.

She posted the letter right after breakfast and walked Meghan to playschool before heading to the hospital. The air raid sirens had been strangely silent for two days now and Doreen thought everyone seemed a little less tense. In previous days, the Germans had begun in earnest to attempt takeover of the British Isles and the presence of the Luftwaffe had been nearly constant. Doreen and other staffers at the hospital had formed their own war strategy over quick cups of tea and coffee. Everyone sensed that if the Germans could strike enough blows by air, the channel crossing would be accomplished and the enemy would be on their soil. Without that supremacy, the Air Ministry and Navy could prohibit any invasion and would surely annihilate any Nazi landing forces. It seemed to hinge upon the Germans' ability to strike by air.

Doreen had been struggling with the idea of evacuating Meghan as Croydon was an industrial stronghold. She couldn't bring herself to think of that reality until now. Yet neither could she reconcile the idea of putting her daughter in harm's way. Perhaps Mother Mary Catherine would have some ideas. Doreen just needed some reinforcing comments on the decision she'd already made.

A few days later, the postman rapped on the door of the Bennett flat, startling Doreen. She jumped up to answer, knocking her sewing to the floor.

"I'm sorry to disturb you, Mrs. Bennett, but I have a letter posted from Hempstead with the return address of the Convent. You said you were looking for a reply from the Sisters. I believe this is it."

"Yes, thank you so much! I appreciate you handing it to me personally. I'm grateful."

"G' day, Mrs. Bennett. I hope that letter holds a bit o' good news for you and your wee one."

Doreen watched him walk away then sat on the front stoop and tore open the envelope.

July 6, 1940

Dear Doreen,

I was glad to receive your letter, though saddened by the contents. I know you must be very worried about Colin and the safety of your daughter as this horrible war drags on. I'm happy that you are involving yourself in some community war efforts as you are not only competent but compassionate as well. Your nursing skills can be used in so many varied ways. I must admit that we feel a bit isolated here in the convent, but many of our sisters are still involved with hospital work at Hempstead Infirmary. More importantly, we have also begun to assist in the transfer of children from London to the countryside, or at least to villages further away from the center of London. In fact, we could certainly use your help in this effort if you've the time and energy. I know you've been very busy, but please let me know if you can help in the evacuation of children. We can also make some arrangements for your own daughter, if that's what it's come to.

I have a younger sister, Margaret, who lives in Kidlington, Oxford with her husband Ian O'Connor. They are lovely people. Ian owns a small sundries shop in town and the two of them take in boarders from the University of Oxford. Their cottage, in the village of Kidlington, is a fair size and Margaret is very house-proud. I know of other children who have gone to Oxford and your daughter would not be without others in her situation. Oxford has no industrial facilities so it should be quite safe and not become a target of German bombs. Some folks accept a small allowance from the government for the care of the children but I know that Ian and Margaret would take Meghan, allowance or not. I have already taken the liberty of sending them a quick note to check on available room in their cottage, as I'm not sure who's boarding with them now. I hope you don't mind my moving ahead with this. You can always change your mind, but I don't see the conditions in London or your area getting any better in the near future. Write back soon or ring me if you get the chance.

With love and affection,
Mother Superior Mary Catherine

For the first time in several weeks, Doreen felt renewed and confident. She had taken a positive step to protect her daughter and it looked as though the arrangements might work out. In addition, she was given the opportunity to help in the war effort in a very special way. With her training in nursing and her experience as a parent, she could offer valuable help in relocating children from London to safer places. At the same time, she could keep an eye on her own daughter, visiting her in Oxford while transporting other children to that area and surrounding farms. It felt like the right thing to do. Even though it would tear her apart to leave her daughter for even a few days, she knew it was right. Someday her daughter would be proud of the sacrifice they *both* made to "fight" in the only way they could. She had complete confidence in Mary Catherine's suggestion. It was the best decision for Meghan.

"Mother Mary Catherine, this is Doreen. I can only talk for a few minutes because the phone lines are continually disrupted. I received your letter and I'm so grateful for the information on the O'Connor's. If they still have room, Meghan and I will be on the train to Oxford the day after tomorrow. I need to inform the staff at Croydon Hospital."

"That's fine, dear. I have not heard from them yet, but I'm sure they will make room for Meghan. Have you thought about my request?"

"Yes, I've considered it and I believe it is the right thing for me to do at this time. I've been involved in several different war efforts, but I wasn't really passionate about any of them. Perhaps because of Colin. But your idea is exciting and I'd love to be a part of evacuating children. In fact, I plan to bring two other children from Meghan's playschool with us on the train. Is that going to be alright?"

"Yes, Doreen, that will fine. I will meet you at the station in Oxford so I can see you, and also so I can help with the placement of the two little ones. I can have a short visit with Ian and Margaret while I'm there. It'll be good to see all of you."

"Yes, Sister, it will be wonderful to see you. I must hang up now, and thank you so much!"

Their goodbyes were cut short as an agitated operator interrupted the phone line. Doreen strode out through the back door to take down the wash, as though everything were perfectly normal. Yet in two days, she would be leaving her only child with strangers and returning to London to help evacuate other strangers' children. It was a curious and unsettling turn of events. She stopped over at her neighbor's and asked the young mother to keep Meghan for a couple of hours. Then she changed clothes, took some coins from the sugar bowl, and headed to the bus stop. She would visit Captain Hollingsworth again before leaving for Oxford. She still hadn't heard anything, but it couldn't hurt to ask once more.

She was met at his office by a young lieutenant who was bent on being as terse and vague as possible. No, she couldn't speak to the Captain, but the lieutenant would answer her question if she were brief; he had other pressing matters to attend to. After a short explanation, she was assured that no more news had come through regarding the status of her husband. His shiny shoes pounded down the hallway as Doreen stood watching him walk away. No more news. She put her gloves back on and adjusted her hat, vowing not to inquire again soon. She would get on with the task in front of her. It was the only sensible thing to do. *It was the only thing that would keep her sane.*

The steady stream of questions from Meghan was beginning to get on Doreen's nerves, but she knew that packing up suitcases and leaving home was difficult for a four year old. As the grandfather clock ticked on, it became evident that they couldn't delay their departure any longer without missing their train to Oxford.

"Meghan, love, we positively must go now. Gather up Max and we'll just make it to the station on time."

Meghan winced and tears welled up in her eyes, but she clutched her bunny and they walked out of their home.

"When are we coming back here, Mummy?"

"I don't know love, I really don't know."

The station was a sea of service colors, khaki, navy and bright blue, swelling in waves of kitbags and cases. Doreen searched for the Oxford platform and dragged both Meghan and their luggage on a rickety trolley that sounded as though it should have been given to the last scrap metal drive. People scrambled in front of them and queues seemed obsolete. Meghan whined in the noise and confusion and Doreen's head began to throb. Perhaps this had been a mistake. Maybe they should have taken their chances and just stayed in Croydon. Older men in tattered clothes carried bundles tied with cords. They were most likely on their way to ammunition factories or mines and uniformed railway staff herded them on with urgency. There were a lot of families waiting to board and just as many waiting to send off their loved ones with hugs and shouts of "goodbyes" mingled with last minute bits of advice. Doreen pushed her trolley forward until they were near the train steps, then unloaded their cases, firmly grabbing her little one's hand. Meghan's whine had grown to an annoying whimper as the train lurched into place amidst clouds of smoke and steam. Doreen wished she had some headache powders in her handbag, but perhaps a cup of tea would do. She glanced over at the canteen trolley where mugs of tea and biscuits were sold at prices she couldn't afford. She'd just have to wait. Once they got settled on the train, things would get better. A lump rose in her throat and she willed it away. This was not the time to let doubt and weakness get the better of her! When a young woman stepped in front of her to board, Doreen spoke up more loudly than she'd intended and claimed her place. It seemed a silly thing to do, but she didn't regret her actions and the young woman moved back, uttering something that wasn't appropriate for Meghan's ears. Her daughter, however, was caught up in her own misery and was clinging to Doreen's skirt as her whimpers became sobs.

Once on the train, Doreen found two seats at the front of the coach and hoisted their cases on the racks above. Their car was near to the engine and the loud hissing of steam seemed to quiet and comfort Meghan. She held Max to her face, sniffing his tattered fur, giving her the scent of home in this alien place. The engineer blew one long whistle and the train left, the acrid smell of the railway accompanying its departure. It wasn't long before an aged man and two small boys came down the aisle, chattering about seeing the boiler room. Meghan perked up.

"Can I go, too, Mummy? I want to see the engine."

The older man paused beside them and offered to take Meghan with him and his grandsons to see the boiler. She knew she was taking a chance, sending her daughter with a perfect stranger. Still, they had to come back through the car so she relented and sent her daughter on a small adventure.

Conversations were flowing around her and she laid her head back, looking down at Max crumpled in Meghan's empty seat. She picked up the bunny and put it to her chest, then closed her eyes. Sleep was out of the question, but a moment to rest and catch her breath would certainly help her headache. Meghan returned a few minutes later, chattering excitedly.

"Mummy, there was fire in that place! The man was putting black coals on the fire and then they turned red! It was *very* hot in there, Mummy, just like that old lady's house where you took the pie that day!"

Doreen lowered her head and laughed. That was so like Meghan. That little imp could remember the strangest things at the most awkward times. The folks seated near them chuckled softly as though they were in need of a reason to smile.

"I'm glad you got to see it, Meghan. And you're right. That lady's house was very warm, indeed, but probably not as hot as the boiler room!"

At this, Meghan laughed out loud and climbed back into her seat as they thanked the man and his grandchildren for the small excursion. The rest of the ride was mostly uneventful, for which Doreen was grateful. The pounding in her head was subsiding as Meghan stretched across her lap and fell asleep, unaware of both the cheerful sounds and soft crying that surrounded them.

The train ride from London to Oxford was normally just over ninety minutes, but it was delayed along the way as transport personnel walked through, examined passengers, and scrutinized the actual rails. Doreen realized that getting anywhere around southern England wasn't easy anymore. Transporting children would be even more difficult with nervous, tearful young ones, leaving their parents and their homes!

Mother Mary Catherine was at the Oxford station along with her sister, Margaret, as the evening sun began coloring the sky. The two women looked physically very much alike, even with several years' difference in their age. Margaret however, had a softer, more grandmotherly look and she knelt down with her arms open wide as Meghan descended the train steps. It was an uncharacteristic gesture in England, yet Doreen knew that the O'Connor's were from Ireland where open affection was common. She smiled at the scene and mused that Anna Bailey must be looking down proudly. Meghan hesitated only a moment, then ran into Margaret's arms as though she had known her well. It was a touching moment and Doreen felt just a small pang of envy. This kind and sensitive woman would be putting her daughter to bed at night and stirring her porridge in the morning. As happy as Doreen was with the situation for her child, she couldn't help already feeling alienated.

"Doreen, you look wonderful. How lovely to see you again!"

"It's wonderful to see you as well, Mary Catherine. I've missed you!"

The two friends exchanged a polite hug.

"I gather you've surmised that this is my sister, Margaret. It seems your little one has already taken to her!"

Margaret stood to face Doreen.

"Hallo my dear. I'm so pleased to meet you. I apologize for Ian's absence, but he couldn't get away from our shop in Oxford. We try to stay open as long as possible, not only for the convenience of our townspeople, but also because the extra shillings help out!"

At this, Margaret threw her head back and laughed heartily. Doreen realized that these folks had no pretense. They were genuine and humorous. What luck for Meghan as she needed some real laughter in her life.

"So, where are the other wee ones you were bringing with you?"

"Their mum changed her mind. I think she's waiting until she hears from a relative up in Yorkshire to see if they can take in the children."

"Oh, that would be better, I suppose, though they best not wait too long. Now then, we just need to board a bus for the short trip to the village – won't take long at all."

Kidlington was very small and there was only just a post office with a few grocery supplies and a tiny news agent that sold only two newspapers and boasted a supply of birthday cards. There were several attached one story homes lining the main street and at least two bus stops that Doreen noticed as they made their way across the barely noticeable village green. Though small, the village was welcoming with lots of flowering bushes and mature trees, a sure sign that it had been settled for a long time.

There was lots of chatter as they made their way to the homey stone cottage belonging to the O'Connor's. It was obvious that their Oxford shop had been good to them, as their roomy cottage stood in stark contrast to the smaller homes nearby. Doreen mused that perhaps they had inherited the house from family, when Margaret announced it was a perfect time for a spot of tea in the back garden. Meghan was skipping up the front walk as though she had never heard all the somber information her mother had so diligently given her before their departure. Her youth had spared her the seriousness of this situation. Doreen knew it would dawn on Meghan when "goodbyes" were said and her train back to London departed in a couple weeks' time. Until then, it was best to let the little one skip and dance.

Ian arrived home at his usual time of 6:00 p.m. and announced his arrival with a loud "halloo". Margaret had started cooking dinner and wiped her hands on her apron as she greeted him in the hall.

"Oh, love, you are right on schedule and I'm so pleased as our guests have arrived. They're out in the garden just now. I insisted that Mrs. Bennett stay here for a fortnight or more to get her daughter settled in and just to relax and regroup, as it were, for her evacuation work."

"Excellent, my dear. Ummm...I smell something quite appealing coming from our kitchen. What are you up to?"

"Never you mind. This is a special occasion, what with my sister Mary Catherine and the Bennett's here. I thought we could spare a piece of pork; it's a good excuse to indulge ourselves."

"Where is Mr. Henderson this evening? I thought he would be here by now."

Margaret's eyes lit up at the mention of their boarder's name.

"He should be here quite soon, I think. I do hope his presence will not upset Mrs. Bennett. She seems a bit overwhelmed as it is."

"You did have Mary Catherine tell her about him living here, didn't you?"

"Of course I mentioned we had a male boarder. Mary Catherine said Doreen was perfectly fine with the idea, and even thought it might do Meghan good, you know, with her father missing and all. Poor child, so many changes in her little life. We'll just have to make an extra effort in assuring her comfort. Now go on out back and greet everyone."

Dinner was nearly on the table when their boarder, Mr. Henderson, walked through the front door, tossing his cardigan on the coat stand.

"Looks like I'm just in time! It's a good thing I didn't stay at the library any longer, I'd have missed the feast that's right before my eyes. What's the occasion?"

"Hallo dear. Glad you're here on time. Our guests have arrived from Croydon and Hempstead. I told you just yesterday that they would be arriving today."

"That's right," he said, giving Margaret a little squeeze.

"I guess, darling woman, my mind is somewhere else these days. Here, let me help you with that."

Doreen, Meghan, and Mary Catherine had taken a few moments to wash up before dinner and now stepped into the kitchen just as the large serving bowls were set on the table. Doreen's eyes scanned the warm, country kitchen, resting upon the cracks and chips in the dishes, embarrassed at her inability to say anything. The strange man helping Margaret finally turned and broke the silence.

"Why Mother Mary Catherine, how wonderful to see you again. You haven't been here in a while. How is everything out your way?"

"We are all fine, thank you, she said, putting her arms around Doreen and Meghan.

"Neil, I'd like you to meet a special pair. This is Doreen Bennett and her lovely daughter, Meghan."

Doreen tried to smile, extending her hand in greeting.

"Pleased to meet you, Mr. Henderson. The O'Connor's and Mary Catherine have told me about you, but not about your business here in Oxford."

Doreen knew her greeting was stilted, if not rude. She felt herself blush, the same way she had years ago as a nun upon meeting Colin for the first time in the Hempstead Infirmary. It must be a curse she would always live with. Yet the man in front of her didn't seem at all ruffled.

"Oh, so they told you I'm a Yank come over here to partake of real tea and honest scones! I'm also enjoying this beautiful countryside, but my official reason is to work on a doctoral degree in political science from Oxford. They say it will look quite nice on a resume in the States someday. And by the way, please call me Neil. 'Mr. Henderson' sounds like you're carrying on a conversation with my late father."

With this the tall, dark-haired man grinned from ear to ear like a schoolboy and stretched his long arms up over his head. Doreen thought for a moment how casual and unassuming this American was and wondered if they were all like that. She had seen American servicemen in London but never close enough to hear their conversations. Perhaps he was the exception rather than the rule. Or perhaps not. She found herself taken back by the accent and his lighthearted reference to his late father.

Margaret broke her reverie.

"Neil Henderson, don't speak so of the departed. And in front of the Mother Superior, no less. Shame on ya'!"

Margaret shook her finger at him as she spoke, a stern yet unconvincing look of disappointment.

"Yep, there I go again. Not even at the dinner table and I've once again incurred the wrath of this wonderful woman. What would I do without you, my lovely lady?"

Neil wrapped his arms about her, nearly scooping her short frame off the floor. Ian motioned the rest of them into chairs as he spoke.

"Can we get on with this meal, you two? Our guests will have second thoughts about staying here with your shenanigans."

Mary Catherine began to quietly giggle, something Doreen rarely heard. It made the Mother Superior's eyes and face light up in a way that was attractive and she looked more like her sister Margaret at that moment. Meghan had been watching the exchanges in silence, also a rare occurrence. The little one settled into her chair and ate as though she had missed several meals. Again, Doreen felt a small pang of envy as Meghan's appetite at home had been poor lately. Perhaps the change of scenery was truly good for the child. It was apparent from the first bite that no matter what the meal, her daughter would be well fed and surrounded by a loving and uplifting atmosphere. That would make the leaving a bit easier, at least initially.

The evening went by quickly with lots of storytelling on Mary Catherine and Margaret's part, and much chatter about routines and rules and favorite things passing back and forth between Doreen and the O'Connor's. It was lively and just what Doreen needed to lift her spirits and take her mind off her already impending loneliness. Her husband was still missing in action and now her daughter would be separated from her, too. She knew instinctively though, that this was the only way for her to keep her sanity and assure her daughter's safety. She had to feel useful and do something towards the war effort, else she thought she could not face another day. It was the only way for her to survive the nightmare of this war. Perhaps evacuating children would help the days go by speedily and news of Colin would be just around the corner. Doreen knew that Meghan would someday understand her absence and possibly even be proud of her mum. She had to take that chance.

The American sat back in a stuffed paisley-print chair, listening to the animated conversation and smiling broadly. It seemed like he was watching a good old movie, one that he hesitated to leave before it was finished. Finally, Ian got a word in and it was directed towards their boarder.

"Neil, tell us again where you are from in the States. I know you've told us before, but the names of places over there just don't seem to stick in my brain. Must be my age."

"Oh no, Ian, it isn't your age at all. I have a hard time remembering places over here. I do well to get on the right bus for Kidlington. Took me a week to recall the name of this place!"

Doreen was surprised at the quickness of the American's response, and his attempt to bolster an older man's confidence. It seemed such a small yet thoughtful thing to do, and she was drawn to really study his face for the first time that evening. He was really quite handsome. His hair was dark brown, very unlike her own Colin's lovely sandy hair. His eyes, in contrast, were a bright blue, rather like an Autumn sky. She thought of Colin's deep brown eyes and wondered just briefly what his eyes were seeing on this night. It was a thought too painful to consider further. This American had skin darker than her own, as though he had been raised upon a farm and spent his youth bailing hay. It seemed a curious image as she remembered his educational pursuits at Oxford. His tanned skin and easygoing manner seemed incongruous with his studious alter personality. He must be a person of many interests and facets. Once again, she saw Colin's face and the single determination that her husband had to be a doctor. She would always know what his passion was, for she had never known him to be anything but a doctor through and through. It was what she loved about him and his passion had never taken any affection or devotion away from her and Meghan. Her thoughts faded and she stared blankly at the man across from her as he spoke in his easy voice.

"I hail from Rockport, Massachusetts, on the east coast. It's near to Boston, which is why I mentioned I came here for the tea. You know that we dumped all the decent tea in the harbor all those years ago and we haven't been able to get a good cup there since."

He chuckled at his own comment and soon the room was alive with silly banter. Doreen smiled in spite of herself, though something was nagging her about this man. The United States had yet to recognize the importance of their involvement in this war. They had continually skirted around sending troops or supplies to aid England in their struggle against the Germans, Russians, and now Italians and here he was just studying and enjoying their countryside! The anger welled up in her as their voices chattered on, a surreal scene passing in front of her eyes. She wouldn't offend the O'Connor's by confronting their boarder right there, but she would find him later and speak her mind!

It wasn't long after Mr. Henderson's tea comments that the party began winding down. Meghan had fallen asleep in her mum's lap and Margaret got up and headed to the kitchen to put the kettle on. Ian carried Meghan up to a spare room and laid her gently on the bed, then turned to Doreen.

"Why don't you just get her into her jammies and lay her down? There will be enough hot water for everyone to bathe in the morning. The wee one is exhausted."

"Thank you, Ian. I shall do that. I'd like to take a short walk about your garden, if you don't mind. I know it's getting dark, yet there's enough summer light to see my way around."

"Of course, my dear, make yourself at home and grab a cuppa on the way out. I believe the rest of us are retiring for the night, except for perhaps Mr. Henderson. Neil prefers to do a bit of reading downstairs before his bedtime."

"Thank you, Ian, and thanks to both of you so very much for your kind hospitality and especially for agreeing to keep Meghan."

"Think nothing of it my dear. We're doing what we are able to in this difficult time. Everyone has a part."

Ian left the spare bedroom and Doreen looked around for their suitcases. The room was done in pale colors, which lightened it some in the darkness of the shuttered windows. There was a brightly colored vase with wildflowers in it sitting on the chest of drawers and an antique framed mirror on one wall. There was one small wooden chair, straight-backed with no arms. It looked it bit harsh and stern in the house of such a lively and warm-hearted couple. Doreen ruffled through the case and dressed her sleeping child in jammies, then headed downstairs for a cup of tea, a walk about the garden, and a quiet confrontation with Mr. Henderson.

She found Neil sitting in the paisley chair, a stack of books and a teacup on the table beside him. Her resolve began to fade as she grew closer. He seemed to emit an aura of genuine affection for his surroundings and she wondered if perhaps she had misjudged him somehow. He looked up from his reading a bit startled.

"I didn't hear you come down, Mrs. Bennett. May I call you Doreen?"

He took her off guard by his request and she paused a moment before speaking.

"Yes, yes of course. I'm afraid we British are a bit formal with names, even in the 20ᵗʰ century. We seem to wait years before using first names so I may forget and use your surname."

Neil paused, trying to read her expression.

"Of course. Only, I probably will correct you anyway, and you'll be calling me Neil in no time. I overheard you earlier telling Margaret that you've agreed to stay here three weeks or so, to get your daughter settled in. Margaret also told me that you're a nurse. I'm sure your services are of great value just now."

"Yes, well, I'm not sure exactly how valuable I am, but I do my best. Mr. Henderson, ah Neil, I'm afraid I had an ulterior motive in coming down for a cup of tea. It had to do with you. That is, I wanted to talk to you before I turn in. Perhaps we should take our tea out to the back garden and walk around a bit."

She turned around and started for the back door.

"I see. I hope there's nothing I've done to offend you this evening. I've been living here for some time now and the O'Connor's and I are familiar enough to get quite carried away."

The sincerity of his voice made her turn around to face him. She noticed how strong his arms appeared as he gathered up the stack of books and placed them under the window next to Margaret's sewing bag. He looked quite muscular for a doctoral student and his skin was tan for someone who spent time inside studying. His wavy hair, neatly combed earlier, now fell across his forehead.

They walked in silence around the garden for the first minute or two, until Doreen gained the courage to speak her mind. She said a silent, quick prayer to the God she had been ignoring and stopped walking. It was dark, but she could make out the outline of his face in the lingering shadows. Her voice sounded like someone else's, a bit too high-pitched and nervous.

"As I started to say, this is a bit awkward for me. Yet I don't think I can sleep tonight if I don't express my thoughts. I hope you'll understand where I'm coming from and won't think me rude. This isn't meant as a personal attack, but rather just to tell you how I feel."

Doreen stopped talking, her eyes focused on his. He was so tall, so close to her and so relaxed. His hands lapped each other, resting in front of him. He didn't move a muscle, didn't try to distance himself in any way.

"I see. And just what are these thoughts that will prevent you from sleeping? I don't mean any disrespect, but I hardly know you well enough for you to have put a barrier between us."

He stared directly into her blue eyes that were so much like his own when on fire with anxiety. It took a few moments for Doreen to respond. The fragrance of the night blew in a cooling breeze across the garden.

"I …I must first apologize if I sound angry or accusatory. I don't really mean to be offensive. It's just that I am so frustrated by recent events."

Doreen glanced up at him before going on, trying to gauge his reaction in the dim and waning light of summer. There was none. He stood as still as before, his hands still resting in front of him.

"You see, my husband has been missing in action since the Dunkirk invasion in early June, and I have no idea where he is or if he is even safe. For all I know, he could this very night be suffering in a German POW camp, or worse. It's been a terrible ordeal for me - and for Meghan. When I met you tonight, I suddenly felt angry, defensive, because here you are, an American enjoying your time as a doctoral student, enamored with our lovely country, while thousands of *our* men are dying and being captured, tortured, oh, God, who knows what else?"

Her voice rose in the thick night air.

"How can you stay here, knowing what is going on and not be involved? How can your country be so blind?!"

She was now moving about the garden agitated, her hands flapping.

Suddenly, he reached for them, pulling them in like a butterfly caught in a net.

"I am sorry, Doreen," he said calmly.

"I know about your husband. Margaret and Ian told me yesterday."

Realizing her discomfort, he stepped back, released her hands and went on.

"Yes, you are right. America has done so little to help in this war, yet I'm certain that soon we will be drawn into this mess whether we like it or not. It's only a matter of time. I know it isn't much, but it's a start at explaining where I'm at."

A dog began barking somewhere in the distance, interrupting the silence. Doreen stepped closer to him, wanting to speak, but he continued.

"About my involvement in this war, I do have something to tell you. The papers I brought home with me tonight were not for my doctoral studies. They were lists of children in and around the London area who need evacuation. This war is only going to get worse before it gets better, and I am trying to put together a comprehensive list of those children that we could take here in the area. I have been searching out homes for them in Oxford and in smaller villages such as Kidlington. My studies are definitely on hold for the time being. I'll finish them someday, but for now I have other more pressing duties to attend to. Please don't let the laughter and my nonchalance taint your image of me. I am very serious when it comes to my cause and, I think, dedicated. I *am* trying to help."

Doreen was speechless. She felt small and foolish and couldn't find her voice but Neil continued.

"I know that my work may seem a small price and sacrifice in comparison to what you're up against. I'm sure I would be equally angry and frustrated if I were in your shoes. But at least I feel I'm doing *something* for the cause."

The dog started barking again, filling in the moment of silence.

"You see, it wouldn't make a difference in my military status if America was in the war or not. I had a very bad case of German measles when I was a child; isn't that ironic? It left me with a serious heart murmur and substantial hearing loss in one ear. I wouldn't be eligible for the draft and I wouldn't be considered for duty even under wartime situations. I take medicine every day for my heart and I live with the hearing loss, and any *other* damage doesn't seem to be of great consequence. Of course, it's nothing like the pain and grief that you live with each day. I can only say that I admire your courage. What I do, it's not enough. It's just the only thing I feel equipped to do at this point."

Doreen felt like a child, one deserving a slap on the wrist for her misjudgment. It was convicting, yet comforting at the same time. She had jumped to conclusions about this man and yet he had been careful to spare her feelings and even empathize with her. There was a reasonable explanation for his presence in this place, maybe even a holy purpose. Finally her words came in a voice of concern and sincerity.

"Oh, Neil, I'm sorry. I don't know what to say. I was so angry with you for your cavalier attitude and yet you're doing the very thing I believe in most, helping the children. Can you ever forgive me?"

"No need, Doreen. Just help your daughter settle in here. I hope you realize she's safe with us. Then return to Croydon and help in any way you can. We're in great need of trained personnel to move these children to safer areas. Margaret and Ian told me that you're to be involved in that process. I am curious, though, just how did that happen?"

"It started with Mother Mary Catherine and the Convent's role in transporting children. I suppose you know as well that I was once a nun in Wycombe Convent."

The surprised look on his face told her differently. It was quickly replaced by a bemused smile.

"Why Mrs. Bennett, you are an interesting lady. I can't wait to hear the rest of the story!"

Doreen shifted uneasily.

"I thought someone would have told you. There were never any hard feelings between the sisters and myself. In fact, I consider Mary Catherine one of my dearest friends, along with a lovely lady at Hempstead Royal Infirmary, Mrs. Markham. She's a wonderful woman, a true inspiration and someone I hope you can meet one day. I know she would be proud of the work you're doing and would help you in any way she could. I am really blessed with some wonderful friends, although you wouldn't know that by the way I've acted tonight."

The nighttime breeze picked up slightly, twirling Doreen's reddish hair across her face. She brushed it back awkwardly.

"I am really tired, Neil. I would love to find out more about the evacuations, but it will have to wait till tomorrow. I need some sleep and I think I won't have any trouble now."

"That's fine. Whenever it works out for you. I will be leaving early in the morning for Oxford to check on another wave of kids. I'll see you at tea time, if you'll be around."

"I'm sure we will be here for dinner; there's no where else to go."

With that, both Neil and Doreen laughed and headed toward the house. Somewhere in the darkness the distant sound of planes pierced the silence of a sky that had once held only stars.

Chapter Seventeen

Mid July, 1940

The next few days were a blur of activities for the O'Connor's and their houseguests. A neighbor held impromptu playgroup for the increasing number of children that arrived in Kidlington. Even as small as the village itself was, the generosity of its people was large indeed.

Meghan made friends easily with her new playmates and spent time helping Margaret in her garden. At Neil's invitation, Doreen traveled to Oxford the second week of her visit to learn the evacuation procedures for children. Aside from the noise of extra children in the parks, Oxford seemed much the same as before the war. Its lack of industry shielded it from being a German target and life was certainly closer to normal than in London. The University helped to lend an atmosphere of studious calm that belied the noise and confusion of survival in London.

Doreen stepped out of the bus and walked the few blocks to Neil's tiny corner office in the basement of Queen's College, one of several colleges within the University. He was standing by the half window, staring out at the ground level when she arrived.

"Come in, Doreen. I'm afraid I'm not being very productive at the moment. We just got a disturbing wire from London, about the increase of air attacks. Probably going to hinder our next evacuation."

She was still standing by his desk.

"Oh, sorry. My manners are a bit rusty, please sit down."

"Thanks, Neil. The bus was warm and stuffy. At least it's cool down here."

Doreen glanced around the small room, noticing the lack of any domestic touches. No pictures on the wall. No vase of flowers. The single bookcase was overloaded with papers and dusty volumes and Doreen felt suddenly like an intruder into this American's life.

"So tell me, Neil, what does your family back in Massachusetts think of your work here? I'm sure they must be proud of you."

Neil hesitated before answering, weighing his words carefully.

"Well Doreen, frankly they don't know exactly what I'm doing just now. They still think I'm working on my doctoral studies. I wasn't sure I wanted to say too much. Besides, it's getting more complicated. Each day I hear reports of more aggressive, hostile action in neutral areas of evacuation like Canada or the U.S."

"What do you mean, Canada or the U.S.?"

"Well, I've discovered that there are transport ships taking children across the Atlantic to homes that will take them in until things quiet down over here. President Roosevelt agreed to help, with the stipulation that they be shipped back as soon as the war ends. I guess you can say we are sort of involved now. In fact, I'm ready to take a group to Liverpool whenever need be. My contacts are in place, and I know the route."

"Is it getting serious, Neil?"

"I'm afraid so. Although as long as the Germans stay away from the outskirts, we'll be able to manage here. Let's not put the cart before the horse."

"What?"

"Never mind."

Neil grinned broadly and strode over to a large thermos on a cluttered, wooden caddy.

"Care for some coffee? I'm afraid I only drink tea at the O'Connor's. I've never had the heart to tell them I prefer coffee. I get this brew from the main office upstairs."

Without waiting for an answer, Neil poured coffee into two worn and faded cups. Doreen watched him, touched by the gesture.

"So Doreen, how have you managed to keep a sense of humor and your head above water with all the unexpected changes in your life?"

"I've had lots of help, actually. Thanks for the coffee. I told you the first night about Mother Superior and Mrs. Markham and their friendship."

Doreen paused a moment, not sure if she wanted to divulge anymore. Still, he seemed so open and genuine, as though she had known him much longer than two weeks.

"Well, I'll tell you Neil, but you mustn't consider me daft."

"I promise."

"I've kept a journal since I was twelve. During my growing up years it was basically a girlish diary. Yet I kept writing as I got older and entered the Convent at eighteen, and it's been a ritual ever since. It's helped me through my anxieties, fears, and frustrations. That sort of thing. Lately it's been filled with short stories on Meghan and the strange or delightful things she does."

Doreen sighed heavily and set her cup on the desk.

"And of course, my fears about my husband, Colin, and this dreadful war news."

Neil walked over to her, dragging the other chair, his tall frame flopping into it with a casual air.

"Do you want to talk about it, Doreen? Talk about Colin?"

"Oh, I don't know, Neil, there's not much left to say. I fell in love with him, the doctor that helped me through my mother's illness and death, the man who caused me to realize I wasn't cut out to be a woman of the cloth. We love each other. We're a family, and then all this happened..."

They reflected in silence. Doreen was ready to change the subject.

"Tell me about your family, Neil. I know your father is deceased, at least from the conversation we had the first night I was here, but what about your mother? She must be missing you so."

"She's deceased as well. They both died in a car crash about ten years ago. I just have one brother and an elderly aunt. Troy and Aunt Ida live in our folks' old house on the outskirts of Rockport."

He got out of his chair and walked over to pour himself another cup of coffee.

"Troy seems happy living there and watching over Auntie. He lives rent-free and comes and goes as he pleases. He has an office job and doesn't work a lot of extra hours so that leaves time for him to 'play.' Aunt Ida's pretty self-sufficient – she's really a grand old gal. I just wrote a long letter to my brother, asking him some questions and telling him my studies are slowing down for time being."

"I'm sorry you no longer have your parents, Neil. I know how that is. I never knew my father and I lost my mum back in 1930. It was a hard time for me. I've no brothers or sisters."

"She must have been a special lady, raising you by herself, and managing to do such a great job."

He paused, reaching for her cup.

"More coffee?"

"No thanks," she said, glancing at her watch.

"I guess we better get down to business. I shouldn't stay too long."

"Right."

He walked over to his messy desk and pulled out a file.

"I have here a stack of papers outlining the evacuation procedures, both the government's 'rules' and my personal setup on it all. I thought we could go over it here in my office, or walk over to the Campus Gardens if you'd rather. It's nice out today, not so hot."

"I think going to the gardens would be fine. Let me help you carry some of these things."

They divided up the stacks of notes and forms and headed out into the warmth of the summer day. A few gray and white clouds drifted above them, making patterns on the old brick and stone walkways. Men dressed in sport coats and carrying leather briefcases scurried along, as if late for something important. Older people were gathered at street corners for a morning chat, the men in their hats and carrying umbrellas despite the warm sun; the women in sturdy shoes with shopping bags on their arms. There were mock orange bushes in bloom, their prickly branches leaning over pavements and their pungent smell riding through the air along with the murmur of conversations and town din. Neil and Doreen sat on a bench in the main gardens and began going through the papers.

"Tell me, Neil, when this war is over and your studies resume, what do you plan to do with all your education? It seems you'll have several options to consider."

"Well I don't know much about my options, but my passion has always been the law and eventually politics. It's become even more important to me lately, as I see the mess this world is in now. I'm not vain enough to think I could make a huge difference, but I'd like to think I could help better at least a few lives along the way. And it doesn't hurt that being a lawyer puts more than just a few potatoes on the table."

At this Neil showed his boyish grin again and Doreen had to smile. It was refreshing to see someone so unafraid to hide behind airs. She wondered if all Americans were like him, willing to show you who they really were. It wasn't that she felt dishonest or introverted when sharing with others; it was that he seemed extreme about it, in a nice way.

"I'm sure you'll be able to someday finish your studies and make your plans come true. You certainly have the energy and drive for it, from what I can see with your evacuation work. I respect you for your dedication to our children, especially when you're a continent away from your own home. I don't know if I could do that."

"Don't ever sell yourself short, Doreen. I believe you could do just about anything. You've already proven that by your courage and stamina in your present circumstances. You never really know what you can do until you have to do it."

"I suppose you're right, but there are moments when I don't want to know how much I can handle."

Neil smiled, nodding silently.

The rest of the day was spent sharing information and shuffling through the stack of papers that frequently blew off the bench in the quickening summer breeze.

There were a lot more "learning" sessions in the next three weeks for all those involved in the evacuation process. Mother Mary Catherine had left for the Convent after one week and had been communicating with Neil and Doreen to stay abreast of the process. Her efforts, and those of the sisters, were growing with each passing day. Neil knew that her position commanded respect and privacy and would go a long way in helping move children quickly. There would be little interference from those in authority. Doreen's connection with the Convent would certainly also help her to get papers processed faster and with fewer questions from overzealous seekers. The O'Connor's spent a great deal of time with Meghan who seemed to be flourishing in the quiet and calm of Kidlington. They took her into Oxford on more than one occasion, showing her their shop and amusing fellow shopkeepers with Meghan's innocent and humorous antics.

Doreen felt encouraged by the scenes unfolding before her and her respect and admiration for the American grew. Having him around actually made her miss Colin more, and yet it was a strange peace and comfort at the same time. Neil's presence was a constant reminder of the man that was out of her reach, the man she had vowed to love forever. It was a strange mix of reality and the fantasy of what should be. A blurring of what she so desperately wanted and what she was faced with now.

Five weeks after their guests had arrived, Margaret walked through the front door with Meghan and began sorting through the mail. Doreen had received a few letters over time, some of them opened by censors. Two were from Mary Catherine and others written by friends in Croydon and Hempstead. She paused as she now took the last letter from the stack. It was from London and had an unfamiliar name on the return address. She swallowed hard and stared.

From: Sub-Lieutenant Graham Lawrence, Royal Navy

Margaret started dinner with a feverish pace, and got Meghan in and out of the bath in record time. When Doreen arrived, Margaret was getting pajamas on her charge.

Doreen held the letter in the palm of one hand and her words were barely audible.

"My God, maybe this is it. Please, God. Let this be it. They've found him."

She tore open the envelope and scanned its contents. Her heart skipped several beats and tears welled up in her eyes. She suddenly found it difficult to breathe and walked backwards into the kitchen as if in a trance. Margaret gingerly stepped into the kitchen, Meghan in tow. There were no words spoken for several moments. Margaret could stand the silence no longer.

"What is it my dear? Have they found your Colin?"

Doreen blinked several times, then lifted her eyes and stared at Margaret.

"I don't know, Margaret. I only know that this man has some information about Colin. He didn't say what it was. I'm not sure if that's good or bad. If Colin had been found dead,…"

Doreen paused and looked down at her daughter, but Meghan had happily occupied herself with a coloring pad and crayons that the O'Connor's left on the back porch shelf.

"I guess I would have gotten an official telegram or phone call if they knew he was dead. I can only hope that this is good news. That perhaps they know where he is at least. Oh God, I sure hope and pray that's what this is."

"What else does he say?"

"This man, Mr. Lawrence, wants to meet with me in London so we can talk. He says he will tell me everything he knows. Doesn't sound too official, does it?"

"No, dear, it doesn't. But he may have a lead. It's better than you've had thus far. Go, darling. Go soon. Your Meghan will be safe and happy with us. You're ready to go back to resume evacuations, anyway. It's time. We'll have a nice dinner together tonight and you can leave in the morning."

Doreen didn't answer right away. Her mind was reeling with questions and thoughts and hopes she didn't dare to share. Her heart was beating rapidly with an excitement that she hadn't felt for a long time. Margaret was right. It was time to go.

Dinner that night was unusually quiet, as though speaking out loud too much might jinx the outcome of the rendezvous with the sub-lieutenant. Still, there was some laughter, always unavoidable with Meghan at the table. Neil was preoccupied and absorbed with thoughts he wouldn't share. After dinner, he and Doreen stood side by side to wash up the dishes, while Margaret read to Meghan and Ian tuned in the wireless for the war news.

"I know you must be nervous, Doreen. Just remember to take everything a moment at a time. It's really the only way any of us can live these days.

Make sure you're listening with your heart as well as your ears to anything this lieutenant has to say."

Doreen stopped drying dishes and stared at him. It seemed such an odd thing for a man to say and yet this was no ordinary man. He seemed to possess an inner quality of tenderness and compassion that she rarely saw, even in her hospital colleagues. His comment was bewildering.

"I'm not sure exactly what you mean, Neil. Listening with my heart?"

"I only mean that, well, try to gauge what sort of man he is and his motive for meeting with you. I'm sure he's honest and has the best intentions. Just try to read between his lines and decipher their meaning for yourself."

"I will. I want to believe he has good news, but I've been waiting so long that I'm afraid to have any expectations."

The clanging of pots and dishes filled the silence of the room as they finished their task. Doreen wiped her hands on a clean towel and walked out the back door. She had to look through the darkness once more to clear her mind. Neil followed her and stood at a distance. Finally Doreen broke the spell of the moment.

"We were out here the first night I arrived. That seems so long ago. Time is suspended in this place, as though everything were almost unreal. I've learned so much during my stay here that I feel as though I've made some sort of transformation. Does that make any sense?"

"Makes sense to me. I felt transformed in this area as soon as I arrived three years ago. I had turned thirty back home and I thought I knew all the answers. Then I got here and realized the questions had changed and I felt dumber than ever. Everything is so old over here. We don't have that depth of history in the U.S. Makes me feel like we Yanks are all teens and the rest of the world grew up a long time ago. It's sobering. I think Oxford is especially like that. All the centuries of learning and debating and probing into difficult issues. It has a sort of eternal feel about it. Like what's going on around us is so temporal. I feel sheltered, in a way. Maybe that's the appeal."

"Sheltered, yes, maybe that's it."

Doreen paused before going on.

"Neil, I want to ask you something very important. Feel free to say 'no' if you don't want the added responsibility, I'll understand. I know that the O'Connor's are loving, wonderful people who would always take good care of Meghan. It's just that I'm not sure they would, or could, take the very difficult steps to remove Meghan from this place if the war reaches further out from London. I know they would protect her as best they could, but gathering up a young one and physically leaving this place, I don't know. What I'm asking you is this: would you see that Meghan is safe, no matter what?"

"Of course I would."

"If that means getting her out of Oxford and into a safer area, could you manage that? I hate to ask you this, but in London I'll be too far away to get her out in a hurry."

"Doreen, I love Meghan. You know that I would protect her at all costs. I promise you that I will take care of her. You can trust me."

Yes, she could trust this man. She knew that the first night she met him. He was more than honest. She would easily be able to trust her daughter with Neil.

"I appreciate it, Neil. Thank you. Thank you from the bottom of my heart. I'll always be grateful for your presence here."

A few moments of silence passed and Doreen stepped closer to Neil. She could just barely see the brightness of his blue eyes and the way they danced in the deepening shadows. She could hear him breathing, his chest moving with a steady rhythm. She thought of the night before Colin's entry into the navy. She had stayed awake most of the night just listening to him breathe, as if that act alone would form an invisible thread of life giving him air from her own lungs when he felt he was choking. She had gazed at the beads of sweat on his chest, a drying memory of the passion they had shared. A vision of Colin was standing in front of her.

"Doreen, are you alright?"

She stepped back, startled by the confusion of emotions and time and circumstance. The envisage was gone. She took several deep breaths and composed herself.

"I think so. I'm just tired I guess. No, that isn't it. I'm frightened. I don't know who I am anymore, or exactly what I'm doing. Tonight everything just seems too overwhelming."

Those words were the last to be said before the tears started. She had tried not to cry often, but it seemed tears flowed more freely the past few days. It was embarrassing and defeating but she couldn't keep back the flow.

Neil made his way to her side and wrapped his arms lightly around her shoulders. His discreet fashion brought no surprise as she welcomed his embrace. He was trying to be comforting and gentlemanly at the same time. It was a nice gesture, one of many he seemed to show. She let out a big sigh and smiled tentatively at him. He reached into his trousers pocket and handed her a handkerchief.

"Thank you. I just needed a moment to feel sorry for myself, but I'm done with that now. I'm not ready to say 'goodbye' to Meghan or to any of you, but it's time. I'm ready to go forward."

"I'll miss you, Doreen. Our friendship has meant a lot to me. I suppose you'll be back soon with a new wave of children, though."

"Get ready!"

Neil stepped back and grinned.

"I'll be ready. Please take good care of yourself. You're an extraordinary woman, Doreen. The angels are surely watching over you. Besides, you have an inside tract with Mary Catherine."

"I'm not sure my 'inside tract' is good anymore! I left the convent, remember?"

"Oh yes, I remember."

Neil stopped without finishing his thought and stared at her. The night air was thick and still and the dampness was heavier than usual. They walked in silence through the back door, leaving the blackness of the night behind them. Above them a curtain fluttered and the shadow of a woman backed away from the window, the concern on her face invisible in the darkness.

CHAPTER EIGHTEEN

It had been less than a fortnight since Doreen's return to her flat in Croydon and already her nerves were raw and she had developed a rash. She knew it was because she hadn't been able to meet with Lieutenant Lawrence yet, given their hectic schedules, and the delay was literally making her ill. Others, unaware of her impending meeting, had their own diagnosis. Her neighbor told her it was due to lack of sleep and not taking time to eat properly. Her priest at St. Thomas inquired of her health and well being one morning after Mass and even Mrs. Markham had phoned, giving advice in a worried voice.

"My dear, I got your last letter and I've been so concerned. Are you sure you've the strength to keep up this pace?"

"Mrs. Markham, I've only been doing this for five days. Except for the initial group of children I sent from London after returning from Oxford, the evacuations have slowed down a bit. My rash is finally going away, thanks to an ointment from the chemist. Truly, I'm fine. I have to do *something*. There are nurses who filled in some of my schedule while I was away, so I've plenty of time to keep at this. How are you doing?"

"I'm quite well, my dear. Just pulling my hair out with too much to do here at the Infirmary. We're so short staffed. I don't suppose you'd consider…"

Mrs. Markham stopped midsentence.

"Oh, I'm sorry my dear. I'm just thinking of myself. I know how much your work with the children means to you just now."

"That's alright, Mrs. Markham. If I could, I'd be there in a flash to help you out. It's just that….things are a bit complicated right now."

She felt a pang of guilt for not sharing the letter from the lieutenant, but she couldn't bring herself to talk about it.

"Now don't you worry about me. I'll get along just fine."

She paused briefly before continuing.

"Doreen, how are things really going in Croydon? I hear the air attacks are getting worse and more frequent. I worry for your safety."

"The attacks *are* getting stronger and more frightening. I'm so grateful that Meghan isn't here. Croydon is certainly a target, with the aircraft factories here. I'm sure it's only a matter of time. But we've all been well trained in air raid drills. My goal is to get at least five more large groups of children evacuated before another big attack. Pray for us, Mrs. Markham."

"I will, dear. The line is breaking up so I must go for now. Take care of yourself. We all love you."

The line crackled and went dead. Doreen stood at her small telephone table, hung up the receiver, and walked to the kitchen table. She truly was working against a time crunch. It was evident that Hitler wanted no less than a full-scale land invasion of Britain, but his Commander Goering had overrated the Luftwaffe's ability to destroy the English air forces. The Luftwaffe had been no match for the Hurricanes and Spitfires of the RAF. Yet Hitler had wasted no time in making another attack, this time over the Straits of Dover when naval convoys were attacked on July 12. Doreen had listened with growing fear as the attacks intensified. London and its surrounding areas were under siege.

She picked up a pen, saying a silent prayer, and began working on the list of evacuees. They were running out of time and there were still so many children. So many lives to be uprooted, disrupted, perhaps permanently severed.

The postman arrived at Queen's College and put the mail in the main office slot. Neil was chatting with the office clerk, glancing often over his shoulder. As the mail dropped in the basket, he hurriedly gathered it up, sorting it as he strode over to the clerk's desk.

"This letter's for me, Jon. I'll see you later on."

His long legs took him out of the office and through the front doors in one quick stride. He stood by a bench and tore open the envelope postmarked 'Rockport, Mass.'

July, 1940

Dear Neil,
    So how are you doing, big guy? Been a while since I heard from you. Sure glad you're alive and still around to give me hell one of these

days. When ya coming back to take your turn with
Auntie? Actually, she's fine and no trouble at all.
I just gotta ask ya now and then! God, it must
be tough living in a place that's one card short
of a full deck war. How the hell do you stand it?
What's happened to your studies? What do you mean,
'they're on hold?' You changing your mind about
all that law and politicking? Probably better if
you did!

Neil stopped reading, laughed out loud and walked over to a spot of
shade. Troy's letters were always better taken in short gulps. He could see
Troy's face, his eyes always darting with energy and mischievousness. He
really did miss the pest. And he knew how grateful he really was to his
younger brother for holding down the home fort. He hoped Troy also had
some answers to the questions he'd written in his last quickly scribbled
note.

Okay, so here's the scoop on the stuff you asked
me about. I double-checked with the county and
city administration offices and had them verify the
information I got. It should be fairly accurate.
The Government has scrapped the laws limiting
British immigration and is allowing unlimited
numbers of their children to come over. Also,
higher-ups in the American Consular Office in
London can grant visas without getting prior
approval from Washington. These temporary visitor
visas have no expiration and they're available to
any young kid up to sixteen years old. The kids'
transportation comes even before other commercial
shipping. The only problem I can see in all of this
is the danger of the Germans attacking these ships
as they set out away from England. I don't know if
Hitler would take a chance on hitting them once
they get into the neutral territory of our waters.
But hell, he's such a madman, who knows?

Neil stopped to shake his head and smile. He missed his brother's blunt
observations on life.

Anyway, that's about all the stuff I have. I
guess you must be about to load up some children
on a boat and send them over here. Whatever you're

up to, be careful you idiot. Just because you can't
be drafted into this stupid war doesn't mean it
can't come back to bite you in the ass. Watch your
backside. Let me know if you need any help on my
end. I'm stateside for the moment, at least until
Uncle Sam decides to piss or get off the pot. Write
back sooner this time. Auntie gets all excited to
hear from you and remembers to take her medicine
for a while. HA!

Love,
Troy

Neil folded the letter and stuffed it into his shirt pocket. He headed back to his office to finish the latest list of evacuees. He knew time was running out. He would soon have to make the decision to send the children far away. Especially one child in particular. He sat down in his desk chair and covered his face with his hands as the sound of shutters slapped against the building.

CHAPTER NINETEEN

London,
August 1, 1940

The pub was crowded and bustling as Doreen made her way to a small, square table in the back. She couldn't believe it was August before she could finally meet with Lieutenant Lawrence. He had postponed their first two meetings, due to 'immediate and urgent orders' that he had to attend to. She had waited in her flat in Croydon nearly two days, not wanting to miss his phone call. After little sleep and much frustration, she returned to London to arrange for another run of children. She'd asked her neighbor to stay in her house to wait for the lieutenant's contact and then phone her at the nursing flats in London. It was difficult using phone lines in the London area, and she prayed hard that her neighbor would get through. The call came; they were to rendezvous at a local pub. The "meeting" finally was going to happen.

She hadn't stopped at the bar to order any lunch, as her stomach was in knots and she felt sick. There were only a few men in uniforms, leaning over the bar, drinking pints and talking loudly. She sat on a wooden bench and looked around her. The décor was actually quite nice, though the ancient beams and walls were in sharp contrast to the cigarette machine and a large wireless set that stood against the side wall. A small billow of smoke drifted from a table a few feet away, and Doreen wished she could have met this Lieutenant in a more private place. As she glanced towards the front door, she felt a strange and cold breeze, an unseen shadow of dread. The same feeling she had felt before. She swallowed hard and willed the damp chill to go away. It lingered nonetheless, and she wrapped her arms about herself.

She knew it was him the moment he entered the pub. She saw the Sub-Lieutenant bars on his uniform and watched him glance about quickly, as if expecting her to be waiting at the bar. She stood up and caught his eye, motioning for him to come over and sit down.

"Lieutenant Lawrence. Hallo. I'm Doreen Bennett. I'm so pleased to finally meet you – and meet *with* you."

"Mrs. Bennett, good to meet you. Can I get you a drink – or something to eat?"

"No, no, I'm fine. But please go ahead and order something for yourself. I'll wait."

He excused himself and went up to the bar, coming back shortly with a pint of bitter and one orange squash.

"I brought you a drink, anyway. Thought you might get thirsty."

He raised his glass, silent of the usual "cheers!"

Doreen hesitated before raising her glass.

"Lieutenant Lawrence, I hope you don't think me rude, but I've been waiting so long to have this meeting that I'm a little anxious to get started."

"I know, Mrs. Bennett, and for that I apologize. I couldn't take a chance of telling you over the telephone; a noisy public place like this is better. It would do us good to pretend we know each other, two people meeting perhaps for lunch or a social drink. You see, I'm speaking to you today off the record, that is, I'm here on my own accord. Usually any information concerning the military, whether it pertains to MIA's or any other official war business must go through the War Department. I know you haven't received any news from them. I hope what I say will be of help to you. We just need to be a bit cautious for my sake."

"I see."

She leaned toward him and placed her hands on the table.

"Here's what I know. Your husband and I were both assigned to the field hospital at Rosendael, France, when evacuations from the Dunkirk beach began. It was an awful mess of confusion and Colin and I got separated for a while. We both ended up together at the embarkation point, where we were transferring the hospital wounded onto two ships."

The Lieutenant's eyes lowered and he looked very tired.

"I was hit by shrapnel coming from enemy aircraft. I went down fast and everything was a blur. When I looked up, Colin was hoisting me over his shoulders and running with me towards the ship. I don't know how he got me there in time. I guess they say fear has a strength of its own. Anyway, he positioned me on one of the ships before getting off again to assist others. Once the beach was cleared of all the wounded and staff, both ships pulled anchor and started back for home, bound for any of our ports we could get to. We left amid heavy attacks by German aircraft.

I remember wondering if any of us would make it. Then, not even ten minutes into our journey the other rescue ship just...it just blew up in a huge billow of fire and smoke, its hull cracking with a deafening sound. We watched in horror as the flames shot toward the sky. Everyone on our boat hit the deck. We lay there eyeing those fireworks as though it were Guy Fawkes Day. We knew it was the end of her. She went down real fast."

The pub noises muted and the only voice Doreen could hear was coming from the man who sat across from her. He paused and took a long drink of his beer.

"It was mad chaos. Men screaming from pain, others crying and thrashing about in the waters, unable to be reached in the deep and high waves. It was hell. All I could think of was getting out of there, getting that boat on the move towards home. I know I went in and out of consciousness."

He reached in his pocket for a pack of cigarettes and offered one to Doreen. She shook her head in a silent 'no;' she couldn't find her voice.

"We were still in shock when the shells came crashing down on us. Our ship was hit and we knew we had to turn back. There was no way to survive on that vessel. We eventually made it to shore. Those who could walk helped those who couldn't and makeshift stretchers were used to haul the badly wounded. Some were even dragged across the beach to the hospital. It was awful.

"Once we managed to get back to Rosendael, a plan was put into place. Those who could make it would return to the beach. They were then put into small, private crafts and taken to the few ships left waiting for them further down the coast. Now comes the part I really wanted to tell you."

Doreen swallowed hard and nodded for him to go on.

"A lottery was held to determine which officers and staff would stay at the hospital with the critically wounded. There were too many injured to move and they needed trained men to stay and doctor them.

He stopped again and took another drink and Doreen cleared her throat.

"I think there were about thirty men who stayed behind and the rest of us left, either by our own power or carried on stretchers, like I was. Some managed to make it only as far as the beach, but the majority of lads eventually made it back to England, myself included.

"Your husband, Colin, was not a part of the lottery. What I mean is, he volunteered right off, allowing someone else to attempt rescue. He didn't hesitate for a moment, which really didn't surprise me. I knew Colin well enough to realize that leaving his post and his patients was never an option he considered. I do know that the Germans overran that area soon after the rest of us headed down the coast. What happened to our men after that, I don't know. I can only guess that they were taken prisoner or…they may have managed to hide out for a while, but I don't really believe they could have escaped the German troops for long. Hitler's brigade, a lot of them just young boys, seem motivated by some demonic purpose."

The lieutenant snuffed the cigarette out in an ashtray. He quickly glanced around the room before looking directly at her.

"I'm sorry, Mrs. Bennett. I don't know whether your husband is dead or alive. I don't know if he was taken prisoner or shot when the Germans came through there. I wish I had better news for you. I'm afraid that's all I know."

Doreen stared straight at the lieutenant, looking at this man who half an hour ago held her future, yet she could not focus her eyes on his face. She sat silently for several minutes, until she found her voice.

"I'm trying to remember his face… on the day he left for this horrible war. Sometimes his smile flashes across my mind. Lately, though, the vision of his face is frightening. His features are distorted and his eyes are red and glazed. It's hideous."

There was an uncomfortable shifting of feet and tapping of glasses on the marked and stained wooden table. Doreen let out a heavy sigh.

"Anyway, thank you for looking me up and contacting me. I know this hasn't been easy for you, either. I'm truly glad that you made it back here alive."

"There's a fine line in a war like this, Mrs. Bennett. Whether it is better to be dead or have to live in your own private hell."

She nodded and stood up.

"Good luck to you, Lieutenant Lawrence. Take care of yourself."

Doreen excused herself and walked to the door, turning to glance at him as he shuffled to the bar and ordered another beer.

The morning of August 18 began with a strange calm in Croydon. Doreen stopped over at her neighbor's very early to deliver a jar of Mrs. Markham's homemade preserves. She didn't really have much time to enjoy the delicacy, and she certainly didn't want them to go to waste. Besides, her neighbor had been more than kind in watching their flat. The street was oddly quiet as she stepped onto her own back porch, and she heard the drone of distant planes overhead. It wasn't an unusual sound, but one that still made the hair on her arms stand on end. She shivered and went into the kitchen with fear in her heart.

Suddenly the skies were a cacophony of sounds, all of them frightening and pounding in her ears. There were many planes overhead, yet she couldn't tell where they were coming from or even how close they were. She ran to her front room and lay down on the floor, just under the windows so any flying glass would pass over her head. The sounds were deafening, though they didn't last too long. She slowly got up when all the noise and commotion were over. She knew what the Germans were after. Hitler wanted to strike the aerodome and aircraft factories. Most likely, he had succeeded. The mere thought left her feeling even queasier inside. She made her way to the kitchen and put the kettle on to boil. This was definitely the time to leave her home for Oxford, to see Meghan and make alternative arrangements for her safety. There would just be time to stop at Wycombe Convent first and gather the children that the sisters were sheltering. The young ones would do much better in the relative calm Oxford countryside, for as long as it lasted anyway. She made her way upstairs to her and Colin's bedroom and vowed to leave the next morning for Amersham.

Doreen did *not* leave for Amersham the next morning. German air attacks had actually begun on August 13, yet Croydon had not been hit hard then. The bombs falling on the night of August 18, though, had nearly paralyzed the city of Croydon. Public transportation was not available for civilians and movement and activities were severely restricted. Doreen knew that it would be several days before she could make her way to the Convent. She tried to telephone Sister Mary Catherine, but the phone lines were also restricted. No matter. She knew that the sisters would keep the children safe until her arrival.

Five days later, Doreen walked up the tree-lined path to Wycombe Convent. It hadn't been that long since she'd been there, escorting children from the relative safety of the Convent to greater safety in the rural countryside. The last time she was here she had intended on taking that group to Oxford, where she could have seen her own daughter. Yet sudden changes in relocation plans had prevented her from heading that direction, and she found herself going in the opposite direction with several children in tow. It was a disappointment she had tried, unsuccessfully, not to show. She vowed now to keep her mind focused on the task before her.

She entered through the front doors of the Convent excited to see the sisters, even more excited to know she would be leaving for Oxford in two days. She could hold her own child and have a lovely visit with everyone! She thought briefly of Neil and envisioned his face just as Mother Mary Catherine appeared before her.

"Doreen! How wonderful to see again. We have quite a bunch for you to transport this time. Are you up to it?"

"Of course, Mother. I'm so looking forward to getting back to Oxford! I'll be staying here for a couple of days to get all the paperwork sorted out, so I've no glitches during the journey. That way I can also get to know each child a little bit which will help with the placement process."

"That's fine, Doreen. You are certainly welcome to stay as long as you need to. I haven't given the children any definite time frame for their leaving. They seem quite happy here. Our custodian put up a big rope swing in the large maple tree out back, and the children have been busily playing. I was so worried the day he put it up that the old gentleman would fall off the ladder!"

Doreen chuckled at Mary Catherine's comment about "the old gentleman" and realized that the Mother still considered herself one of the younger ones. She still had more energy than many of the younger ones!

The rest of Doreen's day and the next one were spent in sharing information and chatting with the children. She felt confident and anxious as she went to bed the night before her departure to Oxford with another evacuation. She lay awake staring up at the ceiling of the tiny Convent room, wondering what ceiling Colin might be staring at. It dampened her spirits to think of him, yet her heart ached if she did not. She tried to keep her thoughts positive though her hope for his return was dwindling. It was a difficult tightrope to walk. She heard the familiar sound of planes buzzing somewhere in the distance, and she pulled the pillow over her ears.

The overhead thunder suddenly grew more intense, as though it was rumbling through her room. Doreen shot up in the narrow bed, beads of perspiration beginning on her arms and forehead. This was too loud – too close! She bolted out of the room, taking the stairs two at a time. She heard someone shouting, "We're under direct fire!" There was chaos outside with shells exploding and the sky was lighting up with an eerie glow. London and surrounding areas were being heavily bombed this time! This was it! The night had turned into a nightmare of searing sounds and screams.

The sisters were running from room to room, gathering up sleeping children and making their way to a basement shelter underneath the cloisters. Doreen was scooping up the little ones in her arms and shouting to the older ones as they ran. It was taking longer than expected to get them all safely in the underground room. The old timbers in the chapel just above them creaked from the vibrations.

Doreen glanced around quickly, making sure everyone was in the shelter when suddenly she heard a deafening crack. She tried to move out of the way of the object, but it came crashing down with a speed and force that she could not avoid. She was flung to the ground, a terrible searing pain ripping through her leg. She tried to crawl away to free herself from the heaviness and excruciating pressure, but she was unable to move. In the distance she heard more screams. The air raid sirens were going off and crying – so much crying! The darkness turned to black as she drifted into unconsciousness.

CHAPTER TWENTY

Mrs. Markham sat close to the wireless set in her small cottage. She had worked long hours at the hospital that day, but her mind would not let her give in to sleep. It was more important than ever to know what was going on. The news spread quickly of the bombing raids on London. There was not a lot of information about the exact location of all the hits, but the wires coming through indicated that several key areas were in chaos and destruction. She wanted so desperately to contact Doreen, but phone lines were down and transportation was at a standstill, except for whatever ambulances and emergency vehicles could get through. People in and around the London areas were staying indoors, next to their wireless sets just as she was, waiting for any more news of incoming German planes. They had been instructed not to attempt evacuation of the City, as the Germans would take advantage of the confusion and blockage of port towns, aiming their vengeance directly upon the civilians as they tried to escape. Those involved in the Civil Defense, Red Crescent, and other wartime organizations were mobilizing defense teams to set up along the Thames and other entrances into the City, as well as along the coastal towns. The war had truly reached a critical stage and Churchill was urging his people to "face their bravest hour." Mrs. Markham adjusted the knobs on the radio and stared at her curtained window. It would be a long time before the former gentleness of the night sky felt like a friend again. It would be a long time before bravery would be reserved for only heroes.

August 25, 1940
Oxford

Ian O'Connor sat immobilized in front of his wireless set, waiting for any new information about the bombings in and around the London area. He lifted his eyes every few minutes to look at Margaret, who held Meghan in her lap. The little girl seemed momentarily preoccupied with her doll, though earlier she had cried when hearing of the bombs. Her caregivers had tried to shield her from the worst of the battle descriptions, yet they had gently explained what was going on. They knew she was very clever, and would know something terrible was happening. Too, the O'Connor's needed to prepare Meghan for any bad news that might come her way.

Neil stepped into the cottage, his head down and his shoulders sagging. He dropped his satchel by the door, walked to his favorite paisley chair and fell into it.

"The news isn't good, Ian. I stopped at the main office on campus to see if they'd heard anything more. The information they had was that several places just outside of London were hit pretty hard, as well as the city itself. They're getting too close for comfort."

Margaret motioned to Neil with a wave of her hand, got up out of her chair and headed to the kitchen with Meghan. There was no conversation in the front room while she got out milk and biscuits and set them on the kitchen table.

"Here, love, you help yourself to a little sweet. Aunt Margaret is going to have a chat in the other room. I'll come check on you in a moment."

"Why is Mr. Henderson so tired, Aunt Margaret? Didn't he sleep last night?"

"I think he's just had too much work to do, love. Now, sit still and I'll be back in soon."

Neil had opened his leather case, pulled out documents and maps, and was laying them out on the floor when Margaret came into the room. Ian pulled his chair over and sat down to look at the papers spread before them.

"This is the pertinent information I was telling you about. I know it seems risky, but I promised Doreen that I would see to Meghan's safety – no matter what the cost. My brother sent me some info on the easing of visa and travel restrictions for children heading to Canada and the U.S. I was able to secure the names of two big ships that are leaving from Liverpool in three days. If I can get train fare for Meghan and myself, I'll take her to the docks and see that she boards safely. I have some connections up in Lancashire, and I'm sure I can get some shipmates to personally watch over her. I know it will break your hearts, not to mention what it will do to Doreen's."

Neil paused and looked into their faces, trying to gauge their true reaction. Even though he had been talking about this for several weeks, it had never seemed to be a necessity, or a reality – until now. The O'Connor's sat quietly, only nodding their heads in agreement.

"I sent off another letter to my brother, Troy, and Aunt Ida, asking them to take in little Meghan. I know my Aunt Ida would love it. She's still in good health and a small one around would keep her young. It would also be great company for her. I trust Troy and Aunt Ida; I would send my own child to them. Troy is really a good guy and he would see to all her needs. I know he likes children. He's even volunteered down at the local grade school on occasion. You wouldn't have to worry about her being safe and well-cared for over there."

Neil paused again and stared down at the papers on the floor.

"I'm afraid the bombings will get worse before they subside. God only knows how far Hitler's troops will actually get on British soil."

At this the O'Connor's shot him a harsh glance and Ian spoke in a raised voice.

"Neil, the Germans will never invade this isle or our own dear Emerald Isle! They may bomb us from the air and attack our fleets in the waters, but they will never take control of our land! You forget that we are a people used to invaders. We are strong and determined."

Margaret wrung her hands nervously and bit her lip.

"I'm sorry, Ian. I meant no personal offense. My concern is for your safety and the safety of Meghan and other children. I would like it very much if you would both go with me to Liverpool, if we can all get space on the trains. It would get you out of Oxford while the bombing is still going on; it might do you good to get further away from all this for a time."

"Thanks, Neil. And I'm sorry I exploded on 'ya. This damn war has all of us on edge. I think it would be good for Margaret to go with you but I need to stick around here. I'm trying to keep my shop open as long as I can, and someone needs to be here in case – when Doreen shows up."

"There's no way I'm going off to leave you alone here, Ian O'Connor! I'll be right here with you, no matter what. Besides, you'd near starve to death if you had to eat your own cooking!"

Laughter broke the tension in the air and Meghan peered into the room from the kitchen door.

"Can I come in now?"

"Of course, my dear. Come sit on my lap and we'll read a good book. We have something to talk to you about, anyway."

Meghan grabbed her favorite book from an old milk crate under the windows and dutifully climbed up in Margaret's lap. Neil was silent for a moment and spoke in a lowered voice.

"I'll need to contact Doreen as soon as possible, which may be a problem. I'm sure sending a wire is out of the question. I may have better luck going back into Oxford and phoning from there."

"Yes, you may. I can loan you my bicycle if the bus is full. A four-mile ride would be easy for you. Sometimes I think all our fancy transportation makes us lazy!"

"Thanks, Ian. I'll let you know. Though I gotta tell you, it'll feel strange not having Meghan on the back with her little fingers digging into my skin! She sure loves going with me on that old bike. Oh, and just for the record, I can't imagine you or Margaret ever being accused of being lazy."

Margaret smiled, readjusting Meghan on her lap so she was facing Neil. The room was quiet except for the chiming of the mantel clock. Neil gave a big sigh, then began telling Meghan about the fast changes she would have in her life. Margaret took a hankie from her pocket and dabbed at her eyes while Ian got up to put on the teakettle. Meghan clutched Max and let the book fall to the floor. Outside, the wind picked up, blowing fallen petals and yard debris across the gardens of Kidlington.

Neil spent the rest of the late afternoon in Oxford, trying to reach Doreen. He thought she was enroute to or from the Convent with another group of children they were sheltering. At least that was the plan in her last letter. He checked the calendar again. Yes, she should have been back in Oxford two days ago. He winced at the idea that she may have still been in Croydon, or worse yet, London proper. He had a nagging feeling.

He picked up the receiver in the Oxford University's main office and asked the operator to try the Convent's number once again.

"I'm sorry, sir. There's no connection at that number. The phone must be out of order or the lines are down."

Neil sighed heavily and continued.

"Can you try to connect me with Hempstead Royal Infirmary?"

Perhaps Mrs. Markham would know something! Hempstead was so close to the Convent. Maybe Doreen got word to her there.

His fingers tapped nervously on the desk as he waited for the operator's reply.

"I've reached the Infirmary, Sir. Go ahead."

"Hello? Hello? Whom I'm speaking with?"

"This is reception. How may I help you?"

"I was hoping to speak with a Mrs. Markham. Is she there?"

"No, I'm sorry. She's gone into London to work with the Red Crescent. Is there something I can help you with?"

"Have you any information on a former convent sister, Doreen Bennett? She married a doctor from your hospital. I'm worried she may have been caught in the latest bombings."

"I wish I had news for you, sir, but I don't know anyone by that name. We haven't had a lot of contact from the nuns lately, as they seem to be involved in a new project."

The line hissed and crackled and Neil knew this conversation was at an end.

"Thank you, anyway."

He hung up the receiver and stood silent. There was no one else to call and he let the afternoon slip away.

The sun was fading fast behind the trees. He grabbed his satchel, ran out the door and got on Ian's bicycle, peddling hard to get home before dark. The faster he peddled, the more his fears surfaced and the sharper the pain was in his weakened heart. He would have to take Meghan to the children's boat bound for Canada and the U.S., without contacting Doreen first. The weight of this responsibility and decision bore down on him like the strong wind he peddled against. Soon the darkening clouds overhead opened up and huge drops of water began pelting him. He buried his head in his chest, glancing up just to see the road. The wind blew harder, causing the rain to hit him sideways and he struggled to keep the bicycle upright. It was stinging his face and ears and drowning out the sound of his own crying.

Meghan had taken the news of her imminent departure quietly and with few tears. It was evident that she really didn't understand the events that would unfold, and she certainly hadn't grasped the idea of being separated from her mother. It was too much for a four year old to comprehend, especially one who'd always felt secure in loving company. The O'Connor's went through all the same evening and bedtime rituals, trying to make Meghan's last night in their cottage as normal as possible. Margaret had gathered up her things and packed them while Ian played make-believe with her, the two of them donning old hats and buying invisible cakes at the invisible bake shop.

Neil arrived home just before Meghan went to bed, shaking his head in a silent "no" as Margaret and Ian searched his face for any news on Doreen. The three adults sat in the front room long after their own bedtime, making sure every detail was worked out.

Neil finally got up and headed upstairs with only a quiet "goodnight." Ian turned to Margaret and motioned toward the stairs.

"Go on up to bed, my dear, I'll be there in a few minutes."

Margaret turned from the steps and smiled at her husband. She knew he would take a few moments alone before joining her in their bedroom. He was a private man, and he would have to deal with this great sadness in his own private way.

Ian stepped outside and stared up into the black sky. He wanted to say something to the God he knew was out there, yet the words wouldn't form. He clenched his fists, then released them and shoved them into his pockets. He wouldn't anger this God just yet. Little Meghan had to get to America and Doreen had to be safe first. Then he'd say what was in his heart. For now, he bowed his head and let the tears stream down his lined face.

The O'Connor's rode the bus with Neil and Meghan to the Oxford train station and stood by quietly while Neil inquired about his reservations. They were to board the 15:00 train for the long ride to Liverpool. Neil stepped back from the ticket window and motioned to a shabby bench that was just outside the doors. If they had to stay for a while, it may as well be out in the sun with the fresh breezes clearing their thoughts.

The four of them sat down on the bench and waited. Margaret took sandwiches and a bottle of milk from her canvas bag and fed her "family" before their departure. Overhead the large starlings appeared, eagerly circling and laying claim to any crumbs that fell to the ground.

At 14:55 the whistle sounded and Neil and Meghan boarded the train. They waved furiously while Ian and Margaret watched until the smoke from the engine was long gone and the heat of the day was waning. The sounds of other travelers were lost to Margaret's ears; she heard only the screaming cries of the black, scavenger birds as they flew to the benches on the platform. She stared for a moment at their eyes and wondered how God had ever made one of his own creatures look so evil.

Only one large, evacuation ship was actually in the harbor at Liverpool, the other one having left some days before. Neil held Meghan's hand and they registered at the purser's office. The ship would be leaving in two days, so Neil made inquiries for a place to stay. He phoned a former professor from Oxford, asking if they could stay in his Liverpool flat for two nights. The older gentleman, a confirmed bachelor, was more than happy for the company. They met at a fish-n-chips shop and brought food back to his cluttered, stuffy place. They wanted to get Meghan to bed at a reasonable hour, as the train journey had made her irritable.

"Neil my friend, you look tired," the professor said as he chomped away at his fish. "Make sure *you* go to bed early yourself, this worrying is not good for the soul."

"Thanks, Cliff, I appreciate the concern."

Neil had barely touched his fare.

"And you should eat, keep up your strength."

"I'm not really hungry, but thank-you."

The professor got up and gathered the remains of both their dinners, taking them into the kitchen and leaving them sitting on the counter. He reached into the cupboard for a bottle of whiskey, scavenged two clean glasses, and sat down across from Neil.

"Ya know, I got a friend who works at the docks. Says those boats headed for America, it can get rough sometimes."

He poured them both a large shot and passed one over to his friend.

"I know...I know."

"Says when they sail, they turn off all the lights. I guess they don't want the Germans to see them, but it sounds like risky sailing to me."

"They do that to avoid attack. It's a blackout curfew mandated by the Navy. There's also ships from the fleet that follow along side them until they are safely out of reach."

"I don't know, Neil. Sounds dangerous to me. Are you sure this is the right thing to do?"

"No Cliff, I'm not sure about anything right now. But from where I stand, the situation isn't getting any better. I promised Meghan's mom that I would look after her and make sure she's safe. That's a big responsibility, especially when you're left alone with the decision."

"Sounds like she's pretty special, this friend of yours."

"Well, I guess so. I've been so busy lately, I haven't given it much thought."

"Aye you have, my friend. Aye, you have."

Two days later, with no news on Doreen, Neil chatted with a shipmate of the large vessel that would take Meghan away from her troubled country. The sailor assured Neil that he would personally see to it that Meghan was well cared for while on board. He explained that the children were assigned in groups to a caring adult, someone from the Red Crescent or a church. The child would have supervision and someone to allay her fears. Still, the sailor promised Neil that he would take extra care of Meghan.

Neil's dreams that night were a disturbing jumble of train whistles and giant, crashing waves; volumes of books stacked much too high on wobbly bookcases, and bombs that kept chasing him as he peddled faster and faster against an oncoming storm. He awoke sweaty and exhausted.

An efficient looking woman met Neil and Meghan as they arrived at the docks the next morning.

"Mr. Henderson, I'm Ethel Headley. So glad you both made it. And who's this lovely little lady?"

"This is Meghan Bennett. She's four years old and quite the charmer."

"Hallo dearie. You and I are going to be best friends."

Meghan smiled tentatively at the stout woman who was already moving towards the ship, talking in a business-like voice.

"I'll explain the procedures as we board and you have a look around. I must inform you of the possible dangers involved in this crossing. The Navy is being stretched well beyond reason so escorts for our boats are not always possible. The children will be kept below decks much of the time, for their own safety. They'll be allowed to come up on deck at the Captain's discretion, for some exercise and fresh air."

Neil stopped and scooped up Meghan in his arms as the escort continued.

"I know this all sounds a bit dismal, but please be assured that we all have the children's best interests at heart. That is, after all, the purpose of our mission."

"I understand. It's just that...she seems so young to do this."

He pulled Meghan closer to his chest.

"There are many younger than she. We'll be fine, Mr. Henderson. Now then, you know that our boat will dock in Canada before going on to the U.S. so Meghan darling, you mustn't panic when some children leave the boat before you do."

Meghan looked up at the woman and squeezed her bunny tighter. Neil lifted Meghan to his shoulder and held her face in his hands. He spoke quietly.

"And sweetie, you remember I told you that my brother, Troy, and Aunt Ida will be at the docks to greet your ship when it arrives in the big city."

Meghan nodded and buried her head into his shoulder.

It seemed that all the urgent items had been discussed. There was just barely time for the really important things to be said as the ship's horn blew, signaling its departure.

"Meghan, I know this is so very hard for you to understand. You must always remember that your mummy loves you more than anything else in the world. She asked me to protect you from bad things, and that is why I'm sending you to my home in America for a while. When all the bombs and fighting here in England have gone away, your mum will bring you back to your own home and your own bed. She wants you to be very brave and to follow the grownups' directions. Please don't ever forget how much you are loved. Now, give me a great big hug and a smooch on the cheek."

Meghan threw her arms around Neil's neck and began to cry softly. There were some things a four year old could understand. Mrs. Headley stood by silently, then lifted Meghan from Neil's shoulder and walked with him as far as the ramp leading off the boat. Meghan wriggled and waved frantically with one arm, her other arm clutching Max. Neil stepped back onto the dock and stood frozen as the steel hull lurched through the quay and headed out into open waters. He was sure he heard Meghan's hysterical cries long after the ship was swallowed by an infinite horizon.

He couldn't go back to the professor's flat. He could not board the train for Oxford. He walked to the nearest open pub and ordered a pint of bitter and a shot of Irish whiskey as the blaring horns of other ships pierced the summer morning.

September 7, 1941

Wycombe Convent had suffered a lot of damage in the early morning hours of August 24, but some of the areas were usable to secure the children and house the nuns at night. Two children were slightly injured when the large, ancient beam had come crashing down just outside of the shelter room, but they had been treated and seemed to be healing nicely. Mother Mary Catherine continued to set up regular prayer vigils, though she herself seemed too busy or preoccupied to attend them. Everything was still so chaotic and unsettled, and she was making several trips back and forth to Hempstead Royal Infirmary. She looked tired beyond time and old beyond her years. The bombing had continued in and around London for weeks, and most always there were the sounds of planes and shells bursting in the distance. The moments of quiet were short and left an eerie calm over the City and the villages surrounding it. It had been nearly two weeks since the devastating attack upon the convent and three weeks since the bombs landed on Croydon. Mary Catherine grabbed the railing and headed into the hospital. Mrs. Markham greeted her with enthusiasm.

"My dear, I'm so pleased you've come early today. I've good news, for a change!"

"Dear God… please tell me that there's been some improvement in Doreen."

"There's been much improvement, for sure. She's awake and talking. Asking about her daughter and the O'Connor's and of course, about you and the sisters. I told her the news on everyone at the Convent. I didn't know if you'd heard anything from Oxford yet."

"I've just heard from the O'Connor's. They say that..."

The nun paused and briefly closed her eyes.

"I'm sorry, Mrs. Markham, but I feel I should say these things to Doreen first, if you'll understand. I'm quite sure she will share everything with you."

"Of course, Sister. I do understand. I'm just so happy that she's finally coherent and complaining about her aches and pains. Her broken leg wasn't the most dangerous of her injuries. At one point, I was so afraid she would never come around. The brain is truly remarkable, isn't it?"

"Yes it is. But so is the heart."

Mrs. Markham nodded in agreement as her eyes followed the sister down the hall.

"Doreen – it's me, Mary Catherine. Thanks be to God that you are finally awake! How are you feeling?"

"I think I'm getting better. My head hurts a bit and this traction on my leg is very uncomfortable, but otherwise I really think I'm on the mend. I've been pestering Mrs. Markham for any news of Meghan and all the folks in Oxford."

"I have news for you my dear. I just finally got a letter from the O'Connor's."

Mary Catherine sat down in a chair next to Doreen's bed and began relaying all the information that she had. Doreen's expression remained the same until she heard the words, "on a boat bound for America to live with his aunt and brother." Doreen's eyes narrowed and her face showed lines of pain but her voice was strong and loud.

"On a boat?! On a ship bound for America?! My God, not Meghan, not yet! Why didn't he phone? Was the situation really that desperate that he made that decision without me? What about the O'Connor's? What did they think of sending my baby so far away from me?"

Doreen's voice grew more intense and she gave no time for response.

"Oh my God, he's sent her away and I have no idea how to reach her! Oh my God, please tell me this isn't really happening......"

Doreen's shouts turned into cries of anguish and her shoulders shook from the loud sobs. Mary Catherine didn't speak. She wrapped her arms loosely around Doreen and let her cry until the only sound left was a soft whimper. Doreen finally lay back on the bed, weakened from her own private grief. She'd asked him to do the right thing – to make the decision she'd have had to make. And he did. Her head pounded furiously and her leg throbbed. But the overwhelming sadness at not being able to say "goodbye" to her only child was the pain that now engulfed her.

Mary Catherine stayed by the bedside and kept a silent vigil for the rest of the day until the night closed in. Doreen finally slept from sheer exhaustion.

CHAPTER TWENTY ONE

September 15, 1940
Hempstead

It was difficult to tell if morning had come, the air outside was thick with a heavy mist, shrouding the hospital in a somber cloak. It didn't even feel like a Sunday, as there were no church bells ringing, nor services Doreen could attend. The walls of the Hempstead Royal Infirmary were beginning to close in on her and she willed herself to heal faster. The doctors had said she could recuperate elsewhere, if she took it easy and kept her leg propped up. She waited impatiently for Sister Julian to arrive to take her back to the Convent. The hospital was kind enough to loan her a wheelchair, a rare commodity. She envisioned herself bumping across the uneven stone floors of Wycombe, a real "terror" on wheels. It was the first time she had smiled in several days. She had heard the news of the night air attacks on Liverpool and didn't know if Neil had gotten Meghan safely on the boat before they began. She knew he would contact her as soon as he could, that mail delivery and phone lines were continually disrupted. Still, she ached with the desire to hear some news about her daughter, something to assure her that Meghan was safely heading to North America.

Her thoughts were racing when Sister Julian entered the room. She could hear the voice, but it took a few moments for her words to register.

" ….And so the doctors say it will probably take about three months for your leg to completely heal."

Sister Julian picked up the medications from the bedside table and put them into a small bag.

"Are you ready to go now?"

"Yes, Sister, I'm ready. I'm afraid I'm not very good company just now. Thanks very much for getting here so early and helping me get back to the Convent and please forgive my inattention. You must be missing Sunday Mass."

The young sister smiled.

"Think nothing of it. Doreen, I need to tell you that Mother Mary Catherine took the liberty of going to Oxford. Let's get you out of here. We'll stop at the reception desk so you can have a word with Mrs. Markham. She'd never let me hear the end of it if we don't."

As Doreen and Sister Julian made their way to the Convent, they heard the familiar drone of planes. They sounded farther away this time, as if they were headed toward the east and south. Doreen felt first a growing panic, then a wave of relief as she realized that they were not coming directly toward Amersham.

Commander Graham Lawrence reread the memo that he'd been given very early in the morning. He was pleased about his recent promotion, but his injuries from Dunkirk had furloughed him from active duty for the next six months, making him agitated. He stood up and stared out the window. The fog was rolling out slowly and deliberately, as though timing its departure in order to give maximum cover for the British fighter patrols which had been put in place from Harwich to Land's End, with squadrons at readiness state. The latest report indicated that reconnaissance planes had appeared in the straits of Dover at 9:00 that morning, coming over the Thames Estuary and Kent. Radar stations reported enemy formations southeast of Boulogne, waiting for their orders to attack and invade. More RAF squadrons had left from Biggin Hill to patrol between Canterbury and Dungeness on the southeast coast.

"Commander Lawrence, Sir."

The lieutenant's sudden presence took Graham off guard.

"Yes, lieutenant, what is it?"

"Captain Belding would like to see all officers immediately in the briefing room, Sir."

"Thank you, lieutenant. Dismissed."

"Thank you, Sir."

The young officer left as quickly as he had appeared and Commander Lawrence strode out of his office to get the latest news on this day of reckoning. Captain Belding wasted no time and minced no words.

"At 11:35 the first wave of one hundred German bombers and their escorts were met by twenty Spitfires as they approached Dungeness. Shortly after that, more enemy fighters were met by five more Spitfire squadrons attacking in the Canterbury and Dover areas. Our reports indicate that visibility was near zero from the flames and vapors, but we know first hand that the ground is littered with burning planes and bodies, mostly

Germans but we lost some of our own. The RAF was ready for the next wave when they got here to London. We hit them hard, men. It was a successful assault."

Commander Lawrence listened to the briefing as though it were a movie he'd seen many times before, but one in which the ending always changed. As the Captain finished his update, the sounds of planes and bombs quieted and a strange calm pervaded the acrid air outside. It seemed the whole war had stopped for lunch! The commander smiled at his own ridiculous thought and left the briefing room shaking his head in private embarrassment.

At the Hempstead Royal Infirmary, Mrs. Markham busied herself filing medical records. Since finding out about the convent's damage and Doreen's injuries, she'd returned to the hospital from her City duties with the Red Crescent. In the uneasy stillness of this early afternoon, she knew instinctively that it was just the calm before the storm, and she was right. Just before filing the last stack, the drone of the German Luftwaffe returned in force. She set off the warning alarm once more and ran for cover. It was not until later in the evening that she let herself believe the reports that came over her wireless radio. The Germans hadn't enough escorts to protect their bombers and the crews had ejected their bombs hastily and without much precision. The victorious RAF pilots had chased Hitler's boys out of the British Isles!

As quiet filled the empty night, she retrieved a bottle of dandelion wine that had been purchased from a church bazaar in happier, peaceful times. Taking a stemmed glass from an antique hutch, she walked outside and toasted the lads' victory over the evil that was more sinister than any devil the darkness held.

Sister Julian gingerly opened the door to Doreen's small convent room, peering in to see if she was sleeping. She knew the last few days had been a blur for Doreen as she adjusted to being in a wheelchair and living in the Convent again. Doreen was awake.

"Come in, Sister Julian."

"Doreen, I've brought you a piece of mail!"

She had received a letter from Neil! It must be about Meghan! It was postmarked "August 29–Liverpool." She wheeled herself over to a small dim lamp and eagerly tore open the envelope.

August 29, 1940

Dear Doreen,

I hope you get this letter. I'm never sure what's going in or out of the post these days. I'm not back in Oxford yet and I haven't been able to get much news from the O'Connor's the past two days. I never even got to find out how your meeting went with that lieutenant that knew your husband. I hope he had some new information for you, and that the whole experience wasn't too painful. You know I would have gone with you to London if things had been different with the evacuations.

I tried very hard to contact you when all the bombing started up in earnest. I had to make a difficult decision and I did so with only Meghan's welfare in mind. You told me to protect her at all costs. I know the price my actions have cost you and I can only hope and pray that you would have agreed with my decision. I truly felt that her safety was in jeopardy so I made the decision to send her to America. I tried to get the O'Connor's to come up north with us and stay there awhile, but they won't budge from Oxford. Anyway, Meghan and I got here safe and sound in Liverpool and stayed with a former professor of mine. I'm not sure what information you have gotten from the O'Connor's or from anyone at the Convent. Everything was such chaos following the horrible attacks. You'll be relieved to know that Meghan was well cared for as she boarded the ship yesterday. They even let me board with her for a little to help her settle in. I told her how much you love her and that you would bring her back home when all the fighting was over. She seemed to understand. My greatest fear now is that something has happened to you. Perhaps by the time you get this letter, we will all know where you are and can arrange to send you regular correspondence if you can't make it up to Oxford.

I have decided to make more trips between the Midlands and Liverpool to escort more children to the boats. There are children in the industrial areas who may be in danger, as the Germans seem hell-bent on destroying any military production sites. I've written to the O'Connor's so they won't expect me back in Oxford for a couple of weeks.

I will also write to the Convent, though I'm not sure any mail is going through there.

If you do get this letter, please write back as soon as possible, in care of the O'Connor's, as I'll return to Oxford as soon as I finish up in these parts. Please take good care of yourself and know that you have been in my thoughts.

Neil

September 18, 1940

Dear Neil,

It was so wonderful to finally get your letter! I have been waiting anxiously for any word from you or the O'Connor's but I realize that mail and phone communication is still so sporadic. It was amazing to read your words, knowing that Meghan has been out of the country for over a fortnight now. I'm sure that putting her on that ship was very difficult, especially since you couldn't contact me first. It was so hard for me to accept at first and Mary Catherine took in quite an earful when she read your letter to me. Yet, you know I trust your judgment, which is why I left you with that burden. My only wish is that we could have known the outcome of the Germans' attempt to land their ground forces here. How could we have known the victory of the RAF and the timing of all this? And yet, I'm sure that there are still dangers here in the U.K.; I am thankful that I have a friend like you who cares enough to make those tough decisions. May God watch over all of us.

May God especially watch over Colin. I'm afraid my meeting with Sub-Lt. Graham Lawrence didn't give me much hope. He served with Colin and was injured when the hospital ships were attacked off the coast of Dunkirk. Lt. Lawrence made it back to England and spent time recovering from his wounds. His news on my husband is not at all encouraging. Colin stayed behind with the seriously wounded, and most likely was captured when the Germans came through that area with their panzer divisions. I don't know what to think, except to keep telling

153

myself that there's still a chance he's alive.
Neil, please pray for him.

I assume the O'Connor's filled you in on my
injuries after getting a visit from Mary Catherine,
if you've been able to keep in touch with them.
I'll be staying here at the Convent for the next two
months, or until my leg is completely healed. I'll
continue to send letters to you at the O'Connor's
until I hear otherwise. I was hoping you'd stay
in Oxford until I'm able to return there, as I
think that's our best chance to get a letter from
your brother. If you receive any word from him,
please try to phone first. If you can't get through
the lines, write back as soon as you can. I miss
Meghan so terribly.

Take care of yourself and give Ian and Margaret
my best regards.

Doreen

The golds and amber browns of autumn were already beginning to splash their colors across the town of Oxford and its college grounds. Yet their beauty was lost on Neil who sat at his small, cluttered desk, his mind whirling with the realization that his work evacuating children was finished. The City Lines passenger ship, City of Benares, was 600 miles out and 5 days into its voyage from Liverpool to North America when it was torpedoed by a German U boat on September 17, 1940. It was carrying 99 children on board. Some had been rescued by HMS Hurricane; others weren't so lucky. This tragedy abruptly halted any further boats from leaving and it was a terrible blow to those evacuating children.

Neil stood and walked over to his messy bookcase and straightened a few books. Perhaps Doreen had been right when she questioned the timing of sending her child away when the threat of German ground invasion had all but been eliminated! Neil had tried to put the whole sequence of those awful events out of his mind, without much success. He felt a growing weight as though the thief of guilt was starting to rob him of his usual cheerful demeanor. If only he had waited just two more weeks to send Meghan away! If only he had been able to contact Doreen before making that critical decision! The O'Connor's had never expressed to him their opinions after the fact, and seemed content to know that Meghan was safe in America. The burden he bore was his own – and Doreen's.

He strode over to the tiny basement window and peered out. He could see the movement of people as they went about their routines. He could see the wind playing with the falling leaves, whisking them away to unfamiliar places. He thought of his own life at this moment. He needed to be in a new place, with a new purpose. Perhaps there would be meaningful work in London. He would stay in Oxford until he received a letter from Troy, assuring him of Meghan's safe arrival, and until Doreen returned to the O'Connor's. He had to see her in person, to see if his actions had put any distance between them and to share with her in person the details of Meghan's departure.

Neil turned around toward his office door, remembering the first day Doreen had come to the campus to learn of evacuation procedures. Here he was thinking about possible distance between them, yet he knew without a doubt that the closeness he perceived had only been in his dreams at night! Disturbing dreams that woke him and left him feeling empty and more confused than ever. He turned back to the window and simply stared, not seeing the campus squirrels scurrying across the grass, preparing their nests for a long winter.

It was dark when Neil walked into the O'Connor's cottage, although it was early and not yet teatime. The long hours of darkness in autumn and winter was one thing he had not grown used to in the U.K. It seemed to taint the evening hours with a strange sadness that prompted a lot of soul-searching. Ian and Margaret were both in the front room, the wireless set humming with a singsong voice and a sewing bag resting beside Margaret's chair. They greeted him quietly.

"Hallo, Neil. You're a bit later this evening. Is everything alright at the University?"

"Yes, love, everything's fine."

Margaret smiled.

"Well then, I'll move myself into the kitchen and start our dinner. Ian, why don't you start the fire? There's a bit of a chill this evening."

Ian peered over his glasses and rose to do her bidding. Neil walked to the kitchen and straddled the cracked, wooden chair.

"Can I help you with anything?"

"You can set the table, if you wish. We're only going to have a stew and some bread this evening."

Margaret kept working at the sink, adding vegetables to the canned mutton she'd been saving.

"Neil, is there anything you want to talk about? You seem a bit upset."

Margaret opened a tin of carrots without further comment.

"I'm not sure. I think the time has come for me to move on. Perhaps go to London and find another useful job in the war effort. My work with the children is finished for now."

This time, Margaret turned to face him, her eyes animated.

"Yes, perhaps it is time, Neil. Though I think you should stay until we hear from Troy."

"Oh of course, that's the plan. It shouldn't be long now. Even in war time, the mail has to get through eventually, doesn't it?"

"One would certainly hope so. I guess that depends upon how many boats are still getting from there to here. About going to London....you know that we would miss you terribly, but Ian and I would be the first to understand."

She dropped her gaze and paused, then lifted her face to look into his eyes.

"I feel as if I need to ask you this question, although you may not like it."

"Go ahead and ask away, Margaret. You've never had anything but my best interests at heart."

"What are your feelings for Doreen, I mean, your *real* feelings? I guess what I'm asking is, do you know where this friendship is going - if indeed it is only a friendship?"

Now it was Neil's turn to lower his head as he considered her words carefully.

"If I told you that my *feelings* for Doreen were always and only plutonic, I'd be lying. And I could never lie to you, Margaret. But if you're asking if I've acted upon those feelings, or even expressed them to Doreen, then the answer is 'no'. I'll admit it's been hard at times; she truly is a remarkable and beautiful woman. But my parents and Aunt Ida put the fear of God into me when it came to being able to look at myself in the mirror and liking myself when I went to bed at night. I'd never do anything to hurt Doreen, nor would I compromise what I think is right, even if that means keeping my emotions, and anything else, at bay."

Margaret laughed.

"You're a fine, refreshing man, Neil Henderson, even if you've never quite had a taste for English tea."

"Jeez, talk about changing the subject. And just how did you know I prefer coffee?"

"I just knew, that's all."

Margaret returned to her task. Neil began speaking about his future plans in London, but she wasn't really listening, her mind drifting back to a scene in their garden. She wondered if Doreen would make it back to their cottage before Neil left, then shook her head with the realization that Neil would most certainly wait for her.

"You okay, Margaret?"

"Yes, dear. Just a bit weary. I think I'll go to bed early tonight."

October 22, 1940

How dreadfully depressed I feel tonight! I know that I'm just going through another time of self-pity and that this time will pass. Still, that doesn't help at this moment, which is why I decided to make this journal entry. I long to be back in our flat in Croydon with Colin's arms wrapped around me and our daughter sprawled across my lap. God, how dismal all this has turned out to be! Not knowing if Colin is living a hell on earth or whether he is looking down from heaven, never to hold me again. Sometimes, I think I cannot bear another day without him. And to be without my daughter hurts more than I could ever describe. I can often feel her little hands, their fingers twirling my hair in corkscrews, her sweet face pressing on mine with innocent and unexpected kisses. To bear a child and be separated from her is my *hell on earth. I often wonder what Colin would think of the decision that I, and subsequently Neil, made to protect her and if he'd done things differently. The sad truth is, I am ashamed to admit that some of Colin's traits are beginning to blur in my mind. One crisp memory I still have is his touch and I fear that it will fade in time, too. I can only hope and pray that the visions and voice of Meghan do not elude me as well. That would be truly unbearable. I cannot write anymore this night. My spirit is in despair. Where, oh God, is your loving Hand in this place and time? How could you leave me so alone?! Doreen*

November 9, 1940

The leaf rake made a rhythmic swishing noise as it moved back and forth across the O'Connor's front garden. Neil had spent the entire morning clearing out leaves that were beginning to compost under the bushes. Margaret peered out of the front window at times, wanting to instruct him to leave the decaying debris so that her rose bushes would be well fed and protected over the winter months. Instead, she kept her distance, not wanting to disturb him. If doing this manual labor would help clear his mind about his future plans in London, then she wanted to allow him some peace and quiet. As soon as he heard again from his aunt and brother, he would no doubt make plans for his departure. He would tell them his plans when he was ready. As the day wore on, she finally stepped outside, her apron over her housedress and a towel flung across her shoulder.

"Neil, it's time for a bit of lunch. Why don't you come inside for some potato soup? You know that mine is the best!"

"Margaret, you are so right to boast! Of course I'll be in. Just give me a few minutes to finish this side of the garden. Besides, I see the postman down the way. I'll wait and get the mail from him."

Neil waited impatiently, avoiding "pleasantries" when the postman arrived, then disappeared around the back of the house. He sat down on the stone bench, worn from time and elements, unaware of Margaret peering intently at him through the kitchen window. He tore open the envelope scribbled in Troy's familiar handwriting. The writing was legible, but distinctly in his brother's hurried fashion.

<pre>
                                    September 1940
     Dear Neil,

     Hi old one! Hope you're dodging the bombs over
     there and staying out of trouble- or least dodging
     bombs…You know what they say about Americans in
     the U.K.: overpaid, oversexed, over there. Ha!
     All is well here. Meghan is doing great. She and
     Aunt Ida have really hit it off. I think Meghan is
     keeping the old lady young and on her toes - she's
     quite the funny little imp. It's hard to scold her
     for anything - all she has to do is look at you
     with those blue eyes and that one dimple and it's
     all over! She doesn't eat much, but Auntie says
     that's normal for her age. She sure manages in the
     cookie department! She still calls them biscuits
     - took us a while to get used to that.
     Auntie took her out shopping one day and
     "Munchkin" asked for the loo. Auntie said all the
     old ladies in the dress shop laughed. Guess this
     language thing is a challenge after all!
     My job's going well - not much hope for
     advancement just now, but hell, who needs to work
     any harder?! I've got a new gal! She's not one
</pre>

I'd bring home to Aunt Ida, but you should see her legs! Actually, sounds like you should see any female's legs. What are you doing over there - going for a degree in celibacy?! I never hear you talk about women - you're making me nervous. Except for Meghan's Mom. God Neil, isn't her husband still MIA? Even you're not that much of a jerk, are you?

Well anyway, don't worry about the kid. She's really fun and well behaved. She's teaching me a few manners and making Aunt Ida laugh a lot. It's good that you got her outta that danger zone. Speaking of danger, take care of yourself, you dog. Couldn't stand the thought of not having you to torment.

Write.

Love, Troy

P.S. I'll have Meghan dictate a letter to her Mom, if I know where to send it. Let me know.

Neil leaned his head on the back of the cold stone bench, sighing in relief. He reread his brother's rare attempt to moralize. He shook his head, shoved the letter back into the envelope and bounded into the kitchen like a schoolboy.

"Margaret, We've got news! I finally got a letter from Troy, one he wrote back in September. Meghan's doing great! Sounds like she's thriving over there, certainly out of harm's way."

"That is wonderful news - just what we've been waiting to hear."

"And there was more in the postman's bag, a letter from Mrs. Markham, addressed to Doreen. You did say Doreen's arriving tomorrow, didn't you?"

"Yes, dear, that's what her last letter to us said."

"Well, I can't wait to give her the news on Meghan. I'll keep trying to phone her until I get through. She deserves to know *today*."

"Yes dear, you're probably right. Just leave Mrs. Markham's letter on the telephone table. I'll dish up our soup now. It isn't often that you're here in the middle of the day and I'd like to enjoy some conversation with my lunch – and hear all about Meghan's 'goings-on'."

They finished their lunch amidst lively talk, their spirits lifted by the recent mail. Neil spent the rest of the day looking at maps and taking notes, forgetting his garden duties. Margaret checked on him as the evening wore

159

on, smiling at his intense concentration – and glad her rose bushes were spared any more intrusion.

November 9, 1940

I'm ready to leave the Convent in the morning for Oxford and I can hardly wait! I was able to receive a phone call from Neil this afternoon. He said Meghan is thriving over there and that his Aunt Ida is so taken with her. I know she's in good hands, and that is at least a great comfort to me. It will be wonderful to visit with the O'Connor's. I'm also looking forward to seeing Neil. The stars are so bright tonight, a rare occasion at this time of year. I keep staring at them and wondering who else is seeing the same stars. How many are clinging to the hope and gathering the brightness of the stars to sustain them in any darker hours to come? Yet tonight I'll try to think of grace and hope amidst this darkness. Even if I'm the only one who is. Doreen

Ian O'Connor closed his shop early and met Neil and Margaret near the train station well before Doreen's train from Hempstead arrived. It gave them the chance to spend some time in the University commons, absorbing the serenity of the ancient stone buildings, as well as the bustling of students weaving in and out of classes. The November sun was still warm and a slight breeze brought down the leaves that clung tentatively to their branches. When Doreen arrived, hallos and hugs were given right away and a few tears followed. They all climbed into the rusted, small Bentley automobile, borrowed from a neighbor. There was just enough petrol to get them home to the cottage.

Doreen stepped gingerly from the vehicle and stopped at the front stoop, still aware of her recovering leg.

"Honestly, Margaret, there were times that I thought I would never return here. I'm so happy to be back. I'm so grateful that you and Ian – and Neil came to retrieve me. It's wonderful to be showered with all this attention."

"My dear, you don't know how many times we have pictured you sitting in our front room. I believe we may have willed you back here."

Doreen stepped into the cottage, leaving her suitcase by the stairs and heading straight to the kitchen, her favorite spot. Soon the teakettle was boiling and there was much chatter and commotion by the warm auger stove. It was an obvious attempt to cover up the absence of Meghan and Doreen felt a bit queasy inside. Suddenly Neil got up and made his way to the stairway.

"I'll take your case up to the room, so you can freshen up whenever you wish."

"Thanks, Neil. I think I'll try the stairs and wash up a bit before I help Margaret with dinner."

"No need to worry about helping Margaret. Ian is making his one and only dish, scrambled eggs and fried fish. Make sure you brag on his efforts, he seems quite proud of this meal."

Doreen tilted her head back, laughing at the vision of Ian making a proper mess in Margaret's kitchen.

Neil sat down in the only chair in her room, the very old hard-backed one, not at all comfortable but sentimental to the O'Connor's. He dropped his head slightly before speaking, while Doreen began to unpack.

"Doreen, I've made a decision that I wanted to share with you, as it may affect how easily I receive letters from Troy and my Aunt Ida."

He continued without giving Doreen a chance to comment.

"I've decided to go to London, to see what I can do there in the war effort. You know that there will be no more evacuations of children, at least not ones that end up on a boat, and there are so few left to place out in the country. I have to do something to help and I feel sort of useless now, staying in Oxford. Although it will be hard to leave the O'Connor's, I think the timing is right. That means that I will need to find a new permanent address in London, or else I can have their letters sent directly to you. What do you think?"

Doreen didn't know why, but his news made her heart feel heavy, as though she just acquired a new burden to bear. It was her first night in this secure and familiar environment, and now she was being asked to consider a new set of circumstances, even though they weren't hers. She turned around to face him, her expression revealing her sadness.

"Neil, so soon? I don't know what to say. I just got here and I was looking forward to spending time with all of you. I suppose I understand your position, but it all seems so sudden. Can you at least stay for a week or two?"

Doreen bit her lip, only just conscious of her own wish coming through her request.

"I don't know, Doreen. I suppose it will take me a little while to secure some kind of official business in the City. I guess I'll take it day by day for the next week or so and see what comes available. I know there are lots of jobs to be done, but I need to secure some kind of salary for whatever I take on. Gotta feed my voracious appetite, you know."

No matter what the situation, Neil always seemed able to inject a bit of humor, Doreen mused. It was one thing she was really beginning to not only expect, but admire as well.

"Yes, I keep forgetting that you're without any British subsidies! Poor man, forced to make it in this world on your own. Somehow I think you'll always manage just fine in that area."

Doreen smiled broadly, hoping he hadn't taken any offense at her good-natured teasing. His quiet chuckling assured her that he hadn't. It was a strange moment, as though they had been friends for a long time with a history of banter and innocent barbs.

"So Doreen, have you made any immediate plans or will you stay put here in Oxford for a while?"

"I'm not really sure. Everything's so jumbled at the moment. I'm certainly in need of something purposeful to fill my time. I love the O'Connor's, but I can't see myself staying here for any length of time. It's too hard to be here without Meghan."

Neil lowered his head and let her words sit in silence.

"Anyway, I would like to get back into some kind of nursing or medical assistance. God knows there's a need. It seems selfish for me to sit around and wait for answers that may never come. Besides, working will make the days go faster and hopefully, living with war more bearable."

"I think you're a wise woman. I only wish I could ease the pain this war has already cost you."

Doreen walked over to him and placed her hand on his chest.

"You know, Neil, I could go with you to London. At the very least, I could look up Mrs. Markham and see what she's up to. What do you think?"

Suddenly, Neil's eyes lit up and he bounded out of the room, calling out as he went.

"Doreen! I nearly forgot! You got a letter yesterday from Mrs. Markham. I'll bring it up to you."

Neil's footsteps rumbled through the house as he skipped down the stairs and grabbed the envelope from the telephone table. Margaret put her mending into her sewing bag and folded her hands on her lap, pondering the scenario that was taking place. She followed his movements with a somber expression as he raced back up the stairs to Doreen's room.

"Margaret, I need a bit help out here," a voice from the kitchen boomed. "I can't find the big iron skillet. Where the devil did you put it?"

"I'll be right there, Ian. Honestly, love, you couldn't find a rock in a stone fence!"

Her husband's plea interrupted the worrisome thoughts that nagged her as she heard animated voices coming from Doreen's bedroom.

"Neil, this is great news! I know I'll find work in London and perhaps I can help you as well."

"Are you sure you want to tackle this job thing with me in tow?"

Doreen bit her lip and nodded.

"I'm sure. Quite sure."

Dinner was filled with lively conversation and lots of "catching up." When the first lull in the conversation came, Margaret asked the two questions that she and Ian had been anxious to ask earlier.

"Doreen, we've wanted to ask you before about your conversation with Lieutenant Lawrence. Neil confided from one of your letters the disappointing outcome of your meeting with him, but have you heard anything more from the man or from the War Department?"

"No, Margaret, not a thing. If the lieutenant did try to contact me after the initial bombings, he didn't get through. I still don't know any more. If ever I get any news, you'll be the first to know. I appreciate all your prayers and concern."

Doreen's voice trailed off and there was another quiet moment before Margaret spoke.

"We were also concerned my dear, about the letter from your friend, Mrs. Markham. We were hoping it didn't contain more bad news."

"No, no it didn't at all. This is actually good news for a change! She's back in London now, doing quite well and involved with the Civil Defense. She's been working all kinds of hours and was writing to see if I would be interested in joining her. She said my nursing skills would be put to good use and that trained personnel are in great demand. There are several first aid stations and rescue posts that need people to serve in all areas, even ambulance drivers. Can you imagine me driving an ambulance?! First I'd have to learn to drive anything!"

Laughter broke out around the table and Margaret rose to clear the dishes and start a pot of coffee especially for Neil. They were all looking for ways to keep the mood light and humorous, trying to fill the void that Meghan's empty chair left.

"Margaret, Ian, as long as we're talking about London, I think this is a good time to let you know that I'm planning to go back there and Doreen's going with me. I figure Mrs. Markham may have a lot of 'work connections' for both of us. We discussed it before dinner and Doreen says she's 'in.' The only thing is, we may have to stay here a while longer so I can borrow the neighbor's Bentley again and teach this Irish lassie to drive!"

Once again, laughter broke out and Ian got up to help Margaret with the dishes.

"Don't despair, Neil. I'll be the best student you ever had! It can't be that difficult. Besides, that old car has so many bumps and bruises, no one will ever notice a few more."

"You may be right about that, Doreen. I'll just make sure to put a crash helmet on before I get in the car with you behind the wheel!"

As soon as he said that, Neil swallowed hard. He hadn't meant to bring up the subject of "crashing" and he looked for any dismay on Doreen's face. Her beautiful blue eyes did her talking more often than not, and they still danced with enthusiasm.

The sky grew very dark as chores were finished, and Neil and Doreen stepped outside in the dank, chilly night. The garden looked abandoned, though Doreen knew that it would resurrect again in the spring, despite its deadened appearance. They walked away from the house and Neil broke the silence.

"Doreen, I know this is terribly difficult for you to be here without Meghan. It's been hard on all of us, but most assuredly you. I really don't know how you've managed; things have certainly not gone your way in these awful times."

Neil stared at Doreen's back as she dug her shoe into the leafy soil of Margaret's rose beds.

"What I'm hoping is that the next few months will bring you some peace and maybe even a moment or two of genuine rest, even if you work with the Civil Defense. God knows you deserve it."

He stepped closer as she turned around, her reaction a mystery in the shadows of the hour.

"I just want you to know that, for whatever it's worth, I'm there for you. You're really remarkable, and I consider it an honor to call you my friend. If there's ever anything I can do…"

Doreen moved up to Neil, putting her hands on his shoulders and leaning toward his face. She couldn't speak. She had nothing to say. She only knew that at this moment and in this place, she was inexplicably drawn to this man. There was no chance for realizing the impact of her action.

Reaching up to him, she drew him to her. There was silence except for unspoken apologies and possible regrets that would never be said. Neil leaned down to meet her and the kiss was a reality neither of them could understand nor avoid. There were no thoughts, no mind-stirring analysis, no future visions. There was only that minute when the blackness of war and circumstance were overcome and even forgotten. That minute when time, in all its fullness, stood perfectly still and only their breathing in and out was part of the warm and comforting reality.

When they pulled away, Neil caught his breath, staring at this woman who had stirred his very soul.

"Doreen, I... I don't know what to say, except that I'm not sure how that happened. I have so much affection and respect for you. Please, for..."

"There's nothing you have to say, Neil. I needed that moment, in just that way. That's all. There's no more to say."

She reached up and stroked the back of her hand against his face, unable to tell whose tear she wiped away.

Somewhere above them a light flickered, a curtain parted and the shadow of a woman appeared. The silhouette remained a few moments longer, then backed away from the window.

Margaret had the teakettle on when Neil and Doreen entered the kitchen. They smiled at her and watched as she finished cleaning up and setting the milk bottles outside on the ledge. They knew it was too late for a cuppa tea. It was too late to do anything but make their way up to their respective rooms and hope for a night filled with sleep too deep for dreams.

Without a lot of other distractions, Doreen's driving lessons went well. She felt fairly confident after two weeks and applied to the Motor Vehicle Bureau for her license. Margaret and Ian had a special dinner, with a sugarless cake for dessert, to celebrate her success. It was also a "farewell" dinner as their houseguests were both leaving for London in the morning.

Try as they might, the evening wasn't as jovial as they had hoped for. As they finished their meal, Margaret stood, wiping her hands on her stained cobbler apron.

"Listen you two, Ian and I will clean up tonight. I think it would be wise for you both to get packed up and ready for London. Morning will come earlier than you think."

"Thanks, Margaret. I do have a few things to do yet, and I'm sure that Neil has papers and maps and more papers to stash somewhere in his case."

Doreen smiled at him with a hint of mischievousness in her eyes. He dug his fist into his chest, as though wounded by the comment, until both Margaret and Ian broke out in laughter. Neil and Doreen went up the stairs together, bantering back and forth. Ian began filling the sink with soapy water.

"What's on your mind, Margaret? You've been as quiet as a goose-down feather today."

"Sorry, dear. I'm worried, that's all."

"Worried about their safety or their relationship?"

"Ian O'Connor! How'd you know?"

"I've eyes haven't I, woman? Just because I don't say as much as you doesn't mean I don't *know*. I've been concerned about those young folks."

"They're not so young, that's the problem. They know the attraction's there. I think they don't know what to do with it. It worries me sick, what with her Colin still missing. I know he's most likely presumed dead by the authorities, yet I've no idea what Doreen thinks. She never talks about it – doesn't even mention his name except in reference to a memory including Meghan. I don't know – I'm not sure how right all this 'going to London together' is. I'm afraid they're in over their heads."

Ian walked over to his wife, wrapping his arms around her shoulders and sighing deeply.

"Listen my love, it's not for us to say. About Colin, remember that each person deals with tragic circumstances differently. She may be grieving for him every day, in her own quiet way. We just have to trust that Neil and Doreen will use their best judgment."

He paused, not sure how to finish.

"Margaret, may God forgive my bold assumption, but I don't believe Colin is coming back. Then again, I've been wrong many times in my life - except, of course, when I married you. That was the single most right thing I've ever done."

The seasoned lovers shared a brief and familiar kiss. Margaret's thoughts, though, were on the recent memory of a long and passionate embrace in their own back garden.

The night ended too soon and the pain of more separations painted the morning sky with searing reds and oranges. The O'Connor's watched the train leaving Oxford for London, once again waving until the tracks were empty. Unable to move, they stood on the platform while the starlings circled overhead, screaming their demands for any leftover crumbs.

Margaret straightened her back and stared up at them, focusing on their eyes. She was glad she had nothing more to give that would satisfy their gluttonous appetite.

CHAPTER TWENTY TWO

London was bustling as the train from Oxford pulled into Victoria Station. Passengers scrambled on as others stepped off, their bags in tow and their faces tired and drawn. The war activity had increased the already fast pace of the City, and its streets looked as weary as those who walked them. The noise in the crowded pubs disguised the fatigue of the ancient stone and timber, the Battle of Britain having aged the very walls and floors.

Doreen and Neil walked briskly to the nearest pub and ordered an early lunch from the bar. She was aware of Neil's eyes on her as she stared at the table against the back wall. She shook her head briefly, trying to erase the thoughts that now plagued her as her appetite suddenly dwindled. How could they have chosen the same pub where she had met with Graham Lawrence?! How could she sit and eat a meal with the memories of that conversation flooding her mind? She had actually enjoyed the train ride, chatting with Neil about their new positions with the Civil Defense program. Now she was sharply reminded of her Colin and his fate. Still no word. Still not knowing whether he was dead or alive. She felt guilty, as her hope for his return was fading with each passing week. Her daughter was a continent away, her husband missing, and she had spent the morning in pleasant conversation!

She closed her eyes and saw her Mum's smile, a brief moment that sent shivers down her back. Yet her Mum's smile spread as her loving face appeared fully. Doreen knew there were no audible words, yet she heard the statement more clearly than the din of voices at the bar.

It's all right, my Lamb. This is the right thing for you.

The moment was gone. A breeze caught the menu board, rocking it slightly and Doreen opened her eyes, frozen. Another moment passed before she turned to Neil without speaking. He carried their drinks to a table and Doreen managed a smile and a "thank you." They ate in silence until he spoke.

"Does coming back here to London give you pain, Doreen?"

"No, not really. It's just that this pub is the place I met with Lieutenant Lawrence."

"God, Doreen. I'm so sorry. If only I'd known…"

"Don't apologize, Neil. I didn't realize it myself until we got in here."

"Are you sure you're alright with this living in London bit and doing this kind of work? It's not at all too late to get back on the train to Oxford."

Doreen managed some enthusiasm in her voice and raised her eyes to his as she spoke.

"No, Neil. I'm fine here. It's good for me to be busy and I'm excited about my new career. I only wish Meghan were here."

Her voice trailed off.

"I know. I'm so sorry. Damn. I'm really so sorry, Doreen."

She nodded. There were moments of silence before Neil broke the quiet with his humor.

"By the way, are you sure you'll not be adding more men to the injured lists, once you get behind the wheel?!"

Laughter broke the tension and Doreen picked up her fork. Maybe she could eat just a little after all.

They each managed to find a dormitory room at one of the larger hospitals near Westminster. It was close to the Unit Station and very convenient to their work and city amenities, making it easy to immerse themselves in daily routines and activities. Doreen discovered that Neil's talents, though not of a medical nature, were varied and supportive. With her driving an ambulance and treating the injured and his skill in handling paperwork and organizing the runs, they were a team from the start. New challenges blew in on the winds of winter and uncomfortable pretenses fell away like the brittle leaves on the trees.

It was a damp and misty afternoon in late February, 1941, when Doreen and Mrs. Markham met for tea at a café near the Thames.

"Do tell me, dear, how is your new career coming along?"

"It's very challenging, though a bit disheartening at times. Sometimes we transport and treat men who've been rescued and transferred here from the port towns. There are days when it's quite dismal. Still, all and all, I feel I'm really contributing to the war effort and that helps me to fall asleep at night."

Doreen sighed and twisted the single ring she still wore.

"Actually, Mrs. Markham, I'm hoping to find Colin in one of my transports. I know it sounds impossible, but I can't help but think that someday I will lean down to treat a wounded man, and Colin's eyes will look back at me."

Doreen peered into her teacup as though the hot liquid would speak her unfinished words.

"My dear, you have every right to go on hoping - and praying - for Colin's return. My only fear in your continued hope is that you will cease to live the life in front of you now. You have gone through extraordinary changes lately and you must learn to embrace the here and now."

"I'm trying. I'm trying so hard not to forget and sometimes…God forgive me, not to remember. Remembering is too hard."

Doreen took a long sip from the delicate china cup and cradled her fingers around it. The clock on the plate-decorated wall chimed three times and the two women glanced at each other and at the café patrons. Mrs. Markham took a biscuit from the porcelain tray, looking at Doreen straight on.

"Doreen Bailey Bennett! You know that when an Irish gale blows through a village, it gathers the good for its own and forces the evil off the nearest cliff. When this horrible war is over and the evil has plummeted, your Colin may not be beside you. But you will always feel him when the wind blows. You must keep your eyes and ears – and your heart open to experience the beauty and wonder that the gale has left behind in the village. You only need to 'be still and listen'."

Doreen's moistened eyes lit up at the Biblical words and she smiled. It was so like Mrs. Markham to remind her of her roots, of her days at the Convent, of Mary Catherine. That's exactly what the Mother Superior would have said.

"And now my dear, if you don't mind my asking, how is Mr. Henderson? I've heard tales of your medical teamwork; how is your friendship?"

Mrs. Markham had rarely been the cause of Doreen's blushing, but this time was an unavoidable exception.

"I….I don't know exactly what to tell you. We've shared a lot of difficult experiences, good and bad. Neil is…so very different from anyone I've ever known. He's so casual and unpretentious, and yet very scholarly and actually sensitive. I don't know, maybe he's just very American."

Both women giggled and the patrons at the nearest table looked over at them.

"Yes well, Americans are certainly *different* but rather nice, I think. Not so much stuff and nonsense, if you know what I mean."

Doreen nodded as she nibbled on the last lemon biscuit, washing it down with nearly cold tea.

"Mrs. Markham, you are the dearest friend I have. As well, I cherish the O'Connor's, and of course Sister Mary Catherine. Yet, *you* are the link to my past and you seem to understand me better than most. How I treasure your being here with me today. I needed your advice. I really just needed to hear your voice. You connect my past and my present."

"I only hope your *future* will be what you richly deserve, as you have always been a favorite of mine. Look for joy in a world that will meet you with cynicism. Don't let the presence of evil overpower your sense of goodness. Cherish the moment, it's all any of us are guaranteed."

The advice spent and intimacies revealed, Doreen paid the bill and they walked into the deepening shadow of the late winter evening. Doreen found herself walking with a lighter step as she made her way to the hospital flat. Her thoughts centered on Mrs. Markham's parting comment. Yet the legend of the Irish gale loomed larger than the actual wind that nearly pushed her down the streets to the empty place she now called "home."

The fog rolled in and out of Trafalgar Square for the next week and the pigeons continued their staunch parade on the monument. New orders were issued from the Civil Defense to their medical teams that more teams were needed at the coastal towns and this news made Doreen's heart beat faster. Perhaps this was a sign that she would find news of her Colin in one of these port cities! She prepared her ambulance for the trip, checking inventory and stocking in supplies. Neil watched her enthusiasm without comment as he sorted through stacks of orders and medical forms. Her face had an excited glow, like that of a young girl on the first day of school. They finished their tasks just before dusk, closing the ambulance doors and standing back to envision their journey.

"Doreen, I want you to get a good night's sleep so you don't crack up this big boat on wheels. We've gotta lot of ground to cover."

Neil grinned and placed his hand on her shoulder, squeezing it lightly.

"Neil Henderson, I should give you the job of driving this old beast – you'd never tease me again!"

Then she paused, her forehead wrinkling slightly.

"Seriously, why didn't you apply to drive instead of doing the truly harder job of keeping all that paperwork in order?"

Neil's eyes focused on her chestnut hair, shining with red streaks as it captured the pinpoint light from the street lamp. He placed his hand over his chest.

"The old ticker, my dear, the old ticker. Didn't want to chance some bizarre medication lapse and put you and others in a ditch."

He laughed and the color rose in Doreen's cheeks. He took a step back from her and sobered his expression.

"It's okay, Doreen. It's never really been much of a problem, but I don't want to ever jeopardize someone's safety."

Doreen lifted her eyes to his, seeing compassion and yet hearing Colin's voice echoing in the reply she'd been given.

"You're a thoughtful man, Neil. Underneath all that laughter is actually a sensitive soul."

"Now you're making *me* blush – and I haven't done that since my fourth grade teacher caught me with a National Geographic filled with photos of half-nude natives."

Shadows of dim streetlights cast by the waning, evening light resembled skinny beings with no heads or feet, suspended across the pavement like some bizarre carnival scene. The dampness of a February night in London was seeping from the dark stone buildings, wrapping its residents in a blanket of chill. Doreen pulled her heavy wool cardigan more tightly around her and turned to face the monument across the wide avenue.

"It's time for us to move on, Neil. Time to hit the road, as they say. I really believe our most important work lies ahead of us."

Doreen stopped to reconsider her last words.

"It's not that evacuating children was less important, but it was a task that was short-lived and I think we did it well, with a lot of help and direction from others. But this next assignment…I don't know… it feels larger in scope and longer in duty. I'm a bit frightened, but it feels right."

Neil didn't respond with words, nodding his head, watching the debris blow across the pavement as the night wind intensified. They stood there, mute. Doreen finally moved toward Neil and spoke.

"Let's go. We both need some rest. I feel tired and weary enough to actually fall asleep easily tonight. No hot milk for me."

She tried to smile, but her attempt was unsuccessful. Neil's eyes stayed focused on the pavement below him as the two friends made their way back to their flats. They walked without words, their shoulders too far apart to touch. Their hearts too heavy and confused to communicate in any way.

June 1941

The warm sun had beat down upon the small coastal village of Gull Bay for most of the day, prompting many folks to take a longer than usual afternoon tea. The scourges of war seemed far away, even as the efforts of transporting incoming wounded soldiers went on around them. It was a paradoxical scene, and one whose strangeness was lost upon the villagers. Tending to gardens and figuring out how best to make a small portion of tinned meat paste last for several meals were the prevalent activities, except for those folks involved in Civil Defense and other "official" war business. The continuous bombing and fires in the city of London did not affect the coastal villagers directly.

Only a few heads turned away from their outdoor repartee to glance at the incoming ambulance. It was a common enough sight and sound in this fishing town, whose ancient history had recorded many struggles and whose recent war involvement had begun to harden its villagers. Still, there were a few eyes and ears that noticed without comment the "new" victims of battle. They knew that most of the men would have received emergency treatment from British medics on the continent, if they were lucky, then transferred by plane or ship to the nearest port town with a decently equipped hospital. Those injured on English soil were treated while in transport. Once stabilized, the wounded were transferred to larger towns where hospitals and makeshift infirmaries could handle further surgeries and convalescence.

Doreen hadn't seen the faces of the two men that she and Neil were taking to the small hospital on the edge of Gull Bay. She only knew that their injuries were severe enough to warrant stabilizing them before moving them inland to a larger facility. They were greeted by a doctor and one nurse who threw open the back doors of the vehicle with routine speed. Doreen and Neil scrambled to the rear to help load the men onto stretchers. The months of working this job had left little room for shock or aversion, yet one man caught all their attention. It was obvious that this soldier had suffered more than a mortar attack or a gunshot wound. More than the injuries of someone having ejected from a plane or having crawled through mine fields. For the first time in several months, Doreen turned her head away and retched. What merciful God would have left this man to *live*?! Why, in all the horror of this war, would a Creator not have taken him Home sooner?! Her anger pumped adrenaline, making her feel even sicker. She let the others wheel him and the other soldier through the hospital doors and stood behind the ambulance to let her stomach recover. The medics in the field had obviously done what they could to get him on a medical transport plane, but their efforts paled at the severity of his injuries. His face was unrecognizable with parts of it gone. His limbs lay limp and dangling and his chest was covered in a blood-soaked bandage oozing with his own insides. His shirt had been torn at the shoulder and the huge welts and bruising was demonic. It was hard to tell where the enemy gunshots had left off and the tortuous Nazi beatings had begun.

Doreen started to regain her composure when a new thought flashed across her mind. What if that had been Colin?! A new wave of nausea spread over her and she crumpled on the pavement in an effort to avoid blacking out. My God! What have we been reduced to?! Where is the sense in any of this? Her shoulders fell and she thought for a moment that tears would begin, but they did not. The whole scene was utterly too horrid to consider any further and she steeled herself against her own revulsion. She stood up and strode into the hospital to find the patient, and to find Neil. It was time to let a doctor do what he could. It was time for them to move on again.

Doreen and Neil hadn't been in London for several weeks and now the roses of summer were in full bloom. It seemed so odd to have such beauty filling the streets of the City, while reports of the war splashed their ugly pictures and predictions across the newspapers. Doreen walked up the steps of the Royal Navy Department and knocked on the door of Captain Hollingsworth. A younger voice answered.

"Come in, please. May I help you?"

"Oh, yes well, I was hoping to find Captain Hollingsworth here. Is he about?"

"No, Miss, I'm afraid not. He's not uh..... not here anymore. What I mean is, you'll not find him about anymore."

The young officer frowned slightly at his own words, knowing that ugly secrets were never divulged from these offices. The public was never to know what tragic consequences were wreaked upon men whose truest enemies lurked only in their minds.

"I can leave a note here for the new Captain. He's out just now, but he comes in often to check for any messages. If you just write down the information you need, I'll see that he gets your note. Would that be satisfactory?"

"Yes, I suppose I don't have much choice, do I?"

Doreen instantly regretted her words. This war was making her and everyone else edgy and rude.

"I'm sorry, officer. I meant no disrespect. It's just that I've not heard a word yet about my husband who was reported missing in action after the Battle of Dunkirk. Is there any way you could check on his status for me? I'd be most grateful. I'm not in London very often now and communication from the smaller towns is a problem."

The officer walked silently over to a file cabinet and pulled open a drawer.

"What is your husband's name, Miss?"

"It's Bennett. Lieutenant Colin Bennett."

Doreen fiddled with the strap on her small handbag as the young man pulled a file from the drawer.

"I'm sorry, Mrs. Bennett. Your husband is still the same status. There's no indication of where he is, or the circumstances surrounding his disappearance. He's definitely still listed as MIA. I wish there was more I could tell you, I'm sorry."

He closed the file drawer quietly and turned to face her disappointed eyes. It wasn't the first time he'd seen that look and it wouldn't be the last.

Doreen's words came out small and tentative.

"Thank you, officer. I appreciate your time."

She turned toward the door, then looked over her shoulder at the young man .

"Do take care of yourself."

It was the only thing she could think of to say.

Neil was waiting for her on a bench at the train station. He didn't need to ask the results of her inquiry, as her disappointment was evident. She sat down beside him and laid her head back against the slats. Without comment, he handed her a letter that had been waiting for her at the large hospital where they had begun their work so many months before. Doreen's eyes brightened up and a smile spread across both their faces.

"It's from Meghan! Well, at least the name 'mum' is in her own handwriting. Isn't she getting to be a clever girl?!"

"Go on now, open it! Did Troy or Aunt Ida do the writing for her? If it's Troy, you'll never be able to read it."

"It looks like Aunt Ida wrote her words down, they look a little wiggly, like an older person would write."

Neil could stand it no longer and scooted closer to her on the hard bench. They read the funny letter together, laughing at Meghan's comical way of expressing herself and smiling at the honesty of a five year old.

```
Dear Mummy,
    Hi to my favorite mummy. I miss you so much.
I know you miss me, too, because you always said
you couldn't sleep right without me around. So
you must be very tired and I hope you find a bunny
like Max to sleep with you. He helps me a lot.
Except when he wakes me up to go to the toilet in
the middle of the night. Auntie keeps a light on
for me so we don't get lost. But really, I think
she keeps the light on for her because she gets
up a lot, too! Now she is laughing. She says you
probably don't need to know when she goes to the
toilet. I like it here very much, even though I
always miss you. I have two best friends, Peggy
and Kate. But they don't share as much as I do.
Uncle Troy says I am the best sharer in the world.
But I think he just says that because he likes me.
He took me to the movies to see Dorothy and her
dog. So now he calls me "Munchkin" because I am
short like the little people in the show. It was
very scary and Uncle Troy said not to tell you we
went there. But Aunt Ida says it's okay for me to
tell.  We have fun going to the park and now I
can ride a bicycle! I only fell down two times. I
love you. I love you.  From, Meghan
```

Doreen smoothed her hands across the page trying to feel Meghan's fingers on it. They both laughed at the picture she had drawn at the bottom of the page. It looked like Troy and Meghan at the park, with a bicycle leaning up against a tree. She had colored red hearts around the tree and her own head was the largest thing on the paper.

"I'm assuming that her self-portrait is a good thing."

Doreen smiled and nodded.

"Yes, Neil. It's a very good thing. Looks like Meghan has a healthy self-esteem and confidence. Other than missing me a lot, I don't think she's been too adversely affected. I, on the other hand, feel as though I'm missing a whole chunk of my life – because I'm missing her growing and changing each day."

Neil shifted uneasily and their silence was much too loud. She stared at the paper in her hands, finally folding it and slipping it into her bag. They ate a quick sandwich and boarded a train bound for Newcastle and their next assignment.

October 1941

Ian turned the volume knob on his old wireless set and leaned his head closer to the speaker. Outside, the winds of an October evening were gathering strength, promising a chill too deep for a late night walk. The voice of the newscaster was familiar, its very sound bringing a little comfort to an otherwise anxious listening audience. The bombing of London proper had slowed since May, yet there were still casualties reported. Ian shifted in his chair as Margaret came down the steps dressed in her nightgown.

"Ready for bed a wee bit early tonight, aren't you love?" He lowered the radio volume as he straightened up to face her.

"I suppose so. I don't know, love. I feel a bit disheartened tonight. Perhaps going to bed early is a good cure."

"Perhaps. It may just be that the dark and dank of Autumn is creeping into your head as well as your bones. Don't let it, my dear. We've a long way to go with this war, and you mustn't let the season get you down.

"What's the latest news?"

"About the same. It's not going well. Hitler's attack on Russia last June has made this war so big in scope. Not to mention how that may change Japan's course from their pact with Russia last spring. It's mucky, all right. I just don't see any early conclusion. I believe we're all in for a long haul."

"Oh Ian, I just worry for Doreen and Neil's safety. And of course, I can't help wondering what's become of Colin. Then there's little Meghan without her mummy. It's just so hard looking at so many lives affected in such dreadful ways."

"I know it's hard, Maggie. But we've got to keep strong. I think what we need is a bit of diversion. I say we go together to Oxford tomorrow and take in a cinema show after I close up the shop. Is it a date?"

"That would be lovely. I'll pack us a lunch in the morning and we can stop in at the fish shop for our supper. I feel better already."

"Good, my dear. Now you go on up to bed and I'll be upstairs in a little while. I just want to hear the end of this newscast."

Margaret leaned down and kissed her husband, then headed up to bed. Ian turned up the volume and sat listening until his eyes felt heavy enough to let sleep overcome his fear and dread.

Outside the wind gathered force, whipping the branches of brittle trees and creaking the windows with an eerie moan. The neighbor's dog whined to be let in and the milk bottles on the windowsills toppled, their shattering glass unheard against the growing gale.

Rockport, Massachusetts
December 7, 1941

Troy Henderson poured a hot cup of coffee from the pot on his aunt's stove and reached up to the cupboard above him. He knew there was still half a bottle of cheap whiskey left over from Aunt Ida's famous whiskey ball cookies. He enjoyed an occasional night out with friends from work and had certainly swallowed his share of beer on those nights. Yet, he never drank at home as Aunt Ida frowned upon having alcohol in her house. Troy was especially careful now that Meghan lived with them and had stolen his heart and his penchant for bad habits. But this night was different. His Aunt's radio blared from the front room, deep serious voices describing with interrupted sentences the horror of the morning. The Japanese had done the unthinkable and the United States had been dragged into the war they had run from for so long. Troy's mind was spinning at the thought of his immediate future. At the thought of his aunt's and Meghan's future. Joining up wasn't the question; it was a certainty. Just where and how and what branch were the only decisions he had to make. That and what to do about leaving his aunt with an active five year old girl, one who needed lots of care and extra attention. He was oddly aware of a strange heaviness in his chest, the weight of these decisions literally pressing down on him.

He poured the whiskey into his coffee and sat down on the green-stenciled wooden chair. He noticed for the first time how worn the pattern was on the kitchen set, and how the colors had faded and been scratched away by buckles and pans and time itself. He looked up at the cupboards, their handles soiled from constant touch, their hinges a dark and rusted amber. The window curtains above the sink were clean, but frayed from years of laundering. The paint around the single-domed light fixture was cracked and never touched up after the globe had been replaced. He realized with a wave of regret that he had never been very handy around the house. It was certainly in need of some fixing up. He took a long swallow of the bitter liquid, knowing that the house would not see any repairs in the near future, at least not from him. He picked up the "Extra" newspaper that still lay on the table, its front page smeared from the water that had seeped from the bottom of Aunt Ida's small poinsettia. His eyes grew wide with an idea, one that would make leaving for this war easier on him and his aunt. He moved to the drawer next to the sink and took out a small piece of paper and a pencil. He would put this advertisement in the local paper as soon as possible.

Wanted to hire: Live-in single woman, no children. Duties: Care for young girl and help elderly person. Qualifications: Must be professional, courteous, and love children. Inquire ASAP by phone at Jackson 20034.

Troy stuffed the paper in his shirt pocket and took the last swallow of his coffee. He got up slowly and walked into the front room where his aunt sat dabbing her eyes with a hankie. He could hear Meghan playing make-believe in her room, telling Max not to be afraid of the munchkins, that they would all have tea and scones together and the monkeys would not get them.

Aunt Ida sat beside the Christmas tree for a long while that evening, at first listening to Meghan and Troy chatter on about "new adventures and changes." As the evening wore on, their chatter quieted to the soft murmur of bedtime stories and finally to the sounds of muffled snores. She knew Troy had fallen asleep on Meghan's bed and she prayed that only Max the bunny would still be staring into the darkness, his eyes ever open to see everything, his soft terry body able to comfort without words. She unplugged the tree lights and pulled the worn afghan across her own body, knowing that tonight she could not sleep alone in her bed. The scent of pine mingled with cooking spices that were still on her clothes. Outside she could see snow softly beginning to fall, though her ears heard the flakes hit the ground like steel balls.

CHAPTER TWENTY THREE

January 1942

Somewhere on the east coast of England, Neil and Doreen sat quietly in a small cafe, staring down at plates of eggs with their hands cradling cold cups of coffee. Neil took a crumpled letter from his shirt pocket, reading its contents over again as Doreen focused on the blackness outside. He stared at the words, trying once more to grasp their full meaning.

December 1941

Dear Neil and Doreen,
Thought I'd write this to both of you, seeing as how you're working together all the time. Sure hope you guys are okay. We don't hear from you as often as we used to, but I guess it must be getting really difficult to get the news across the ocean. Just wanted to fill you in on the "happenings" around here. By the time you actually get this, I'm sure it will be well into the new year, so hope you were able to celebrate the holidays in some special way. I know Christmas must be especially hard. It wasn't too easy this side, either. I'm leaving for boot camp in two days. Joined up with the Navy. Couldn't stand the thought of traipsing around the hills and valleys of Europe, thought I'd take my chances on sloshing around on a ship. Sure hope I get my sea legs real fast. (What an ugly picture that paints - me hanging over the boat's side…)
Anyway, here's the scoop. Aunt Ida and I hired a wonderful, single woman to live here and take good care of them both. Her name is Beatrice Moore.

She's thirty-seven and recently moved to Rockport from northern California to "discover new places and faces," as she said. She gave me some letters of recommendation and everything seems in order. She and Meghan are really hitting it off. She does a little cooking if Auntie asks, otherwise she stays out of Auntie's turf and only does those chores that are on her "list." Munchkin really seems okay with all of these changes; she's quite the little trooper, that one.

You don't have to worry about Miss Beatrice. We did a lot of interviewing and she seems perfect for this job. Munchkin sure likes her. She and Miss B go out on day trips when the weather's good and go sledding when it snows. Miss B actually got Meghan a new PF Flier for Christmas, as my old sled was fairly worthless from years of abuse.

I don't know much else to tell you except that we're all doing okay through these difficult times. God, I sound like an old man. My former girlfriend says I acted like one.

Maybe I'm destined to be old before my time. I guess that beats the alternative of never growing old. Oops, sorry. That was a bit weird and maudlin. You two take care of yourselves and have some fun once in a while. Let me know your news via Aunt Ida. She'll forward my mail to a UPO address while I'm still stateside, unless it's a letter from my old girlfriend. Ha… (Aunt Ida didn't think much of her…) Be good. Write.

Love,
Troy

Doreen finally broke his reverie.

"Neil, what do you think this all means for Meghan? Is she in danger over there?"

"I don't think so. I'm sure it means that Troy will be shipping out soon. I really think Meghan will be fine with Aunt Ida."

"At least they're far away from the west coast. I just hope this doesn't mean a longer war."

"Actually, it means a war fought on more fronts. It'll mean our guys will be over here soon, fighting in France and Germany, as well as in the Pacific."

The conversation stopped as their eyes met briefly, but a blaring siren interrupted the moment. They took a quick gulp of coffee and grabbed some cold toast. The sky was still very dark as Doreen opened the ambulance door. The vehicle seemed to have taken on a life of its own overnight, one that was sinister and foreboding. She shivered and climbed in, pulled out the choke, and started it without comment to her teammate. Neil finished the toast and brushed his hands on his pants. As the ambulance sped away, its driver noticed that her partner was still brushing away crumbs that were long since gone.

The rain was streaming down steadily outside as Neil and Doreen leaned back in the torn and stained sofa, one of the few comforts in the Southend-on-Sea Hospital. The emergency runs had slowed in the past two days, allowing medical personnel a much-needed break. January had been a dismal month with days on end of rain and casualties coming in to several port towns. Doreen was glad to see February come, hoping that her spirits would improve with the new month. Yet it was the letter she held in her hand that lifted her from the doldrums. She caressed the paper, trying to envision Meghan's face, trying to hear her daughter's voice.

"I knew we'd hear from Troy sooner or later. Doreen, I'm sorry that it always takes so long to get word back and forth. I know you must go crazy sometimes, thinking about her and what she's doing, how she's growing up so fast."

"You don't have to keep apologizing to me, Neil. I know this whole situation is not your fault. I've told you that before. It just keeps getting more complicated and I get more frustrated. This bloody war has upset so many lives, destroying some and forever changing others."

Her voice trailed off and a phone rang down the hall, startling both of them.

"Doreen, I know it's not my fault – not really. There are so many times, though, that I wish I had never put Meghan on that ship. If only I'd waited just a couple more weeks, I'd never have had to make that decision at all."

"You can't continue to beat yourself up about it. You did what I asked you to do, to protect Meghan at all costs. None of us knew how long the bombings would last. London was hard hit for months after you sent her to safety. You of all people know there've been countless other bombings in outlying areas. Who knows if Oxford may still become a victim?! You made a very difficult choice and one I would have chosen had I been able to be there. I admit I was upset – even angry at first, but that was more about not getting to say 'goodbye' to her, plus I was still not quite in my right mind from the convent bombing. I'll always be grateful to you for taking action. Besides, it appears she's doing quite well with Aunt Ida and now Miss Beatrice, and I really think it's still safest for her to be stateside."

"I know in my head that you're right, but sometimes it's hard to accept."

They listened in silence to the water pelting the windows, willing their minds to clear and their tired backs to relax. In the distance, the changing pitch of a siren wailed its imminent arrival and the old sofa was abandoned.

They met the ambulance with two stretchers and threw open the back doors. Doreen retrieved a white, wooden case holding several drawers and questioned the medic who was feverishly working on one victim.

"Why haven't you opened this case for some morphine powders? What are you treating him with?"

Doreen's voice was high-pitched and agitated, not efficiently calm as it usually was in any emergency.

"Doreen, step back."

Neil's firm demand took her off guard and she backed away from the open doors, allowing the two men to transfer both victims to gurneys and wheel them inside. For a moment, she stood frozen, her eyes wide with disbelief at her own volatile reaction and Neil's harsh command. He was right. She needed to step back on this one. The letter from Troy had unnerved her more than she thought. It had transported her to a place where she could *see* Meghan, yet it had left her feeling as though she were only looking through a window, unable to reach inside and touch her daughter's face.

The sounds of the gurney's wheels clacked loudly on the linoleum and forced Doreen back to reality. She raced to catch up, vowing to concentrate first on the patients and apologize to Neil and the medic later. She spun into the small emergency cubicle, parting the curtains with a flick of her wrist.

The man that now lay on the hard, sheeted bed was moaning softly, his arms heavily bandaged and his shirt soaked with blood. She walked up beside him and turned to the medic for instructions.

"We need to stabilize him first before we continue any assessment. He's still in shock. His wounds are serious, but not immediately life-threatening."

Doreen began setting up an IV and caught sight of the man's face. It had been a lifetime ago, but she knew this face. She knew the curve of this jaw, the shape of his features. She stroked his matted hair and whispered softly, wanting only to comfort him, not frighten him with her sudden appearance.

"William. William, it's me, Doreen. I'm right here beside you, William."

She waited for any response, but the only sounds that came from his mouth were the soft involuntary moans of a nearly conscious man in excruciating pain.

She looked up at Neil, who was lifting the other victim onto a bed, then returned her gaze to her childhood friend. She and William had come full circle now. He had left Hempstead to follow a dream that was never fulfilled and she had left to follow hers only to have her dream interrupted. Her mum had left this earth too soon and his Da hadn't gone on to his reward soon enough. Now they both were in the same nightmare, unable to wake up from the horrors that had chased their rainbows until the colors all ran together, creating a dark and ugly shade. How she wished at this moment that at least his dream could have turned out differently. He had struggled so hard to break the stranglehold of disappointment that had choked his early life. Now he struggled for life itself.

Doreen finished her tasks in silence until the emergency doctor and two nurses flew into the room. She left as quickly as she'd entered, stopping only to wash her hands, glancing over her shoulder at the patient whose clothes were being cut away with careful precision.

Neil was waiting for her in the hallway. He didn't say anything, and for that Doreen was grateful. The rain had slowed to a fine mist and the evening set in reluctantly, the sun still trying desperately to break through the clouds and deepening shadows. The pungent, greasy smell of frying fish and chips hung in the damp air and the cries of seagulls covered the soft sobs that Doreen could not swallow.

Chapter Twenty Four

Dear Doreen and Neil,

It was good to hear from you. I wanted to put this note in with Meghan's, just to catch you up on things that she may never include in her " news." I know you've probably written many more letters to us than we actually receive, but I assure you that every one we get is treasured by your Munchkin. She makes me read them over and over to her. Aunt Ida has a little trouble writing and reading small print these days, so she asked me to do some of the "communicating" between us. You will be pleased to know that Meghan has learned her ABC's and can already count to twenty. She is very smart and a sweet child, too. Aunt Ida is strict about manners, so she is growing to be quite the fancy little lady. Aunt Ida even had a "formal" tea party for her, with several of her friends over for special cakes and finger sandwiches. It was quite a scene. I guess it's a fairly common practice for girls in this part of the east, a sort of training for later social introductions. At any rate, it was fun for the girls and especially fun for Aunt Ida. She's not as agile as she was a few months ago, so indoor activities are easier for her.

Now that the weather is nice, Meghan and I have spent a lot of time at the local parks and the zoo. We ride bikes together and, I'm afraid to admit, eat more than our share of ice cream from the Good Humor truck that circles the neighborhood. We're looking forward to summer when we can go to the swimming pond at the far side of town. I hear it's the place to be on a hot day!

> Aunt Ida is already talking about enrolling Meghan in Rockport Elementary School this fall. It may be a year earlier than some children go, but Meghan is definitely ready for formal education. As a side note, both Ida and Meghan said to tell you that they are very proud of the difficult work you are doing over there.
>
> We're all hoping and praying that you both are well and taking good care of yourselves. Continue to write when you can.
>
> Respectfully,
> Beatrice

Doreen's eyes stung from the tears that had streamed down her face and now lay dried and salty on her cheeks. The letter from Beatrice had been too upsetting to read more than once. Now Doreen had to face driving an ambulance with extra supplies to Bath, the scene of a surprise German raid the day before. Her mind was reeling with the thought of Meghan starting school without her there to see her off. She took the letter from her cardigan pocket and put it up to her lips, pressing it to her skin to feel Meghan's touch or smell her scent. Perhaps her mum had been wrong with her advice from the grave. Perhaps what she was doing was *not* the right thing after all. Maybe she should have tried to somehow get to America to be with her daughter! It should be *her* taking Meghan to the zoo and eating ice cream! It should be *her* that enjoys a summer of swimming and bike rides! Her neck and head felt too heavy to lift up and her legs trembled as though carrying a great weight. There had still been no word on Colin, still no end in sight to the horrible carnage that kept coming at her from all directions. She looked at her ambulance, its chassis streaked with tar and months of road dirt. At that moment, it seemed like a Madam, waiting to drag her back into a life that held only prostitution and regret. She shivered.

God, I don't have the will to pray. I don't have the will to move. You must do it for me this time. You must reach down and carry me across the street.

Neil opened the back doors of the ambulance, putting in the last of the supplies, and met Doreen as she fumbled for the driver's door. She knew she looked terrible, her face red and swollen from crying, her eyes glazed with the pain of sadness too deep for words. Neil took her arm gently and guided her around to the passenger's side. She didn't object. His hands felt strong and secure. She was vaguely aware of the fact that he wasn't really authorized to drive, but she sank into the seat without objection. Neil started the engine and sped towards Bath, glancing at Doreen as she continued to stare into the distance. Overhead, the clouds thickened with the smoke from bombs mixing with the moisture of the spring day.

The fragrance of early primrose wafted through the O'Connor's windows and Ian settled into his chair to hear the morning news. It had been more than two weeks since they had received a letter from Doreen and Neil, and listening to the war news seemed the only way to feel connected to them. Outside, Margaret was already pegging out her wash, pausing to speak to neighbors over the back fence. She could faintly hear Ian's wireless set crackling as it warmed up. The muffled voice coming through faded in and out, as though avoiding the discouraging and unpleasant bits.

"The top of the news for today, May 1 : The War Department has reported that British troops have evacuated Mandalay following serious hits from the Japanese. It isn't known at this time how many casualties were suffered, nor if any troops were dispatched into India. The Japanese presence in the Philippines has caused …."

The voice crackled with static and Ian fiddled with the tuning knob for a moment. He turned the set off and headed to the kitchen to pour a large cup of coffee from the chipped granite pot. This was not the day to hear more bad news from the front. Today he would open his shop before normal hours, then come home early to help Margaret set the rest of their garden in the ground.

Rockport, Massachusetts
September 1942

Ida Jenkins pinched off the dead blooms from the large potted mum that sat on her front porch. The warm, early September sun had resurrected the plant and she carefully watered its roots and leaves before calling through the door to Meghan. She hadn't expected to feel so bereft on the little one's first day of school, yet her actions revealed an anxiety that wasn't part of her usual demeanor. She had carefully packed Meghan's school bag and starched and ironed her red plaid dress until it nearly stood on its own. She made sure that she had all of Meghan's favorites for lunch, and promised her a quick lunchtime picnic. Now all that was left was walking her to the door of the brown brick building and bidding her a "happy first day."

Meghan stepped out on the porch, her bag in her hand, her face scrubbed, and her hair pulled back neatly in a big red bow.

"My sweet Munchkin, you look adorable. Are you all set to go?"

"Yes, Aunt Ida. I even brushed by teeth an extra long time today. Do you think I look alright?"

"Yes Meghan. You are definitely ready. Let's go now before you're late. I'm sure you'll like your teacher, Miss Kerns. You know how much I like her and I'm sure you'll have lots of fun in her class."

Hints of red and yellow were visible on the maple trees that lined the street where the Henderson house sat. As she walked back, Ida considered the years she had been living in her sister's house and the times spent with Neil and Troy. They had been happy times for her and gave her the chance to be a mother. The Autumn always made her question the choices she had made as a young woman. Perhaps it was the earth preparing for decay that prompted the memories of a proposal turned down. Usually new seasons brought up happy thoughts of the single life, lived well and to her own liking. Yet the older she got, the more she battled with the doubts that plagued anyone with dreams and life experiences left unfulfilled. She saw Beatrice from a distance, her blond hair flying around in the breeze that had picked up since daybreak.

"Beatrice! Hi! I wasn't sure if you wanted to go with us this morning, but it was getting late so I walked Meghan to school myself. What are you up to already?"

"I'm going to get some crabapples from the Sager's yard. Thought I'd make up some jelly today. They have to be picked before the rot sets in – or the squirrels eat them all!"

"That's a great idea. Let me know if I can help you. I could at least help clean up the kitchen."

"Oh, and I didn't plan on going with you this morning. I thought it might be best if you and little Munchkin went by yourselves."

"That was nice of you. Beatrice, if you don't mind my asking you a personal question…"

"No, I don't think so. What's on your mind?"

"It's just that, you're so good with Meghan. I was wondering how is it that you've never married and had a family of your own? I mean, you're a very attractive woman with many talents and a wonderful personality, surely you must have had a man in your life at one time."

Beatrice shifted on her feet and didn't respond right away.

"I'm sorry if I've asked you too personal a question."

"No, no it's alright. What about you? Have you ever been married?"

"No, Beatrice. I was in love once, but that was a long time ago. Anyway, I've had a good life here with 'my' boys. So, what about you?"

"I suppose I've never married for the same reason that you never did. There was someone special, but it doesn't always work out the way we intend for it to. And in looking back, it was best for me that it didn't."

Aunt Ida nodded in agreement, then posed her next question more quietly.

"What about your family? You never speak of them at all, or any of the friends that you left behind when you came from California. We've very little insight into your life before you came here. Were you close to folks back there?"

Beatrice stared into the older woman's eyes and spoke more loudly than necessary.

"I'd love to stand around and chat with you, but I really would like to get started on this project for the day. We'll catch up some other time. Once Meghan gets home for lunch and rattles on about her morning, I'll be quite interrupted in my work. I'd like to finish cooking and canning the jelly before school lets out for the day."

The color rose in Ida's cheeks.

"That's fine, dear. I'll let you get on with your apple-picking."

Beatrice picked up a bushel basket and left quickly for the Sager's. Ida watched her go with a strange uneasiness, then shook her head and headed inside with her own agenda: baking sugar cookies for Meghan.

The Sager's yard was quiet except for the chattering of squirrels scrambling to finish their winter store before the snows fell. Beatrice picked unbruised crabapples as quickly as her hands could work, her tiptoes balancing precariously on a rickety, wooden stepladder. A vision of the man who had rejected her affections and devastated her, peered through the leaves, his face blending in with the gnarled branches. The sunlight now streaming through the top of the small tree momentarily blinded her, like the stark, institutional fluorescent bulbs of the "home" she had left out west. She teetered for a moment, then regained her balance and grabbed at the apples, ripping their stems from the twigs with unusual force. The uneven colors on the fruit looked very much like the experimental streaks of dyed hair that had once adorned her head. Just beyond the tree, Mrs. Sager's white coats flapped in the morning wind, their empty arms flailing. Beatrice froze. Sheets. Of course. They were sheets hung out to dry. She turned back to her task, but the man's face continued to laugh at her through the twisted, uneven branches.

188

November 1942

Dear Mummy and Neil,

I was so happy to get your letter! Miss Beatrice says it won't be long before I'll be able to write letters all by myself. I love school but it's too easy for me. Miss Kerns said I could be her special helper because I always finish my work faster than the other kids. Peggy and I play hopscotch on the playground, but I don't play with Kate anymore. Miss Beatrice said she doesn't have nice language. Aunt Ida says that's because her daddy doesn't talk nice, either. Anyway, school is lots of fun. Miss B and I went to a Halloween party at the big, white building in town. I forget what it is, but it had lots of toilets in it. Aunt Ida came to school for our Thanksgiving feast and brought food to share. We pretended we were pilgrims and Indians and I got to wear a pilgrim hat that Auntie made for me. After school that day, we all went out to a big farm and rode in a wagon with lots of straw in it. It took Miss B a long time to get all the straw and tangles out of my hair! But she didn't yell at me. Aunt Ida says it will soon be time to write a letter to Saint Nicholas and tell him I've been good. I hope you've been good, too, Mummy, so you will get a present and I hope Daddy gets a present, too. I'm sure you will get a present, Neil. Aunt Ida says you are a good boy and St. Nick will not forget you. Aunt Ida knows a lot about being good. I am making Miss B a present, but it's a surprise! We are going to send your presents up to your friends' house in that other place away from the big city. You know, the people that we lived with, but Aunt Ida says they will not get there by Christmas. I'm sorry. I miss you very much. I love you. I love you. I love you.

From,
Meghan

London, England
December 1942

Mrs. Markham gingerly turned over the envelope in her hand, trying to decide what to do with it. It was a risk to send it to Oxford and she didn't want this letter to be lost. It had come to the hospital in London where she and Doreen had worked together earlier in the war. Evidently Lieutenant Lawrence, now a Commander, had sent this correspondence to the last address he had for Doreen. She ached to know if there was any news inside about Colin. She would locate Doreen as soon as possible, even if it meant traveling to the coast to find her. The last she'd heard through "official" channels, Graham Lawrence had been shipped out with sailors to the coast of Africa to stave off Hitler's advance. The headlines of the last week had brought discouraging news about the Germans' invasion of the unoccupied zone of Vichy, France, and about their further advance into Tunisia. It was possible that Lawrence had some news about Colin that had filtered through the French underground! She sat down on the bench outside the hospital, considering whether she should open the letter and read it. She could always try to phone the O'Connor's with the news, as Neil and Doreen kept closer contact with them because of letters to and from Meghan. The early dark and dampness of the November evening set in while she considered her options. She went to bed convinced she should send the letter to Oxford.

Kidlington was unusually quiet this winter day and the O'Connor's sat in silence, waiting for the phone to ring. The unopened letter from Mrs. Markham lay beside the receiver. Doreen's phone call from Plymouth to the large London hospital had been brief, but certainly significant. Upon instructions from Mrs. Markham, the staff notified Doreen of the letter from Commander Lawrence, which had been forwarded to the O'Connor's. The loud ring of the phone finally interrupted the uneasy quiet of the day.

"Hallo, Kidlington 886755, is that you, Doreen?"

Ian thought his wife's voice sounded peculiar, too high-pitched and nervous.

"Oh Margaret, I'm so happy to be speaking to you. I thought I'd never get through the line. I've been trying all morning. How are you and Ian?"

"We're doing quite well, my dear. Things have slowed down considerably at our shop, so Ian doesn't keep the long hours that he used to, which is just as well. Are you and Neil both healthy?"

"Yes, quite. A little more than worn out, I must admit."

The line crackled and Margaret held her breath.

"Margaret, before something happens to our connection, please open the letter and read it to me. I can't stand waiting any longer. Is Ian there with you?"

"Yes love, he's right here listening."

Margaret opened the letter carefully, as if hesitating could influence the contents.

```
Dear Mrs. Bennett,
    I sincerely hope this letter finds its way to
you. You don't need to know from where I'm writing,
though I will tell you that mail in this part of
the world seems to be a luxury that they don't
know about. Especially from a boat in the ocean.
    I've had some word about Colin through special
lines. I can't divulge the details of my connection.
I know you must be going mad with wondering what's
happened to him. I wish I had good news. Please
brace yourself.
```

Margaret heard a soft whimper over the line. She stopped reading to clear her throat and give herself and Doreen a moment to gain composure.

```
    Colin and the men who were left with him, both
patients and other staff, were taken prisoner by
the Germans soon after the Dunkirk battle. They
ended up in a POW camp, somewhere just over the
border into Germany. The source that had this
information said that the prisoners had been
beaten and tortured, and that there was little
hope that any of them survived the ordeal. At
any rate, there has been no more news on the
camp itself, and no other sightings of any of the
other prisoners. It's possible that the German
command tired of their POW post and obliterated
any evidence of the camp itself. Of course, that
would mean not transferring any prisoners - too
much effort.
```

Margaret paused and turned to Ian, her hand covering the mouthpiece.

"Ian, I don't think I can go on. This is dreadful."

Her shoulders were shaking. Ian gently took the phone from her trembling hands.

"I'll finish the letter, my dear. This is too much for one person. I hope that Neil is standing beside Doreen. What she must be feeling....."

"Doreen, this is Ian. I'm going to finish reading the letter, but only if you want me to."

Doreen's voice sounded small and pathetic.

"Yes, Ian. You may as well finish it. Surely I've heard the worst of it."

```
    Please excuse my bluntness; too many years of
officer memos, I guess. Please also bear in mind
that this is not official notification of anything.
It's all based upon information that's coming
through the lines. You know, of course, that there
could be huge holes and mistakes in this report.
I pray there are. Your husband was my companion
as well as my shipmate. I just thought you'd want
to know what I heard. I'm sorry, I wish it could
have been different news.
    Please take care of yourself, Mrs. Bennett.
You're a brave woman and I know Colin would be
very proud of you. I know for sure that he loved
you - more than anything.
                         With respect and regards,
                         Commander Graham Lawrence
```

There was silence on both ends of the phone line. Ian dropped his head and closed his eyes, waiting for any response from Doreen. All he heard was a soft moaning cry, then the sound of a deep voice in the background.

"Doreen, is Neil there with you?"

"Yes, I'm here, Ian. I made Doreen sit down on a bench here. She's very pale and doesn't look well at all. Is Margaret okay?"

"I think so. This is a terrible blow for Doreen, for all of us who love her. That poor dear, I don't know how much more she can stand."

"She's stronger than you think. If there's one thing this lady has, its resilience. Listen, I'm going to hang up now. I think she needs a little assistance, you know, a cool rag on her head or perhaps a strong shot of Irish whiskey. I promise not to leave her alone today. I really miss you and Margaret. Please stay well and remember that we're thinking of you."

"I'll pass that along to Margaret. Neil, whatever you do, please keep an eye on that little lady. She means the world to us, as do you. You're the son and daughter we never had."

Again, silence on the line as the two men absorbed the last few comments. Then it was time for a quick goodbye as the line crackled loudly and broke up. Ian stood motionless, staring at the phone, then gazed out the window without speaking. Margaret finished wiping her tears with a worn out hankie, took her husband's hand in hers, and led him up the stairs.

"I'm so very tired, my dear. Please help me get into bed for an afternoon nap. I don't think I can manage on my own. I'm just so very tired."

Ian O'Connor helped his only love onto the bed, removing her shoes and laying her head gently upon the pillows, fluffing them the way she always did for him. Then he lay down beside her and rocked her until her quiet snores had lulled him to sleep as well.

Neil sat down on the bench beside Doreen, guiding her head to rest on his shoulders, then taking her trembling hands in his. Her cries were not the loud and anguished sobs of someone nearing the edge. They were the soft whimpers of a grief too deep to be heard, a despair of one who was already in the abyss. It was the most horrible silent scream he'd ever heard. He could only wonder what kind of love could rescue this perfect soul whose inner strength and resilience had crumbled like bricks reduced to particles of sand.

CHAPTER TWENTY FIVE

Rockport, Massachusetts
September 1943

Aunt Ida watched as Beatrice and Meghan walked hand in hand, making their way to school as the sun peered through the changing leaves. Another Autumn arrived and there was no end to the raging war that swallowed up families and spit them out in fragments. She studied the darkening spots on her hands as the postman greeted her cheerfully.

"Ida, I've got something special here for you! Looks like you've heard from that soldiering nephew of yours. Hope he's staying out of trouble. He was always a challenge, wasn't he?"

"A letter from Troy?! Thanks, Henry! Oh, and you're right. That one is still a challenge, but I wouldn't change a hair on his head. They're both good boys – always have been."

"Hope it's not bad news. I've got to move on now. Take care of yourself."

"I will."

She clutched the letter as the postman continued down the street. Ida realized, with a strange sadness, that she didn't even know Henry's last name. She knew only that he had never married and that he took his job very seriously. Taking her glasses out of her pocket, she adjusted them on her nose and began reading.

```
Dear Aunt Ida,
     Hello classy lady. I have no idea if you will
ever get this, but I'm writing it anyway, 'cause
it makes me feel like I'm just around the corner
from you, hanging out with friends and drinking
a beer. I'm somewhere in the Pacific, can't tell
you where but it's hot and humid. Even when we're
out at sea, the breeze sticks to your skin like a
salty, leather glove. It makes it hard to breathe
```

and I can only imagine what we must smell like. But no one seems to care much about personal hygiene out here. Staying alive is the order of the day. I'll tell you, Auntie, when we are able to make land,there are some beautiful places in this part of the world. Trouble is, many of them are filled with the enemy and that takes them off my list of places to go on vacation!

You'll be happy to know that we still have some grub, such as it is. If I never see another dried meal… What I would give for some of your homemade chicken and biscuits. I gotta tell you, aside from the physical beauty of the places we've been, this is an ugly war. I won't go into details though, as I really can't describe the sick scenes that keep playing in my head. It's hard to sleep and harder yet to stay awake. But don't worry too much about me, only the good die young! Ha!

Seriously, I'm okay, Auntie. I miss you and Munchkin and wish I could be home by the holidays, but of course that's not gonna happen. Just tell the little one I said "hi" and give her a big hug from me. Tell Beatrice I send my regards, too, and hope the three of you are well and holding down the home front.

You might ask our priest if he would say some extra prayers this week for my buddy and his family. Nathan Swanson was killed in action a few days ago. It stinks - he was one of the best.

Take care of yourself, Auntie, and remember that I love you and Munchkin and Neil. I'll be back there annoying you as soon as I can.

Missing you,
Troy

Croydon, England
Late June, 1944

The Croydon Royal Infirmary had been filled to capacity with patients for the past three weeks. The Allied troops' landing on the beaches of northern France had turned the tide of the war against Hitler, but his attacks on Great Britain had taken a new twist. The newly developed

German V1 bomb had created havoc around London and surrounding areas. The staff at Croydon hospital had been working non-stop to treat the injured of all ages from this slow-moving "doodlebug" bomb. It came into view, hovered until it ran out of fuel, then exploded. It was impossible to determine just when it would explode, and some folks even ran out into the streets to watch it with grisly curiosity.

Mrs. Markham had returned to her old post at Hempstead Hospital some months back, finding that she had more responsibility than ever. It had been some time since she had heard from Doreen and Neil, but intermittent bombings and the influx of wounded soldiers had kept the Civil Defense Corp constantly busy. Medical personnel worked endless days and nights.

Mrs. Markham peered into the mirror over her small bathroom sink, examining the folds and creases that had silently changed her face in the past five years. The soft June breeze fluttered the curtains on the window that faced out to the Infirmary. She had always wanted to find a nicer cottage, away from the direct path of the hospital, away from the sounds of wailing ambulances. Yet she never had. Her cottage was humble, like herself, and it had been paid off for quite some time. She walked to the window and breathed in the night air. It was a bit clearer here than in London proper, and the fragrance of flowers just in bloom met her by surprise. She peered up into the sky, wondering at that moment where Doreen and Neil were spending their night. Wondering how their friendship had survived the horrible sights and sounds and strains of working with wounded men, women, and children. Especially the children. She thought of little Meghan and wondered what she looked like now, and if she spoke with an American accent.

A bright light twinkled oddly in the distance, moving toward the hospital in a circular pattern. Her heart began beating faster and beads of perspiration spread across her forehead. Yet she couldn't seem to move, transfixed by the growing, sputtering buzz that accompanied the light. It was getting closer and louder and sounded like a growling motorbike. Mrs. Markham froze with fear. The deadly V1 was now hovering above her cottage, like a giant bug waiting to devour its prey. Snapping to reality, Julia Markham ran out the back door of her home, running as fast as her arthritic legs would take her, but the bug exploded, as if on cue, sending its deadly guts flying through the air and raining down upon the woman who burst into flames like a fireball. The dark night heard only one scream, unfinished and swallowed in the searing heat.

Chapter Twenty Six
London, England
May, 1945

The noise in the pub was deafening, but joyful and exuberant. So many years of waiting for this day had brought the British people to the point of frenetic celebrating. The evil that had sculpted the horrific face of destruction, terror, and death had, in the end, taken over the artist himself. Hitler was dead. The war in Europe was virtually over and the Allied troops had declared victory. Although war still raged on in the Pacific against the Japanese, the immediate threats to the people of the British Isles were over.

Doreen sat with her back against the ancient, stone wall of the pub, her hands drumming on the old square table as she took in the scene. She was in no hurry today as she waited for her dinner to arrive. Her eyes focused upon a tall, dark-haired man whose strong back bent over the bar as he retrieved drinks. She noticed with some amusement, that the hair at his temples was graying. He turned and glanced around for her table, a broad grin on his face. It was the same grin that she had seen so many times in the early days of their acquaintance, but which had become more rare as time went on. Now it spread across his face like a half moon, unabashedly exposing a joy that could not be contained.

He strode to the bench and took his seat beside her, still smiling.

"Doreen, I know you don't drink as a rule, but today we *are* celebrating. I brought you a gin and orange squash. What do you say we toast to the end of this awful chapter in our lives?"

"I say, what a brilliant idea! Just don't let me drink this too fast or you'll have to carry me back to my hospital flat."

"God, I don't know if I could manage that!"

They both broke out in laughter and raised their glasses to the ancient, beamed ceiling.

"Neil Henderson, I toast with you to the end of this war in Europe. May it soon be over in the Pacific, as well, bringing Troy home safely, and may God grant that we never see another war again."

Their glasses clinked in the air and they both took a long sip.

"Cheers! I toast to you, Doreen Bennett, for having been the best team partner I could have had, and for your extraordinary perseverance."

Doreen raised her glass again, her heartbeat quickening with the magic of the moment. For the first time since hearing of Mrs. Markham's death, she felt the wonderment of life again. So many large events had changed her life. Her marriage, the birth of Meghan, the tragedies of her mum, Father Loughry, Mrs. Markham, and her own dear Colin had molded her life and her passions. Yet it seemed to be the little moments that made up living. Tea at the O'Connor's, learning to drive, treating an injured soldier, crying over a letter, and walking amongst the city parks seemed larger than their moment in time. It was the embracing of all the smaller bits of everyday life that pruned and nurtured, that tore and healed, that ultimately sustained her. She looked at this man who had been her constant friend and companion for five years. The one who had laughed and cried with her. The man who never took, only gave. The one who still let her grieve for the man she'd first loved. Perhaps it was just the day itself that filled her with the spirit of new life and hope. Perhaps it was the strange and girlish excitement of sharing this celebration with a true soul mate. Whatever the reason, Doreen felt years of sadness and burdens peeling away like layers of deadened skin. She felt the new layer tingling with radiance. Tomorrow she would face responsibilities. Today, she would raise her glass and make a toast to the man whose eyes spoke what his words did not.

"To new hope, Neil."

"Yes, to hope. And another toast to you, Doreen, for all you've taught me, for all you've been to me."

Doreen's cheeks reddened and their glasses paused mid-air before the toasts were complete. They sat a while longer, finishing their meal and taking in the celebratory scene that surrounded them. It was as though neither of them knew the right moment to stand up and head for the door. The request of an older couple to sit at their table finally prompted them to move and Neil stood up first.

"Please, sit down. We were actually leaving now, so the table is all yours. Enjoy! Oh, and drink one for me!"

Doreen rose, gathered up their cardigans, and took Neil's arm as they walked into the din of revelers in the streets. The whole of London had been transformed into one huge party. Doreen stopped to take it all in, afraid it might fade at any moment. Neil stood still, his eyes focused only on her.

"Neil, I've an idea. Let's stop at the Savoy and see what's going on there. Let's see how the other half celebrates!"

"Sounds good to me. Just remember, you can only order one drink at their prices!"

"I probably don't need another drink, anyway. I just want to see the lobby filled with people. It'll be fun!"

The lobby *was* filled to capacity. There was little room just to stand and watch, but the scene before them was mesmerizing. Neil found a spot against the reception desk, guiding Doreen to stand in front of him.

"This is really something, isn't it?"

The desk clerk's voice interrupted their thoughts.

"Aye, it's something alright. Nothing like I've ever seen."

Doreen looked up at Neil, unable to find voice for the words she longed to say. She took both his hands in hers and drew them to her lips. He gazed at her without response, then turned and spoke quietly to the desk clerk.

"Yes, sir. We have just a few. I guess you'll only need one, though."

Neil turned around to Doreen and smiled weakly. She watched him fill out the registration card, knowing that neither of them could speak of the feelings that would create their own magic while the victory celebrations carried on far into the night.

CHAPTER TWENTY SEVEN

Rockport, Massachusetts
June 1945

The sun was already warming up the sidewalk as Meghan and her friends waited for Miss Beatrice to take them to the ice cream shop downtown. Miss B said it was too nice out this day to go to a movie, but that she would stop at the park with them for the afternoon.

Summer days were often spent with Beatrice and Meghan exploring one thing or another. Sometimes Aunt Ida went along, when she was feeling up to it. It seemed to Meghan that her aunt tired more easily than ever before. Miss B, however, assured her that she shouldn't worry. Still, they both watched her with concern.

The postman stepped around the group of girls gathered on the sidewalk in front of the old Henderson house. Ida Jenkins got out of the front porch swing and walked down the steps to take the mail from him, greeting him with a smile.

"Hello Henry. How's life treating you today?"

"Not bad Ida, not bad. I see that young one of yours has a lot of friends. Other than that, how's she getting along? I see her playing out on your porch sometimes. She's quite a little character."

"She's doing pretty well. And you're right. She's an adorable imp. She keeps me laughing. At our age, that's a good thing, don't you think?"

"Certainly is."

The postman shifted his mailbag, rocking back slightly on his feet.

"Henry, I know this may seem a bit odd, but I've never known your last name. I don't how I got to calling you Henry right off the bat."

"It's Murphy. I think I'm the one that made the introductions years ago, telling you to just to call me Henry. I've never stood on formalities. Besides, I've always felt comfortable with you, Ida. You never treated me like I was just your civil servant. Somehow, I knew you were always a friend."

Ida blushed slightly, her smile broadening as she slipped the mail into her apron pocket.

"Make sure you give a knock when you come by tomorrow, I'll have my sugar cookies fresh from the oven."

"I'll be here with bells on, you can count on that."

She watched Henry continue down the street, then took the mail out of her pocket. She'd been expecting a letter from England any day now with news of Doreen's plans for herself and for Meghan. It was hard to know just what Neil would write or what his plans called for. Taking the mail inside, Ida headed to the kitchen to make some lemonade. She'd been so thirsty of late and the heat had bothered her more often. She stopped suddenly when a pain shot through her leg. It was a peculiar sensation, and one she'd never felt before. It subsided just before Meghan came bounding into the kitchen.

"Aunt Ida, are you making lemonade?"

"Yes dear, but I thought you were going to get ice cream with Miss Beatrice and your friends."

"We are, but I'm thirsty right now and I don't know when she'll be done working at her desk."

"Alright, that's fine. But could you and your friends come inside to get your glasses, the heat is bothering me so today."

"Of course, Auntie. I can help you make it, if you wish."

"That would be very nice, honey."

Meghan cocked her head in surprise. Aunt Ida rarely asked for help in her kitchen. It was her own special place and she preferred to take care of food and drink things herself. She looked at her aunt anxiously, then took the lemon juicer from the cupboard and began squeezing the fruit.

The month of June continued to heat up, allowing all of nature's things to grow. Meghan stood at her window, watching the young birds in their nest that sat sheltered in the curved branches of a maple tree.

"Meghan, are you ready to go yet?"

"I'll be downstairs in a minute. I don't know why we have to go shopping this morning when it's such a pretty day outside. You always say I should play outdoors when I can."

Beatrice didn't answer, not wanting to continue the conversation by shouting up the stairs. She closed the notebook and shoved it hurriedly into her desk drawer, looking over her shoulder as she did so. Meghan rumbled down the wooden steps and threw open the front screen door, letting it slam.

"I'll be on the porch with Aunt Ida, Miss B."

"I'm ready to go, let me just grab my handbag."

Beatrice glanced at the desk, then gently closed the screen door behind her and held out her hand to Meghan.

"Let's go, Munchkin. The day is wasting."

"I still don't know why we have to go on such a beautiful day. Why can't we wait for a rainy one?"

"Two reasons. First, you desperately need a new bathing suit. A nine-year-old girl needs a proper fitting suit and your old one is not appropriate anymore. Secondly, I don't relish the thought of going in and out of shops on a rainy day. It won't take us long, I promise."

Ida shooed them down the steps.

"You go on, Meghan. When you get back, we'll have a nice snack on the picnic table. The roses are starting to bloom and it's beautiful out back. Have a good time!"

Meghan kissed her aunt on the cheek and skipped down the steps, dragging Miss B by the hand. Meghan rarely did anything in a tentative fashion.

Ida watched them until they were out of sight, then stood up to go in. Her legs felt a bit weak and she steadied herself on the porch railing before pulling open the screen door. She sighed as she noticed that the screen was tearing in the corner. The flies and wasps would soon be a real problem inside. As she closed the door she looked over at the desk she had "willed" to Beatrice's care. A small slip of paper stuck out of the top drawer. She had never invaded anyone's privacy, except for an occasional snoop around Meghan's room for soiled laundry or overdue library books. Her first instinct was to walk away, but the tiny bit of paper looked too out of place for Beatrice' habits so she pulled open the drawer and pushed the paper in completely. As she adjusted the old drawer on its track, her eye caught sight of an envelope with a return address of California. Beatrice had never shared any personal history, even in all the years she had lived with them. The subject had not come up again, following Ida's inquiry on Meghan's first day of school three years earlier.

Ida picked up the envelope and turned it over in her hand, feeling at once both a twinge of guilt and a strong inclination to peer into its contents. Her decision was cut short by another painful jab in her leg. She caught her breath, closed the drawer, and made her way tenuously to the sofa. She was still resting there when Beatrice and Meghan came home, their arms laden with shopping bags and a bouquet of flowers for Ida. Meghan flew to the sofa and put her hand on her aunt's forehead.

"Auntie, are you alright?"

"Yes, dear. I'm fine. I think I will make an appointment with Dr. Ellis tomorrow. I've just been a bit too tired lately. Don't you worry, Munchkin. Now let me see your new bathing suit. In fact, why don't you model it for me?"

Meghan took her suit out of the bag and headed upstairs to change. Beatrice and Ida watched her, both of them laughing at her exuberance. Beatrice's eyes caught the desk drawer and she paused to stare at it. She thought she had quickly closed that drawer earlier, leaving a small bit of paper showing. Yet now the drawer was closed neatly, with no scraps hanging out. Ida watched her with anxiety. They were both interrupted in their thoughts by a small-framed model who sauntered down the stairs in a blue bathing suit.

Breakfast dishes the next morning were washed and put away before Aunt Ida ever emerged from her bedroom. She had asked earlier to not be disturbed, so Beatrice and Meghan finished the early morning chores and went outside to hang up clothes that still lay in a basket by the back door. Beatrice heard the familiar whistle of the mailman as he clanged open the mail slots on each porch. She straightened her back and walked briskly towards the front sidewalk.

"I'll be right back, sweetie. Just going to get the mail in for Aunt Ida. You finish hanging up the laundry."

There was a bill from the local grocery store and an invitation to a church picnic. There was also a letter addressed to both Meghan Bennett and Ida Jenkins, with a postmark from London, England. Beatrice shoved the letter into her dress pocket and quietly slipped upstairs to her room. She locked the door and slit open the envelope.

June, 1945

Dear Meghan,
    Neil and I have wonderful, exciting news! We are both coming to America very soon! My darling daughter – how I long to see you and lift you into my arms. I hope you are not too big for that! I can't believe I'm finally going to see you after all this time. I love you so very much, you are my life. I know this has been difficult for all of us, but soon we will be together forever! I don't

know exactly what our plans will be once we've visited with Aunt Ida and Beatrice and of course, meet all of your friends. I can't wait! We have a few things to finish up here and I will need to get a passport to travel to America, so it may be late July or early August before we get there. I'm sorry to tell you that Daddy will not be able to come with us. Please remember that he has always loved you; it's just not possible for him to join us. I will explain the reason why when I see you. Please take extra good care of yourself and give Auntie and Miss B hugs from us. But most of all, know that I am hugging and loving you with all of my heart.

Always,
Mummy

Dear Aunt Ida,
    We decided to put both letters in one envelope so they would reach you and Meghan at the same time. I can't tell you how excited I am to be coming back home! Have you heard anything lately about Troy? I suppose he's still in the Pacific somewhere; I sure miss the big pest. Can't wait until we're all reunited. I'm also anxious for you to meet Doreen in person. You probably feel as if you've met her already. I don't know what her plans are after getting her daughter back and visiting in Rockport for some much needed R and R. I hope you are well and having a great summer. I miss you a whole lot. But don't let it go to your head! Just make sure you bake plenty of sugar cookies for me the week we arrive home. I love you bunches, Auntie.

Neil

Beatrice folded the letters and put them back in the envelope. This was certainly news! It was time for her to get busy. It was time to make special preparations! Outside, the pure strains of a child's singing voice floated on the summer breeze and the laundry moved in rhythm to her song.

CHAPTER TWENTY EIGHT

Lunchtime came and went without any sign of Aunt Ida emerging from her room. Meghan had never known her to stay in bed so long. As Miss B sat at her desk in the front room, Meghan skipped upstairs in a hurry to get to the bathroom. She stopped at Aunt Ida's bedroom door and knocked. There was no answer. She turned the knob slowly and pushed open the door, peering in sideways. Aunt Ida lay very still on the bed. So very still. Too still!

"Aunt Ida! Aunt Ida! What's the matter? Are you alright?"

The old woman lay perfectly still, her eyes half closed, her lips pursed as if frozen mid-sentence.

"Miss Beatrice! Miss B, come quickly. There's something wrong with Auntie! Please! Come up here fast!"

Beatrice bounded up the steps, her heart pounding, her head spinning. God, she didn't want the old woman to die!

"Ida, Ida, can you hear me?"

Ida Jenkins continued to stare through slits in her eyelids, not moving, not reacting. Meghan fell in a heap on the floor beside her bed, sobbing uncontrollably.

The doctors said it was a massive stroke. There was no way of telling how much damage was done, nor what kind of recovery they could expect. He asked about next of kin. Beatrice assured him that she and Meghan were the only ones available to work with, as Ida's nephews had not returned from the war. The prognosis was not good. Besides the loss of major motor skills, her speech and ability to reason and communicate was severely compromised. There wasn't a lot of hope for rehabilitation.

Meghan sat with her legs swinging in the waiting room chair, her hair unusually disheveled and tangled. The lights were bright and the room was stuffy with a stale odor that she had never smelled before. She tried to overhear the doctor as he spoke to Beatrice, but his voice was droning on in soft monotone. She heard a fly buzzing by the window and turned to watch its antics. She knew with certainty that Aunt Ida was not going to be okay.

The next few weeks dragged on with daily visits to the hospital. Beatrice and Meghan tried hard to be there at lunchtime so they could feed Aunt Ida. It was difficult to watch the once vibrant woman drool and spit her food out as they spooned it back into her mouth. Meghan drew her pictures and told her stories that she had read in school. Beatrice spent more time talking with doctors and nurses, and sometimes people that Meghan didn't recognize.

"Good morning, Miss Moore. I understand that you asked to speak with me."

Beatrice stared at the nursing home's administrator who suddenly appeared in the doorway of Aunt Ida's hospital room. He was considerably shorter than her, with very blonde hair and ears that seemed proportioned for a much larger man. She smiled and extended her hand.

"Yes Mr. Tanner, it's good to meet you. I wanted to let you know Miss Jenkins' family circumstances, in case there were any questions or decisions that needed to be made on her behalf. I've already spoken to Ida's doctor concerning this."

"I see. And you are related to Miss Jenkins?"

Beatrice paused to rehearse her lines.

"I am, but a bit removed by generations. You see, my grandmother and Ida were second cousins. Ida only has two living relatives, her nephews, and they are both overseas in the war. There is no way to contact them, nor have we heard from them. With her condition as it is, I was certain you would want me to sign some forms that enable me to make important decisions on her behalf. It would be a shame to have complete strangers choosing her future options. Do you think you could arrange for that?"

"I don't see why not. Did her nephews give you any kind of documents, indicating their concerns and wishes? Given her prognosis, you can understand my asking you that."

"Certainly, I understand. No, they did not. When they left, Auntie was in good shape. It probably never even occurred to them."

"I see. Well, under the circumstances I'll have my secretary draw up the papers immediately, giving you rights to make decisions for her, should her condition get worse."

"Thank you, Mr. Tanner."

Beatrice's heart was pounding as she returned to Ida's room and plopped down in the chair. Meghan was chattering away to Aunt Ida but the old woman's gaze was focused on the other face in the room, a face that was flushed with more than the heat of the day.

July was hot and sometimes Meghan wished she could go swimming more often, yet she felt lonely if she didn't visit Auntie every day. Some days her friends asked her to play at their houses and this was a welcome invitation for Meghan - and a relief for Beatrice.

August was just around the corner when Miss B sat Meghan down on the sofa in the front room one morning. A storm was gathering in the distance and the thunder was only a muffled rumble.

"I'm scared, Miss B. I don't understand what's happening. I thought that Aunt Ida would be better by now. I thought Mummy and Neil would have written or called by now to tell us when they were coming here. I don't know what's going on anymore..."

Her words trailed off as the tears began to fall. One thing she knew, this was not how it was supposed to turn out.

"I know you are frightened, Meghan, there are so many things happening in your life. But I will always be here for you. Aunt Ida loves you so very much and she wants the best for you. She just isn't able to communicate with you now. You must trust me. I have had to make a very difficult decision. Aunt Ida isn't going to get any better than she is now. In fact, she will most likely get worse."

Meghan let out a loud shriek and stood up with her hands on her hips.

"No!! That's not true! She will get better, just you see! We have to wait a little longer! Please, don't say that she won't get better...."

Her voice trailed off in sobs that wracked her small frame and Beatrice ached at that moment for the little one's pain. And for her own pain, too.

"I know this is so hard for you, my sweet one, but we must place Aunt Ida in a home where people know how to care for her properly. They know what medicines she needs. They know what kind of exercises she needs to keep up her strength. They know how to communicate with her and we do not. Aunt Ida is not only hurting, she is frustrated and needs us to make important decisions for her. You must help me in this. We must do this together."

"I don't want to put her anywhere else. It doesn't make any sense to me. I'm sure that Mummy and Uncle Neil will come soon, and maybe even

Uncle Troy. They will know what to do. Please don't send Aunt Ida away. I would miss her so…"

Once again, Meghan's tears began and Beatrice stared at the floor, wringing her hands. This was harder than she ever thought it would be! There was no easy way to finish this conversation.

"Meghan, you are too young to understand all of this. I have to make a decision. Aunt Ida needs to be in a convalescent home, not in that hospital and not in this house. She won't be far away. There is no other way to help her. She needs for us to make this tough decision for her. Please don't hate me and please…don't make this any harder than it already is."

Meghan continued crying for a while, then looked straight into Beatrice's eyes.

"Okay, I guess you are doing the right thing for Auntie. It's just so hard. I want to help you pack up her things."

She paused before going on.

"Do you think that Auntie understands what we are doing, that it is for her own good?"

Beatrice hesitated before answering, then plunged ahead with the news that she had been waiting to tell.

"Meghan, I believe Aunt Ida will be happy with our decision. She knows that she needs help that we cannot give her right now. She can always have visitors. And there's more you need to know. You see, we have to make a journey! I received a letter from your mom and Neil, saying that they are arriving in Canada in one week, and that we need to meet them there. It is important that we greet them when they arrive, because your mother has important, official papers for you. We must see them at the boat dock. Then you and your mom will be returning to England – to your home! It'll be a fun trip for us – and a great reunion for you and your mom! I know it will be hard to say 'goodbye' to Auntie, but you can always come back and visit her and Uncle Troy."

Meghan's eyes grew wide. She stepped backwards and shook her head.

"You mean, I will be going back to England to *live*? I can't wait to see my mum, but what about my friends and Auntie and you? I don't want to leave here – not just yet. This is where I live now. I'm not ready to go away from here! Can't Mummy stay here with me in America?!"

"I don't know, darling. All I know is, she needs for us to meet her in Canada. You have a few days to prepare for the trip and also spend time with Aunt Ida. Although she can't talk, I know she loves seeing you."

The words that would change her life were loud and heavy on Meghan's ears. She focused upon Beatrice's face, then turned and walked slowly from the front room out onto the porch, letting the screen door slam. The air was sticky and thick and Meghan's breath came in short gulps. She listened to the thunder closing in and glanced up at the large maple.

Its leaves were whipping back and forth in the wind, showing their veiny underside – a sure sign of a bad storm. A sure sign that a pelting rain would soon rattle the glass in the open windows. A rain that would either dispel the humidity, leaving a sweet, clean fragrance or compound its stifling hold, causing even the heartiest of plants and people to wither from its weight.

Ida Jenkins stared out the window. The walls of her room were beige and there was only one picture placed above her bed. It was a paint-by-number of horses. Ida had always hated horses. They frightened her with their snorting and their sheer size, and the way they took off at full gallop without warning. Across the Home's yard two people came into view. Ida's mouth tried to form a smile and her heartbeat quickened as they approached the wide, steel doors of the West Rockport Convalescent Home.

"Auntie Ida! I've missed you so much."

Meghan threw her arms around the old lady, knocking the crocheted afghan from her lap.

"Meghan! Be careful that you don't send Auntie flying out of her chair."

Ida's eyes squinted and one side of her mouth turned down, the only response she could make.

"How are you doing Ida? Hope you've settled in here okay and that you have everything you need. It's not a bad room at all, is it?"

Ida watched as Miss B skirted around the small room, her heels clicking on the chipped tiles, her hands reaching down to pat the bedspread and chair cushions. Meghan watched her too, mesmerized by this sudden flurry of movement. Beatrice Moore rarely moved that fast. It looked like someone had wound her up like a toy and she was spinning out of control. The visit was not a long one. All of the news about the trip to Canada had been shared on the last visit. Then, Meghan had chattered on about seeing her mum and Neil again, and about the party Beatrice had given for all the neighborhood friends. This time the child sat next to her without saying much. She held Aunt Ida's hands in hers and occasionally stroked the gray hair that was uncombed and in need of shampooing. A nurse stepped into the room briefly, checking vital signs and recording them on a clipboard before she spoke.

"Ida, I'll see to it that an aide comes in this evening to give you a shampoo. How about a manicure as well? You'll probably feel a lot better when you go to sleep tonight with a little cosmetic attention."

She smiled, then walked out without looking for any reaction on Ida's face.

Beatrice had stopped flitting about and shook her head in agreement.

"I think it's wonderful that you get such good care here, Ida. I know it seems they're a bit short-staffed, but I think they do quite well for you, overall."

She stood without further comment for a few moments, then raised her shoulders and spoke.

"I know this is going to be terribly difficult on all of us, but we have to leave now. We have a train to catch and we dare not miss it. Our things are all packed and ready for the taxi to take us to the station. Please, Meghan, give Aunt Ida a big kiss and hug. We really do need to go now."

Meghan did as she was told. The real and honest expressions of affection had been said so many times and in so many ways that this last farewell scene was superfluous. Still, Beatrice had insisted that they make this final visit. She stood next to the window and brushed away at her eyes, wiping them on her skirt. Meghan hesitated before standing up and took Aunt Ida's face in her hands.

"Aunt Ida, no matter where Mummy and I end up, you will always be my special Auntie and you always live inside my heart. I love you so much. I wish you could talk, but I think I know what you're saying. I can read what's inside *your* heart. I'm not going to say 'goodbye', I'm just saying 'see you as soon as I can.'"

Meghan backed out of the room, throwing kisses as she went. She stood in the hall waiting for Beatrice, tears streaming down her face.

Ida Jenkins watched her go, her eyes moistening and the words she really longed to say sitting just inside her lips, silent and trapped. She tried to sort out the events of the past week, but her mind kept wandering between Meghan's childhood and her own.

Beatrice knelt beside her, taking hold of the veiny, paper-thin hands.

"Believe me, Ida, I know how hard this is for you. I know exactly what it feels like to be held inside a place that you don't want to be. Poor soul. I know what it's like to be trapped inside your own head, without a path to take you away from the thoughts and fears that haunt you day and night like a thief without mercy."

Beatrice swallowed, looked up at the ceiling and continued.

"And those lights. They're always so bright. They hurt my eyes. They make me feel like sleep will never come. Don't you get so tired, Ida? Don't the lights and these horrid, blank walls make you so tired?"

Ida stared straight ahead, unreactive.

Beatrice sighed heavily and dropped the old woman's hands, standing up with stiffness in her head and shoulders.

"Don't you worry that confused head of yours, Ida. I plan to take good care of Meghan. I love her, you know. We're going to have a fun trip together - to see her mom and Neil, of course."

Beatrice smiled, then turned and walked briskly out of the room. Ida's head slowly turned, seeing only the empty doorway, her hands now clasped tightly in her lap.

The clickety-clack of the wheels and the train's gentle rocking had lulled both Beatrice and Meghan to sleep. The air had cooled as the Canadian border approached and the train came to a dead stop for border checks. Meghan woke up and pressed her nose upon the streaked glass, trying to glimpse just where they were.

"Miss B, we must be close to Canada! Look at all the men in the uniforms! I hope it doesn't take us too long to find the boat docks where we meet Mummy."

"I don't think it will take us long at all, dear. The docks are just over the border. As soon as we get settled into a room for the night, I'll phone to see when the boat is due in."

Meghan settled back into her seat, making pictures of the happy reunion on her drawing pad. She was quietly absorbed in her own thoughts as Miss B lugged their suitcases into the lobby of a small, unimpressive hotel, just down the street from the wharf and the bustling activities of the Toronto waterfront.

"I'm going to grab us a couple of sodas and call the dockyard to see if they've information on the arrival time of the ship. You stay right here in the room, I'll just be downstairs in the lobby."

Meghan nodded and flopped herself down on the soft, squishy bed, her strawberry blonde curls bouncing in rhythm.

Beatrice strode to the phone booth in the lobby, opened the door, and stepped into the tiny enclave. She picked up the handset, putting it to her ear. The silver-haired man behind the lobby desk watched her with curiosity. She hadn't deposited any coins and her lips weren't moving. She only stood in the booth a few moments, then came out and headed towards the desk.

"We'll only be staying just this night, sir. Since we're leaving early in the morning, I'd like to pay for the room now."

"Certainly, miss. The little girl you came in with said the two of you were meeting her mother at the docks tonight or tomorrow. Did the ship arrive early, if you don't mind my asking?"

"No. I just found out that her mom won't be arriving at all, so we are leaving at first light. Oh, and could you please send up some extra towels? I want the child to enjoy a long bubble bath tonight, and there are only enough for our morning baths."

Beatrice smiled and thanked him, then headed up the winding stairs to tell Meghan the tragic news. She stood at the door to practice her frown then walked in with her shoulders slumped. Meghan was curled up in a plaid armchair with Max pressed against her chest.

"That didn't take long. Where are the sodas, Miss B?"

"I'm sorry, dear. I'm afraid I got distracted. You see, I made the phone call to the boat dock and spoke to someone in charge. He had some very bad news. Come sit on the bed with me, dear."

Meghan crawled out of the chair tentatively and sat down next to Beatrice, the bedsprings squeaking intrusively.

"What is it, Miss B? You look so sad."

She squeezed Max as she waited for the response.

"Your mom and Neil were to be on the HMS Whitby, the ship that would bring them to America, but they never boarded. Their friends contacted the ship's captain just before the ship pulled out of the Liverpool harbor. What they told the captain is going to be hard for you to hear."

Beatrice wrapped her arms around Meghan and took a deep breath.

"Meghan, your mom and Neil were both killed in an automobile accident on their way to Oxford, to say 'goodbye' to the O'Connor's. I'm so very sorry."

She paused, looking directly into Meghan's face.

"My mummy – and Neil, they're both *dead*?"

She buried her face in Max's scrubby fur, and began trembling from her shoulders. The tears weren't coming yet. Beatrice knew that they would, as soon as the horror of her news finally set in.

"I know you've had so much to cope with in your short life. I promise you that I will be here for you, that I will always take care of you and love you as though you were my very own."

She paused to gage Meghan's reaction, but the child's face was still covered by the bunny who'd shared her sadness so many times before.

"You and I will be a family, honey. I won't leave you alone. I don't know when Uncle Troy is coming back from the war, and Aunt Ida is not able to take care of you. For right now, I think it's best we go where I know people who can help us."

"But will we never come back?"

"You let me take care of all those details. I'm so sorry you have to suffer through this awful time."

Meghan put Max down beside her and rooted her anguished face into Beatrice's chest. Beatrice held her in the same position for most of the night. Never eating dinner or changing into pajamas. Ignoring the light knock on the door, signaling the delivery of extra towels. She rocked her back and forth trying to comfort this child whom she had come to love so dearly.

The bells in the Catholic church down the street chimed three times before Meghan finally began to cry. The tears were still coming when the café across the street opened for breakfast at 7:00 a.m. Beatrice took a cool cloth, washed the girl's face and guided her out the hotel's front door to see if a pot of hot tea and some toast could help. The clouds had gathered overnight and the dampness of the morning chilled them both as they made their way to a table by the window. Meghan sat Max the bunny on the seat beside her. She nibbled on her toast and sipped a bit of tea. Beatrice watched her without talking, not able to find any words to say. Outside, the seagulls screamed, their cries piercing the silence and competing with the church bells. Meghan looked out the window at the hovering birds, then peered toward the church. She shuddered and pushed the tea and toast across the table, softly mumbling that it was cold. Everything was so cold.

Chapter Twenty Nine

Kidlington
Oxford, England

August 7, 1945

The morning was already in the grip of summer heat when the train from London arrived at the Oxford station. Neil and Doreen stepped off the coach car, shielding their eyes from the glare of the late morning sun. They walked in silence to the O'Connor cottage, still absorbing the events of the day before. America's decision to drop an atomic bomb upon the city of Hiroshima, Japan, had repulsed Doreen. She pondered the absolute devastation and horror that the people of that city would be forced to deal with. Yet deep down, she knew with certainty that this action would mean the end of the war, that a Japanese surrender would be imminent. This madness could finally be put behind them. She and Neil had exchanged uncomfortable words about this the night before. Their conversation played back in her mind as the two of them made their way past old men and women puttering in their front gardens, and mothers and children sunning and playing behind back gates.

"Doreen, I understand your feelings about all the innocent people that died and are suffering, especially after all we've seen in this war. But you have to understand why it was necessary."

"No, no I don't. I never want to understand why something must happen that causes so many innocents to hurt and grieve. Where is the humanity in any of that?"

"That's the problem, Doreen. There is little humanity in war. It comes of an evil we were never meant to know. It comes from souls too twisted and tormented to grasp the sanctity of life and love and everything good. I have to tell you, as the war in the Pacific continues, Troy's chances of ever coming

214

home alive diminish. God, sometimes I get so afraid that he will come back home in a body bag."

"I'm sorry, Neil. I never meant to upset you. You never talk much about Troy, except to mention all his antics when you two were younger. I know you're afraid. I know what it's like to fear that you'll never see your loved one again. But I still don't believe that others must suffer to save me from pain. Maybe it's a hold over from my convent days. Maybe it's just that I believe if we're persistent, good will eventually overcome evil."

"I understand what you're saying, I just think that sometimes 'good' needs a little help. We saw that in Europe, now we're seeing it in Japan."

The conversation had ended there, but the strain had gone on through the night and was now stifling their spirits more so than the heat of the new day. Doreen squinted as the familiar form of two people came into view and the tension dissolved into jubilant shouts of friends reunited. She thought Margaret and Ian looked a bit older, but they were as energetic as always. The hugs and tears and constant chatter was cleansing and comforting. They all walked arm in arm into the cottage and sat down at the marred kitchen table, enjoying Margaret's lamb stew and drinking tea well into the afternoon.

"So tell me, you two, what are your plans now?"

Margaret raised her eyebrows at her husband in a silent scolding.

"Now Ian, don't be asking these folks what their plans are when they've just arrived. I want to keep them here for awhile."

"Well actually, we are going to stay here for a few days, at least until the war situation plays out. I thought I might hear something from Troy."

Doreen shot Neil a sympathetic glance, focusing on his eyes longer than she intended to. The earlier tension had melted away in the warmth of the love that permeated the O'Connor's home. Besides, she knew she could never stay upset with a friend so dear. A friend who'd come to be more than just that. Someone who knew her, perhaps better than she knew herself.

"Once all the commotion is completely over, we plan to go to America. I'm going with Neil to Rockport to be with Meghan. I can't wait! I don't know what my plans are after that, except that I may have a difficult time taking Meghan away from Auntie Ida and Beatrice! Her letters always say she's happy, though I think she'll be very excited when Neil and I arrive. I'm hoping she got the letter. I haven't heard anything, but mail may still be slow."

"When we leave here in a week or so, we're heading back to London. Doreen wants to check on the status of Colin, perhaps try to meet with

Commander Lawrence once more. We're also going to stop at the Convent on the way back."

Margaret stopped scraping dishes and wiped her hands on her apron.

"My dears, I'm not sure what you'll find when you get there. That area was pretty badly hit. Mary Catherine wrote to me quite a while ago, saying the sisters had relocated. Some moved in with relatives, most of them are somewhere in Lincolnshire. I don't have any more news on any of them."

Doreen sighed and rose from the table, her hands quickly placing dishes in the sink. Ian finished his wife's thought, a habit formed from years of marriage.

"Although it may be a good idea for you to go there anyway. Get some closure on that important part of your life. Besides, maybe a little of that reverence and holiness will rub off on this bloke, here. Couldn't hurt!"

The men's laughter was contagious and once again the quiet tension of an emotional moment was broken. The rest of the day was spent in alternating conversations of sad and joyful experiences. The sun was reluctant to set on this summer evening and the four friends sat in the back garden long into the night. Ian's wireless sat without comment, its usual humming hushed in preference to the murmur of voices and the sounds of the night singing their constant song.

The smell of bacon floated through the upstairs window and Doreen woke with a start, trying to sort out where she was and how late she had slept. Margaret was busy as usual, moving about her kitchen with quiet enthusiasm.

"Good morning, Doreen. Did you sleep well?"

"I slept like a rock. I've missed this fresh Oxford air."

Margaret chuckled.

"I didn't realize our air was so fresh. I suppose compared to London, it's quite nice."

She poured two cups of coffee and motioned for Doreen to sit down.

"Do you mind if I ask you, how did you continue to keep going all the time? How could you keep treating wounded, looking for your own Colin, missing your Meghan? It's just mindboggling to me that you could keep your head above water, as they say."

"My faith, first of all. And Neil. I don't think I could have managed without him. There is one thing more."

Doreen closed her hands around the hot mug and continued.

"I've kept a journal since I was a girl. Well, it was a diary as I grew up and I filled it with all sorts of nonsense. But I kept on writing as an adult. I guess it was a way for me to communicate with myself, and with God. Even with my mum after she died."

Doreen paused and took several sips of the rich coffee. Margaret didn't speak. It was a gift she had, knowing when to talk and when not to. Doreen had always needed to fill silence, even with her writing when she could not speak. Neil was a lot like Margaret and Ian. He often just sat without comment, filling the void without words. His presence was enough. Doreen smiled at that thought then looked up at Margaret.

"I'm a bit frightened, Margaret. I'm scared to leave England, and scared that my daughter won't know me anymore. I've been in so many frightening situations in the past few years, but this is different somehow. I'm not sure why. I'm aching to hold Meghan, but I'm afraid to make this journey. Something is nagging at me, a fear that is gnawing away at my insides."

"Sometimes those feelings are hard to explain. Don't ignore them, but don't let them overtake you. Perhaps you should tell Neil about your fear. He's a good listener and just that alone may give you some comfort and peace."

"You're so wise, Margaret. I've missed you so. It was hard after Mrs. Markham's death. I just kept praying that you and Ian were all right. I couldn't have managed if either of you had been lost."

Margaret waved her hand in the air.

"We're too crotchety for that. Now's the time for you to get yourself in gear for your journey to America. You'll have to send us photos of you and Meghan and all the folks over there."

"I will, I promise. Being here with you and Ian and Neil is giving me courage as we speak. Thank you, Margaret."

The two women embraced as sunlight burst through the yellow-checked curtains above the old porcelain sink.

Once again, the O'Connor's walked with their friends to the train station. They had all sat beside the wireless the day before, listening to the news of Japan's surrender. Ian had brought out a bottle of dry sherry and they toasted this final victory. They raised a toast to Troy and his safe return. They toasted to friendship and new beginnings. They laughed at old jokes and hugged and cried and went to bed drained and exhausted. Yet the freshness of the morning woke them all with a new kind of exuberance and hope. Life would be good again.

They reached the station just in time for Neil and Doreen to board the train. One more round of goodbyes were said. One more round of hugs were given. Ian and Margaret stood waving, peering into the brightness of the morning as their "children" left for new adventures. As they left the platform, Margaret glanced at the starlings that were gathered on the bench. They stood fairly still, merely shifting their skinny feet and staring at her. She smiled to herself when she saw that there were no crumbs left for them. The benches had been wiped clean and the litter was gone.

The garden fountain at the remains of Wycombe Convent had long since dried up and stood like a limestone monument, surrounded by bricks and wooden beams and piles of debris that waited patiently to be swept away. What had been moss covered cloisters were piles of broken stones, their arches lying awkwardly like discarded limbs. Doreen shuddered. She had been warned of the convent's destruction, she just hadn't imagined the extent of it. The cemetery lay undisturbed like a testament to the strength and resolve of the sisters in their earthly lives. The red oak that Doreen had cried beneath so many years before was still standing, its trunk rough and knobby, its limbs shading the grave markers.

She found Sister Agnes' grave and kneeled down to brush away the sticks and leaves. Scenes came flooding back of quiet walks and chats, of morning vespers and evening prayers. So much quiet time. So many opportunities to commune with God, with nature, with herself. So much time spent studying and learning and teaching. So much energy given at the Hempstead Hospital, treating and training others, and getting to know the man she married. Colin. What about Colin? The realization hit her that leaving England even for a short time would mean some kind of acceptance that he was never coming home. She focused her eyes upon the Sister's name etched in the stone, an eternal reminder of her presence on earth. What kind of eternal reminder could she have for Colin's presence on this earth? Did she even need one? Perhaps not. Maybe his presence in her heart and the creation of life in their daughter was enough, just as Meghan's invisible presence had sustained her the past five years. She smiled and formed the words, "thank you, Sister Agnes." She had received a true blessing in this holy place, a place that bore the scars of a time too horrible to remember and too horrible to forget.

Neil waited outside the door of the navy captain's office, his feet tapping on the hardwood floor and his fingers drumming on the edge of his chair. His emotions were confused and his eyes weary from a poor night's sleep. He knew without a doubt how badly Doreen wanted good news on Colin. He also knew without a doubt how he felt about her. His hope for her good news and his own feelings of guilt were crossing paths in his foggy mind.

She emerged with a somber face. Neil took her arm and guided her outside into the hazy sun.

"Doreen, I'm sorry."

"Thanks. I gave them the Rockport address, just in case there's ever any word."

They walked in silence for a few minutes as they headed to Victoria Station.

"It's time. I'm ready to make that phone call to your Aunt's house to tell her we're on our way. I'm really ready now."

They found an empty phone booth just outside of the station and Neil spoke to the operator. Doreen propped open the booth door and stood listening to the clicks and relays of signals sent across the ocean.

"I'm sorry, sir. There's no answer at that number. In fact, the number has been disconnected. Shall I try again?"

"Yes, please do. I know I gave you the right number, it's the house I grew up in. We've had that phone number for years."

Several more clicks and a voice on the other end of the line repeated the same information. The phone had been disconnected and the number was now invalid.

"Maybe she changed numbers. Let me give you the name and address and see if you can find a new number."

Doreen's face was showing worry and Neil's voice was sounding agitated. Still no luck. There was absolutely no phone connected at that address.

"Thank you for trying."

Neil hung up the receiver slowly and turned to face Doreen.

"I don't know what that means, but don't panic. Maybe Auntie decided it was too costly to keep the phone. We'll remedy that when we get there. Let's just pack up and arrange for passage on the first ship out of here."

Doreen nodded, her mind reeling and her voice caught in her throat. She didn't want to sound like a doomsayer, so she didn't speak her thoughts. There was something wrong here, the same feeling she'd expressed to Margaret. It wasn't fair to fill Neil's head with all kinds of unpleasant scenarios. It was best to get their affairs in order, pack up, and leave with a sense of hope and expectation.

They ate dinner in their favorite pub that evening and the conversation was light, not touching upon the end of their impending journey, but only on the beginning of it. By the time they made their way back to their flats, Doreen's heart felt a bit lighter. It was only after she climbed into bed that her worry returned. She lay awake most of the night, unsure of how to cope with yet another fear that was holding her joy hostage.

The lights of the city still blazed long into the night, flickering into Neil's open window. He sat with his hands wrapped around a large mug of black coffee, staring out into the darkness and replaying the phone booth scene again and again in his mind. They would leave as soon as possible. Or even sooner. Somewhere several streets over, a siren screamed its awful song. Neil shuddered and closed the window, trying to block out the wailing melody.

Chapter Thirty

Rockport, Massachusetts
September 1945

The sun in late September was warmer and gentler than Neil had remembered. It seemed to massage his weary back as he and Doreen walked up the front steps of the Henderson homestead. He was expecting to see Aunt Ida sitting on the porch swing, as she often had done when evening set in.

He glanced around at the leaves and dirt that littered the porch. His aunt had always kept her porch swept and tidy. Cobwebs hung like drapes across the dirty windows and the front door was pulled shut. Everything looked out of place and suspended in time.

"I gotta tell you Doreen, the house has never looked so unkempt or uninviting. I'm not sure what's going on, but this is very peculiar."

Neil pulled an old skeleton key from his pocket and unlocked the door.

"Aunt Ida! Beatrice! Meghan! Where are you?! It's us, Neil and Doreen, we're here!"

His shouts were met with only the hum of the old refrigerator that greeted them from its usual place.

"Meghan! It's me – Mummy! Where are you?"

Doreen turned to Neil, sighing heavily before she spoke.

"There's certainly no one here right now."

Neil didn't respond as he crossed the front room and entered the kitchen. He opened the refrigerator door only to find that it was emptied. Nothing. Not a scrap of food or drink inside. The kitchen table was set for two persons, the placemats and napkins layered with small particles of dust. He walked over to the cupboards and opened a door. There were boxes of cereal, a can of coffee, and a few cans of vegetables staring back at him, but little else in the way of food.

"Neil, what's going on?"

Neil whirled around, startled by her presence and quickly closed the cupboard door.

"I'm not sure, but it's more than odd."

A steady drip from the kitchen faucet made a hollow sound as it hit the sink in rhythmic beats. Doreen looked at Neil's worried eyes, a sinking feeling overtaking her earlier optimism. She rarely saw this expression. They moved upstairs and found the closets nearly devoid of clothing. Only a few items remained, thrown across bent hangers like discarded remnants. There was little evidence of which room was Meghan's, except for a growth chart that had been penciled onto the wall just behind the door. Age 4…Age 5…Age 6… Doreen shivered even though the warmth of the day had made the room stuffy and hot. She glanced over at Meghan's bed. Max the bunny was gone. Meghan had always put Max on her bed, insisting that it was his home. No matter what, her bunny had to stay on her bed unless she was holding him. Doreen knew it was Meghan's need for security and stability, as Max's place remained the same though other things kept changing.

"Neil, her bunny is gone. He always sat on her bed. Meghan isn't here. I don't believe any of them are here. The question is, where are they?! Why didn't they leave us a note or send a letter or something?!"

Doreen's voice was sounding more frantic with each question. Neil shrugged and shook his head in confusion and disbelief. This was not like Aunt Ida. She would never do this.

CHAPTER THIRTY ONE

Their footsteps echoed loudly as they ran down the stairs and out the front door, the screen door slamming with a haunting familiarity. The squirrels under the maple tree scattered in several directions, their scolding chatter unheard by their intruders. Neil found Mr. Sager at home and waited anxiously for him to open his door.

"Why, as I live and breathe, is that you, Neil?"

"Sure is, Mr. Sager. It's good to see you again."

"Well, come on in and bring that pretty lady you have with you. Sit down here on the sofa and we'll chat for a while. Can I get you something to drink? A soda or a beer?"

"No thank you, at least not for me."

Doreen shook her head, barely hearing his offer.

"Actually Mr. Sager, we just got into town from London and we were hoping you could tell us where in the hell Aunt Ida and Beatrice and Meghan are."

Mr. Sager's expression sombered.

"Oh Neil, don't you know what's going on? Don't you know about your Aunt's stroke?"

Neil's eyes grew wide and his heel began tapping on the floor, the sound muffled by the worn out rug.

"Please Mr. Sager, I don't know anything about any stroke. Just tell us what's going on over there. Doreen's come over here from England to reunite with her daughter for the first time in five years. Tell us what you know."

Neil's voice had become louder than necessary, with a definite edge to it.

"I'm sorry, Neil. Your Aunt Ida had a stroke way last July and now lives in the Rockport Convalescent Home. I hate to tell you, but it was a bad one. She doesn't get around at all on her own and she has no speech. My missus goes to visit her once in a while. We're not really sure she understands very much, can't really communicate in any meaningful way. I'm so sorry you didn't know."

Neil heard Mr. Sager's voice, but the room around him was spinning and he felt nauseas and disoriented.

Doreen stared at the old man, feeling part of a surreal nightmare. The walls of the room were closing in on her and she was struggling to breathe.

"I know that Troy hasn't come home yet, but he's due back any day, according to what the townsfolk are saying. As far as Beatrice and the little one go…"

The old man paused and cleared his throat.

"As far as they go, I can only tell you that they're gone. No one knows exactly what day they left, or anything about where they went. I can only tell you for sure that it was soon after Ida's stroke and they haven't been back here. The missus and I have kept an eye and ear out for their return but we haven't seen hide nor hair of either of them. In fact, no one's been over there. You can probably tell by the sorry state the place is in. I'd have tried to keep it up for you, but my health hasn't been so good. Sorry I can't tell you more.

Doreen let out a small cry and Neil jumped up from the couch.

"Doreen, let's go. We'll start at the Home. Then we'll hit the church and school and every place else we can think of. We'll find out where they are, I promise."

He gently lifted her trembling frame from the couch. They briefly thanked Mr. Sager and went out into the deepening shadows of the warm, Autumn night, unaware of the colors that the sunset was painting across the sky.

The once welcoming kitchen in the Henderson house now felt like a room from an abandoned movie set. Everything was in its place - and yet out of touch with reality. Neil guided Doreen to a chair and took two cans of soup from the cupboard and a loaf of homemade zucchini bread from the freezer. Doreen sipped the hot soup and picked off small bits of the bread, staring at the curtains as they fluttered in the night breeze. The warmth of the day had given way to a chilly evening and Doreen shivered.

"I guess it's time I close this window back up. I opened it earlier to air the place out, but it's getting mighty cool."

"Neil, I just want you know…I'm glad that you're here with me through all of this. I couldn't do it alone."

"I know you would forge ahead with the same resolve you've always shown. It's part of why I admire you so. Besides Doreen, I feel responsible for this whole mess. If only I'd never put her on that boat…."

He paused to watch her reaction, but her face was expressionless.

"You know that I wouldn't let you struggle through this by yourself. We'll find her, Doreen."

She nodded.

"You know, I suppose it's possible that the two of them went on a small trip somewhere, maybe just to get away."

Neil hesitated and shook his head.

"I don't think Beatrice would have taken her out of school for a vacation. She always seemed keen on Meghan doing well in her classes. And besides, Aunt Ida and Meghan should have received our letter and responded somehow. But then again, who knows?"

They finished their light supper in silence. The long journey from the boat docks in Boston had finally caught up with them. Neil piled the dishes in the sink.

"I'll wash these up in the morning. Let's get some sleep. I'll sleep in Troy's old room, even if it is painted lilac and smells like a perfume counter. Maybe I'll do some snooping around while I'm at it. See what I can find out about this Beatrice."

He grinned and Doreen forced a smile.

"Okay Neil, but just don't let me see you wandering the halls in a nightgown."

He gave her shoulder a squeeze.

"You have the choice of either Meghan's or Auntie's room. Let me know if you need an extra blanket, I'll get one down from the hall closet"

"I think I'll take one. I feel chilled tonight."

He handed her a soft white comforter that usually went on his aunt's bed when Autumn came. Even after having been washed, it still smelled of her lavender powder. A vision of his aunt staying in a sterile room alone passed before his eyes and he suddenly felt chilled and a bit weak. They stood in the hallway in a moment of awkwardness, then hugged briefly and turned toward their rooms. Neil stepped into Beatrice's room, then turned around to find Doreen still standing in the hall, her eyes focused on him.

"Are you alright, Doreen? Damn, what a stupid question. Of course you're not all right! What I meant was, is there anything else you need - for tonight?"

Her silence and her stare made him shift uncomfortably. She reached out her arm towards him and the comforter slipped to the floor.

"Neil, please, don't go in just yet. You're right. I'm not okay. I'm not all right at all. How could this happen?!"

The stillness of the empty house was instantly shattered by her desperate pleas.

"This is not fair!! Where is my baby, Neil? She's supposed to be *here*! She's supposed to be in this house waiting for me...."

Her voice gave way to sobs, and she crumbled to the floor.

"Doreen, I don't know what to say."

Neil could find no words of comfort and he sat down on the floor beside her, wrapping his arms around her shoulders. She continued to cry until her breath came back in short gasps, her lungs grabbing for air as if she were drowning.

Neil's face was stained with tears of his own. Why had he sent Meghan away?! Why had he been so hasty in his decision?! The silent reprimands assaulted him as surely as if they'd been hurled in an audible, angry scream.

"Doreen, I'm.... I'm so sorry."

Though her voice was weak, her anger was apparent. Yet it wasn't Neil who bore the brunt of her rage.

"Where is God in all of this? Where is this God who's supposed to be watching over us? Where was He when Colin was captured? Where was He when my Meghan was taken away, just when I was so close to holding her again? Just where in the *hell* is this God of ours?"

Neil sat frozen, unable to respond.

"Please don't tell me that God is here, that He will make everything right again! Don't tell me about His hand reaching down to make miracles. Where is *my* miracle?! Where?!"

His voice was quiet and apologetic.

"I don't know. Truth is, I don't know where God's been these past few years. I've never had your faith. I can't give you any answers. If He's in this room, I can't feel Him."

Doreen's voice softened, the anger transformed to quiet desperation.

"I can't feel Him, either. I just feel so cold. So incredibly cold."

Doreen's grief found company on the hardwood floor and Neil's closeness made her skin sting like a thousand needles were making their mark. The clock in the downstairs hall struck two times and Doreen shifted her position.

"I need to get up, Neil. I'm tired. Really tired."

Neil stood up and helped her to her feet.

"I'll get you settled in Auntie's room. Come on, hon."

"No, Neil. Please don't leave me alone tonight."

Tears began to stream down her face again and she shook her head and wiped them with the sleeve of her blouse.

Neil willed his heart to stop racing and his thoughts to stay focused.

"If that's what you want, Doreen. If you're sure."

"I'm sure."

"Honey…I want you to know that I would never do anything to hurt you. It's been so hard for me to watch you suffer silently for so many years and in so many ways. I wish I could have protected you from all the bad things that keep happening to you."

Doreen let out a tiny whimper and pulled his hands to her chest.

"Neil, you're so kind and your love and goodness has been tested to the limits. It's not just that I don't want to be alone. It's that I want to be with *you* tonight. I can't face the morning without you."

Her hands fell to her side and she buried her head into his chest. He only paused a moment, then wrapped his long arms around her and guided her into his aunt's room.

"God, I don't know what to say. I really don't."

"Don't say anything."

They sat on the bed and Neil continued to rock her, wrapping the white comforter around both of them. As the clock chimed three an owl hooted outside the window accompanying other nighttime rhythms. Inside, the comforter slipped to the floor as limbs and hearts found their own warmth wrapped around each other, making their own rhythms long into the night.

The sun had been up only a short time when Doreen and Neil walked briskly to the Rockport Convalescent Home. A robust woman in a floral skirt and a white blazer greeted them as they pushed open the heavy metal doors.

"Good morning. May I help you?"

"I hope so. We're here to see my aunt, Ida Jenkins. We were told she was brought here last July after suffering a stroke."

"Oh yes, I see. May I ask what your relationship to Miss Jenkins is?"

Neil's annoyance was evident.

"She *is* my aunt. I guess that makes me her nephew."

Doreen glanced up at him and noticed that he wasn't grinning.

"I'm Neil Henderson and this is Doreen Bennett."

"Yes, of course. I heard rumors of Miss Jenkins' nephews. I knew one had joined up when the war broke out. Are you one and the same?"

"No I'm not. That's my brother, Troy. I'm surprised that you were never kept informed of our whereabouts."

"Well, I do recall the lady who brought your aunt here. Quite attractive, maybe in her late thirties. I'm not sure what relationship she was to your aunt, but I'm sure it's in our records."

"That would be Beatrice Moore, my aunt's housekeeper and the little girl's nanny. She's no relation at all. Do you have any idea where the two of them are?"

"No, I'm afraid I don't. I can tell you, though, that they haven't been here for quite some time. You'll need to ask our administrator if you want more information."

"We'll certainly do that. Right now we'd like to talk to my aunt."

"You're welcome to visit her, but I'm sure she's not awake yet. She sleeps rather late. I must also tell you that you will be able to talk to her, but she will not be able to answer you. According to the nurses, she can't communicate in any meaningful way and doesn't even seem to understand conversation. I'm sorry you've arrived here in Rockport to find her in such a way. Pity, really. I heard she was very active and sharp before her stroke."

They stopped in front of Room 148 and Neil hesitated for a moment. Doreen took hold of his elbow and pushed open the door. Their fears were met with the reality of Aunt Ida's condition. She still lay in bed, her eyes open and focused on the stark, white ceiling. There was a pungent smell of urine and the odor of stale air mixed with soured perfume. Doreen's first reaction was to open the one small window immediately, but she stood beside Neil, waiting for him to make the first move. He took a deep breath and walked over to the bed, motioning for Doreen to let some air into the room. While he bent over the bed to speak softly to his aunt, Doreen struggled to unlock and raise the window. It had evidently been a while since Ida had enjoyed any fresh air. Doreen turned to watch as this gentle man lifted his Auntie into the chair next to the bed. He took both her hands in his and motioned for Doreen to sit beside him on the crumpled bed.

"Aunt Ida, it's me, Neil. I've come home from England. And this is Doreen. You finally get to meet her in person. We didn't know about your being here. I'm so sorry I didn't know before now. I've missed you so much."

He stopped, trying to gage if there was any recognition at all. Doreen felt the beads of perspiration beginning to form on her forehead and down her back. Was it the stuffy heat in the room, or the sadness that was spreading across her once again? Coming to Rockport had already brought one unhappy event after another. She placed her hand on Neil's and tried to give him a smile. His lips turned up slightly, then he sighed and went on.

"Aunt Ida, we both feel terrible about your stroke. It must have been awfully frightening. You know that we love you very much."

Again he paused, watching for any sign of response. She looked back at him but there was no glimmer of understanding, no movement indicating that she even knew who he was. Doreen watched with a heaviness pressing on her shoulders as Neil's eyes moistened and his long arms draped around his failing aunt. As Neil continued trying to make some connection, Doreen's thoughts shifted back to Meghan. To Meghan and Beatrice. Where were they?! Did his aunt know *anything* about their whereabouts? If so, wasn't there some way for her to communicate what she knew?! She knew she shouldn't be frustrated with Aunt Ida, but she was unable to completely separate the present reality with the hopes that she had pinned on the dear old woman. This was not what she had prayed for as dawn had broken! Her mind was reeling and her heart was hurting from the confusion and the emotions of the early morning hour. Doreen got up from the bed and walked to the window, wanting the muted September light to reveal the answers to the mystery. She turned and stared at Neil, his soft and simple words filling the silence of the room, his arms still wrapped around Ida's shoulders. Doreen turned back to the window and silently mouthed her growing anger at God. This was not the way it was supposed to end, not at all what she'd kept praying for. This was not at all fair! A crow flew to a high branch on the oak tree that lined the path they had treaded earlier. She watched as it settled in, its head bobbing back and forth, its loud caws interrupting the morning like the ugly shrieks of one in pain. The bird's cries became louder, filtering into the room and catching Neil's attention.

He took his arms from Auntie's shoulders and covered his face with his hands.

"She doesn't seem to even understand what I'm saying, let alone have the ability to answer any questions. I don't think she even knows *who I am*. It's so hard to see her this way. Not to mention that she can give us no help with finding Meghan and Beatrice."

Doreen moved toward Neil, kneeling down beside him, then smoothing Ida's wrinkled gown. Her short burst of anger was softening as she saw the anguish in Neil's face. He was dealing with two tragedies at once.

"I feel so defeated, Doreen. For the first time in a very long time, I feel totally useless. I wasn't there when my Aunt needed me and I've no idea what to do for her now. I can't help you either, and I should at least be able to do that."

Doreen glanced at Ida, looking for any expression. There was none. The old woman's eyes stared straight ahead at the beige walls.

"Even worse, I feel so responsible for Meghan. I can't place her in your arms right now and I don't even know where to begin looking."

He lowered his head as a loud silence filled the room, broken only by the ticking of a small, plain clock on the wall.

"Neil, this is not your fault. None of this is your fault. Yes, I'm angry – but not at you. We can't give up. We may not be able to help Aunt Ida, but we have to get on with searching for Meghan."

"You're right, but I still feel responsible for all of this mess. I never should have let her..."

"You can't think like that. You did what I asked you to do."

She looked at Ida again, half expecting to see *some* sign of affirmation.

He stood up, offering his hand to Doreen and they finished talking to Aunt Ida as though she could understand. They both kissed her goodbye, then walked out of the room to face the rest of the day.

The crow flew from the tree to sit on the windowsill. He carried on a scolding conversation, his head turning first to the tree, then towards the old woman who stared back at him without emotion.

The school principal ushered the guests into her office, motioning for them to take the two hard-backed chairs in front of the large, cluttered desk. Doreen looked at the framed diplomas and a sloppy watercolor of the seaside that hung above the desk. She wondered at that moment if the principal even knew who Meghan was. The playground was crowded as they came in and the sounds of children playing made her wince.

"Mrs. Bennett, I know this is hard for you to hear, but your daughter was not enrolled for this school year. Miss Moore came into my office last summer requesting her school records, saying that Meghan was moving to another location. I believe she said out west somewhere, but I don't remember exactly where. Once a child has been released with a guardian, we lose track of them. We have so many children who come and go each year, it's hard to keep up with it all. We especially had many transfers before and after the war. I assumed that Miss Jenkins had approved the transfer of Meghan's records, though I found out later she suffered a stroke. I understand she's still in the Home."

"Yes, she is. Mrs. Byrne, I realize that you can't keep track of all children who come and go from your school, but Meghan is an English citizen, now in the care of a woman who is not even a relative. We've no idea where the child is. Anything you can give us would help. We seem to be getting nowhere."

"I understand and I give you my sincere apologies. Miss Moore had recently been listed as Meghan's guardian and we never had reason to question the legality of that. She was also very involved with Meghan's school activities, as was your aunt. The two of them seemed to have worked out a wonderful team effort to raise her with a love of school and people. I don't personally know all of the children as well as I'd like to, but I knew Meghan. She's a beautiful child, inside and outside. She was always well mannered and kind, and the other children loved being around her. I know many of them miss her. The teachers miss her spunk and sense of humor."

"Mrs. Byrne, would it be possible to talk to any of the other children? Perhaps they heard Meghan say something during summer playtime that would give us some information."

"Yes, I think that can be arranged. I would like to contact those children's parents however, just to get their permission. You do understand, don't you?"

"Of course."

Doreen shifted in her chair, glancing up at Neil. He nodded in agreement and the principal began making phone calls.

Talking to the children had given them a glimpse of Meghan's personality and character, but there was nothing about Beatrice's plan or their whereabouts. They stopped in at all the local shops, showing the old photo they had found in Aunt Ida's bureau drawer, but no one knew anything about their disappearance. Beatrice and Meghan had vanished without leaving any clues.

After a full day of searching, Neil and Doreen stepped into the brightly lit restaurant that sat on the edge of the town square. They took their seats at a table that still needed clearing, opened the plastic menu, and ordered quickly. They ate in near silence, their voices tired and their spirits low. Doreen finished her coffee and took Neil's hand from across the table.

"Let's go back to the house. The phone's been reconnected. We'll start fresh tomorrow."

"Okay. Tomorrow we go straight to the police and give them all the information we have, such as it is. We should have started there. I just hated to go that route until we checked out the whole situation. Now this horrible thing is even more real."

"I know, but it's past time to get some help. We've given Beatrice Moore the benefit of the doubt. I just want to find my Meghan."

It was well past dark as they made their way to the house. They both stopped a few feet away from the porch. A lamp was on in the front room! There was also a light shining from the upstairs bathroom window! Doreen's heart skipped several beats, then began pounding wildly. Perhaps they were home! Oh God – maybe they were in there reading on the sofa!

She missed the puzzled look on Neil's face as she hurried up the steps and threw open the unlocked door.

"Meghan!! Meghan, is that you?! Are you here?!"

Her voice sounded frantic and nervous as it rang through the night like an alarm. Neil stepped in just behind her, almost afraid of what he might see, and not knowing what that fear was. The room was empty, but there were sounds coming from the kitchen. Doreen froze, unsure how to face the next few moments. Her silence was met with a loud and boisterous greeting.

"Hey, hey! Who's that lurking in my front room?!"

From around the corner of the kitchen peered a face familiar to Neil and a voice that brought immense relief.

"Neil, you old dog! You're back! Jeez, it's great to see you! Thought I'd never make it back here in one piece. How 'bout you? When did you arrive?"

The sight of his brother standing with all his limbs intact and smiling broadly made Neil's breath catch in his throat. The words wouldn't come, but the hugs were easy and the tears flowed unabashedly. Troy was home in one piece, along with his humor.

But the few moments of their intense joy were sobered by the shadow of the woman standing behind them, her face a mixture of relief and devastation. Neil stepped back from his brother, feeling instantly guilty with the realization that his gain was Doreen's loss.

"Doreen, this is Troy. Need I say more?"

Neil smiled uncomfortably as he stepped back, allowing Troy the chance to give Doreen a long hug.

"It's certainly a pleasure finally meeting you face to face, Doreen. I really feel as if I've met you a hundred times before. By the way, how the hell could you stand this guy so long?"

"Troy, this is a *real* lady, not like the ones you never bring home!"

"Sorry. I think the Navy destroyed all those manners Auntie was keen on. Speaking of Auntie, where is she? Where's Munchkin – and Beatrice? I expected to find them eating dinner when I got here. I was hoping to grab my first home-cooked meal with them, but I haven't seen a hint of anybody – 'til you came in. And what's the deal with the house looking so lousy? I promise it wasn't like this when I left. What's going on?"

"Troy, Aunt Ida had a severe stroke last summer. She's in the Convalescent Home."

"Damn. Poor Auntie. Have you seen her? How is she?"

"Yes, we have. She doesn't even know me, and she has no ability to communicate or understand. It's so damn bloody sad to see her that way.

"God Neil, that's horrible. I knew nothing about that! Maybe Beatrice sent a letter that I never got. I swear that Auntie was fine when I left. Everything was great when I left. So what the hell is the deal with Beatrice? Why isn't she here with Meghan? I don't know what the hell is going on!"

Neil looked over at Doreen and sighed heavily before answering.

"Troy....Meghan's gone. Evidently Beatrice took her and left town, and no one knows where they are. Beatrice left no clues. We've been searching since we got here the night before last. Sit down and tell us what you know about this woman. Do you know where they could be? Anything in her reference letters that might help?"

The color drained from Troy's face.

"No. I can't believe she would just take off with Meghan. I mean, she seemed like such a respectable lady, and it was clear that both Auntie and Munchkin liked and trusted her. This is awful. This is all my fault. Doreen, I'm so very sorry. I had no idea....And poor Auntie. She couldn't possibly have known about this. She'd never have left Meghan out of her sight. She loves her so much."

The joy that had filled the room only moments before was gone, replaced by a heavy burden that bore down on all of them. Neil placed his hand on Troy's shoulder. It was so unfair that both their homecomings were tempered with such sadness.

Doreen spoke before Neil could form the words he longed to say.

"This is not your fault, Troy and it's not Neil's, either. It certainly isn't your aunt's. How were you supposed to know what this Beatrice would do? I mean, none of us could have predicted this. We didn't get a sense of her instability from any letters sent back and forth. Not from school staff or neighbors, either. You don't suppose she'd hurt Meghan, do you?"

They both answered in unison.

"No."

Troy glanced around the room, taking a deep breath before offering his opinion.

"I really don't think she'd ever hurt Meghan. From what Auntie wrote to me, Miss B and Munchkin were very close and Beatrice seemed to genuinely love her. I sure don't know what's going on in her mind, but I can only guess that she's taken Meghan to live with her somewhere."

Without speaking, both brothers wrapped their arms around her and they stood entwined until the clock chimes broke the spell of the moment. The clock rang several more times as they sat long into the night, making a plan to search for Meghan. As the new day heralded with just one chime, a cold and blowing rain began outside, soaking the fallen leaves, signaling the ruin of the remaining mums.

The phone in the Henderson house rang loudly at 8:30 the next morning as the three of them were finishing breakfast. Neil jumped up and answered it quickly.

"Hello. Yes, yes, I see your point. This is good news. We'll be at school as soon as we can."

He hung up the phone and relayed the conversation as quickly as he'd heard it.

"One of the girls who used to play with Meghan at recess was absent yesterday. She said Meghan had told her a secret about going away. The principal wants us to talk to this kid firsthand."

Doreen put down her fork and ran upstairs.

"I'll be ready in ten minutes!"

The little girl sat straight in the chair, staring at the principal with a worried expression as Neil, Doreen, and Troy opened the office door and stepped in.

"Tell them the secret, Peggy. It's okay. This is Meghan's real mommy and we need to know what she told you."

"Meghan said they were taking a long trip."

"Where were they going on their trip? Can you remember *where*?"

"It was someplace far away. I think she said it was a different country, but I don't remember which one."

Neil looked directly at Doreen as he spoke.

"They couldn't have gone overseas, could they?"

Miss Byrne stood up behind her desk and walked over to her student.

"Peggy, think, honey. Was it England or Mexico?"

"No, I don't think that was the place."

"What about Canada?"

Peggy's eyes opened wide as she considered the sound of that word.

"Canada. Yes, I think that's what she said. I think I remember now. They were going to a place in Canada so they could meet her mom and friend when they got off a boat. She was very excited to be going to see her mom and also the big ships that would be there."

Doreen stood up suddenly and motioned for Neil and Troy to follow her. Canada - of course! It was fairly easy to cross the border into Canada!

"Let's get going!"

She turned to face the child as they walked out the office door.

"Thank you, Peggy. But are you sure there's nothing else at all that you remember? Anything?"

"No, only that Meghan told me it was our secret and I should never tell."

Peggy's eyes began to tear and Miss Byrne walked over to her.

"You did the right thing, honey. It was right of you to tell us what you know about Meghan's trip. Thank you very much for being so brave and honest."

The police chief was polite but preoccupied when they met with him later in the day. Some pranksters had played havoc with the street signs in town the night before, and the chief seemed more interested in finding out their identity than searching for information on Beatrice Moore, even though a kidnapping was involved. Neil and Doreen's patience grew thin and the chief's slow pace angered them. Troy had gathered up what papers were left from Beatrice's initial interview with them and two letters of recommendation he found in the bottom drawer of Aunt Ida's wardrobe and gave everything to Neil. Unfortunately, there was not much else to go on. After heated exchanges and more urging, the chief put out an all points bulletin and made some phone calls to the larger city police stations in the northern regions, asking them to contact officials on the other side of the border, as well as the west coast, where Beatrice had said she was from. Neil gave them her name and description as well as Meghan's. It was just after three in the afternoon when a call came through from the main San Francisco police station.

"Yes, yes I see. That's all you have for me. I guess it's a start. Thanks."

The chief hung up the phone and ran his hands through his thinning hair.

"I'm afraid they didn't give us too much to go on, but they said she once lived in San Rafael, just outside of San Francisco. She hasn't lived there in years. She was picked up a few times for vagrancy, but no criminal records. Not even a speeding ticket."

Troy's reaction was swift and defensive.

"Vagrancy! I don't get that at all. When I hired her, she sure didn't seem like the type not to have a home and roots somewhere. Someone's got to have known her in that town."

"It's possible she just listed that town as her place of residence. It's hard to tell where exactly she's from. I do think it's a good idea, though, that if she can't be located in Canada, you try looking on the west coast. She may just return there at some point. It's a big place, California. She probably feels as if she could lose herself and Meghan out there as well as in Canada."

Troy glared at the chief, annoyed with his reference to "getting lost."

The chief continued.

"The trouble with her staying over the border is that she most likely couldn't find employment there without a work visa, and that would be hard to get just now."

Doreen watched the exchange like it was playing on a movie screen. It was too unreal for her to grasp.

After two more hours of questions and no answers, they left the station and headed home. As they neared the house, Troy recognized the postman and waved him down.

"Henry! I gotta talk to you!"

"Troy! Well, I'll be, you two did make it back here. Good to see you, boys. How are you doing?"

"We're okay, Henry."

"And how's Ida doing? I sure miss that woman. Your aunt is a wonderful person."

"She's not good. No change from what they tell us."

"Ah…that's sad. Such rotten luck. But who's this lovely lady?"

Neil spoke up quickly.

"This is Meghan's mother, Doreen Bennett."

The postman tipped his cap.

"Wonderful to meet you, Doreen. You have an incredibly charming child. She always made me smile."

"Henry, do you have any idea where Beatrice and Meghan are?"

"No, sorry. I thought it very odd that one day they were here, and the next day the house looked empty. I received notice to keep all their mail at the post office, that they would not be in town to collect it. Very peculiar. I thought at first they'd gone on vacation, but I knew better after a few days. Ida, and Beatrice as well, always seemed keen on getting the young one off to school. The whole thing seemed not right, somehow."

Henry shifted his mailbag and shrugged.

"Sorry I can't tell you more. Well, it's good to see you boys. Good to meet you, Doreen. Sure hope you find Meghan. For what it's worth,

Beatrice always seemed attentive and loving around the little one. Let me know if I can help. Give your aunt my regards."

Henry tipped his cap again and moved on down the street and the Henderson boys escorted Doreen into the house. It was time to make other plans.

Doreen scrounged around the kitchen and set a respectable dinner on the dining room table while Troy and Neil spread maps and notebooks out at one end. The brothers stood up as she came to the table and sat silently as she offered the blessing. Troy peered up at Neil, whose eyes were focused not on the tablecloth, but on her. Their dinnertime was filled with talk of trains and buses and what to pack.

Troy wiped his mouth and leaned back in his chair as he spoke.

"I promise to check on Auntie at least twice a week, more if I can. I've got to secure a job and get my life back together. I'll stay here and hope that one of them gives us a call. Maybe Meghan will slip away and phone here, you never know. So when are you two heading up to Canada?"

"Probably day after tomorrow. I want to wait until I can get through to the O'Connor's in Oxford. Perhaps they've actually heard something, you can't tell."

"I'll want to talk to them too, Neil. I miss them both terribly, especially Margaret. She was really like a mother to me."

There were a few moments of silence before the chatter and planning began again. An hour later, Doreen watched with some amusement as the "boys" did up the dishes. The seriousness of the evening waned as the brothers swatted each other with dishtowels, leaping around the kitchen like children once again.

It was a bittersweet scene for Doreen. In an instant, a similar scene from her own kitchen in Croydon played before her eyes. Colin. She could see him dancing in their tiny kitchen with Meghan's feet planted on top of his and a dishtowel draped around his shoulder like an ascot. She could see the curve of his mouth as he sang off-key, serenading his daughter like a royal suitor. She could see his sandy hair, ruffled and mussed from wee hands that had earlier caressed his head and neck in innocent fascination. She could see his dark, penetrating eyes as he focused on the child he loved so dearly. The laughter that now filled the Henderson kitchen was drowned out by the song that played in her ears as the memory took hold of her, at once both cleansing her sorrow and soiling her hopes.

Neil found her sitting on Meghan's bed, clutching the pink pillow that his aunt had lovingly embroidered. He sat down beside her without speaking or touching. Sometime before the owl began its late night litany, he laid her across the bed, covering her with a soft, rose-colored quilt, then settled into a chair next to the bed. He stroked her hair as the clock chimed through the hours of the long night.

Ida Jenkins' head turned at the sound of voices in the hallway. Neil and Doreen opened her door quietly and stepped in.

"Hi Auntie. We wanted to see you before we go away. We're taking a trip up to Canada. Auntie, I'm going to show you a picture and if you can respond in any way, please do, even if it's just a nod."

Neil took a photo from his jacket pocket and sat on the edge of her bed.

"This is a picture of Beatrice with Meghan. You remember Beatrice, don't you? She's taken Meghan on a trip of some kind and we need to find them both. We think they've gone to Canada. Do you know if this is true?"

She looked at her nephew, blinking just once.

"She knows something. I know she does."

Doreen sat down on the other side of the bed and took the old woman's hands in her own.

"Aunt Ida, do you know anything about Beatrice taking Meghan away somewhere? To Canada?"

Nothing audible came from her lips. Doreen stared into Ida's eyes, willing her memory to return, yet knowing with certainty that her mind and body were both being held prisoner. She had seen that same empty stare many times before, when tending the wounded. That same blank expression worn by someone completely helpless.

A small tear made its way down Auntie's face, traveling down one of the many creased lines that made her appear even older than she was. Neil put the picture back into his pocket and motioned to Doreen.

"We'll go now, Aunt Ida. We never meant to upset you. We know how frustrated you must be. I don't know what you can comprehend anymore, but I do know that you're sad now, and I feel badly about that."

Neil winced. He turned to wave to his aunt, but her eyes were now focused on the window and whatever she saw outside, or in her own confused and captive mind.

CHAPTER THIRTY TWO

October 5, 1945

This has been such a difficult week for me. Neil and I made it to Canada. We started in Toronto because of Peggy's reference to Meghan seeing the big ships. We went from hotel to hotel, asking questions, searching for any clue at all. We finally found the place where we're certain that they stayed. It was wrenching for me to be in the same place as my lovely Meghan was, yet not be able to find her there. The man behind the hotel desk told us that he remembered a woman with a small child, and that they were to meet someone getting off a ship. My heart is aching with the fear that Meghan may have thought we didn't come to meet her. The hotel man was kind and insistent that they left as quickly as they'd come. He didn't know where they were headed. Mum, I'm so scared. Please help me feel your strength. I need so much more than I have right now.

Lamb

Troy watched silently as Neil piled suitcases into the trunk of the car, then spoke abruptly before the last one found its place.

"This may be a bad time to ask you this, but I've been curious about you and Doreen. What I mean is..."

"I know what you mean. You're asking me if we're sleeping together."

"No, actually, I was going to ask if you love her."

Neil tipped his head and grinned.

"Okay, okay, and also I was wondering where Doreen's going to end up once you two get back from the west coast. Just where will she be living – or sleeping for that matter?"

"You really get to the point, don't you?"

"Yeah, the Navy taught me that."

"Well, to answer your first question....Yes, I think I love her. It's awkward because of her husband's status. That, and I'm not sure how she feels about me. I think she's going to stay in the Sager's extra room when we return. They've been looking for a new renter and they won't charge her much. As far as the other question, I'm not answering that one."

Troy laughed.

"This trip of yours to San Francisco, it's a long shot, isn't it?"

"Probably, but one worth taking. We've certainly talked to the police enough times in the past few weeks, without any results. I do hate leaving Aunt Ida just now, she's failing so fast."

"Don't worry, Neil. Call me when you get a chance and I'll keep you posted on her condition. We'd better go inside now. Doreen probably thinks we locked *ourselves* in the trunk."

San Rafael was a quiet town with quaint shops and good seafood brought in from the neighboring harbor of San Francisco. Neil and Doreen spent the waning days of autumn walking and asking questions, following every small lead they were given.

"Let's ask in here. It looks like the kind of place a young woman would want to work."

Neil guided Doreen through the door of a small gift shop. The walls and shelves were cluttered with candles, knickknacks and baskets filled with dried flowers, filling the stuffy room with an odd collection of scents. Doreen wrinkled up her nose, stifling a sneeze before she could speak.

"Have you had this shop here long?"

The matronly woman behind the counter nodded.

"Yes, I've been here for quite some time. Is there something I can help you with?"

"We were hoping you could give us some information on a lady that lived in this town several years ago, maybe even grew up here. Her name is Beatrice Moore. We only have this one, small picture."

"Beatrice. Nope. Can't say I ever even heard of her. Why are you looking for her? Has she done something wrong?"

"Yes. She kidnapped my daughter in Massachusetts and we've come out here to search. The police know all about it, but they don't have any leads for us. We know she was arrested for vagrancy, but other than that, there's no other record of her. It's like she barely existed. I've got to find her. She's got my daughter."

Neil studied Doreen's face as she spoke, waiting to finish the explanation.

"Please mam, think hard. Anyone at all you can think of that might have come into your shop that wasn't a regular in this town? I mean, it's a small place. Thought maybe people around here all know each other."

"Well, you're right about that. Only thing I can think of...there was a young woman who actually worked here very briefly several years back. I think she may have even gone to our high school for a little while, 'cause she came in looking for an after school job. She didn't work out. She was nice enough as I recall, but very unpredictable. You know, I think she went into the hospital for something after she quit here. Honestly, I don't remember her name and I never heard anything else about her. Sorry I can't be of more help."

"Thanks very much. We'll keep asking around. Maybe we can jog some more memories."

"Good luck. I really hope you find your daughter."

The steps of the local hospital brought back unpleasant memories for Doreen as they walked up to the large, steel entrance doors. The lobby was well lit and the tiled floors smelled slightly of an antiseptic cleaner. A picture of Mrs. Markham flashed briefly before her eyes. They approached the information desk and repeated their story. The young receptionist walked over to a different desk and made several phone calls, then returned to answer their questions.

"All I can tell you is that we've never had a woman admitted to our hospital by that name. Even if we had, we couldn't release any medical information on her. Hospital policy, of course. It's certainly possible that the name she goes by is not her given name. Many people who are treated for sensitive issues, such as addiction or psychiatric problems, move on to other places with a new name for themselves. It's a way of forgetting a difficult past. I sure can't say if that's the case with your Miss Moore, but it's a thought. I wish I could help you further."

As the weeks passed, nothing turned up to indicate where Beatrice Moore may have lived or worked, or even resettled. It was obvious she hadn't been in the area for quite some time and there was very little evidence of her even having been there at all. They explored all the surrounding towns without discovering anything new. Troy kept in touch, phoning often to check on their progress and to say that Aunt Ida's health was in sharp decline.

It was a wet and windy day in early December when Doreen spoke the words that Neil was afraid to say. They sat in a small café sipping hot chocolate, watching cars splash along the narrow main street of San Rafael.

"We've reached a dead end here, Neil. I believe it's time to go back home to Rockport."

Neil's ears caught the use of the word "home" and he smiled only slightly, nodding in agreement. They would be returning "home" together. At least he would be able to stay beside her as they sorted out what to do next. Her voice continued as he pushed his eggs around on the cracked china plate.

"Besides, your aunt's health is getting worse by the day and we need to see her again. She may not live until Christmas and I think it's important that we're there. We've also run out of money and we can't continue like this. It's too hard for me. I'm not ready to give up searching for Meghan, but I need to go back now. Maybe we'll get some fresh ideas on what to do next. And you Neil, need to get back into school. I think it's important for us to focus not only on finding Meghan, but on getting back to some sort of plan for ourselves."

Doreen blushed slightly, realizing what assumptions her words may have made, but Neil seemed caught on her idea of leaving.

"I think you're right. It's time to go back home. I do need to see Auntie. Maybe her advanced state will prompt some sort of new, miraculous recollection. It's happened before with old people who suddenly remember things when they near the end of their life."

Neil laid his fork down and took the last swallow of cocoa.

"I miss her so much, the way she used to be. I wish you had known her then. I know she never would have allowed Meghan to leave our home. If she does know what's really going on and just can't communicate it, she must be devastated and so incredibly sad and frustrated. I pray that's not the case."

They paid their bill, packed up their things at the hotel, and walked to the bus station for the long journey home. As the bus pulled away from San Rafael and headed to the train station, Doreen stared at the trickle of rainwater that was winding its way down the streaked window. It gathered in a tiny pool and spilled into a new stream, darting and zigzagging to the bottom of the metal strip that brought its journey to a halt. As she lifted her eyes to adjust her wool hat, she felt a cool breeze across her neck. The heater was on in the bus, but the breeze was chilly enough to demand her attention. She took her scarf from her lap and wrapped it around her shoulders, then removed her hat and laid her head on the strong shoulder of her traveling companion. As she drifted into a fitful sleep, another drop of water on the window began its journey, unnoticed and unable to avoid its final destination.

CHAPTER THIRTY THREE

Kidlington
Oxford, England

November 1948

Ian O'Connor set the shovel beside the back door of their cottage and stomped his boots before going inside. It was very unusual to have snow this early in the season and the dampness had chilled his feet and hands. He smiled at the scene that awaited him in their cozy kitchen. Margaret was humming softly and rolling out pie dough. The smell of lamb stew filled the room and Ian's stomach rumbled. Margaret turned, prepared to scold him for wearing his boots inside, but she thought better of it as she saw the tender look on his face.

"I declare Ian O'Connor, you're going do yourself in working so hard out in the cold. Please take your boots off love, and come and get warm by the stove. We'll have our tea in a few minutes, soon as I can get this pie into the oven."

"Smells wonderful in here, my dear. The postman finally made it and walked around back to give me our lot. I've got good news! Looks like we've heard from Doreen and Neil. Shall I open the letter and read it while you finish up?"

"Yes, of course dear! Can't wait to hear all of their news! Perhaps they've even got news on Meghan."

"Don't get your hopes up. It's been three years and there's never been any word before now."

"I know, I guess I just can't give up the idea that we'll all see her again. Anyway, go on with the letter while I pop this into the oven."

November, 1948

Dear Ian and Margaret,

Sorry we haven't written to you for a while. Hope you have been enjoying good health and staying warm. We've been well and quite busy. I'm excited to tell you that Neil has only half a year to finish his law degree! He's been working like a madman, studying nights and days and taking extra classes. I think his extensive Oxford classes in political science helped him move along faster, as he was able to test out of some requirements. He's certainly ready to join the ranks of the employed! It looks as though he will have an offer from a highly reputable firm on the outskirts of Boston. It will mean commuting from Rockport, but he doesn't want to move. Ever since Aunt Ida died, he's linked to the old house more than ever.

We like this quiet town and my job at the hospital is ideal. I'm hoping my work visa will be extended again, or better yet, made permanent. I love nursing here and lately I've been branching out. What did you think of my article I enclosed in our last letter? I've been lucky to have several medical articles published in the hospital's local report that goes to the board and all personnel. I think it's because they want an "outsider's" view on procedures and research in the medical field. They can still think of me as an outsider as long as I can continue seeing my work in print! I'm hoping to get something published in the New England Medical Journal one day. Wouldn't that be a thrill?

Are you still going to the shop each day, Ian? Margaret, do write and tell me about your church and charity work. I love hearing what your day-to-day activities are; makes me feel as if we're just around the corner from you. We both miss you terribly.

I know you keep hoping to read some good news on Meghan and I wish I had some to write. We've had no leads in a very long time. Sometimes the emptiness is overwhelming and I spend the evening crying. I keep trying to see her in my mind as she would look now. I'll bet she's beautiful - and impatient to face her teen years. I can only hope that she's well - and well cared for.

On an equally sad note, I phoned the Royal Navy in London again last week. There's never been any more information on Colin and the rest of the men he was with. I was told that the legal waiting time to declare a missing person as deceased is now past. It seems like such a dreadful decision to make, but one I may have to deal with soon.

On a happier note, Troy has found a new job in Boston! He's going to live in the city and work for some company that handles corporate employee searches. It doesn't sound like his "cup of tea," but he said the money was good and it was time to grow up. I know that Neil will miss having him in the house, as he's such comic relief from all the pressures right now. I hope you can meet him someday, he's quite a character! We all love him, though. He's looking for a small apartment, not too far from the law firm where Neil will work. He teased me about my finally moving into the house with Neil and giving up my room at the next-door neighbor's. It's been lovely staying with Mrs. Sager these past three years. I know she needed the company after Mr. Sager died so suddenly. Still, living in the Henderson homestead would be very special. We'll see…

I think I've gone on long enough. You must be ready for a cuppa after all of this. Please take care of yourselves and remember how often we think of you with great fondness.

Love,
Doreen (and Neil)

Ian folded the letter and laid it on the kitchen table next to the stewpot. Margaret poured some tea and they sat down together to ladle out the hot meal that would warm their stomachs as the letter had warmed their hearts.

The light snow continued to fall throughout the evening and Ian turned up the gas fire as Margaret sat down to answer Doreen's letter. She looked around their front room and noticed for the first time how worn their furniture had become. Then she smiled with the realization that it was worn from years of friends gathering to sit and chat. Worn from years of sitting beside the man who still held her hand as they walked upstairs to bed.

December 23, 1948

    I can't believe another Christmas is upon me, and I am spending it yet again without my daughter. No matter how hard Neil and Troy and all of our dear friends try to keep me busy and focused on the season, it never works. I can never face a holiday without the haunting ache that Meghan is <u>not here</u>. She should be with me. We should be celebrating this holy season together. I think I've worked out my anger at God. At least, I guess the three of us have worked through it together. I still will never understand, but I'm starting to accept that Meghan is not going to be a part of our everyday lives. Yet she will always be the most important part of my life. She will live in my mind and my heart each day. It's just that, though I will never give up the struggle of finding her, I have to move on with my life somehow. I can't continuously look for her to walk through the front door. I can't keep planning "vacations" with the purpose of searching for her. It's too hard now. It's too draining. God, forgive me, but I've not the energy to keep searching everyday without any leads or results at all. I will always keep looking for her in some way or another, but I can't continue with the weekly phone calls and monthly visits to authorities. I have to face reality now, and it hurts so much. It hurts so much. Lamb.

Rockport, Massachusetts
March 1949

    The spring twilight cast strange shadows on Mrs. Sager's Venetian blinds. Doreen placed the phone receiver back on its cradle and stared at the shadows, trying to change them into friendlier pictures. The dim lighting that Mrs. Sager insisted upon was suddenly irritating to Doreen. Her thoughts were on the well-lit house next door. Yet perhaps her irritation was really because of those thoughts. She walked out into the chilly evening with just her cardigan on to escape the bad lighting and the Mrs.' inconsequential chatter. She sat down on the back stoop of the Henderson house, drawing her sweater around her shoulders. Earlier that day she had finally done what her heart had never allowed before this. The phone conversation she'd just had with Troy was a sad attempt to hear someone else say, "it's okay, you did the right thing." She didn't know why she had called him, but he didn't question whether or not Neil knew of her decision. Troy was always able to see things from a clear perspective. He seemed to possess an insight that some people never gained, as if he had seen so much more than even Doreen or Neil. His words had comforted her as she mulled over the finality of her earlier actions.

It had taken several attempts to reach the Royal Navy Department in London. She learned that the captain she'd last spoken with had retired from his post and moved out to the countryside. All of his reports and previous contacts, along with those of the late Captain Hollingsworth, were gathered neatly in folders that still lined the file drawers. Even with those papers, it had been a long and tedious procedure, one filled with more questions and legal jargon. The new charge was finally able to grant her request, speaking in a quiet and serious voice. With just seven words, her past was dissolved into a blurred memory. Yes, Mrs. Bennett, we will honor your request.

We will declare your husband legally *dead.*

The harshness of those words had surprised her, even though she had said them in her mind many times before. Was it because the words sounded so unfeeling, or because they just sounded so final? Legally dead. What exactly did that mean? Was he just a form of dead? Was he MIA-but-dead to the Navy? Was he not *really* dead to those who loved him? Or was he dead in the way that meant his soul and body no longer roamed the earth, but only his spirit? The weight of these questions had pressed down on her for the rest of the afternoon. Her chest ached and her head pounded with the sound of her own heartbeat, a beat that was erratic and sharply uncomfortable. Her hands remained sweaty, no matter how many times she wiped them on her uniform skirt.

She stood up suddenly and stepped off the Henderson porch. The crocuses that now struggled to force their way through the hardened earth were lost on her as she walked briskly down the sidewalk. She had no destination in mind. Only the need to walk and walk, facing no one and avoiding seeing or hearing any signs of new growth and rebirth.

Finally the chill set in her hands and feet and her pace slowed as she made her way back. She stopped and stared at the houses in front of her, realizing that she could never walk far enough away from the pain that had lodged in the deepest part of her. She could never get away from the anguish of losing Colin. She could never escape the haunting nightmare of losing her child. She didn't really want to escape nor get away from those wounds. She only wanted to be able to go on. To start living again with some sort of feeling. To heal enough that she could face the nighttime without being drowned in a wave of dread and fear. She wanted to come up breathing and assure her survival.

It was dark when Neil got home and Doreen listened from the Henderson's back steps for the familiar sounds he made. Doors banging, pots clanging as he began making dinner. Very soon he would make his usual trip to his neighbor's and knock lightly on the door. He would ask them both for dinner. Mrs. Sager would politely decline, having eaten much earlier in the evening to "keep her blood sugar on track." Doreen would smile and say, "Yes, thank you. Be right over." It was an almost nightly ritual. But tonight, it seemed both oddly out of place and wonderfully comforting. She was quite chilled by the time he opened his back door.

"Doreen, how long have you been sitting out here on our stoop? It's dark and cold. What are you doing?"

"I was thinking. I was just sitting here thinking. But now, I guess I'm just waiting for you."

Neil extended his hand to help her up and looked at her without speaking. She moved closer to him, her head lowered and the sound of her voice inconsistent with the levity of her next words.

"You know, I'm not really sure how we started this routine. I never ask you over for dinner. I haven't cooked for you since December, when I only made my mum's Christmas pudding. I wonder why that is."

Her voice trailed off and Neil paused before answering.

"Maybe it's because I'm a terrific cook."

She glanced up at him, watching the grin spread across his face.

"Come on Doreen, it's cold out here."

Neil turned on the oven and started the coffee pot. Doreen sat at the kitchen table, watching him. She closed her eyes for a few moments, then stood up.

"I called the Navy Department in London today."

Neil turned from the stove.

"And?"

"There were a lot more questions and a lot of waiting while the new guy searched through all the files. It was a long process. I know it was time to do that, but it was still very hard to hear them say the words. So hard to finally let go. I didn't know what to do after that phone call, so I called Troy and then I walked."

Doreen paused, unable to avoid the knot in her throat as tears streamed down her face.

"Troy didn't offer me any advice. He just said he thought I did the right thing. That it was time to move on."

Neil stood silent for a long time and sighed heavily.

"Doreen, I know this is incredibly hard for you but I think you did the right thing."

They stood perfectly still as the hum of the refrigerator filled the silence.

"My only question is, are you ready to move on, Doreen?"

"Yes I am. I really am."

The oven clicked quietly as it continued warming up and the coffee began percolating through the glass knob on the pot. The kitchen seemed to have its own ears and eyes.

"Neil, you give – oh I don't know, direction and meaning to my life. You've always given me more than I've been able to accept- or give back- before now."

Neil swallowed hard, then moved forward and gently put his arms around her as she continued.

"What I'm trying to say is, making that phone call today meant that I had to face what's been too hard to say until now. I do love you. I really do love you."

"I love you, too, Doreen. I have for a very long time. I know it's been a sad and emotionally draining day for you, but do you think that soon we can start making some plans for the future, for *our* future together? I'm so afraid that you will disappear from my life, and I could never bear that."

Doreen nodded silently. The sounds of the kitchen continued their strange song while her thoughts darted back and forth from future to past.

As she dished out their dinner onto antique china plates the lace curtains in the dining room fluttered, shifting the direction of the steam that rose from the hot platter of roast. The candle flame sputtered slightly and a drop of wax rolled down its silver holder.

"I guess I'll need to work on the storm windows this summer. They seem to be drafty. I never noticed that before, but of course the house is getting old."

"Yes, Neil. The *house* is getting old, but the *home* will be new."

They finished their meal and curled up on the old sofa to listen to the owl once again, reminding them that at least one thing in their lives would forever be consistent while others would never be the same.

CHAPTER THIRTY FOUR

May 1, 1949

Dear Doreen and Neil,

My dears, how wonderful to hear that you two are getting married soon! We are so very happy for you. Thank you for your invitation to the grand event! We've been able to save some pounds in the past four years and we can't think of a better way to spend it. We will arrive in New York and take a train to Boston in time for your big day. I'm so excited to get our travel plans in order, and of course buy a new dress for the occasion. I may even get Ian to finally get a new suit, but I wouldn't wager on that one!

We're also anxious to meet Troy. From what you've written, he seems like quite the character! Please let us know if we can be of any help to you in the meantime.

Things have been going quite well at our end. Ian still goes to the shop to make sure everything is "as it should be." I think he just needs an excuse to keep busy. He's never been as keen on gardening as I've been, so the shop keeps him from getting under foot.

We went to London several weeks ago. It was back to its hopping pace. It was nice to see the City again, but we were glad to get back to the peace and calm of Kidlington!

Take care of yourselves and we look forward to seeing you soon.

With love and affection,
Margaret and Ian

It turned out to be a sunny Friday in June and the Henderson home had taken on a festive air as Neil and Doreen prepared for two special occasions. Troy bounded up the steps of the old house, yelling as he entered.

"Okay, where's the new law graduate?! Where are you, Mr. Lawyer, are you already out taking advantage of vulnerable people?"

"Troy! We're out here in the kitchen! Get your sorry self out here and help us get ready for the crowd. They should be here soon and we're not ready yet."

"Hey, lovely lady, how are ya?"

"I'm nervous as a cat. I can't believe we're having Neil's graduation party and our wedding on the same weekend. We must be daft!"

"Well, look at it this way, you'll get all this company in and out in one shot. That can't be all bad. Speaking of company, when are the O'Connor's coming in? Will they get here today?"

"I certainly hope so. It depends if their ship docked on time and they got on the right train. I can't believe they're actually coming – I can't wait to see them! This is the first time they've ever gone anywhere farther than four hours from home. They'll be exhausted and hopefully not too seasick. I know it must have taken a huge pile of their savings to buy the tickets. Yet, I suppose it's a good excuse for them to treat themselves. They've spent their whole lives doing for others."

Neil nodded in agreement as he lightly slapped his brother on the back.

"What do you say, Troy, if I put you in charge of picking them up from the train station? I told them it would probably be you at the station as Doreen and I would be going crazy at this point. Besides, you need to make yourself useful if you're going to eat our food and sleep in your old room this weekend."

"Yeah, yeah, I hear ya. At least my room's a decent color again."

As soon as he made the remark, Troy bit his lip. It was hard not to say something that brought up painful memories of Beatrice and Meghan. His brother, however, seemed oblivious to his comment and Doreen was out on the back porch.

"What time do I need to leave for the station?"

"They're due in at noon. You can eat before or after you get them, there's a dish of macaroni and cheese in the oven. You'll be glad to know that Doreen made it – not me. There's also some of Mrs. Sager's apple cobbler on the counter, help yourself."

Troy smiled at his brother who seemed unusually focused and perhaps a bit too organized for his own good.

The sound of Troy's squealing tires was Neil and Doreen's signal to greet their arriving guests and they both hurried to the front porch. Neil was shaking his head and muttering, mostly to himself.

"Maybe I shouldn't have sent Troy to get them. They may have made it safely here, only to die of fright riding with the 'terror'."

Ian emerged first from the car, turning to help Margaret crawl out from the backseat. Troy unloaded the suitcases and the joyful chatter began.

"I can't believe you've made it! You both look terrific! We've missed you so much. How was your trip?"

"Great, Doreen, just great! A bit long for two old folks like us, but nice nonetheless."

Margaret scowled at her husband. "Wait a minute, Ian, just who are calling old?"

The laughter began and the four friends hugged before going into the house to share memories and catch up on recent news as they sat around the kitchen table. Troy quietly finished the chores that needed to be done before more guests arrived that evening to celebrate Neil's law degree. Then he left for town to pick up the wedding ring that would adorn Doreen's finger on Sunday. As evening drew near, the O'Connor's excused themselves to freshen up before the party.

Neil spoke up to avoid any confusion.

"You'll both be staying in my room, it's all ready for you. I'll be staying in the small room and Troy's got his old room back for this weekend."

Margaret glanced at Doreen and smiled. Letters back and forth had made it clear that Doreen was still living with Mrs. Sager, but very soon she would live in her own home. Her's and Neil's. The hole in the fabric of Doreen's life would be mended, the stitching strong yet always visible, forever a reminder of the torn threads.

Sunday dawned with clear skies and a warm breeze. The church was simply decorated with vases of early wildflowers and the pews had sprigs of fresh greenery draped across their ends. The wedding was short and the guests followed the bridal couple back to the house for a luncheon and lots of loud, cheerful conversation. They cut the cake and spent the afternoon visiting with each person, taking time out to open gifts. As the afternoon sun slipped behind the horizon, Dr. and Mrs. Neil Henderson thanked their guests for coming, then sat down on the sofa, their faces a blend of exhaustion and excitement.

Margaret's voice interrupted their reverie.

"You two go on upstairs and get your clothes changed. We'll clean up down here."

Ian stifled a smile and stared at his wife, hoping she wouldn't say anything more. But his gaze didn't seem to deter her.

"Now if you get hungry later on, just come on down and I'll fix you a plate. I'm sure you didn't eat much lunch, with the excitement and all."

"Thank you, Margaret. You're a doll!"

Neil grinned at Ian, who stood shaking his head in slight embarrassment.

The newlyweds left the room, both aware of all the eyes following them. Doreen giggled as they reached the top of the stairs. Margaret shooed Ian and Troy out to the kitchen, where the mess waited for their attention and Ian waited to speak privately to Troy.

"You know, Troy, I had a thought. Doreen wrote that you work for an employee search company. I'm guessing that means that you look for people to fit a specific job that a company needs filled. Am I right about that?"

"Yep, that's it. I try to hook up people who have certain skills and experience with companies that need to hire someone."

"Is there any way you could use your experiences to help look for Meghan?"

"I don't know. To be honest, I never thought about my job in any way other than looking for employees. Looking for a missing person is a whole other ballgame, but one I've become more experienced at. God knows I've tried hard in the past few years to find Meghan, but any possible leads always come to a dead end."

Troy winced at his own term.

"That might be, but it couldn't hurt to try from a completely different angle. Do you have any connections out on the west coast?"

"Not directly, but I could ask some folks in the office to help me out, on our own time, of course. Might give us a new lead. I'll start looking into that first thing Monday morning."

Ian tossed the dishtowel over his shoulder and spoke his mind.

"I think that's a great idea, Troy. But I wouldn't say anything to Doreen or Neil about it just yet. Maybe when there's a glimmer of a lead, but not until you at least get that."

"You're right, Ian. The last thing I need is to give them more false hope."

The rest of the kitchen crew's conversation centered upon the events of the weekend. It was already the early morning hours when Neil and Doreen poked their heads into the kitchen. The mess was gone, the teapot was steaming on the stove and both Margaret and Ian motioned for them to sit down.

"I left a pot of soup on the counter. Won't take but a few minutes to warm it. Sit yourselves down and join us. How about some tea?"

"God, you two, what are you still doing up? Aren't you exhausted?"

"A little. But we love all this excitement!"

As the lights in other houses went out, the lights in the Henderson house continued to shine long into the night as the friends shared the food that nourished their hearts and their souls. It was a meal that would need to sustain this group of friends long into the nights to come. It was the simple sustenance that would feed them well into the years that would follow.

Boston
July 1949

Troy's secretary set the phone down on the cradle with a heavy hand and sighed audibly.

"Mr. Henderson, I've placed that call for you - again. You should be hearing from him this afternoon. I forgot about the time difference and the custodian answered the call. He said he'd leave a message on the vice-president's desk and mark it urgent. He sounded sincere enough. I really don't want to phone our company's home office again for your personal business. It's the third time this week."

Troy looked up from his desk as she continued.

"I *know* that you're working on something, but I don't like being asked to compromise my position by making your personal phone calls on company time."

Troy smiled as he took a pen out of his mouth.

"I've got to hand it to you, Miss Beeman, you sure know how to speak your mind."

The young woman stared at her boss for a few moments, then returned to the stack of papers waiting to be filed.

Troy put the pen back in his mouth and considered what might be the outcome of the call from the vice-president of the home office. It was at least a chance to see if anyone in the northern California region had ever heard of Beatrice Moore. He had sent a copy of the two photos of Beatrice, as well as some old snapshots of Meghan. Not informing Neil or Doreen of his actions had weighed a bit on his shoulders, but it was certainly not worth telling them if nothing came from yet another search.

It was nearing two o'clock in the afternoon when he got the phone call and the summer heat made his hands even sweatier as he answered the ring.

"Mr. Henderson, this is David Sanders from the home office in San Francisco. Sorry your call to our vice-president wasn't returned earlier. I'm a department manager here and I just got done weeding through Mr. Roberts' mail and messages. You see, Stuart Roberts had a serious auto accident a few days ago, and I'm not sure he's going to pull through. Obviously that's why you didn't hear from him. Anyway, maybe I can help you."

"I'm sorry to hear about Mr. Roberts, I hope he makes it. I know he's been in that area and with the company for years and years and probably has a lot of friends and relatives. That must be hard on all of you."

"Yes, it is. And you're right about friends. He's a good man and we all respect him here in the office. As far as relatives go, he was married once, but they've been divorced for quite some time and they never had children. I know he has a brother who's an architect and lives somewhere up the coast, but I don't think they see each other. Some kind of falling out, I guess. Enough personals, now what can I do for you?"

"I was hoping to get any information I can on a woman named Beatrice Moore. She left Rockport about four years ago and kidnapped my brother's wife's daughter. My brother met the little girl's mother in England during the war and they sent her daughter, Meghan, here to the states to live with my aunt and me. Of course, I joined up and went to the Pacific, leaving Meghan in the care of my aunt and this Beatrice. To make a long story short, my aunt suffered a stroke and Beatrice disappeared with the girl. I certainly didn't think she would kidnap the little one! God, it all turned out to be such a mess. I've done a lot of searching for them in the past few years, but I always come up empty-handed. Both my brother and the girl's mom have looked to the point of desperation. I wouldn't say they've given up exactly, but all their searches have gone nowhere. I just thought I'd try once more."

"I see. How did you think Stuart Roberts could help you?"

"I know it may seem irregular, but I was hoping that he could use some of our corporate search guys to check out if this Moore woman was anywhere in that area. The one thing we do know is that she used to live out there. I keep thinking she may return for some reason, family or whatever. Maybe your people could look for her under the guise of searching for a woman to fit a particular job, whatever that would be. I don't have any concrete plan for this, but any help you and your co-workers could give me would be great. I feel so lousy about the situation;

it was my fault for hiring this Beatrice. The girl is a wonderful child. I can't imagine what she must think, how abandoned she must have felt, when all the while her mom and many others have been searching for her for years.

"How old is the girl?"

"She would be thirteen now. Is there any way you can help? I'll personally pay you whatever rate your guys get out there."

"I think we can try. Let's not worry about the payment part of it just yet. We'll see how much time goes into this. It could be we run into a dead end real fast."

Troy absorbed the last few words in silence.

"Okay, yeah. That would be great. The photos and particulars should be on Mr. Roberts' desk somewhere."

The sound of shuffling papers filtered through the phone line.

"I've got them right here. The little girl is beautiful, you're right about that. Does her mother know what you're up to?"

"No, and I want to keep it that way for now. They've had enough disappointments trying to find her."

"Sure, okay. I'll be in touch as soon as I have any information for you. I'll also let you know if Mr. Roberts recovers."

"Thanks, thanks a lot. I may phone you again if I think of anything else that might help in the search. I'd like to actually get out to San Francisco soon and talk to whoever's got the info. It'd make me feel better to be there in person checking on it. I'll let you know my travel plans, if you could set up an appointment for me. Oh, and I'm sorry to hear about Mr. Roberts."

"Thanks. We'll get started on it, Mr. Henderson."

Troy hung up the phone and walked to his office window. He could smell the harbor a few blocks away, the humidity carrying the odor of fish and salt through the hot, sticky air. The street sounds outside made everything seem so normal. But it wasn't. It would never be until Meghan was back with her mom.

"Troy, why is it again that you're headed out to the west coast?"

It was barely noon when Neil poured his brother a cold beer, then took his own soda from the table, motioning to the porch. They sat down on the new swing and Troy took a long gulp from the pewter stein.

"I told you, I've got some business out there at the home office. I'm going to take a week vacation while I'm at it. I hear northern California is beautiful. Why are you so worried? Afraid I won't come back to Boston to face another winter?"

"Well, that crossed my mind."

Neil didn't say what had *really* been on his mind since hearing of his brother's trip. Troy would be in the same area where he and Doreen had looked for Beatrice and Meghan that terrible autumn of '45. Perhaps there was another reason for the business trip. Still, he hesitated to ask his brother anything more as Troy was fairly close-mouthed about his personal life.

"So Neil, how's the law practice coming along? Got any clients yet?"

"Yeah, actually. The head of the firm said I was off to a good start, whatever that means. Anyway, the hours are a bit long right now but that should improve soon. I'm still getting the hang of this corporate law stuff. I always saw myself as a public defender, but reality set in the further I got into law school classes. At least if I lose a case now, it's some rich guy's money that goes down the drain, instead of some poor man's life."

"How do you know what that rich guy's thinking? He could get desperate if he lost his money. Besides, that rich guy's probably going to be you one of these days."

"Oh, I wouldn't count on that. Doreen gives away enough money, I'll never have to worry about that! She's the conscience in our family. I think she's trying to bring socialism to the masses all on her own. Gotta love her, though."

"Especially if she keeps feeding me every other Sunday. Hell, I may never have to get married! I can come here for my fix of home-cooked food and domestic atmosphere."

The brothers slapped each other's backs and laughed, only to be interrupted by a call from the dining room. Dinner was on the table. Doreen poured lemonade into glasses and smiled as she heard them stomping through the door, their laughter barely subsiding.

The chicken she had so lovingly prepared was devoured in a matter of minutes and the conversation was as lively as the pace of the meal. When her plate was nearly empty, Doreen pushed her chair back from the table and watched and listened as the two men she loved bantered back and forth like teenagers. It was a scene that was repeated whenever Troy came in from the city. But today, their voices and smiles blurred as she focused her thoughts on her only daughter. Where was she having Sunday dinner? What was her favorite meal now? Would Meghan ever have a sister to spend the afternoon with? Doreen saw her own childhood flash before her. She had been the only child in their small home and her diary had helped her cope with lonely hours. Perhaps Beatrice would be sensitive enough to give Meghan a diary. Maybe Meghan wasn't an only child. Maybe Meghan wasn't even with Beatrice anymore. Doreen shuddered and folded her arms, her fingers clutching her elbows. She rose from the chair and picked up her plate and glass.

"No way, beautiful. This old, ugly brother of mine is gonna help me do dishes. It's your turn to relax. Dinner was delicious, as usual. What's for dessert?"

"Ice cream with fresh strawberries. Do you want it now?"

"No, we'll clean up first and work up another appetite. You look a bit pale, Doreen. Are you okay?"

"Yes, I'm fine."

"Why don't you take a short walk, then settle yourself in the porch swing. We'll holler when we're done."

Doreen smiled. She remembered her mum saying that only cakes get done; people *finish*. She walked out into the afternoon sunshine, heading to the park to watch the children and grandparents weave their lives together in a way that parents never understood.

The park was crowded with "children" of all ages. Grown men hopping on and off the merry-go-round, old ladies waiting in line for the ice cream vendor, parents chasing their children in games of tag. She sat down under a massive oak tree whose bark had been stripped away in places, but whose trunk still stood strong and proud. She leaned her head back and closed her eyes. Soon the warmth of the afternoon sun and the mix of happy voices lulled her to sleep.

The next voice she heard startled her and she tried to jump up to see where it was coming from. She didn't remember the water. How did she get to the water? The boat was waiting for her and the voice she had recognized was calling to her from the boat's deck. It was a frantic voice and she tried so hard to reach the boat. The closer she got to the walkway, the further away the vessel drifted. She was reaching out her arms, trying to grab hold of the rope that had secured it to the docks, but her arms weren't long enough. The harder she strained to reach, the softer the voice became. It was clear that her place was on that boat, yet she had chosen to spend the afternoon sleeping under a tree! How could she have been so stupid?! How could she have missed the sailing, and that voice, was it her mum's? No, maybe it was the voice of a child. Of course, it was Meghan's voice! She let her aching arms fall to her side as she saw herself begin to sob. No, perhaps it was *her* voice calling out. The boat was barely visible now and Doreen covered her face with her hands, her body wracked with the pain of desperation.

"Lady, lady…Are you alright?"

Doreen struggled to open her eyes, not sure if her hands were still covering her face. When she was finally able to see the figure before her, her hands were laying innocently across her lap and a young boy stood at her side.

"Lady, I'm sorry to bother you, but I was worried that you were okay. Are you alright?"

Doreen's breath came in quick bursts and her heart was pounding in her chest.

"Yes, yes, I think so. I'm sorry. Did I do something to you?"

"Oh no, mam, it's just that you were crying in your sleep and well…I thought it would be better to wake you up. It sounded like you were having a really bad dream. Can I get you anything?"

Doreen shifted her weight away from the tree trunk, sitting forward and shaking her head in confusion.

"I'm really okay. I guess I *was* having a bad dream. I just need to get up and walk around a bit. I'll be fine. I'll be fine in a little while."

The boy scampered off to the jungle gym. Doreen stood up, brushed her slacks off and looked up at the canopy of oak leaves that had shaded her from the hot sun. She could see light through a small gap in the leaves and a hint of color seemed to dance across the sun's rays. Maybe it wasn't true color. Maybe it was just the reflection of everything else that gave the appearance of color. She lowered her head and stared off into the direction of the ice cream vendor. His popularity had grown and the line was longer now, but no one seemed to mind. They all seemed content to wait. They knew that sooner or later it would be their turn. They might not get exactly what they wanted, but there would still be some treat in the freezer. They would pay for it and go back to enjoy the rest of their day.

Doreen searched her pockets and came up with a dime, just enough for a single scoop cone. She couldn't go back to the house for dessert just yet. She needed time. Wiping the tears that still lay in the corners of her eyes, she walked slowly over to the vendor. She had the rest of the afternoon, plenty of time to wait her turn. Enough time to watch the happy scenes before her as she contemplated what choices may still be in the vendor's cart.

The clanging of the trolley bells alerted Troy that his stop was coming up soon. He grabbed his briefcase and hopped off the bus as it pulled to the curb. He turned around to watch it, amused by its quaint appearance as it continued down the long hill. He was glad he'd tossed a sweater into his other small bag as it seemed the evening would be cool. Boston was hot in the summer, but San Francisco seemed to have forgotten what July was supposed to feel like. He followed the directions on the small piece of paper and headed to the corporate office.

He was greeted by a secretary who politely showed him into Mr. Sander's office.

"Good afternoon, Mr. Henderson. Glad you could make it out here. Are you going to take some vacation time while you're here?"

"Good afternoon! Please call me Troy, if you don't mind. I'm not one much for formalities. And yes, I'm actually on personal time now. I couldn't really justify this trip for pure business, so I'm also on my own expense account as well. I'm hoping you can direct me to some good cheap places to eat."

"I sure can. This city's loaded with great food. Hope you like Chinese, it's the best here in San Fran. Don't forget to check out this little fish shop on the wharf and the Ghiradelli chocolates, of course."

"Of course. I've got to bring some of those back for my sister-in-law. Actually, Mr. Sanders, she doesn't know, of course why I'm really here. I just feel certain that being here may give us some clues about Beatrice Moore and hopefully, Meghan's whereabouts."

"Please, call me David. I truly hate to tell you this Troy, but Stuart Roberts died last evening. He hung in there longer than any of us expected him to, but I guess his injuries were too extensive."

"I'm sorry for your loss, David."

"Thanks. It will seem weird around here without him. But I do have a bit of news."

"What's that?"

"My secretary, Marcy, who used to be Mr. Robert's secretary, came up with a quirky idea. She said that Stuart went to every one of his high school class reunions. I guess they had them every five or ten years. Anyway, she thought maybe if this Beatrice Moore lived in the area, she might have gone to high school with him. You said she lived for a while in San Rafael, right?"

"Yeah, according to police records. I can't say she actually *lived* there, but she was picked up for vagrancy, of all things. So she must have been there for a while at least."

"Well, here's the deal. Marcy said that Stuart Roberts was from that town and likely went to San Rafael High School. We could start by looking at old yearbooks, see if this Beatrice is in any of them. I'd ask Stu's ex-wife, but I'm not sure she's even in town yet, and if she is, this is a bad time to approach her."

"Yeah. Your yearbook idea sounds great, though Beatrice may be a lot younger than he is."

"Could be, but at least it's a start. And don't forget that she may have assumed a new name."

"Yeah. Anyway, do you think we could also track down his estranged brother you mentioned? Maybe he'd know something."

"That's a good idea, but where to start looking? The upper northwest is a big place, and I really wouldn't know how to begin. There must be thousands of Roberts in just northern California, let alone Oregon and Washington. Let's start in San Rafael first and see what happens."

The bus ride to San Rafael grew warm and stuffy. Troy took one of his notes on the search and folded it into a fan, waving it wildly as he stepped off the bus. The high school was not too far away and at least walking gave him the chance to get some breeze. There was only a skeletal staff in the office, as school was officially closed for the summer. The women behind the counter eyed him suspiciously as he opened the door and stepped in.

After much explanation, the yearbooks from past years were spread across a conference table in the now vacant principal's office and Troy began his search. He found Stuart Roberts' picture, but not his brother's. Perhaps he was a lot younger than Stuart, or the family had moved to another location. There was no Beatrice Moore, either. The only name remotely close was Betty Maury, and she was dark-haired and heavy set. He kept looking until his eyes began burning and the ladies in the office interrupted him with a final "we have to close up now." He thanked them for their time and walked out to look for a room to spend the night. The only hotel right in town was small and run-down, with lots of trucks parked out in front. Troy walked briskly to the nearest bus stop and took the ride back into San Francisco. At least he could enjoy a good meal as he pondered his next step.

Doreen was writing feverishly, her papers and books scattered across their sofa, when the phone startled her.

"I'll get it, Doreen. Keep working so you don't lose your train of thought."

Doreen smiled as the pencil continued scratching. She knew without a doubt that not all husbands would approve of their wives carrying their work home with them. Still, Neil had never complained of her evening work on articles for medical journals. She knew it gave *him* an excuse to catch up on new legal briefs, though he would never admit that he brought work home. She also knew that her published work was a source of pride for him, too, as he had mentioned it at the law firm's recent picnic.

"Hey, Troy! How are you out there in God's country?"

"Doing great, though it was a long trip and I'm ready for bed while everyone else is just having dinner!"

"So how was corporate Fancher Executive Searches? Did you meet any big shots?"

"Yeah, yeah, but actually the president recently died. Anyway, they're all nice people. Not snooty or anything. I'm getting ready to eat in this Chinese place that the new boss recommended. Smells great. Everything okay there?"

"We're fine. Troy, you just left yesterday. Not much happens around here in twenty four hours!"

Troy laughed.

"You've got a point."

There was a pause in the conversation as the brothers each considered divulging what was really playing in their mind. Troy broke the short silence, starting up the subject of what to bring back to Doreen. After a few suggestions, they said their "goodbyes," keeping the talk to a minimum to avoid the costly charges. Neil hung up the phone and walked over to Doreen, pushing away papers to find a seat. Her pencil kept writing as she spoke.

"Did he have anything interesting to say?"

"Not really. Said it was a long trip yesterday, but he was looking forward to this Chinese dinner tonight. He sounded good."

Doreen put her pencil down and looked up.

"You know, he's right in the same area we were in when we searched for Meghan that first autumn here. You don't suppose he's out there for reasons other than business?"

"I certainly wouldn't put it past him. Honey, I know he still feels responsible for Meghan's disappearance."

"You know I've told him a hundred times that it wasn't his fault. Nor yours. Nor any of ours for that matter. He didn't take Meghan, Beatrice Moore did!"

"I know that and so do you. But Troy seems unable to separate himself from the whole thing."

They sat silently for a few moments. Neil put his arm around Doreen's shoulder and gave it a slight squeeze.

"I know I've said this before, but it probably needs repeating. Hon, I have never believed that Beatrice took Meghan for any other reason than to love and raise her. I don't believe she would ever hurt her or leave her; she was just desperate for a child. According to everyone else, Beatrice always loved Meghan as if she were her own. I'm sure she's taking very good care of her."

"That's my constant prayer. It's just that…I'm her mother. It's me who should be taking very good care of her. I should be the one helping her through these difficult in-between years. I should be the one to buy a dress for her first dance. It should be me cleaning up all the messes that she and her friends make. What if she thinks I just abandoned her?"

"We've been through this before, Doreen. You know Meghan would never think that. I've said before that Beatrice must have made up some tragic story, something that would mean she could never see you again. If she loves Meghan as much as everyone said, and I believe she does, she would have had to convince Meghan that you were not alive. Then Meghan's only option would be to go with Miss B."

"In my head, I know you're right. But…damn it, Neil. It's all so wrong! It's so unfair! If only you would've waited just a bit longer before shipping her off …damn it, Neil!! It *is* your fault. You should have waited a few more days!"

Never before had she let those words surface directly at him and now they were drowning both of them like waves of water spewing from a stagnant well. Neil sat frozen as her wails of grief washed over him. The outcry had choked off his breath, but the worse stranglehold came from the pain that now gripped their home and would leave marks far outlasting those spoken words.

The early morning sun burst through the windows and Doreen pulled the bed sheet up over her face. She could smell coffee perking and heard Neil rustling around in the kitchen. She rolled out of bed, avoiding the mirror that would reflect her swollen eyes. She grabbed a light robe and treaded softly down the steps. They ate breakfast in awkward silence, but as the sun moved across the sky the routines of their day brought a gentle cleansing. By evening, the air was thick with heat and humidity and a summer rainstorm brought relief – and solace.

The lure of the beautiful city of the Golden Gate distracted Troy more than once in his weeklong quest for information on Beatrice Moore. Still, with the help of local police, he was able to post her picture in public buildings. She had been listed initially in Rockport as a "missing person," but her status had been changed to "kidnapper" with the urging of the Boston Metropolitan Police Department. Troy was more familiar with the San Francisco transport systems than he cared to be, going from one small town to another within a two hundred mile radius. There was no new lead, no other information. The possible link of Beatrice attending high school with Stuart Roberts had gone nowhere. If the Roberts boys had ever known Beatrice Moore, it was far too late to seek their input. Then there was the whole question of her name being an alias. Without real proof of her acquaintance with Stuart, City Hall had refused to allow Troy access to any of the Roberts' records. Without that, and without their parent's names, it would be nearly impossible to find Stuart's brother in the vast northwest. Impossible to discover if Stuart's brother ever knew Beatrice Moore. For every step forward in the case, Troy knew he was taking two steps back.

He sat on Fisherman's Wharf, peering down through the wire fence at the fish that swam below. He had tried and failed. It was time to go back home. It was time let go of the feelings of guilt and helplessness. Maybe Doreen and Neil had finally given in to the reality that Meghan was not coming home. If they still believed there was a chance, they never said so. Too many years had gone by without any more concrete piece of information. Perhaps that was why ending this trip weighed so heavily on him. He didn't know exactly what they thought; it was too painful to bring up the subject.

The sun had been shrouded in clouds for most of the day and as evening rolled over the harbor, the damp fog of the bay settled in. Troy stood up and stared out at the water. There was an answer somewhere. He just didn't have any more time to spend on the search. Or maybe it was his heart that couldn't afford the expense. Maybe that's why Doreen and Neil rarely mentioned their loss. The pain was still chipping away at the inside, but the outside had to remain strong to avoid a total collapse of their hearts - and their spirits. God, what an awful paradox to live with for the rest of your life.

The plane that brought Troy into Boston was an hour late, but Neil and Doreen were both at the gate to greet him. He could see their faces clearly as others pushed their way past him. They knew. Of course they knew. He'd forgotten the bond he shared with his brother, a bond that spoke when voices did not. They wanted to see hope on his face and all he could do was smile weakly, hug them both, and shake his head "no." The three of them stood embraced, the rest of the travelers disappearing from their sight. The loudspeaker announced the next flight, bringing them back to reality. They turned toward the terminal exit and walked out into the fading sunshine, their silence speaking louder than words, and their arms linked in the comfort of the human touch.

CHAPTER THIRTY FIVE

Rockport, Massachusetts
May 1960

The reflection in the vanity mirror wasn't what Doreen was hoping for. She ran her fingers across her face, pausing at her eyes. When had the wrinkles become so unkind? She was used to looking at laugh lines, but the ones that now creased her skin weren't laughing. They were deep and appeared without fanfare – and without permission. They looked almost sinister, as though they knew a dark secret that she hadn't discovered yet. She took a comb from a gold-plated tray and tried to tease the top of her hair just a bit more. She could hear Neil singing as he finished donning his tuxedo. His voice was strong and cheerful, even if a bit off-key, just like Colin's had been.

This would be another of those difficult evenings for Doreen. She always found corporate gatherings stressful, full of inane pleasantries and uncomfortable stares. Yet the worst were the probing questions about the all the lawyers'children. How were they doing in school? What university were they attending? Did they make captain of the varsity team or when was their "coming out" party? Were they married yet? Doreen had never been able to stay in one conversational circle too long, afraid of facing the questions she could never answer. It was expected of Neil to mingle and talk with as many people as possible, especially since he had made known his political ambitions. He was always careful to keep Doreen at his side, yet there were many times when she found herself standing isolated, wondering if anyone had read her latest article on cancer research or if they just thought her dress was too tight. For a moment, her mind wandered back to the Croydon Hospital parties held before the world had gone mad. She and Colin had moved about the crowd, arms linked, sharing private laughter at some of their co-workers' antics. It had been such a different time then. Such a long time ago.

"Doreen, are you nearly ready? I can't be late tonight."

"That's for certain, dear. It would never do for one of the guests of honor to be late for his own award presentation."

"You just love saying 'guest of honor', don't you?"

"Of course. I've always been your biggest fan in the courtroom, and I'll be your biggest supporter in the arena of long-winded American politics."

"You've certainly got the 'long-winded' part of it correct. We should keep our campaigning to a minimum like your country does."

Doreen smiled at his reference to her citizenship. His upcoming leap into politics could cause concern over the British passport she still held. But that was a discussion for later. Right now she had to slip into the black dress she hoped would disguise her true shape.

"You look beautiful."

Neil zipped up her dress and they went arm in arm down the stairs.

"Neil, I completely forgot to tell you we received a letter from the O'Connors today! It wasn't as long a note as they usually write, but they send their heartiest congratulations on your award from the firm. They said they wish they could be here with us, but to give you a hug and their best wishes. You can read it later after we get home."

"I hope to be doing other things when we get home tonight. I'll catch up on their news tomorrow."

Neil gave her his standard grin and she laughed at his not so subtle declaration.

"Come on you, we'll be late. Is Troy going to make it tonight, to see you get your award?"

"I think so. He likes to check out the single women scene."

"I think he's in the wrong place for that! But then again, you never know!"

The street had an eerie glow this time of night. It was not dark enough yet for the streetlights, but the sun had set and shadows danced through the blossoming trees. Doreen pulled her shawl across her shoulders as they climbed into their car to make the short trip to Boston. It felt a bit chilly for May, but her nervousness would make her warm by the time they got to the awards banquet. She spoke sentences in her mind that would be easy to recite when faced with the hard questions that came after dinner and too many drinks.

"So my beautiful sister-in-law, how are you surviving this evening?"

"Oh Troy, thanks for saving me from the woman who's now making her way over here. Pretend we're involved in some deep discussion."

"You want *me* to pretend that?"

"Come on Troy, be a sport! Neil's been held captive by old Dr. Anders for the past twenty minutes. He's not going to rescue me any time soon."

"Okay, okay."

They both casually turned around, trying to look very serious and making their mouths move without sound. As soon as the woman in pursuit changed directions, Doreen giggled like a schoolgirl.

"That was perfect, Troy. You're the best!"

"Actually Doreen, I really did have something to ask you about. I'm not sure how to say this, but when I saw Neil for lunch last week, he didn't look so good. He looked really tired, and bit pale. Have you noticed that at all?"

"I have, a couple of times. I think he's just been working too many hours again. It doesn't help when I'm also consumed with my work because he uses that as an excuse to keep late hours. He doesn't feel guilty working so much if I'm in the same boat."

"Well, just to be sure, talk him into seeing a doctor soon, will 'ya? You can pretty well talk him into anything."

"Except a vacation!"

When Neil joined them later, Doreen looked carefully into his eyes. He did look unusually tired tonight. Could be all the excitement of the evening. Perhaps it was the glasses of champagne. She vowed to call the doctor herself on Monday morning.

Neil and Doreen looked for Troy as they left the festivities and saw him in lively conversation with a red-haired woman whose dress was possibly a little indiscreet, but whose smile seemed genuine. Troy caught their eyes and waved at them, his animation giving them permission to leave without interrupting him. Doreen laughed, then took her husband's arm and went out into the night, exhilarated by the lights of the city and her single glass of champagne.

There was a soft light burning in the front room as they walked through the door. Doreen always left the old hurricane lamp on when they were out. She hated coming home to a dark house.

"I'm going to get a tall glass of water before I come upstairs, Neil. I won't be long."

"Get one for me, will you please? I'm so thirsty tonight."
"Champagne will do that to you, love."

Doreen looked up as Neil tripped on the stairs.

"Are you alright"?

"Yes hon, I'm fine. I'm just so very tired. If you don't mind, I'd like to postpone our after celebration activities as long as you're willing to take a rain check."

"Of course, casanova. Go on up to bed and I'll be there in a few minutes."

Doreen took a pitcher of ice water from the refrigerator and filled two glasses. She picked up the envelope from the O'Connor's and took the letter out. Their words always made her feel at peace. She unfolded the paper and reread the letter.

May 1, 1960

Dear Doreen and Neil

Hallo to our dear friends! We hope you are both keeping well and content. This will be just a short note this time, as I want to get this posted so it arrives on time to say, "congratulations" to you Neil! A little bird told us of your award and we are so proud of you. Wish we could be there to share the moment with you. We must also add that we are equally proud of the writing you've been doing, Doreen. Thanks for sending us the articles to read, even if we don't understand the medical terms. We've been keeping all our neighbors informed of both of your accomplishments. Honestly, I think that sometimes they get rather jealous of our having something to talk about besides the weather and the naughty schoolchildren who tear up their gardens playing football!

We had quite a lovely afternoon in Oxford today. There was a May Day celebration on the Commons, complete with the maypole and children with their streamers in hand. It was such fun to watch them weaving their way about the pole and giggling all the while. I hope you will not find my next comment too painful, but it did bring back memories of watching Meghan play during the summer she lived with us. There were many days during the war and strangely, even more days since, that the vision of your lovely daughter engaged in innocent child's play sustained us. Not only sustained, but nurtured us, as though her short presence in our lives was meant to continue giving us joy as only a child can do.

Ian only goes to the shop once in a while now, just to see if the new owners are following the many instructions he gave them. Of course, they are not. But I reassure him each time he goes there that his honesty and integrity is a legacy that others will not forget, no matter what the new owners do.

I should be honest myself, now, and tell you that I took quite a fall the other day. I injured my hip, but I'm on the mend now. Nothing broken, just my pride a bit bruised. Ian fusses over me like a mother hen, nearly drives me batty. Never mind, he always means well! That's all our news for now. Again, congratulations on your award and accomplishments. We think of you often with great affection.

                                    Love,
                             Margaret and Ian

Doreen folded the letter, laying it on the table for Neil to read with his morning coffee. She realized with a twinge of regret that he had been in bed for a while now and she had promised to be upstairs much sooner. She took the glasses of water and made her way up to their bedroom. Neil was indeed in bed, but he still wore his tuxedo shirt and his socks, and he lay there without covers. She walked to the side of the bed to cover him and loosen his collar. The small table lamp shone on his face - it was an ashen color and his skin was wet with perspiration.

"Neil! Neil! Are you alright?"

There was no response. Doreen's adrenal system went into high gear. She flew down the stairs and grabbed the phone, dialing the ambulance service as quickly as her fingers could.

She returned to their room and began CPR, but her mind and her hands couldn't concentrate on the task – there was too much at stake.

It was only five minutes before they arrived and she watched in horror as they worked over him. The clock downstairs chimed two times and it seemed her heart was beating loudly enough for everyone to hear. As a nurse, she knew what she was seeing. They were continuing giving him CPR and massaging his heart. The same heart that had prevented him from serving in the U.S. Armed Forces. The same heart that had stolen hers while he made his own war contribution a continent away from home.

She followed the stretcher as they carefully maneuvered the stairway and put him into the back of the ambulance.

"You may ride in the back with us, Mrs. Henderson. He's stabilized for now."

Doreen blinked away tears and sat on the floor of the ambulance as it sped away. Troy. She would call Troy as soon as she could. She hoped the redhead had not been so intriguing after all.

It was after four in the morning when the doctor opened the door of the emergency waiting room.

"Mrs. Henderson, your husband's doing well. He had a heart attack, but he's going to fully recover. There was some damage, but nothing that should be of too much concern, as long as he gives himself a long recovery time and takes better care of himself. I'll go through all the specifics with you later in the morning. Right now, I suggest you get some sleep."

"Thank you, doctor. Thank you very much."

Doreen let out a big sigh and turned to face Troy whose face had been devoid of color for the past hour. He extended his arms and gave her a hug, his body shaking with emotion.

"It's okay, now Doreen. He's going to be all right. He's too ornery to let this get him down. Besides, he knows I still owe him money from our last poker game. He's not going to miss the chance to harass me about that."

They both attempted a smile.

"I know you're right. I was just so frightened, Troy. I can't go through this...not again."

"You won't have to, the doc just said he's going to get better, it'll just take time."

They looked in on Neil, then left the hospital at the insistence of the intensive care nurses. Doreen knew the nurses were right. What she needed now was to take care of herself so she'd be able to care for her husband. Then it would be her job to make sure he took care of himself.

She sent Troy upstairs to sleep in his old bedroom and put the kettle on for some hot tea. She would go to bed later. For now, she needed to sit down and sort some things out as her mind was reeling with the events of the previous night. It would be dawn soon. Maybe the light breaking through the clouds would help her determine her next steps. The teakettle whistled and she poured the hot water into a small pot. She watched as the tea ball floated around, bobbing up and down like a swimmer playing in the waves. She took a spoon and stirred the brown sugar that floated from the bottom and dissolved into the liquid.

Her mind drifted from Neil to her daughter. It was soon going to be Meghan's birthday. She would be twenty-four now. Had she ever gone to college? Perhaps she was married and even a mother herself. Where was she living and what were her friends like? Doreen took a swallow of tea, then rose to get a notebook and pen from the kitchen "junk" drawer. She sat down, took another drink of tea and began writing down ideas and thoughts as they crossed her mind.

Neil would need lots of attention for the immediate future and she would need to be at home with him. It would give her the perfect chance to do what her inner self had been considering for quite awhile. The fear that had gripped her in the earlier hours of the morning had forced her to look squarely at her past and her present. Fear had a way of revealing things that were always just out of sight. Nearly visible, yet not quite recognizable. She had almost lost her second husband, the man who had pulled her away from the edge of despair. Now it was time to move *him* away from that edge, and then to step back and remember her precipice. It was time to deal not only with the reality of the present, but of the past as well. It was time to let the wounds heal completely.

She watched the sun send its early rays through the kitchen window, a promise that the clouds had dissipated for the time being. The new day seemed to speak its own wisdom. The trouble with always moving on, as she had become so adept at, was that the constant motion interrupted the healing process. The very ability to keep going in the face of pain and grief could also mask the depth of the injury. It could prevent the process of feeling that hurt, of letting the air reach the wounds instead of keeping them covered. It was time to revisit the past to keep the wound from festering and never healing.

Troy found Doreen on the front porch, still in the dress she had worn to the banquet the night before. She had on Neil's Aran cardigan and a tartan wool blanket spread across her lap.

"Are you doing okay, Doreen?

"I think so."

"You never went to bed last night, aren't you totally exhausted?"

"Yes. I'm finally tired enough to sleep. Exhausted enough to stop fighting the inevitable. It's time I go in and rest for a while. I've got a long road ahead of me."

"Yes, you do. We all do."

They walked through the front door together. She walked slowly up the stairs while he went to the kitchen, opened the refrigerator door and stood staring at its contents, unsure of what it was he really wanted.

CHAPTER THIRTY-SIX

Rockport, Massachusetts
November 1964

The television cast a strange, blue beam that darted across the room, bouncing off the curtains and furniture like an uninvited dragonfly. Doreen sat on their new sofa, intently watching the news and trying to make sense of all the turmoil. Neil's position as a state senator had catapulted them both into the arena of politics, just when the world around them was exploding - yet again. Doreen had tried unsuccessfully to dissuade Neil from entering the legislature. Yet the more she said, the more passionate he became about making a difference the best way he knew how. Quietly mulling over his decision, she had realized how like Colin he was in that respect. Both men strived to live their passion. She only wondered at what cost.

The war in the rice paddies of Vietnam was escalating every month, with more and more young Americans joining the services or being drafted to serve on the other side of the world. Doreen often sat on their porch, contemplating how she felt about that conflict. She was a war widow and reconciling her views with that of those around her was difficult at best. Civil unrest was certainly not new to her, but now it came packaged differently than she expected. There was also the whole issue of racial unrest prompted by the injustice she had watched many people endure for decades. She hoped that having more time to absorb all the changes and uncertainties had given her a broader perspective on events and their effect on others.

Staying at home for the past four years to help Neil recover and to work on her own project had given her a chance to think. More time to complete the task she had begun when it was no longer possible to avoid it. Even after Neil had returned to the office full time and went into politics, she resolved to keep going until her project was finished.

The voice that spoke from the television screen mechanically reported the latest statistics that had just been released from the Pentagon. Doreen rose from the sofa, turned the set off, and walked outside on the porch. The trees had become barren and the wind was more intense than earlier in the day. The shutters on the old Sager's house rattled like a cry for attention. She looked over at the now empty house and wondered instinctively how Ian was doing. They hadn't heard from their Oxford friend in nearly two months. His last letter had arrived just as the trees had begun to change into their regal costumes. The letter's contents had been such a shock. His written words still played in her mind like an old newsreel, one that touched her so much more than even the disturbing scenes on television. The lines repeated in her consciousness without invitation – without warning.

```
                                September 10, 1964
My dearest Doreen and Neil,
    It is with great sadness that I write this
letter. I wish I could avoid telling you, but I
know in my heart that I must. I wanted to phone
you, but I knew it would be so difficult for me to
say to you and too difficult for you to hear. This
way you can absorb what I have to tell you in
your own private way. My lovely Margaret died two
days ago. She seemed fine when we went to bed, but
she passed on while asleep; I didn't even know it
until morning came and I couldn't rouse her. It
was dreadful for me, but I know now that it was a
peaceful way for her to go. I just didn't get to
say "goodbye" which I suppose will haunt me for
a long while. We laid her to rest this morning in
the old churchyard here in Kidlington. It was a
lovely September day and there were certainly lots
of folks in attendance. Did my heart good. Please
don't worry about me, as I shall be fine. I'm going
to keep myself busy and my mind focused. I'm so
sorry for the grief you will bear, as I know how
much like family we four have been. And yes, I
will be grieving with you. Do remember, though,
that Margaret and I both led a long and wonderful
life together. If you can say that when you are
our age, you will have indeed been blessed.
                          With fondest affection,
                          Ian
```

One question had plagued Doreen since the news of Margaret's death. Did Meghan have any memory of the O'Connor's? She had taken so naturally to Margaret and Ian. Did she ever remember even having lived with them before boarding that ship? She answered herself the same way each time the thought occurred. Yes, she would have remembered the people who made her feel safe and secure in a world full of fear and uncertainty. Doreen pictured Meghan and Margaret sipping tea in the O'Connor kitchen, giggling at a shared secret.

"Hey love, what are you doing out here?"

Neil's head was poking out from his car window as he drove up in front of their house.

"I'm just thinking about things."

"About what a wonderful husband you have?!"

"Certainly! And what my wonderful husband wants for dinner this evening."

"How about if I take you out to dinner?"

"Does that mean we're joining Troy and his new 'right one' – again?"

Neil laughed as he closed the car door and walked up the porch steps.

"Actually, I was thinking we'd go out alone. And yes, Troy does have another 'right one' and she may really be it this time. Let's hope so, he needs someone to keep him out of trouble. We've done the best we could!"

"Neil, you're terrible! But I *would* like to go out to dinner with you alone tonight. I've some important things to share with you."

"I hope we have something to share *after* dinner as well."

"Is that an invitation for dessert?"

"You might say that."

Doreen shook her head and laughed at this man who never changed.

Neil watched as his wife began changing into a brown, wool dress. After fifteen years of marriage, she sometimes seemed like a new bride. It was only one of the reasons he loved her so. He knew she had something important to tell him concerning the private project she'd been at so diligently for the past four years. Yet as he gazed at her in the twilight that peeked through their bedroom window, he hoped she wouldn't mind if they dined later in the evening. He got up from his corner-reading chair and quickly unzipped the dress she had just donned.

"Maybe dinner could wait just a while longer. You always look so incredibly beautiful by twilight. I've never understood how it is that I just look older each year yet the passing seasons only make you look better. How did I ever get so lucky?"

Doreen let her dress fall and wrapped her arms around his neck.

"I'm never sure if luck has such a hand or not. We are blessed, though. Very blessed. We have each other, which is more than many people have. I love you so very much."

As darkness fell, the dress remained on the floor and the dinner was forgotten.

Sometime before the owl began his nightly song, the soft murmur of voices drifted through the room as Doreen finally shared her news with the man who loved her intensely.

Neil opened his eyes, trying to wake up and focus. He pondered the words he'd heard in the late night hours.

"Doreen, are you absolutely sure? I know it may seem like a good idea to you, but do you really want to dredge up all those painful memories and actually speak to total strangers about them?"

Doreen scowled at Neil and rose quickly, shaking her head in frustration. She opened the bedroom curtains and morning light streamed in.

"You just don't get it, do you? You've let me work on this project for years without asking me much of anything and now you're trying to tell me it's wrong for me to do this? How can you possibly question this?"

"Because I'm thinking of your emotional well-being, that's why. I don't know why you'd want to dredge up all those sad events in England when you have a new life here. Damn, you've had a new life here for many years, what's the point of going back to the old one?"

"What's the point of sharing my own war story at a conference in London where it all began? God, Neil, that's such a dumb thing to say. I thought you'd be proud of me for finally being able to verbalize my story; it's the only way I can finally close that haunting chapter of my life."

"Geez, I hope you don't think of our meeting up as a bad chapter in your life."

"Don't be ridiculous. You sound childish when you say things like that."

Neil picked up the clothes that had been left strewn across the floor the night before and hung them in the closet before responding. The clock next to the bed ticked loudly and downstairs the grandfather clock chimed eight times.

"I'm sorry, Doreen. It's just that, you know I've always been sensitive about a lot of stuff related to that time. Sometimes it's still awkward for me, knowing I wasn't your first love, knowing all the mistakes I made after we met, the mistake of sending Meghan on that ship. It's just that…I don't want you to hurt all over again. Hell, *I* don't want to hurt all over again."

"Honey, that's why I'm going to London for this conference; I need to tell my story out loud. I need to verbalize the pain that war brought to my own life. I need to say that the terrible hurt is not the final feeling."

Neil walked over to the bed and guided Doreen to the window.

"Have you noticed the leaves changing already?"

Doreen sighed without responding.

"You do know how very proud of you I am, don't you? I mean, if this trip is the culmination of all that work you've done for the past four years, then I truly hope you find a peace when it's all over. I hope that part of your life will finally find its place as a sad time, not a haunting nightmare that never ends."

"I can only try. I have to try. It may be all I can do from here on out. But remember, I do love you. I love our life together. I just have to do this. I'll only be gone a week or so and it's not until the beginning of May. We have *plenty* of time to let this settle in."

Neil nodded and wrapped his arms around her shoulders as the morning sun danced playfully across the colorful leaves of the sturdy maple.

CHAPTER THIRTY SEVEN

Seattle, Washington
December 1964

The janitor's footsteps echoed down the long hall as he began his morning shift at the Seattle Sun newspaper. He pushed the long-handled broom almost enthusiastically as he hummed Christmas carols, glancing at the decorations that were on each office door. The newspaper presses were clanging loudly and he stood for a moment to watch them through the glass partition, then took a rag from his pocket and wiped down the window. The sight of the large gears and belts in motion halted both employees and visitors as they stopped to watch in wonder. There was something magnificently dynamic and yet mesmerizing about the presses in action. The sound of voices from the editor's office prompted the janitor to continue on with his task. He paused at the open door and polished the brass plate that read: *Richard Meyers, Editor-in-Chief.* The men in the room waved at him and resumed their conversation.

"I tell you, Hank, it's terrific. The girl's got some real talent. I think we should let her fly with it, and give her the bigger project as a follow up."

The assistant editor lowered his head, shoving his hands in his worn sport coat.

"I don't know, Rich, she's so young. I'm not sure she can handle the real scope of your new idea. I'll admit she's a talented writer and her piece is first-rate, but I guess I'm just a bit concerned with her perspective on this next one."

"You've got a legitimate concern, Hank. But I think you're wrong about the age thing. She seems to possess a depth in her writing that's unusual, even for seasoned journalists. I believe we should give her the chance. Hell, what have we got to lose? We don't have anyone else we can release for this next piece. Our writers are swamped as it is with everything else going on right now. I wish we could hire one more, but we can't. She's the one."

Hank Thomas knew when he was beaten. He raised his head and stared out the window at the city below them. Seattle always looked so dismal in December. He turned back to his editor and nodded in agreement.

"Okay, Rich. This is your call. Go ahead and give her the shot. I'm sure she'll do a great job."

Richard Meyers watched his assistant editor walk down the hall and sighed. He knew the cause of Hank's concern and it had nothing to do with Meghan Robert's age or lack of experience. It had everything to do with envy. She was good. Damn good. Hank Thomas was getting nervous. Rich sat down at his desk, wound up the plastic Santa and watched as it bounced around, skipping over the nicks and grooves in the old wood. He would tell Meghan at the Sun's Christmas party. That was a perfect time to tell her how pleased he was with her writing and what her next assignment would be.

The Seattle Sun only had offices for the chief, assistant, and section editors. All the other gopher writers sat at small desks in cubicles, separated by five-foot barriers that served as bulletin boards from the inside. The noise of typewriter bells and phones ringing added to the confusion of people scurrying about the room like ants on a hopeless mission to keep their anthill from crumbling. Visitors to the "think and ink den" were always amazed at the prospect of being able to think in this environment. To the writers, the cacophony was both stimulating and soothing at the same time. There was a sense of belonging, even in the competitive world of news journalism, and the bustling activity served as a catalyst for creativity and truth seeking.

This had been Meghan Robert's working home for five years and she thrived in this "captivity." At twenty-eight and single, she put many more hours into her work than she did her social life. She'd never considered the cost of her dedication. She loved to research a subject and put her heart into writing about it with energy and commitment. She stood in her cubicle staring at the picture she had esconded from her dearest friend – and lover. His photo-journalistic work had already secured him several awards and she felt privileged to have one of his best shots tacked up on her board. It had inspired her on more than one occasion to cover her latest assignment with more than just a casual, mundane report. The world was moving so fast and in so many different directions. It was such a different place than it was when she had gone to college at the University of Washington only a few years earlier.

She glanced up at the picture of the Beatles her dad had given to her only a few months ago. She could never quite figure out Paul Roberts. He had said the English group was a passing fad, yet he had insisted that she include something about their influence on young people in her recent article on the British music invasion. Meghan smiled as she considered yet again how serious and stoic her dad seemed on the outside, yet how childlike and flexible he often was. She wondered if that was because he didn't seem to have had much of a childhood – at least not that he shared. Not at all unlike herself. Her own childhood had seemed to really begin when she and her new mom had moved to Marysville, just outside of Seattle, though she was already nine years old by then. They had always been a family of the here and now. Neither she nor her mom had talked about the earlier events in their lives. It was as if once they settled in Marysville, the time clock had begun anew. Even after her mom married Paul Roberts while working as a secretary at his architectural firm, the subject of past histories rarely came up. Her "new" dad seemed perfectly content with silence on that subject.

Meghan listened to her colleagues ramble on Saturday nights about their extended families and all their obligatory activities. On more than one of these nights, she sipped her wine and listened to their complaints, wondering what it would be like to have an extended family. As far as she knew, her mom and dad were the extent of her living familial links. It didn't exactly sadden her, but it felt strange nonetheless. What was her beginning? The thought made her uncomfortable when she considered the passage of time and what endings would look like.

As the Beatles stared back at her, the editor-in chief peered over the top of her cubicle.

"Can I interrupt your thoughts?"

"Of course, Mr. Meyers. Step in and grab a corner of my desk. I'd ask you to sit down, but my chair needs repaired and it slopes down to the floor. My legs are getting their exercise keeping me from sliding off it when I type."

Rich Meyers laughed and saddled up on the corner of her cluttered desk.

"I'll mention that to maintenance. I just stopped by to see if you are coming to the Christmas party tomorrow after work?"

"I planned on it. Was there something I needed to get done before I come?"

"Oh no, that's not at all what I meant. I just wanted to talk to you about a project."

"Well, I can stop by anytime today or tomorrow if that's more convenient."

"I want you to spend today making any corrections on your article for this weekend's edition. I was hoping to see the copy for final approval before you leave the office tomorrow. I don't want to take your time talking about your next project until this one's put to bed."

"Sure. No problem. I hope to have it on your desk first thing in the morning."

"That's great, Meghan. By the way, great protest photo! Did your friend snap that one?"

"Yeah, he's good, isn't he?"

"Yes he is. Do you think we could get him to come work for the Sun?"

"I don't know. He's a free spirit. He's getting used to this freelance work. He's kind of a lone wolf."

"I see. Not totally unlike yourself?"

This time Meghan laughed and nodded as Mr. Meyers slid from the desk and left, peering in at other cubicles for a quick "hello." She sat down in her sloping chair, propping her feet against the thin, metal crossbar under the desk, and took her article from its folder. There wasn't much time to polish what she considered her finest work, her masterpiece: *"The Vietnam War and Its Effects on the New Generation"*. She hoped that it would grab more than just the attention of the Seattle Sun employees, maybe even be considered for an award in the newspaper world. She began typing her corrections, but her mind was slightly distracted by her editor's words. A new project! Whatever it was, she hoped it would be as challenging as the one she now completed.

Meghan walked into Mr. Meyers' office on Friday morning with a folder tucked under her arm. He was sitting at his desk looking at a recent issue of *Time Magazine,* muttering under his breath.

"Excuse me Mr. Meyers, I knocked but you didn't hear me."

"Come in Meghan. Sorry, I was engrossed in this article. Whatever happened to 'ask not what your country can do for you'? Hell, I don't know. I used to think I was pretty liberal in my political views, but all this war protest stuff… I hope your article can help me understand where these young folks are coming from. I've been working hard to stay unbiased, as all good newspapermen are supposed to do, but I guess the riots and the campus unrest is just more than we bargained for when it comes to free speech. But hey, why am I rambling on about this to you?"

"I do understand what you're saying, Mr. Meyers. Sometimes the end result doesn't seem to justify the means. Other times, it does, but I guess young people have been saying that for centuries. You of all people know that a lot of their protests in the past weren't recorded because of their lack of status in the communities. Now we've reached the point that we afford young people the opportunity not only to voice their opinions, but also to have them recorded and disseminated. It's a different world now."

"Yeah, I know. Good thing I have someone your age turning in this story rather than an old goat like myself."

"Old goat, huh? Well, keep your youthful head on while you read my work. You can tell me later what you think. I had actually planned on taking a vacation day today, then show up for the Christmas party later, if that's okay. I've still got three days of vacation to use before the end of the year and if you're going to put me on a new project, I'll probably only get to take just today off. I worked late last night to do my final corrections."

"It seems to me you've already missed the best part of a vacation day – sleeping in! Go on and get out of here, Meghan. I'll see you tonight."

She gently closed his office door and walked out into the drizzling rain, putting on her hooded jacket as she walked to the bus stop. She should get some holiday shopping done while she had the chance, but instead, she took the bus straight home.

Meghan walked into her apartment, stopping at the thermostat by the door to turn it up slightly. Her cat greeted her with meows of protest for not having been fed. She opened a can of chicken livers and scraped a small portion into the cat's bowl, then washed her hands and started the coffeepot. She looked around her sparse kitchen, noticing with just a twinge of regret that she had never bothered to hang much in the way of pictures or plaques. Maybe having barren walls gave her the opportunity to create pictures in her mind. She laughed at the absurd thought. Not hanging pictures was just easier than shopping for them and tacking them up! She preferred to spend her off days driving up to Mount Rainer to hike. Sometimes she just sat under a large pine and stared out, gazing up at the snow-crested tops of the mountains and feeling the wind whip across her face, tangling her reddish blond hair until it looked like a handful of straw.

She poured herself a mug of coffee and stretched out on the worn couch, looking up at the only picture in her living room. It was a picture of the English countryside and she had bought it at an arts fair in Crescent City on her return from San Francisco. She remembered how dizzying her trip to San Fran had been, and how out of touch with reality she was when faced with the "flower children" and "free love" spirits she had encountered there. Yet, *they* seemed out of touch with the rest of the country as they took the lead in this new era of generational conflicts. She thought about the contrast in lifestyle when she stopped in Crescent City. It seemed so far removed from the activities of San Francisco, but she knew it was only a matter of time before many places experienced wildly different events, resembling those in the Bay area.

She stared at the picture longer, remembering the comfort and peace she felt when this oil painting of England had caught her attention. The picture had sparked one of the earliest yet still vivid memories she had, that of living with the Irish couple in a village outside of Oxford, England. The artist had captured the colors so precisely. The bright green fields, delineated by ancient stone fences and sheep that grazed unaware of intruders; the clouds' ominous warnings of frequent weather changes that villagers accepted without fuss, and the local post office that belied the social changes they fought so hard to avoid. The painting held a small cottage, its chimney crooked and its front gate slightly offset, with laundry hanging out to dry in the back garden. The artist wasn't particularly skilled at realistic portrayal, though it was obvious that he intended a true replication of what he'd seen. Still, it was the content and the colors that had intrigued her and had brought her back to the artist's booth a second time to look. It was the link to her past that made her purchase the painting. It spoke of a past she could only bring to mind when dreaming at night, or when triggered by one of her senses at the most unrelated times.

The cat jumped into her lap, spilling what was left of her coffee.

"Kit! You're such a troublemaker."

She set her cup on the end table and began scratching behind Kit's ears as the cat purred and the sounds of the city below grew louder. They both fell asleep to the lullaby of screeching cars and ships' whistles and the steady drizzle that tapped on the roof of their unadorned, yet cozy abode.

It was nearly dark when Meghan awoke and she rose from the couch, dazed from the long, uninterrupted nap. She couldn't remember when she had slept so long during the day, except when she had a bad case of the flu two years earlier. She grabbed a glass of orange juice from the refrigerator and slipped into the shower. There was no need to eat anything, as there'd be plenty of food at the party. She put her hair in a French twist and stepped into a dark, green dress and black pumps. She was a bit giddy for the first time in a long while, thinking about the impending conversation with Mr. Meyers. She felt like a schoolgirl just before a dance. She stroked Kit's back on the way out and promised to be home early. Kit just blinked at her and settled back onto the couch.

It was a dismal night to drive anywhere, but taking her car was certainly preferable to going by bus. Besides, the buses didn't run late in the evening and Meghan wasn't sure what she'd do after the office party was over. She thought about calling Ryan, but he had a photo shoot early in the morning down by the docks. He probably wouldn't be available to "party" after 10:00 p.m. She smiled at the thought of Ryan partying *anytime*. He was even more serious about his work than she was. Still, he could be fun when the timing was right. He certainly was more interesting to talk to than any employees at the Sun.

He had been born in Hawaii while his father was stationed with the U.S. Navy. His dad had been killed in the attack in December of 1941. Meghan and Ryan often talked about how similar their very early lives had been, though their conversations were never maudlin. Instead, they were filled with the smallest of recollections of their past. There were discussions of family ties and the effect World War II had on children of their generation. Her late-night talks with Ryan had helped her form more than one impression of the Vietnam War's effects on a whole new generation. She smiled as she thought of the way they finished each other's sentences.

The parking lot behind the Seattle Sun was nearly full when she arrived and she could hear lively music well before she got close to the door. She walked up to the large room that served both as a cafeteria and a media-conferencing room. The dividers were drawn back and the room had been transformed. It was always decorated for the annual holiday party, but this year the "party committee" had outdone themselves. Meghan wondered how many company hours had been lost to the planning of this one event.

The tables were spread with food of all colors, textures, and tastes. Seattle prided itself on being cosmopolitan and banquets always included an array of the exotic as well as traditional fare. The beer keg was at one end and bottles of wine were protruding from oversized metal tubs like bowling pins suspended in their fall. She filled a plate with seafood and Indonesian chicken and poured herself a plastic tumbler of white wine.

"I was afraid maybe you had a better offer for entertainment tonight."

She turned to find Mr. Meyers smiling at her and she offered him a shrimp from her plate.

"Here, take one of these. I'm afraid I got a little carried away. This place looks great, Mr. Meyers. This is really wonderful."

"Don't thank me. It's my predecessor that started this whole thing. If it were up to me...no, never mind. I'd do it even if it weren't tradition. I love seeing everyone having a good time and loosening up a little. God knows you all work hard meeting deadlines all the time. A party now and then is good for the soul. Now finish up your food and dance a little bit. I'll be sure to catch you in a while. I want you to have some fun before I start 'talking shop' with you later."

As quickly as he had appeared, Richard Meyers was back into the thick of the crowd, his voice booming above the noise of the band that played from the other end of the large room. Meghan found a table occupied by only one other couple, and they weren't at all interested in starting up a conversation. She sat down and began picking her way around the plate of food that suddenly seemed unappealing. Her thoughts were on the conversation she would have later with Mr. Meyers.

Writing for a living was a curious thing. It could elevate a person to the highest of highs, or lower them to a place beneath not only their dignity as a person, but a basement level that ensured their failure as a professional writer. In actuality, there was very little middle ground, but most reporters considered themselves somewhere in that middle ground anyway. The truth was, someone who made their career out of using words and phrases to shape someone else's view of the world, insular or not, was constantly subject to the whim of the "expert." Whoever that was. To be an expert in the world of journalism meant that your talents had been proven and if your views were not accepted but the facts were there, all the better. That was what sold newspapers. That was what the public demanded in a democracy where every voice is supposed to have equal time.

Meghan ate the shrimp last and wished she hadn't let it grow warm. She thought about the first time she'd tried shrimp and had buried it in her serviette. It was while she was at the cottage in Oxford. The lady had opened a tin can and offered it as an appetizer before one of their special dinners with her mum and Neil. It was strange, she very rarely thought of Neil. She could only remember a few times spent with him that fateful summer, though the memories were good ones. Then there was her departure from England. Even as young as she was, she remembered that ship. It had been a devastating moment in her life and one Meghan had tried for a long time to forget after arriving in the States.

She took the last swallow of her wine, then sat back in the chair and watched her colleagues behaving with foolish abandon. She wished she could express that kind of freedom. She looked out into the room and smiled at the long conga line, men and women moving alike, who seemed not to care who their partner was or even if they had one. In the blur of the noise and whirling bodies, a vision of the Irish couple dancing in their front room flashed before her eyes. She had often wished she could remember their names, but no more so than on this night. It would have been so nice to have communicated with them over the years, sharing with them all her growing up experiences. Letters to her from England that were read by Neil's aunt disappeared after Uncle Troy went to war. Her "new" mom had taken care of all the correspondence that went back and forth across the ocean. After moving out west, her requests for those early letters had been met with "they've come up missing." A little girl's memory was no match for the battle with time. When she initially asked her mom for the Irish couple's name and address, the reply had been: "They've moved to a new location, just like we have, and I don't have a clue how to find them, especially from a continent away." It was the same story with Uncle Troy, like they all just disappeared. Her mom's certainty was something that had always bothered her, but subsequent inquiries had yielded no new answers. Maybe it was just as well. Perhaps in finding them, her life would have been interrupted with painful memories and even more loss. If her mom knew their whereabouts, she may have shielded her from that knowledge out of love and concern for her adjustment to permanent life in the States. A strange uneasiness crept into Meghan's thoughts as she gazed out once again at the party going on around her.

The band seemed louder than before and the dim lights made the whole scene surreal. It was right that the rest of the world should be celebrating, it just rarely felt like something Meghan could do. Celebrating always seemed a bit scary, as though it was tempting the fates.

She was considering what fates those might be when a hand touched her shoulder. She jumped in her seat and spun around to see who it was.

"I'm so sorry I startled you, Meghan. You were certainly deep in thought. Why aren't you up dancing, anyway? Don't tell me you don't dance!"

"Hi, Mr. Meyers. Yes, I do dance, but I'm afraid my energy level is waning after the past two weeks of work. When I left your office today, I went home and fell asleep on the couch for the rest of the afternoon. See what an exciting life I lead!"

"Speaking of exciting lives, I'd like to sit down with you for just a moment to talk about your next project. I know this could wait until Monday, but I was hoping to get your reaction tonight. I'd like to announce your next article at the staff meeting first thing on Monday. Do you mind?"

"No, not at all. Have a seat, or do you think we should go out into the hall for a bit more quiet?"

"That's probably a good idea."

The hallway reverberated with the vibrations of the music, but it was at least quiet enough to carry on a conversation. Meghan hoped it wouldn't take too long, as her feet were still aching from days of pounding the pavement. Her boss stuck his hands into his pocket. He took a deep breath and began.

"You did such a magnificent job with your article on the Vietnam War. I thought you might want to expand on the war theme with an intimate look back at World War II. This upcoming year is, of course, the twentieth anniversary observance of the end of the war. You seem to have an unusual ability to probe people's minds on sensitive and difficult subjects. Since there has been a lot of backlash in Europe surrounding the Vietnam War and our involvement over there, it would be interesting to examine the differences in reactions to the two wars from both the American and European points of view. I really haven't figured out an angle for all of this, but I guess that would be your job. What you do think? Does it sound like something you're interested in?"

Meghan's eyes lit up for the first time all evening and her mind was already spinning with possibilities. It was a good thing she had slept all day as she certainly wouldn't be able to sleep much the rest of the weekend!

"Sounds great! I'd love to do it!"

"Good. I thought you'd jump at this one. Personally, I can't think of any other writer I'd want to do this piece, except for myself, of course."

Richard Meyers laughed.

"Actually Mr. Meyers, I have some interesting information for you that you may not have known before. I was born in England. My biological dad died in the Battle of Dunkirk and my mum died in an auto accident right after the war ended. She was responsible for the evacuation of children from the London area and for placing them in homes out in the country. How about if I start stateside and get some research done while I wait for a new passport? Then I could start the other half of this project by covering England's point of view – from England! I'd love to have the excuse to go back there, this subject seems tailor made for me."

"That sounds just fine. If you don't mind my asking, how did you end up as Meghan *Roberts*?"

"The Roberts adopted me when I was ten years old."

"I see. Is your return to England going to be a problem for your folks, I mean, the link to your past and all?"

"Heavens no. To be honest, my adoptive folks are wonderful people, but we've always kind of gone our own way and done our own thing."

"I can understand that. Seems like that's more the thing these days, anyway. I'm really glad to know you were born in Britain. That should give you a unique point of contact with the locals, especially the older folks who lived through World War II. Get their view on how it was then, and what they think of Vietnam, the protests, and what this current conflict looks like to them."

"Thank you, Mr. Meyers, for giving me this incredible assignment and for trusting me with it. I promise I won't let you down. I'll get started right away!"

Energized, Meghan felt obligated to walk back into the party and to mingle with her co-workers. Perhaps it was the desire to please Mr. Meyers who seemed so intent on everyone else having a good time. She walked up to the bar and poured herself a soft drink. Returning to England – and at the newspaper's expense! She didn't make much money just yet but she felt as though all her long hours of hard work would someday pay off. Until then, it was wonderful getting to work at a job she'd been trained for. Not everyone her age was so lucky. She made her way towards the band and was quickly whisked onto the dance floor. Her feet and arms were moving in rhythm to the loud music, but her head spun from the sheer excitement of the secret she couldn't share just yet.

Seattle, Washington
December 24, 1964

The sky was oddly lit with the lights of the city in the distance and they cast a peculiar glow through the parted blinds in Meghan's living room. The cat paced across the couch, trying to attract her owner's attention. The hum of an old Christmas album crackled softly from the small dining area where a record player sat upon a black wobbly, tubular stand. Her record player was one of the very few things she had brought with her from the Roberts' house. Most of her furniture she had purchased a little at a time, much of it from thrift stores. Meghan never thought it was important to worry about the looks of her furnishings, though she did take some care in her personal appearance. Her clothes were casual but classic, not at all in keeping with the fads that came and went. Her strawberry blond hair was long and wavy, but usually pulled back to keep it out of her eyes while she worked. On this night, though, her locks hung down in front of her face. Perhaps covering her eyes would keep her from seeing the empty room that stretched before her. It was not the first Christmas Eve she had spent alone. Her parents had taken a trip on more than one holiday and Meghan was fairly used to their explanations of "time alone" and "business ventures." Still, on this night in particular, the sounds of the families below her and the noise outside her windows made her feel less than celebratory. She knew she was a loner and that had always been okay. Yet she couldn't seem to come to terms with the immense quiet that now interrupted the songs floating from the well-worn album. Ryan was spending the holiday at his brother's house, where his whole family would now be engulfed in wrapping paper and empty Christmas punch glasses. She smiled as she imagined Ryan's demeanor in the midst of all that togetherness. He also was a loner, yet seemed to enjoy the infrequent visits with his extended family. She replayed in her mind his invitation to join him for their festivities. Her answer had perhaps been a bit too hasty. Kit jumped off the couch and went straight for the shiny red balls that hung limply on the lower branches of the plastic Christmas tree. It suddenly seemed ludicrous that she had bothered to put up the artificial tree, as it seemed to symbolize all that Meghan found distasteful about the new-fashioned ways of celebrating a sacred event. She watched Kit persistently paw at the shiny orbs until they fell off one by one. Having been successful in her small rebellion, Kit jumped back upon the couch and settled on Meghan's lap.

"Kit, you're so adept at annoying me, maybe that's why I love you so much, you silly old cat."

Meghan sighed. It was Christmas Eve and she was talking out loud to a cat. There was no turkey in the oven, no presents beneath her plastic tree, only a few greeting cards taped to her refrigerator and a sprig of fake greenery laid across the living room windowsill. She brushed her hair away from her face and continued her conversation with the only living creature that was close enough to hear.

"You know, Kit, I remember Christmases that were a lot different than the one we're now spending together. The first one I can remember well was spent with Aunt Ida and Uncle Troy. I'm sure she died a long time ago and the last thing I heard, Uncle Troy was playing in the ocean somewhere in Hawaii. Funny, Kit, I'm trying to remember my real mum's face. I can't remember exactly what her voice sounded like, but I think it was lively but *gentle*. You would have liked her, Kit. I'm sure she was as strong and independent as you are and would most likely have spoiled you with too many bowls of milk."

Meghan breathed out deeply and stared into her tiny kitchen. It was now lit with just one small bulb over the sink and there were a few dishes in the drainer, long since dry.

"Some soup, Kit. That's what I need. A little soup and maybe a cup of tea. I rarely drink tea, but coffee sounds so harsh. We need something soft tonight. Yeah, some soup would be good. Let's see what's in the cupboard."

Meghan scooped up her cat and carried her to the kitchen. There were plenty of choices when it came to the soup, but her tea tin was empty. She took a pencil from the junk drawer and jotted down "tea" on her grocery list.

She settled down in front of the plastic tree, her mug of soup in one hand and a glass of dry sherry in the other. She'd read recently that proper English ladies drank sherry in the evening, especially at the holidays, so she'd bought a bottle of inexpensive sherry, just to see if her roots were still English. Drinking the sherry hadn't made her feel particularly proper but it had tasted good nonetheless. The bottle had sat in her cupboard ever since, her tastes usually moving towards drier wine. Still, the warm liquid seemed appropriate on this night, creating a stream to something or someone in her past. The album made a quiet swishing sound as the needle stuck in the last groove. Outside, she heard the very faint bells of the Catholic church she had attended upon occasion. The bells seemed so far away, yet she knew that they were really close by, just lost in the city din and the revelry that continued down below, unrelated to any sacred observance.

"Merry Christmas, Kit."

The cat raised her head, then pressed against Meghan's arm and sipped from the sherry glass. They sat together long after the soup was cold and the chimes had quit. Meghan stood up and headed to her bedroom, pausing to glance at the picture above her couch. The lights in its English cottage were always lit.

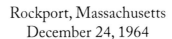

Rockport, Massachusetts
December 24, 1964

A quiet snow had begun earlier in the evening, promising a white Christmas even as the stubborn grass still poked through the scant covering of snow. The church bells were now ringing, offering their Christmas greetings as the parishioners left the sanctuary. Doreen and Neil had walked to the late night service, as the church was only a mile away and the temperature hadn't dropped before they left the house. Now that the night was full upon them, Doreen shivered against the growing dampness. A curious thought crossed her mind as she took Neil's arm and walked more briskly against the growing wind. How had she managed to stay warm all those years of growing up in England? It was always damp, even in the summer after several days of sunshine. The ancient bricks and stones held in the winter cold for centuries, never fully warming up to the temperature around them. She didn't remember being cold too often then. Yet now, the slightest drop in degrees or dampness settled in her bones. She frowned at the thought that perhaps her age had something to do with it.

"You sure are walking fast, Doreen. Are you cold or just nervous that the priest may have realized how long it's been since you've been to confession?"

Doreen smile was lost in the darkness but her response was as quick as usual.

"I think he's probably more concerned with the date of *your* last confession. At least mine was in this decade."

"And we won't even mention Troy's last time in a church."

"Yes, but it won't be long now before he steps inside one, unless they plan to marry outside somewhere!"

They both laughed and walked the rest of the way in silence. The colored lights on their porch sparkled and they could see their Christmas tree shining proudly through the front window. It was the biggest tree they'd ever gotten and the neighbors had teased them unmercifully.

"Are you ready for a glass of champagne, hon?"

"I think so. I'm just going to go up and get ready for bed first. Maybe my flannel pajamas will take the chill out of my bones. I'll be back down right away."

"Take your time."

Neil watched her climb the stairs and went to the kitchen to retrieve a small package he had placed upon a shelf much too high for Doreen to ever use. She had been very quiet during the walk to and from church and hadn't even commented on the choice of hymns they had sung. Perhaps the small gift would cheer her even as Christmas morning greeted them. He knew that her thoughts had been on her daughter, as they were at every holiday. He ached with the pain she must have felt seeing the children sleeping or sprawled across their parents' laps during church. It would never get any easier to usher in a holiday, never knowing anything more of Meghan. So many attempts to find her over the years had come up empty-handed. Doreen had finally chosen to take a rest from those efforts. It was too draining on them both and only served as a hurtful reminder of the reasons the two of them had met in the first place. It had been such a different time in their lives and so many seasons had come and gone, molding and shaping their relationship into a purpose all its own. And yet, in a few short months she would be reflecting upon those seasons once again. Neil swallowed and tried to shake away his negative thoughts on her impending trip.

He slipped the wrapped package into his pants pocket and opened the refrigerator door to get out the cold champagne. Taking the delicate antique flutes from the china hutch in the dining room, he placed the celebratory items on the polished table and waited for Doreen's return.

She changed quickly and started out of the room when a photo stuck in the side of her vanity mirror caught her eye. It was a picture of Meghan, taken with Mrs. Markham's camera in the early years of the war. She was holding Max the bunny and smiling a bit too broadly and her pinkish blond curls stuck out from under her favorite hat. She had always looked like such a little imp in that hat. For just a moment, Doreen wished she'd had a more formal portrait taken then, but money and time for such luxuries were both scarce in those days. It was enough that she even had one photo of her lovely daughter. She didn't really need a reminder of her face. It was only the memory of the wee voice that had faded through the years. Doreen looked down at her red plaid pajamas, remembering a similar plaid nightgown that the O'Connor's had given to her daughter when they first arrived in Kidlington in the summer of 1940. It had been just a bit too long and Margaret had lovingly hemmed it in a hurry so Meghan could wear it to bed on the second night of their stay. It was only one of many gestures that had assured Doreen that these folks would be both loving and attentive to her daughter's needs. For the next few moments, a flood of memories now filled her mind and time stopped its incessant march. Visions of Saint Nicholas' visits to Meghan floated unabashedly through her consciousness and her focus was lost in the recollection. How many Christmas Eves had Doreen endured, knowing that she had missed watching her daughter grow up?! How many years had she spent knowing that someone else had severed the cord that bound mother and daughter together?! Doreen felt the small stab of anger that the years had not completely erased, and the Priest's recent words of "charity and forbearance" scraped in her ears like a broken tin bell. She sighed deeply and her legs were weak with the heaviness of the burden she would always bear. Taking a deep breath, she started down the steps to toast in the Christmas Day with the man who rarely complained of her moodiness; a man who had absorbed her anger with his own sense of guilt.

"Neil, don't pour that champagne just yet! I think I'd rather have a glass of sherry."

Neil turned to watch her descend the steps and guided her to a chair next to their Christmas tree.

"That's a fine idea, hon. I'll get out that special bottle that Troy gave us on our anniversary last year. You sit right here and enjoy the lights on the tree and I'll take care of pouring our toast."

Doreen heard his words, yet was unable to respond with much more than a small nod. Her eyes now focused on the colored bulbs that cast a blurred glow, transforming their front room into a place set apart from the rest of the world outside. It was safe here, and it was okay to silently grieve for the gift she had once been given but which had then disappeared from all her holidays. Here in her home and on this night, she could feel her loss. She could also be reminded of how deeply she was loved. She could begin this holy day remembering that weakness was okay sometimes, but that strength can grow amidst weakness. She could cry and rejoice and toast to the past and the future.

The fragile sherry glasses were emptied and the tree lights dimmed. Outside, the dark blue of the sky dissolved into hues of the promised morning, but the wind sang a mournful lullaby.

Kidlington
Oxford, England

December 24, 1964

The wind was whipping against the shutters as usual when Ian O'Connor settled into his chair to read a while. He wasn't used to being up this late at night and the sounds seemed a bit foreign, even in the home he'd lived in for nearly sixty years. The clouds had gathered early in the day and without the stars, the night sky was now pitch dark. He looked up from his book every few minutes to gaze at the small evergreen he'd brought inside. It had one gold star on the top and a few homemade ornaments for decoration. He hadn't felt at all like putting up a tree this year, but changed his mind as he heard Margaret's voice scolding him.

"Ian O'Connor! Just because I'm not with you is no reason to slack on your holiday duties. You get that tree up right away, old man. Do you hear me?"

The strange thing to Ian was that he *did* hear her. He heard her voice more often than he would have admitted if anyone had ever asked. In turn, he actually found himself talking out loud to Margaret as though she were in the next room. It was a strange transformation for a man who prided himself on being a very reasonable person. Yet each time he felt a bit silly at their "conversations," he reassured himself that age grants certain privileges. Talking to departed loved ones was one of those. As he took a sip from his tea mug, he smiled at the memory of their last Christmas together. Margaret had been concerned about the lack of food donations

293

for the church Christmas bazaar. She had bemoaned the fact that the younger women just didn't seem to be pulling their weight when it came to helping raise the funds that the church gave back to the local village. When he had gently reminded her that some women were raising children and working outside the home, she had softened her tone and apologized for being a "cranky old woman." They had both laughed at her words. Ian's Margaret had rarely been cranky in her life. She was as steady as rain and as patient as Job.

Ian brushed a small tear that had settled in the corner of his eye. It was Christmas Eve. He would not give in to sad thoughts or pity. His focus had been on the same page of the book for a few minutes and he knew he could not read right now. He rose from the chair and went over to the hutch. He opened the glass doors and took down the bottle of sherry that his neighbor had given them last Christmas. He and Margaret had toasted each other on their anniversary and had shared a few glasses with friends over the past year. There was still plenty left for him to enjoy a glass while he ushered in the sacred morning. He would greet the holy day alone. He cranked up the gas fire to take off the chill that had settled in over the course of the evening. He hadn't realized until now that their cottage was quite cool. It suddenly occurred to him that over the years their guests were most likely uncomfortably chilly, especially in the colder months. He recalled hearing requests for extra blankets and duvets on more than one occasion. Strangely, he had never really felt the chill through the thickness of his cardigan - until lately.

He brushed past Margaret's armchair, glancing over at the sewing bag he had never removed from the corner of the room. Why he'd left it there, he didn't know. It certainly wasn't waiting for him to use its contents; he could just barely sew on a button! He supposed it gave him some measure of comfort, as though she were truly still there or at least coming back soon. He paused to touch the lace doily that lay draped across the back of her chair. It felt rough from years of washing and starching and Ian wondered how it could have been comfortable on the back of her head. Then he smiled as he remembered how she sat forward, bent over her work. She rarely leaned back in any chair, as that would show a hint of lethargy. Margaret O'Connor was constantly in motion even when she sat physically still. Her mind clicked from one thing to another with the precision of a Swiss watch, and he had never ceased to be amazed at the intensity with which she lived life. He, on the other hand, could be quite content to sit without his mind in motion. He pulled the doily off her chair and lowered himself into the cushion. He had sat in her chair just once right after she died, hoping to feel her presence or smell her lingering powder. He had only sat a few seconds, getting up with sadness that he had somehow invaded her private space. Perhaps she was still sitting there, waiting to silently say "goodbye" to the man and the home she had loved and cared for.

Yet now, on this night, he planted his feet on the floor and held the sherry glass in his lap, his elbows touching the armrests where Margaret's had done for so many years. Outside, the wind picked up again, making too mournful of sounds for such a holy night. He glanced over at the clock on the mantle and realized with some concern that the morning had arrived hours before. How did he lose track of so much time? Had he fallen asleep in his chair earlier and missed the twelve chimes that heralded Christmas Day? He raised the glass of sherry to his lips and spoke aloud, feeling neither foolish nor frightened of his own peculiar behavior.

"A toast to the Christmas Day, my lovely Margaret."

He took a long sip of the silvery drink.

"And a toast to you. You know how much I miss you. You certainly must know how much I love you. You have always been the light of my life. I'm trying, my dear. I am truly giving this situation my best effort."

He stopped, sighing deeply, and took another sip.

"It's just that this cottage is so quiet without you. And I must admit, although you will scold me even as I say this, but I am so lonely without you. It's such a mystery to me how full a room can be with two persons and how utterly empty it is with only one."

Ian paused again, wiping away a tear with the back of his blotched, wrinkled hand.

"I'm trying, love. But tonight I'm so very tired. I'm already tired of rattling around in this place by myself."

The clang of a milk bottle startled Ian from his reverie. He had forgotten that there would be no milk delivery for two days and the wind had tipped the glass bottle over. He knew he should go outside and take it from the ledge, but he couldn't seem to make his body move out of her chair.

Just as the hint of dawn approached, Ian O'Connor fell asleep. The empty sherry stem lay in his lap, the sticky residue of the drink clinging to the sides of the glass. The wind had died down, unnoticed by Ian as he played back pictures in his mind before giving in to fatigue. His mental photos had taken him on a journey filled with recollections of small moments and larger events shared with the woman he had loved for so long. It was a bittersweet way to welcome the holy day. Christmas morning came to rest gently upon his shoulders, as quietly as it had come so many centuries before.

CHAPTER THIRTY EIGHT

Seattle, Washington
March 1965

The bells and clacks of the typewriters reminded Meghan of miniature trains that were speeding away to exotic destinations. She sat back in her desk chair and stretched her neck from side to side. Sometimes the small space of her office cubicle was conducive to creativity, making her feel protected and safe in letting her free thoughts find their way to the page. Today however, the cramped the area was confining and she only felt frustrated and restricted. She wished she could jump aboard one of those make-believe trains and journey without obligations. The deadline for the first installment of her latest assignment was in twenty-four hours and she still wasn't finished. It had been her idea to begin her coverage of the twentieth anniversary of the War's end from stateside. She was attempting to link American memories of World War II to the current reactions surrounding the Vietnam War before she tried the same comparison in the U.K. She had known it would be difficult but it seemed important to bridge that gap somehow, if only to recognize the immense differences between the two settings and times before looking for universal themes. She picked up her coffee mug and stared down into the cold, black liquid. It looked more like syrup at this point and she realized how long it had been since she'd been out of her chair. There was no point in staying any longer. It was a reasonable time of day to pack it in and go home. Maybe the comfort of her own place could inspire her to finish the writing.

She loved the feel of her old typewriter at home. Its keys were worn smooth and had an almost sensual feel. Ryan had thought her observations on the old machine were nearly ridiculous until she forced him to admit that his well-used camera had a similar appeal. They had laughed until their sides ached at the revelation that both of them had more intimate contacts with black boxes than with other people. It was one of the things that kept them together, albeit rarely, as their schedules were demanding. She smiled at the picture of him hunched over his camera, then shook her head as she remembered the last time she'd gone into his dark room. He had scolded her for nearly ruining the roll of film he'd just finished shooting, but had relented as her visit in the dark room continued for reasons unrelated to photos.

Her apartment was chilly even though the day had been fairly warm. She routinely left her windows open, even at night, and the early morning air kept her place cool most of the time. It was only in the winter that she had to sleep without the fresh breeze, and then her apartment was damp and cold. She tossed the stack of mail on the kitchen table and plopped into a chair. Kit was meowing loudly, seeking both attention and her evening meal. There was one large, heavier envelope in the stack and she opened it first. She'd been getting anxious to receive her passport as her trip to England was past due. The envelope contained the only productive thing she could claim all day – her passport had arrived! It'd been such a struggle for her to apply as her original birth certificate had been lost sometime after arriving in the states as a child, and her adoption certificate had certain irregularities. She had asked her parents why there was not more in the way of identification for her and their answer had been vague. She was glad her dad knew a lot of people in Seattle as their connections had certainly speeded up the process. Meghan thought it was always peculiar that she and her parents' lives focused on the immediate all the time. There was rarely mention of events and times past, and even less said about the future. They had not even spoken much about her choice of college and majors. As much as she loved and admired her parents for the good life they had given her, she wished at that moment that they had *lived* that life *with* her. She turned the passport over in her hands several times before opening it to glance at her photo. It was a typical "mug shot," but it would get her back to the U.K. and that was all she needed. She got up and took a boxed pizza mix from the cupboard and started making some dinner. Perhaps a pizza and some chocolate bars would inspire her to finish the installment.

Kit arched her back and settled awkwardly on Meghan's lap as the old typewriter kept up its rhythmic pace. The pizza pan still lay on the table, its few contents long since cold, and a small pile of paper and aluminum foil lay crumpled next to it. The clock's hands ticked quietly while the sounds of the city faded into an occasional siren and screech of tires. Meghan pulled the last page from the roller and pushed the chair back from the table. Now she was ready! Finishing this first article meant she could focus now on her trip to England. She could turn her energies to packing and picking up last minute necessities.

April 10, 1965

The traffic into the Seattle airport had been heavier than Meghan or Ryan had expected, and she was glad they'd left on time for a change. Meghan hoisted her large suitcase out of the trunk and walked into the check-in line while Ryan parked the car in short-term parking. She was grateful he'd been able to rearrange his schedule to take her, as she hadn't wanted to go by herself. Airports could be such lonely places. At least this way she would have someone to have a drink with and walk her down to the gate. She would have someone to turn around and wave to, like most of the other travelers. Her parents were not able to join her, though as usual they hadn't given her a sensible reason. They had praised her recent articles, yet seemed reticent about supporting this new project. They rarely asked many questions and didn't seem interested in getting too involved in her activities. She reminded herself that it had always been that way in their home, but there were times when she longed to have parents who questioned and even meddled.

There were two open chairs at the bar by her flight gate and Meghan sat down, throwing her jacket on one of them. She ordered two beers and watched the people around her, wondering where they were headed and why. Some were loud and laughing and others talked in quiet whispers, as if someone could actually hear their conversation over the noise that echoed and bounced off the walls. The beer was icy cold and she hoped it would help her sleep for a while on the long flight.

"Thought I'd never find a parking spot. This place is a zoo. Hey, thanks for the beer. Good idea! Are you hungry? I can order some fries or a sandwich if you want."

"No thanks, not for me. I think I'll get plenty to eat on the plane. Get some for yourself if you want."

"Nah, I've got some leftover stuff at my place that will be growing things if I don't eat it soon."

Meghan shook her head and shrugged.

"I swear Ryan, someday you're going to die of ptomaine poisoning from eating the food in your fridge. Why do you think I always ask you over to *my* place?"

"So, did you make out some kind of itinerary for your time there?"

"Sort of. I know there are certain places and people I need to talk to, but I'd also like to let the research flow naturally and guide my feet, as they say."

"Meghan, what are you going to do about looking for clues to your early years in England?"

Meghan set her mug down and paused before answering. She had told him what little she could remember of her time there, but he had never brought up the subject before she did. Even when asking her about the assignment and her unique perspective, he hadn't mentioned the idea of searching into her past. She had indeed given thought to finding out whatever she could and she smiled at the idea that Ryan knew her so well. It was good to have someone know you from the inside out, even if it was scary at times. It was hard to be exposed and vulnerable, but really knowing someone required that level of openness. Now, more than ever, she was recognizing the power of semantics. Words really did have a life of their own. It mattered what words you chose to say or write. It mattered because understanding the true meaning of those words meant that your voice and pen reflected what lay beneath the surface. They revealed what others may not have heard or seen before. They had the power to change minds and hearts. It wasn't enough to use words as a gift to be opened. It was more important to wrap the package and then open it together layer by layer, sitting side by side on the floor.

"I've thought about it quite a bit since I first got the assignment. I'll definitely give it a shot, but I doubt I'll get very far. It's been so long. The chances are slim, so I'm not going to spend much time on it. My focus will be on my work. I have a lot to do in a short time so there's little time for detours."

Ryan nodded and took a long swallow of his drink.

"Well, whatever you find out, you know I'll be here when you return."

Meghan smiled and put her arm across his shoulder.

"Yeah, I know."

The loudspeaker boomed in the background announcing the next set of flights and several people at the bar got up to leave. Meghan finished her beer and motioned for the two of them to walk to the gate. Ryan gave her a long hug and a brief, warm kiss, then waved as she made her way to the plane. She turned around twice to wave again, thankful he was still standing there, then settled into her seat and stared out the scratched window. She couldn't decide if her tiny space was cozy and comforting or frighteningly claustrophobic. Either way, it would do until she stepped out at the airport in London and hailed a black cab to carry her to her future – and her past.

San Francisco, California
April 1965

The corporate offices of Fancher Executive Searches were bustling as personnel and their clients wove in and out of doors like the long ribbon on a maypole. President David Sanders glanced out of the window facing the hallway and watched the action with some amusement. He could see animated faces and mouths moving and arms waving, but the sounds were not clearly audible through the glass. It was like watching a silent film with an added dull soundtrack of indistinguishable quiet crowd noise. He knew he hadn't been at all productive on this morning and the scene before him was just another excuse to avoid getting back to his work. It was nearing lunchtime so he took a paper bag from the bottom drawer of his desk and set it between piles of papers. What would be in the bag was always a mystery. He knew his wife hated his long hours and late nights, but she never complained and continued to surprise him with a lunch that brightened his day. He took the thick sandwich from its wrapper and picked up a newspaper from the stack that constantly adorned his desk. He enjoyed reading articles from other area newspapers, as it kept him abreast of what businesses on the west coast were doing. It was also a good way to keep informed of the brightest new graduates and company hires in a field that was too crowded with idealistic hopefuls.

Glancing over the latest news on Boeing, his eyes focused on a second page article in the Seattle Sun about the Vietnam War and Americans' reflection on it in the light of World War II anniversary observances. It was intriguing and well written, with insights and a maturity that made it worth the read. Halfway through the article, he glanced at the byline. "Meghan Roberts." It wasn't a writer he'd heard of before, but he usually paid attention to facts on business news rather than articles on conflicts around the world, unless they pertained to business interests. The end of the article focused on the writer's upcoming assignment in the U.K., where she would get the British perspective on both the Southeast Asian conflict and reflections on the big War that had nearly devastated the great city of London. David Sanders laid the paper and his sandwich aside and rose from his chair. He walked to the window that looked over the city and stared at the traffic below. This Miss Roberts seemed to possess an uncanny sensitivity to the hard memories she was about to bring back. She was obviously a gifted writer. Meghan. Where had he heard that name? Meghan *Roberts*. A Fancher employee from out east had come into his office years ago asking for help in locating a missing young girl named Meghan. Sanders rubbed his chin, a habit he had when concentrating.

His own predecessor, Stuart Roberts, had had an estranged brother living somewhere on the northern west coast. They initially thought Stuart or his brother might have known Meghan's kidnapper, but the investigation went nowhere, perhaps due to Stuart's death. Any connection seemed very unlikely after all this time. Sanders walked back to his desk, picked up the phone and called the offices in Boston.

"This is David Sanders from Corporate in San Francisco. I'd like to speak to Troy Henderson, please."

It wasn't long before Troy answered the phone.

"Mr. Sanders, this is a surprise. What can I do for you?"

"Troy, you remember several years ago when you ask me to give you some help in locating your niece - your brother's wife's child?"

"Yeah, sure I remember. It was about fifteen years ago, I guess. Nothing came of the search."

There was a pause before Sanders' response and Troy's heartbeat quickened.

"Well, I know this is probably a long shot, but I just read an insightful article in the Seattle Sun, written by a Meghan Roberts. She seemed to have a real understanding of the effects of war and her next assignment was to cover England's view of Vietnam *and* World War II remembrances. I recall that we discussed the possibility that Stuart Roberts or his brother may have been a school chum of Meghan's kidnapper. I don't know, seems like a crazy link, but with her first and last names both ringing a bell, I wanted to give you a call nonetheless."

Troy took a deep breath before answering and got up to pace the floor as he pulled on the long cord that stretched across the polished floor tiles.

"That does sound a bit far-fetched, but I'm glad you called me. You never know...There could be something there. Even if there's not, no harm done."

Troy knew as soon as he said it that the harm had already been done. Even as full and wonderful as Neil and Doreen's lives were, he knew that there was not a day that went by without at least a momentary thought or prayer for the daughter that had disappeared. Not a day went by without Troy feeling a pang of guilt and responsibility for that disappearance. He supposed that a nagging conscience had affected his life more than anyone knew. It was the reason he had never married. There was one real love he had, only just a year ago. She backed out at the last minute, claiming that something in his life prevented him from total trust and intimacy and that she couldn't marry him until he rid himself of the hurt or fear that held him captive. At first he'd been devastated by her change of heart, until he came to terms with the honesty of her words. She was right. For all the richness of his own life, he had never been able to shake the demon that strangled his ability to accept love without fear. A demon born from his own decision that resulted in several lives being torn apart.

"I hope for all your sakes that there's some connection, but I certainly wouldn't hold my breath on it. There are so many variables."

"You're right about that, Mr. Sanders. I'll contact the newspaper myself and see what I can find out. If I don't hear back from the editor, I'll assume I'm on a wild goose chase. It's good to have perseverance, but sometimes…."

Troy stopped, unsure what to say next.

David Sanders twirled his pencil across the grooves in his desk, searching for an easy end to the conversation.

"You may be right, Troy. It's not that we ever forget. We just have to move on, as they say. Let me know how it all works out."

"Yeah, I will. Thanks Mr. Sanders."

The two men hung up their phones and moved about in silence, as if the rest of their unspoken words could be heard cross country like some futuristic telepathy.

Troy picked up the phone and dialed the Seattle Sun.

"I'd like to speak to the chief editor, please."

Assistant Editor Hank Thomas hesitated, his hand holding the receiver firmly.

"I'm sorry, but Richard Meyers is not in the office today. Some sort of outside appointment, I think. Can I help you?"

Now that Meghan Roberts was bound for London on assignment, Hank Thomas wandered in and out of offices like he was looking for something he'd misplaced. Others on the staff watched him with a mixture of dismay and curiosity. He had never been a likeable guy, always watching everyone else's moves and reporting any odd or unprofessional behavior. Richard Meyers made it known that Hank's observations were not taken very seriously, still Hank Thomas had the knack of getting other staffers into trouble. On this day, he had taken on the job of quickly answering any phones that rang. This call had come in on Mr. Meyers' line.

"I'd really like to talk to your editor-in-chief. May I ask who I'm speaking with?"

"I'm one of the assistants to the editor. What is it you need to know?"

"I was calling to inquire about a Meghan Roberts who writes on your staff. Is she available to speak with me?"

Hank Thomas' eyes widened and his hand on the plastic receiver began to perspire.

"She's not at all available for quite some time, I'm afraid. She's on assignment in Europe and won't be back here for weeks. Is there something you needed to ask her? I mean, if it's about an assignment or a story to cover I'm your man, as they say. I've a lot of experience and as assistant to the editor, I have inside tracks."

Hank's voice had become more agitated.

"I really just wanted to speak to the person who hired her and then see if I could speak directly to her."

Troy hesitated and decided to continue with his next question.

"You don't happen to know where Meghan Roberts grew up, do you?"

"No, I don't. I'm not even sure Meghan is her real name. Hard to tell with novice writers. They seem to find a popular name and go with it just to stay current, if you know what I mean."

Troy's shoulders dropped as he considered the words he'd just heard. Of course. Writers changed their names all the time. It was likely that either one or both of her names were made up. There was most likely no connection at all between *his* Meghan and this woman. How ridiculous for him to think that there would be any link, after all this time and without any more to go on than that. Troy's neck felt warm and his stomach was churning. It was good that the man at the other end of the line couldn't tell how foolish he felt right now.

"Yeah, I see your point. Well, just tell your editor to call me if he has any personal information on her that he'd be willing to share, if I explained my situation. I don't want to bother him if there's nothing he has for me, and I certainly don't want to invade her privacy."

"I'll give him the message."

Troy hung up the phone, grabbed his briefcase and walked out of the office into the afternoon sunshine. He needed some time in the park or maybe down by the water. Just some time to consider why he was still clinging to branches of hope on a tree that had long been withering.

Hank Thomas hung up the phone and pondered the conversation. Of course that man wanted Meghan to do a special article on *something*. Why else would he have been asking about her? It wasn't just about where she was from and other personal information – it was about an offer for an article! He stared at the pad next to the phone then turned and walked out of the office, the message recorded only in his own mind.

The pungent odor of fish hung in the air around the Boston harbor, a familiar smell but one that still caught Troy off guard as he tried to make his way across the broken bricks and crumbling cobblestone. The once active harbor area had been reduced to blight and economic ruin. Now construction crews worked amidst the fishermen's gear and the crews' own debris mingled with the remnants of years of neglect along the harbor's edge. The genesis of a new waterfront was now taking shape and many folks observed the daily progress, stepping over the litter and avoiding the workmen's tools and supplies to watch the transformation. It was a curious scene and one that Troy felt connected to, as his office was nearby and he wanted the waterfront revitalized for business *and* personal reasons. It was also mesmerizing just to be near the water and hear the waves lapping, sometimes crashing against the retaining walls. He often thought some folks kept vigil in this area just trying to feel the ebb and flow of the harbor, reveling in both its history and the promise of a contemporary beat. Still, on this day Troy found the curious onlookers more than just an annoyance. They seemed an intrusion on his personal world. He needed the sounds of ships' horns and the purposeful shouts of commercial fishermen to reassure him of the normalcy, even validity of his *own* life. He needed to give the Seattle editor time to return his call. He needed to give himself time to accept the outcome. Either way it turned out, he would once again have to come to terms with a choice he was forced to make so many years ago and so many worlds away. The aimless folks and their meanderings were in sharp contrast to the singular reason for *his* presence at this place. This was where he could clear his mind. This was where his senses were fully engaged. This was where he could let the breezes and sights and sounds empty his thoughts by their sheer energy and draw.

He stopped when he got to a pay phone at the outer edge of the pier. He picked up the receiver, deposited a dime, and dialed the familiar number. A gull flew over his head, screeching unpleasantly. He wondered how God had given such a beautiful bird a voice that was so grating. It was only one of many paradoxes he had called God on lately. He didn't know if God was still listening to him, but Doreen had hinted that maybe He was. That woman was still a mystery to him. She still believed. She still practiced the faith in a God who had allowed such painful losses in her life. She still gave so much to a life that had taken so much from her. She still loved his brother with a passion that defied reason. God, to be so complete while living with such a void!

He let the phone ring for a while and hung up. It was probably better he hadn't gotten through to the Henderson house, he didn't really have anything to say. Besides, Doreen was getting ready for her trip to London and Neil had been a bit touchy about it. Troy turned and stared out at the water, remembering the last time he had eaten dinner with Neil and Doreen. She had set the dining room table with china as usual and they had eaten and laughed until their both their stomachs and their faces hurt. Doreen had looked a bit tired, but her good spirits were genuine. After dinner, he and Neil had gone through their usual bantering while washing up the dishes. They'd all sat on the couch together and belatedly toasted Neil and Doreen's anniversary with champagne. The whole evening had seemed so wonderfully normal. So validating.

Troy paced in his office, realizing with dismay that he'd been totally unproductive for the past three days. He expected at least a phone call from the Seattle Sun's editor as a matter of courtesy, even if the guy didn't have any personal information on Meghan Roberts that he could divulge. Troy took out the bent and cracked copy of the only photo of Meghan, the one he'd always kept in his wallet, and stared at it. Damn, he was going to try once more. He picked up the phone and dialed the Seattle Sun.

"Chief Editor's office, may I help you?"

The woman's voice was soft but professional.

"Yes, I'd like to speak to the editor if I could. Is he in?"

"Just one moment."

"This is Richard Meyers. What can I do for you?"

"Mr. Meyers, this is Troy Henderson from Fancher Executive Searches. I was wondering if you could give me any information on an employee of yours by the name of Meghan Roberts. I understand she's in Europe on assignment for awhile."

The line was quiet as the editor considered his response.

"Well Mr. Henderson, we do have an employee by the name of Meghan Roberts, but you can understand that I can't give out personal information to a stranger. We have a strict policy here about privacy and security."

"Of course, and I understand your position. I'm not asking for her address or phone number. I just need to know something of her background or where she grew up, or even her parents' names."

"I see."

Richard Meyers replayed the beginning of their conversation. *Fancher Executive Searches.* Of course. He really just wanted to know her educational and work experience. He was a professional recruiter! His true respect and fondness for his young employee was overshadowed only by his desire to keep her talent on staff. Besides, he really *didn't* know very much about her personal past, except her birth and early childhood in England. She was a very private person. He certainly wouldn't jeopardize her trust by divulging anything to a total stranger!

"I'm sorry. I really don't have any information for you. You must understand that even if I did, I'm not at liberty to say."

"Of course. Perhaps I can contact her when she returns."

"Perhaps."

"Thanks for your time."

Troy hung up and flopped into his chair. This was going nowhere, at least not while the young journalist was still in Europe. Maybe when she returned he could try again. Or maybe one more attempt would only delay the inevitable and he'd have yet one more disappointment – one more reminder of the burden he'd always carry. This last clue was really an unfounded hope. He couldn't pursue the lead any further, nor could he ever mention it to Doreen or Neil. He would let it rest. The search had wearied him the way it had worn down the two people he most loved and respected.

Seattle, Washington

The soft sound of the cat lapping the milk in her small bowl interrupted Paul Roberts' thoughts. It had been a long time since he'd sat quietly enough to hear a cat drinking patiently, its small, rough tongue able to bring in only tiny sips at a time. As per usual, Beatrice was gone. She filled her day with countless activities, even when *he* had a day with nothing planned. They had traveled so much together, especially in the past few years, that he didn't begrudge her outside interests. Still, there were times he sat at home with the television blaring away, waiting for her return and not understanding why she still had such a hold on his life. He got up and walked to their newly remodeled kitchen, picked up Kit and brought her back to his recliner. He was glad Meghan had asked them to keep her cat while she was away on assignment in London. He was honored she'd asked them as she was very attached to the beast. Beatrice hadn't been thrilled, but he had insisted that they do this favor for Meghan as she rarely asked them for anything. Meghan had been able to take Kit with her when she'd traveled to San Francisco to research her last big article. This time she needed help as her boyfriend- what was his name?- was shooting photos in Nevada and couldn't care for Kit. The cat came over and jumped up next to him. It was strange how just a fluff of fur could give such comfort, soothing him in a way he rarely experienced. He could feel her tiny heart beating rapidly against his chest, her tail swishing against his arm like a miniature broom. He smiled at her occasional cleaning swipes, her head bobbing and twisting to keep herself meticulously clean. Cats were strange animals. They liked you on their own terms, but then with tenacity and boldness. Not unlike some people he knew. Perhaps even his wife. When Beatrice chose to exhibit enthusiasm at your presence, she was charming and captivating and made you feel important. It was the reason he'd married her. Yet, unlike the warm critter that now slept on his chest, she rarely got close to anyone.

The clock on the mantel of their fake fireplace chimed five times and Paul stood up to go pour a drink. He brought Kit with him and set her down on the top of the bar, but she jumped down and sauntered back to his chair. A strong scotch and soda would help the time pass. As he sat back in his chair and repositioned the cat on his chest, he counted the number of times they'd been in Meghan's apartment. Five, maybe six times? How had the years gone by without more visits between them? How had they come to this point? He thought about his brother, Stuart and the ridiculous argument that had caused the rift in their relationship so many years before. He couldn't even remember what they'd quarreled about, but he was only just going into his teens and Stuart had left home without any reconciliation between them. How had they come so far in their lives yet left the important far behind them, never looking back to retrieve it? Kit shifted her position and curled up on his legs. He knew the answer; it was just hard to face it. His small family had always chattered about things but rarely communicated. They had gone many places together in the earlier years, but never shared their feelings on what they'd seen or experienced. They had eaten in fine restaurants and attended sporting events; shuttled back and forth to lessons and school meetings, yet had rarely discussed starving children or the importance of back alley ball games. Lessons and meetings were carried out with precision, yet there were few celebrations of accomplishments and even fewer hugs or warm pats on the back. They had been a family of going and doing, not of being and sharing.

Paul Roberts took a swallow of his drink and stared at the blank television screen. The nightly news would be starting now. Perhaps he could concentrate on the world's events. It was so less frightening to get the war news and civil rights protests, to hear of campus unrest and economic woes than it was to consider the absence of the thread that should have tied his family to each other all these years. Watching the nightly report was less painful than yearning for the openness- and the closeness- that should have woven them together. As the sun danced in shadows across the window shades, he glanced down at the cat who chose to stay close to him. He got up and clicked on the television, then settled back and finished his drink, cradling the cat as she buried her head in his side.

London, England
Late April, 1965

The sun was struggling to break through the clouds as Meghan stepped out of a black cab in front of her small hotel in Earl's Court. She glanced around her at the row of small hotels and private flats that made up this mostly residential neighborhood. There was a small off-license shop on the corner and the local post office stood across the street.

"You'll find the tube station close at hand, Miss. It's quite convenient for gettin' around, though I'd not travel by yourself after dark, if you know what I mean."

The driver smiled and winked as he passed by with her suitcase, delivering it into the lobby.

"Yes, I know what you mean. I'll be very sensible."

This time it was her turn to smile at him, knowing how important being "sensible" was to the English. She had done her homework and felt ready to begin this monumental assignment – as soon as she had a nap. It had been a long flight and the traffic getting from the airport had made her journey even longer. All she really wanted now was a hot bath and a little sleep.

Her room was small but nicely furnished. She trudged down the hallway with her bath articles and filled the old claw-footed tub. The spigot and handles were brass and porcelain and looked as though they were the original ones that came with the tub. She tossed her towel and clothes across the heated drying rack and settled in for a good soak. As she laid her head against the back of the tub and steadied herself with her feet at the front, her mind drifted to the last conversation she'd had with her parents. It had been short, mostly giving instructions for taking care of Kit and giving them her hotel information. Her dad had started to question whether she'd planned on exploring possible places she may have been in as a child, but her mom had quickly interrupted him.

"Don't be insensitive, Paul. Of course she doesn't want to dredge up all those hurtful memories."

The truth was, Meghan *wanted* to spend time visiting places she had tried so desperately to remember. Her mom had never thought it important to save information about her early years in England or Rockport. She had always told Meghan that "going back" wasn't mentally healthy, that it was only important to know who you were and where you were going *now*.

She turned on the faucet and added more hot water, watching the steam fog over the small mirror above the sink. Maybe it was all the old stone and brick that passed in a blur as the cab had woven in and out of traffic. Maybe it was her assignment that required her to deal with the past. Whatever it was, she felt a nagging desire to preface her research with a bit of exploration into her own personal history. She knew only a few things about Oxford, most likely memories from the few letters her mum was able to send across the ocean to Rockport. One memory lingered though, and concerned the couple that she had lived with one summer. Meghan couldn't remember their names. She always thought her mom might remember but if she did, she never said. They must have been special people – at least to her real mum. She vaguely remembered another lady who stayed with her on occasion while her mum was at work, but names and distinct faces had been lost through the years. There was also something to do with nuns though their connection to her was unclear. So much time had passed.... so little to go on.

Meghan closed her eyes and slept until the water went cold and a sharp knock on the door awakened her.

"Would you mind hurrying up, please? You've been in there for quite some time now."

Startled and a bit embarrassed, Meghan stepped out of the tub, dried quickly and dressed. It was time for some dinner.

The rain started sometime in the middle of the night, spritzing through the curtains of the open window. She could feel the dampness beginning to spread across the floral duvet, but jet lag and a full stomach were making it difficult for her to awaken. She struggled to sit up, leaning over to close the window while her eyes tried to focus in the near dark room. The lights from the street below cast a grayish glow outside and Meghan shivered from the chill that now enveloped the room. It was amazing how the day had been comfortably warm and bright yet the night revealed a dank and foreboding nature. She was learning- perhaps relearning- that England was a study in contrasts. She had already been greeted with polite familiarity, but there was a business-like efficiency of words and actions that could be considered curt. The view of the countryside from the plane was of lush green, rolling hills, yet in contrast stood the black coal-scarred buildings set on littered streets. Her dinner had been bland, but the beer and the tea were first-rate. She laid her head back on the pillow, turning over several times to find the warm spot. She thought she saw a light go on in the hallway outside her door, but there was no noise except for the occasional clang of an anxious radiator.

Her mind began spinning, still reeling with the motion of the plane as it dipped and swayed. She saw herself on a bicycle holding on to someone's back and a ship passed by them. It was on fire and people were screaming and jumping into murky, black water. A man in a uniform stopped to ask her if she wanted to stay with him in his photography dark room. She told him that she didn't know how to print pictures, but he assured her that he had all the photos he needed. He took out a wallet and began flipping through his collection, showing her bright red phone booths and clothes pegged out to dry. There was an old woman pouring hot milk and a younger lady piling books and chairs in front of the door, her eyes set with tears and her face twisted in pain and confusion. Someone knocked at the door and the phone rang. It rang and rang until Meghan screamed for someone to answer it but no sound came from her mouth. She slipped through an open window and ran next door to the school. Her teacher was there, but all the wooden desks were being broken up to throw on the fire. It was so cold and the teacher kept writing on the board. She just kept writing and writing and no one was listening to the screams or the cries for help to get home again. She only wanted to get home again. Where was the other lady? She was still piling up things to keep her out! Why was she not looking for her? What happened to the man with the pictures? Why had he jumped into the water that was now burning? Everything smelled so heavy. So hot. So hot.

The pounding of her own heart woke her up and Meghan shot up in bed, whimpering and sweating profusely. She couldn't focus and her breath was coming in short gasps. The walls of the stuffy room were swaying like the dips of the plane. She sat there until she could put her legs over the edge of the bed and stand, then moved to the tiny sink in the corner and drank a full glass of water. The early morning sounds of the city were beginning and she opened the window to let the cool air flow across her face, drying her tears and her sweat. There was no possibility of going back to sleep. Meghan opened the wardrobe door and pulled out her robe. Another bath, some breakfast, then it was time to catch a train to Oxford.

Chapter Thirty Nine

Victoria Station was a confusing sight, with people running in all directions and the changing train schedule signs clattering like wooden blinds as they turned over in rapid succession. Meghan stood in the midst of it all and watched, her eyes darting back and forth between the array of moving legs and swinging arms and the kiosks filled with stands of brightly colored scarves and postcards. It was morning rush hour and the platforms were lined with anxious commuters who had already fought their way through the underground "tube" trains. Meghan was beginning to regret that her day had started so early as jet lag was already creeping in again. She found her way to the ticket booth and waited patiently in the queue, sorting through the unfamiliar coins and bills in her wallet.

She found a seat by the window and hoped no one would occupy the seat beside her. She only wanted to watch the city dissolve into the rolling hills and conversation was not a priority on this morning. She'd be interviewing almost non-stop for the next few weeks, but right now it seemed more important to absorb in silence. The train picked up speed as it got further from London and Meghan felt soothed by the constant clack of the wheels. She caught an older man staring at her from time to time, but she smiled politely and turned her head away without comment. He was of Indian descent, she was sure, and probably wondered what a "nice" lady would be doing traveling out of London unescorted. She felt a bit awkward and young for her years.

It wasn't a long walk from the Oxford station to the center of town, and already the shops and cafes were filled with students and various collegiate-looking older folks. The colleges that made up the campus of Oxford University were spread out all over the town and gave the whole area the aura of a huge schoolyard, each with its own "playground." Meghan took some photos and stepped into a cafe for some much needed caffeine.

"I'll take just a cup of coffee, please, with sugar and cream."

The server smiled and nodded, then moved to the next table before going to fill a small silver pot. Meghan guessed she must have been in her forties, but it was hard to tell with the matronly skirt and blouse the woman was wearing. There was a cobbler apron tied loosely around her generous waist and her shoes were black and sturdy, the kind much older women wore back on the west coast. She seemed polite enough, though her movements were abrupt and her words lacked the "chummy" pleasantries of coffee house waitresses in Seattle.

"Your coffee, miss. White with sugar. I'll leave the pot. Just flag me down if you wish more. Will that be all for now?"

"Yes, except..."

Meghan hesitated, unsure how to phrase her question.

"I was wondering how long you've lived here, whether or not you were here during World War II?"

"I've lived here all my life. I was born here. What is it you're wanting to know?"

Meghan noticed a softening in the server's voice.

"I lived here very briefly during the summer of '40, just before the Blitz. There was a couple that housed me, billeted as you say, somewhere outside of town, I believe. I don't remember their names, but I know he owned a business in town, a small shop I think. I was just wondering if you might have any recollection of a shop owner that took in a young girl at that time."

"I'm afraid that's not much to go on. Lots of folks took in children from the City. Still, let me ask our cook, Heath. He's been here for quite some time. He may know something."

She made her way to the kitchen door, stopping along the way to pick up plates and leave small white checks on the tables. It wasn't long before she returned, setting down a china plate covered with a scone.

"I think you should try this, it's quite lovely and it will give you a little boost of energy. Now then, Heath says he remembers a man who owned a sundries shop not too far from here, but it's been closed down for a few months now. Thinks the chap may have bought it quite some time ago from an older gent, but he doesn't remember the name. He said you should check a couple more places, as someone's bound to at least remember the surname."

"Thank you. Please, tell your cook that I appreciate it very much."

"It's not mine to ask, love, but is there an important reason you're so keen to find these folks?"

"They might hold a small clue to my early childhood here in England."

"I see."

The server stood for a few moments without speaking, then sighed and placed the check next to the scone plate. Meghan glanced down discreetly, noticing that only the word "coffee" was scribbled on the paper.

"Miss, if you don't find them, perhaps it's for the better. Sometimes the past is best put behind us."

She shrugged as she spoke again, a smile spreading across her tired face.

"Listen to me. That bit of advice from one whose country is still fighting the Napoleonic Wars."

With that, she tilted her head back and laughed, then left the table without further comment.

Meghan paid and left the cafe, heading toward a chemist shop that looked as though it had weathered more than a few years. Its proprietor's name was proudly displayed over the door and an elderly man stood hunched over some shelves behind the front counter.

"Excuse me, sir, I wondered if I might ask you a few questions."

The man turned around and stared at Meghan.

"Aye, what is it?"

His short, curt question took Meghan off guard and she swallowed before going on.

"I was hoping you could give me some information about the *original* owner of a sundries shop that was close by. I don't remember his name, and I've no idea how long he had his shop before selling it. I hear the shop's been closed for a few months now so I'm at a loss for details."

"Aye, the last owner sold it right quick and moved to the Cotswold's. He was quite standoffish, that one. And just why would you be wanting to see the original owner?"

"I stayed with this couple for a few months during the war before being shipped over to America. I've no living blood relatives, and I thought this man may be able to help me answer some questions about my early years."

Meghan stopped. The chemist turned back toward the shelves he'd been filling, his voice muffled as he spoke.

"Well, seeing as that's your purpose, I'll tell you. There was an Irishman by the name of O'Connor that originally owned the shop a few doors down, but he hasn't had the place for years. I know he and his wife lived in Kidlington, just a short bus ride outside of town. I heard it said that his wife died last year and he took it right poorly, as they say. It's a small place, Kidlington. You should be able to make inquiries there, if you've a notion to keep at it."

Meghan's heartbeat quickened. His gruffness did not distract from the importance of his words.

"Thank you, sir. You've been a big help."

She thought for a moment about asking him where the bus station was, but decided against it. The town center was relatively small and the station was probably a few steps away from there.

The bus that left for Kidlington was crowded and Meghan shared a seat with a young man who nervously fidgeted with a canvas grocery bag that he held on his lap. He seemed uncomfortable, perhaps a bit embarrassed about his shopping errand. Daily living on the west coast of the United States was indeed a different scenario than here! Time moved at a different pace in this place.

Meghan headed straight for the small Kidlington Post Office, bracing herself against both the strong breeze and another reticent encounter. She was greeted, instead, with a friendly face and a welcoming voice. The lady behind the counter was tall and slim and her face glowed pink, either from spending time outside in the gardens or from the wind that blew steadily across this small village. The woman wiped her hands on her skirt and stepped around the counter to face her.

"Yes my dear, what is it I can do for you today? You must be a visitor in our little village."

"Yes, I am. I just arrived in London yesterday from the States and took the train to Oxford this morning, then the bus here. I'm a little tired and I was wondering if there was any place to get a cup of tea? I'm afraid the coffee I had in Oxford this morning has long since worn off."

"There's not much left here anymore, my dear. We're in a right slump just now. But there is a nice pub just across the Green. It shouldn't be occupied with the 'regulars' yet, and they have some lovely homemade soup. You look as though you could use a bit of nourishment."

Meghan shook her head in agreement.

"I certainly could. By the way, I think the countryside – and your village is very pretty. You wouldn't happen to know what time the last bus leaves for Oxford, would you?"

"Of course, my dear, half past five. You won't want to miss it, as there's really no place to stay here. They used to have rooms above the pub, but they've been turned into flats. You're probably better off anyway, as they never were much to see."

The woman laughed and adjusted the pins that held her hair securely in a twisted bun.

"Oh, I don't plan on staying in Oxford, either. I've a hotel room in London and I need to be back there tonight. I actually came here looking for a bit of information. Perhaps you could help me."

"I'll do what I can. What would like to know?"

"Did you happen to know the O'Connor's? They used to live here and I believe they were the couple that took me into their home during the war. I was very young and only with them a short time before I was evacuated to America. Can you direct me to their place?"

Meghan tried to determine if her request would be met with kindness. The woman's head lowered and her eyes focused on the wooden floor, as though counting the slats.

"My dear, I'm so very sorry. I can direct you to their home, but you'll not find them there. Margaret O'Connor died last autumn. The Mr. was so lost without her. They were so very close and only had each other. I know they took in boarders and helped evacuate children during the war. It's been so long now, the names of their boarders have faded from my memory."

"And Mr. O'Connor? Where is he?"

The woman took a step closer to Meghan and wiped her face with a hankie from her skirt pocket.

"He's gone, love. He died shortly after Christmas. They were wonderful people. I'm so sorry they're not here to see you, how lovely you are and what a confident and independent woman you appear to be. They'd have wanted to know that you survived all of that horrible war stuff and indeed, it appears, certainly thrived. What about your parents?"

"They've both been dead for many years and I've no other living relatives that I know of."

"I'm truly sorry. I wish I could be of more help."

"Thank you. You're the first to have asked about my folks. You're very kind…."

Meghan felt tears welling in her eyes. She didn't know if it was due to frustration or fatigue, or if she was beginning to grieve for the couple she had wanted so desperately to talk to. Was she truly feeling grief for the *O'Connor's* passing or for the death of her hopes of reconnecting with her past? She'd considered the possible outcomes of finding the O'Connor's but never the possibility that they were no longer living! Now that the reality was before her, she ached with an emptiness that only *knowing* would fill. It was fairly certain that she would never know anything more about that part of her life. She was weary from both fears and expectations. This finality was a lot to bear.

She cleared her throat.

"Can you tell me where their cottage was?"

315

"Yes, of course."

Meghan got the simple directions, thanked the woman, then waved and walked outside, shielding her face against the growing wind. She reached the cottage quickly and stood just staring at it, as if the activities of the family that now lived there were just temporary and the O'Connor's would reappear. There were no particular memories that came flooding back, yet Meghan felt drawn to peer into the windows to look for pictures of her past replaying like old movie frames. Resisting the urge, she stood across the way and stared a while longer. She was finally here, the place where her life had taken such a sharp turn, and everyone was gone. As the wind whipped across her face, it dried the tears as soon as they fell.

It was a very long trip back to London. She grabbed some fish-n-chips from a corner shop near the hotel and went back to her room. Stepping inside, she immediately opened the window, hoping that the cool night air would help her eat quickly and sleep soundly. There were no strange dreams on this night. Her mind was as drained as her body. She slept until the small alarm clock woke her in the morning, its bell clanging and causing it to shake across the nightstand like a wound up toy soldier.

Meghan woke with a start and sat up straight. The wind was howling through the narrow streets like a banshee on a wild ride. It was a good morning to be inside somewhere and the National Museum was the place to start.

It was strange to her that certain facets of her mum's life were only just now surfacing from her memory. The myriad of facts that made up the history of her own life were a blur and incomplete at best. The early years of her birth parents' lives were even more obscure. Still, Meghan's curiosity was stirred by the memory of a convent and it was this thought that ran through her mind as she boarded a bus to the museum. She wasn't sure what the memory held, but it was worth pursuing.

Her inquiry about convents in and around London during the war brought an immediate response. The historian led her to a section on war-damaged churches and convents across the country.

"This may help. What exactly are you looking for?"

"I'm trying to locate a convent close to London that helped relocate children during the war."

"There was one in the small village of Amersham, just outside the City. It was bombed during the war and never rebuilt. I believe there's a school on the property now."

It didn't take very long to get to Amersham. Meghan approached the school grounds, hesitating at the black fence that surrounded the property. What ghosts did she expect to find? The place looked as though it had been there much longer than recent years would attest, probably due to the darkened stones that it was constructed from. It resembled an old puzzle with its salvaged pieces chipped and thrown together offset like a toddler's tower whose builder had given up on a reasonable design. A variety of sounds drifted from the open unscreened windows and Meghan began to feel she was intruding. She opened the gate and walked across the concrete playground to the door marked "Headmistress."

"Yes? I'm Miss Atherton, the Headmistress here. May I help you?"

"My name is Meghan Roberts. I'm from the States and I'm here in the U.K. on a newspaper assignment for the Seattle Sun. I have a few days before I begin my work and I have been visiting some places that may hold a clue to my early childhood days in England. I believe this is one of those places."

Meghan stopped to give the woman a chance to respond. She watched her shuffle some papers on her desk. A few moments passed before the woman walked out from behind the desk and faced Meghan, her hands folded properly in front of her. Meghan continued before she lost her nerve.

"I was hoping that maybe you, or someone here at the school, might know some history of this property."

"I see. I've been here for quite a few years and I'll tell you what I know. After that you may want to visit one of the several historical societies in London. You may get more information from them."

Miss Atherton moved across her office to straighten a picture on the wall. It was an inexpensive print of a hunting party and the dogs strained at their leashes with fierce, angry faces. It was a strange print for a school filled with young children.

"As you obviously know by now, this area currently houses a First School, though many years ago a convent sat on this land. From all I've heard, the convent was heavily damaged during the war. Fortunately, most all of the sisters evacuated safely, many of them to Lincolnshire. I doubt there are any still living up there, but you could inquire at one of the larger Roman Catholic churches in London. I think the Corpus Christi church in Covent Gardens may be a place to start."

"Do you know anything about the convent's role during the war?"

"I'm not sure what you're asking for."

"I know that there were nuns from some convents that helped evacuate children to the countryside. I guess I was hoping there may be some connection between *this* convent and my own evacuation just before the Blitz."

"And just what would you gain by this information, seeing as the convent is no longer here?"

Miss Atherton's question was blunt.

"If there was a chance I was at the convent that stood on these grounds, I would like to contact any wartime sisters still living and talk to them about my past, and whatever history on my parents they may remember."

"Ah yes."

Miss Atherton walked to the single-paned window and stared out.

"I'm sorry, dear, but I have absolutely no specific names to give you. Like I mentioned, it would probably be best if you contacted that parish in London. They might be able to help you."

"Thank you. I'm sorry to have taken your time. Would you mind if I just walked about the grounds for a while longer? I promise I won't be in the way."

Miss Atherton turned and glanced sharply at Meghan indicating she thought her request entirely unreasonable.

"I suppose that would be alright, but only for a little while. As a rule, we don't allow strangers on our school grounds. I hope you understand."

Meghan nodded, unable to verbally respond to this woman who made her feel like a naughty six-year old.

"Miss Roberts, you might want to consider the ramifications of this search of yours. Sometimes it's best to let the past stay in the past. Sometimes we find out things we wish we hadn't."

Now it was Meghan's turn to shoot a disapproving look at the headmistress as she turned toward the door. She resented this stranger doling out unsolicited advice. It was *her* past to discover, *her* life to reclaim! Why was everyone else so keen to discourage her search?!

Meghan closed the office door more loudly than she meant to. The wind had picked up once again, sending a chill through her as she meandered across the brick paths and worn play areas. Her gaze finally caught sight of a blur of white in the distance. It was hard to tell exactly what lay beyond the "official" school property, but it looked almost like a building, or stones that once made up a building. As the white picture came into focus, Meghan realized what she was seeing. A cemetery. The convent's cemetery. Its white headstones were actually varying shades of gray and yellow, some even darkened black from the years and the weathering mixed with coal soot. Many of the stones leaned to one side, without the strength to stand up straight. They were all alike in shape and form and the writing, when still legible, contained the same number of words. Just the names and dates inscribed, nothing that revealed anything else significant or personal about their lives. Just an inscription to prove they once occupied space on this earth and now lay nearly indistinguishable in a sea of anonymity. What an awful fate!

Meghan's heart began pounding as she whirled around, the stones bending like waves and flooding over her, drowning out the sounds of children's voices in the distance. What if she were laid in the ground someday without knowing any more of her own roots?! What if she continued through the motions of daily living *without knowledge of her past*, just as she been raised to do, only to be boxed and tagged with no more fanfare than just the elements whipping across her name year after year?! Without knowing – and feeling the generations who continued to live through her, their spirits weaving threads that helped create who she really was. And her name?! She didn't even know which name to assume! What would the stone say? They would have to decide which name to inscribe, which name to be weather beaten by the elements!

Meghan's breath was coming in short bursts now and the wind seemed to push each gasp back into her throat. The darkening sky bore down on her and her legs crumpled beneath her. The tears that had sat on the surface now exploded, the ghosts around her listening with anguish to the familiar sobs.

The train ride back to London was unpleasant. The full car was overly warm and Meghan's head pounded. A young woman with an infant and a toddler on her lap kept encroaching on Meghan's seat, apologizing each time in a squeaky, annoying voice. The toddler's hands were sticky and he kept putting them on Meghan's jacket and the baby smelled from an unchanged diaper. She laid her head back on the soiled headrest, closed her eyes, and willed herself to think of her favorite place. It was a small, quiet beach south on California's Route One coastal road and one that she drove to whenever she had more than four days off work. There was a beachfront bar and surfers and nothing else much going on. The perfect "get away." The noises of the train faded as fatigue overtook her and she napped. When Meghan stepped off the train in London, she vowed to avoid any further trains for a few days. That would give her time to research the convent and visit the Imperial War Museum.

The city was bustling with shoppers toting canvas bags. Men in dark suits with umbrellas over their arms strode briskly down the crowded walkways. The vendors in kiosks touted newspapers and snacks and black cabs veered around corners with amazing speed and agility. It felt good to be back where there was so much living going on. It was a picture very different from the English cottage painting that hung over her couch at home. This was a blur of colors and textures and sounds that defied exact description, yet you somehow knew what everything was around you, even if it passed you with a dizzying pace. Meghan stood in front of Trafalgar Square and stared up at Admiral Nelson standing proudly on top of a tall column. A triumphant pose for the man who gave his life in battle and secured yet again England's place in naval history. Yet Meghan knew from her own homework that even with many victories on the battlefront, this place hadn't always been self-sufficient in other ways. England's dependence on the rest of the world for food and other life necessities could have cost them the war. Still, there was a defiance that had seeped into the very stones and moss in this place, a quiet strength that seemed embodied in the granite of the man who loomed larger than life.

The Corpus Christi church in Covent Gardens was quiet and locked when she arrived. It was probably teatime for the priests, a short break for them before evening Mass. In a way, it was a small relief. Meghan didn't feel empowered enough to approach the subject of the convent just yet. Perhaps a good, hot pub meal and a couple of half-pints would soothe her, giving her just enough peace of mind to face her self-appointed project *tomorrow.*

The evening was setting in with a cool nip in the air that seemed just like Seattle in the spring. Meghan peered through the windows of a pub bedecked with heavy braided curtains, drawn aside to let light through during the day and pulled closed at dusk to keep out the damp chill. There were folks gathered at tables and at the bar and a smoky pall hung in the air. There was one short, wooden stool at a half-table against a far wall and Meghan sat down to look over the menu. A crumpled newspaper lay on the floor by her feet and she picked it up to see if it was current. It had obviously been well read by the lunch crowd and would be tossed at closing time. She hadn't taken the time or energy to read much of anything since she'd arrived and she felt a strange twinge of guilt for not having picked up a London paper to browse. It was something newspaper people did constantly, not only to keep abreast of happenings and views in other places, but also, Meghan suspected, to confirm their own prowess. Something to do with egos. She unfolded the paper to catch the headlines before going up to the bar to order food and treat herself to a foaming English bitter. It wasn't surprising to read that there were several activities planned in and around

London to kick off the commemoration of the twentieth year of the end of the war. Obviously the Brits took this very seriously and that would be a great help to her. She went up to the bar to order. The bartender smiled at her accent and asked her more questions than were probably necessary, then she sat back down with a glass of bitter in her hand.

The inside pages had schedules of events and Meghan read them carefully, hoping to find something that might serve as a good basis and catalyst for examining the war in light of the conflict in southeast Asia. Her eyes focused on one event in particular that seemed interesting, though it probably would not give her anything on the Britons' view of Vietnam. It was a lecture series at Greenwich Towne Hall, being given by several authors who had written in one form or another of their wartime experiences. The talks weren't until tomorrow afternoon, which would give her plenty of time to sleep in a bit, then maybe do a little shopping. It was one day she could call her own before her work began in earnest the following day. She had come so far already and been given a tremendous opportunity. The pressure would be on. But tomorrow...tomorrow she would claim back the soul that was nearly lost at the cemetery, the soul that nearly faded into the ghosts of a past she couldn't even claim.

She smiled at the prospect of tomorrow filled with nothing in particular. What a wonderful treat for herself! She took a long sip from the small beer glass and suddenly thought of Ryan. It would be late morning in Seattle and he would be running around trying to get a photo shoot in before the noonday sun spoiled the lighting. For just a moment, she tried to feel his presence, to be bound by some invisible thought wave as though the two of them were communicating by a process that no one else would understand. Least of all Ryan. She wasn't sure if she loved the guy or not, but he seemed as close as she would ever get to a soul mate. She wondered if he had felt a heaviness in his chest while she laid a continent away sobbing, surrounded by the crumbling white stones. Had he felt a twinge of pain, or even an ache as her emotions came to terms with realities? Ryan had told her once, just once, that she could never really love until she learned to love herself. She had responded angrily that she couldn't love herself without ever knowing who *she* really was. That evening had ended badly with both of them harboring resentment for days afterwards. The subject had never come up again until his brief words at the airport. Still, tonight she could hear his voice mumbling something unintelligible and see the way his eyes danced when they made love. Maybe she did love him. Maybe it was the one *real* thing she had in her life. She got up and ordered another beer, musing that it seemed so silly to serve women such small glasses when the men just got the whole pint all at once!

She finished her meal and hailed a cab back to Earl's Court. The fare was extravagant, but she didn't feel like taking the underground and her feet ached from too much walking. She drew a hot bath, determined to ignore any requests from the other side of the bathroom door. This night was the beginning of her "free" day! A good long soak was not too much to ask for.

CHAPTER FORTY

The sun was shining brightly through the thin curtains of the hotel window when Meghan awoke. The intensity of the light made it seem she had slept in very late, but her alarm clock read only half past nine. There was plenty of time to wander about London and still make the two o'clock lecture series. Realizing she missed the hotel breakfast, she grabbed some extra money from the small safe in the bottom of the old wardrobe, dressed quickly, and walked out into the modern hubbub of the ancient city. Her heartbeat quickened at the possibility of capturing the essence of London for herself before she worried about taking its pulse for her article.

Her destination was the War Museum, which necessitated a long tube ride. Once there, she wandered around gazing at displays, reading them occasionally but mostly just watching other people as they toured the exhibits. An eerie quiet prevailed in the section that chronicled horrible war atrocities and Meghan decided it was time to leave. There would be time for her to absorb that whole aspect of the war, but today was not that day. She walked back out into the sunshine, glad that the forecasted rain showers had not moved in yet.

She made her way into the pub that purported to be Dickens' favorite and ordered a cold sandwich and an orange squash for lunch. Watching the businessmen go in and out in their similar suits confirmed that she had brought the wrong clothes to look professional! The pub was warm despite the old stone, walls that had held in centuries of London dankness. This May Day was turning out to be an example of London at its finest: sunny and warm. She pulled the torn piece of newspaper from her jacket pocket to check once more on the location of the authors' lectures. Greenwich. It was getting late and there was a bus to catch to Towne Hall. Still, it just felt good to be free of deadlines and clock-watching for one day!

The bus dropped her off two blocks from the hall and Meghan began having doubts about spending a beautiful afternoon inside a stuffy building. Still, the program sounded interesting and she could always slip out at any time. A speaker was already talking from a podium on a small stage and Meghan felt a bit awkward at her late arrival. A stern man in a cardigan much too heavy for the day stood at the entrance and motioned for her to be seated; he seemed annoyed at the slight interruption from the banging of the heavy doors behind her. For the second time in only a few days, she felt like a misbehaving child and quickly slid into a seat near the back. She glanced at the older lady down the aisle and realized with dismay that she didn't have a program. Never mind. She could get one later when there was a break in the action, if she even stayed long enough to require one.

The older man at the podium was bent over, his hair very white and his shirt a bit rumpled. She took a notepad from her small, leather bag and stuck the pen in her mouth as she listened to his words. He had served on a ship in the Pacific and was explaining how isolated the men were from all the action on the home front, and how that affected their ability to readjust when they returned to England. His words came painfully slow; perhaps time or an injury prevented him from speaking in a manner that was easy to listen to. The gathered audience was nodding politely; dozing off or showing any frustration with the pace of his words would be too offensive, even in this modern age of speed. It was a delicate moment and Meghan pondered the sensitivity that people showed at times, especially for older folks. She started writing down that particular observation, noting that she may learn something valuable from watching and listening to those around her, as well as those relating their stories. How some folks shuffle their feet uncomfortably or turn up the corners of their programs while pretending to listen. She turned to look at the older woman once more and was surprised to find her knitting as she sat. That was odd. She hadn't noticed the bag of yarn on the lady's lap when she'd first glanced at her. Strange what the eyes saw when they weren't really looking.

A figure in the very back sat hunched over in a wheelchair. He seemed to be napping. A young man in a patched corduroy sport coat was scribbling intently on the back of his program. Perhaps he was covering the event for a university paper or an underground rag. Either way, he was taking his task seriously and paused only a bit to chew on the end of his pencil. Meghan smiled. She preferred pens in her mouth. The heavy doors opened yet again and an overly dressed middle-aged woman sat down in a chair nearby. She had a large, gaudy handbag that looked like it came from Harrod's basement sale. Her glasses were black and very pointy and made her face look like an aging cat. Her lipstick was bright red, much too bright for a woman whose skin was wrinkled and lined from years of holidays in Spain. Meghan mused that she looked rather like a marionette that might speak if you pulled on her purse strap.

It was with some surprise that Meghan realized another speaker had been introduced. It was an older man again but he appeared so different from the last. He stood tall and was sharply dressed in a suit, complete with a handkerchief protruding from the jacket pocket. His hair was speckled with some gray and his skin was relatively smooth for someone of his age. Perhaps he wasn't that old. She found herself drawn to the sound of his voice for a while, until the woman with the yarn dropped her bag on the floor. It made a loud thud from the large knitting needles that now rolled under her chair. Meghan stifled a chuckle, then wondered with some embarrassment why she had found that a bit amusing. The older woman, obviously flustered, was shifting in her chair and trying to retrieve the bag while still maintaining some decorum. Meghan turned around to see if the stern man at the front doors was going to come and help. He just stood without making a move, statuesque, an unpleasant expression etched in his stone face. Meghan slid quietly over to the woman, keeping her back lowered to avoid blocking anyone's view. She quickly retrieved the bag and its contents and placed them gently on the lady's lap. The woman smiled and silently mouthed "thank you." Meghan smiled back, then returned to her seat and began writing down her take on the "statue man." He might be an interesting character to weave into her observations on London. Nothing to do with the war, particularly, but an interesting character nonetheless! She was scribbling furiously in her own brand of shorthand when she realized that the speaker's voice had changed yet again.

The deepening shadows outside had dimmed the room's natural light, a sure sign that the rain would be moving in by evening. The old chandelier lights were missing a lot of bulbs and were not enough to make the speaker easily seen now from the back of the room. It was obviously a woman, but beyond that it was hard to tell much else. Her voice was pleasing, almost melodic in the way her words found pitch and rhythm. The voice was strong but not aggressive and Meghan wondered if this woman was a singer at one point in her life. She seemed very confident, yet she moved around the podium as she spoke like a child who couldn't stand still. It was a strange combination of experience and innocence. Meghan found herself actually listening to the woman's words, hoping to solve the enigma of this paradox.

The words that flowed from the speaker were an artful combination of facts and feelings, events and observations, and they were powerful in a way that Meghan couldn't describe. It was as though the very essence of this woman's soul was being released into this room of strangers. The lilt of the voice and the richness of her vocabulary were mesmerizing. It was like opening a present or being let in on a secret. Meghan felt suddenly small and far away; the enormity of what she was hearing made everything else so insignificant. No, not really insignificant. More like she and everyone around her were being embraced by arms that knew how to hold with an intensity that was almost frightening in its honesty. To be able to present a historical account of your life with a vulnerability that made the listener both enchanted and uncomfortable was a gift indeed! This was someone worth staying to hear.

"......And the hardest part after the fact was realizing that I never got to say goodbye. My mum died when I was still a young woman and I had always thought that to be the most difficult time of my life. That event, more than any other, prompted me to stay in the convent when my heart and my feet were aching to move on to another place, another frame in life. Then I faced the uncertainty of my beloved's return. The manner in which he was lost was too horrible to internalize. Somewhere inside myself I knew he had whispered 'goodbye,' but I still refused to say the words out loud. My lack of response may have been why I never could hear his voice again. Yet the loss of my only child was so much harder to comprehend – and accept. This was different altogether. There was something so out of sync, so jumbled in the timeline of life's events. An unfairness that defied even spiritual explanation, if ever we are capable of being gifted with omniscience in a world so limited by our own self-imposed minuteness.

"I guess that's what war does to people. To nations. It stretches that perfect line we all ascribe to until the line is no longer there. It seeks unreasonableness to the point of chaos when we are screaming for reason and order. It tangles that lifeline we live on into knots that choke off our ability to breathe fully, to see correctly, to hear with complete understanding. And finally, it tears the very threads that ensure – and validate- our own existence.

"My daughter's life was in jeopardy and yet I believe to this day that I was not capable of sending her away to safety, though I thought I was at the time. In reality, I would have paused at the moment of decision like a dazed moth not able to fly away from the consuming flame.

"And so, the worst of that moment was that I had given that awful decision to someone else to make. It wasn't that I felt his choice was wrong, though I'll admit I've thrown angry words at him more than once. It was only that I had burdened him with a weight that should have been my own. I was already too weighed down with loss, knowing in my heart of hearts that my husband would not be returning. I guess I couldn't shoulder one more weight.

"I have learned since that it is only in accepting what we believe we cannot bear that we finally discover the kind of strength that is born only from, and in, our weakness. A strength that has been forged from pain and fragility carries its own unique properties. It teaches us to catch our breath in short gasps if need be, to see while our eyes are still closed, to hear even while the noise around us is deafening. It's a fortitude that shores us up when the waves have washed away the pier beneath our feet.

"And in the end, I believe that the knotted mess from our struggle to do more than just survive, comes undone as a circle, no longer rigid with a beginning and an end, but instead beautifully wound around us like a delicate yet strong necklace, like a warm, woven wrap around our shoulders; a completeness with an eternal quality that provides us with the ability to feel both secure and adventurous."

Meghan sat perfectly still, as any movement would destroy the hypnotizing moment. The only thought of her own was that she wished she had been paying attention to the beginning of the talk. She had missed so much of the woman's story, a story that seemed vaguely familiar in a haunting way that made her skin painfully tingle. It was like meeting the speaker's soul after it had already been searching the room for someone who was truly cognizant of the gift it was giving. Meghan's mind was racing, replaying the woman's words like a tape reel even as she continued to absorb each new revelation. Her pen lay across her lap now, silent and unproductive. She realized at one point that her mouth was partially open and she swallowed hard and rewet her lips. The sound of the wind outside was only a minor annoyance and the rain was now falling with usual, British determination. Its rhythmic pulse was accompanying the voice like perfectly tuned tympani, emphasizing her words with a beat that was indistinguishable from the soft, percussive movements on the stage.

"After I came to terms with my husband's fate, I let time assuage the searing wounds, pouring myself into my nursing duties and filling the void with war's demands. Yet it was only after I went to America that I finally faced my deepest pain. After many years, I had to accept that what I held most dearly in my life, my daughter, would never be mine to hold again. It was in this pain that I realized I was truly blessed and loved by a man who accepted me unconditionally. Yet, the effects of the war continued through the years to challenge the strength of that circle that kept me from falling off the edge. Again and again, the war's devastation hit me like bombs that exploded without warning after years of lying dormant. It was only the ability to move and bend inside that circle that saved me from my own bouts of anger and helplessness. If the world around me, my world, had stayed rigid each time I'd fallen, I'd have broken too many times to get up again.

"I have often thought of the movie, based upon a book, that came out at the beginning of that horrible time. Four friends go in search of a wizard who can make their lives whole and right again. It is only after they recognize – and accept his weakness that the real miracles happen. It is because of the wizard's vulnerability that he knows the real strength that lies inside each of them. He has been there. He can now give them the beautiful gift of perseverance and confidence that was inside of them all the time. They only needed to rediscover those gifts."

The speaker paused, letting her head drop, her feet planted in one spot. She was lost in the picture she had just created and wasn't ready to move on yet.

Meghan swallowed hard then smiled slightly at the recognition of those four movie characters that were her own personal favorites. She stared at the woman, feeling a bit uncomfortable at the silence and the stillness that now occupied the stage and pervaded the entire room.

"My daughter was warmly welcomed into a loving circle of friends in Oxford at the start of the war, while I was still with her. Later, she was accepted by others who welcomed her into *their* circle and loved her so completely. One special friend called her 'Munchkin,' I suppose because she was so small and lively. Yet as I stand before you today, that name seems more appropriate than ever. For you see, the Munchkins knew all along that the wizard would help the four friends. Though they didn't know how he would do it, they believed he would find a way. I think my young daughter believed that others in their "wizardly" roles would encompass her, protect her, and love her. I know she had a childlike faith that allowed her to see that goodness was just a hug away. I have to believe that that security, and a stuffed bunny named Max, gave her strength, that love gave her hope."

There was a soft rustle as the pen and notebook fell from Meghan's lap. Munchkin! The memory of being called Munchkin was sifting into her consciousness like a falling object, lightly at first, then crashing down inside her very being. It was at once frightening and overwhelming, like watching a skydiver just over your head. A bicycle, something about riding on the back of a bicycle in a small town. Just like her nightmare! A woman's hands were stitching the hem of something and there was a large sewing bag in the corner of a room. Tea. Lots and lots of hot tea served at a marked, wooden table adorned with a pitcher of flowers. A ship. The large ship that seemed to be moving in slow motion as a man waved frantically from the pier. More pieces of the nightmare that had haunted her! Meghan stared at the far away face on the stage, now nearly unseen in the dimness of the large, shadowy room. The bunny! Max the bunny who still sat on her pillow in Seattle! Meghan could feel a warm hand stroking her hair while she clung to the toy that had always soothed her. Someone had called her Munchkin long after the woman with the gentle hands and the melodic voice had disappeared. *This man had held her and had bounced Max the bunny on her lap as he sang the Munchkins' song to her.* He had told her stories of the loving woman across the ocean and her friend who were helping so many others be safe and recover from wounds of war. The speaker's next words were lost to Meghan. Her heart began pounding wildly and the revelation resonated with truth, a certainty too strong and powerful to ignore. She was on her feet.

The sounds in the room were reverberating against the pounding of her heels as she raced down towards the stage with a driving need. The murmuring grew louder but Meghan heard only one voice. It was truly a familiar one, finally breaking through endless years of silence.

The rain was pounding on the ancient roof, but its sound was drowned out by cries born from years of anguish now transcended and reborn in a single, suspended moment of joy and completeness.

EPILOGUE

The wind outside had picked up making the rain come down hard in horizontal sheets. The official doorkeeper at the lecture hall was shuffling the programs that lay on a cracked, wooden table in the back. He seemed ill at ease with the scene on the stage that was unfolding before him and he buttoned up his heavy cardigan. Turning his head, he caught sight of a waving hand in the far, back corner of the lecture hall. The doorman's stern face softened a bit as he answered the quiet summons. He walked over stiffly and leaned his head down to hear the instructions being given him, then straightened up. Returning to the entrance, the doorkeeper pulled open the heavy doors and walked out into the rain, raising his hand to attract the attention of the nearest cab driver. He came back inside and fidgeted uncomfortably, waiting for the man in the wheelchair to start moving toward the door. Instead, the man sat silently, the wheelchair still in place.

He was aged well beyond his years; the silver-gray hair and deep lines in his face had been there long before they should have been. Time had stolen so much. His right arm trembled involuntarily and caused the whole side of his body to shake. He stared straight ahead, his smile tentative, hinting of sadness too deep for the genuine sparkle in his eyes. His face was a paradox of someone to be both pitied and celebrated.

Though he sat unmoving, his mind was racing. He could see her locks of reddish chestnut hair spilling out from the crisp white band that could never quite secure them. There was a snapshot of a child gliding across the room with her feet planted on his, a dishtowel ascot wrapped about his neck, while the bluest of eyes watched them both with amusement. He felt the brush of a soft hand and smelled the fresh coffee brewing in their tiny kitchen. He heard the chimes from an old grandfather's clock breaking into his perfect world. Ringing, ringing until his ears ached from their incessant clang. Breaking in without permission, compelling him to leave for a hell never bargained for. Forcing him to be a part of that moment that had lasted an eternity. Severing the cords that bound so many lives together. He had stared out that grimy window of the train as mother and daughter stood helpless on the platform, their presence diminishing in a swirl of mist and smoke. Time had stolen so much.

He swallowed and tried to rewet his lips, but his mouth was parched. Still, in his mind he could taste his lover's tears that had danced, with desperation, a ballet that would never be repeated. He blinked several times, sighed heavily, and wheeled himself to the entrance.

The sound of the howling storm rose above the din of the evening traffic as the man was lowered into the backseat of the cab. The passenger faced forward as the heavy doors of the hall clanged shut, his tears unnoticed and his face blurred by the rain that pelted the windows as the car sped away.

LaVergne, TN USA
01 November 2009
162614LV00003BA/4/P